Life Sentence

J. M. R. Gaines

J. M. R. Gaines
FREDERICKSBURG, VIRGINIA

Copyright © 2016 by John Manley Roberts Gaines.

All rights reserved. No part of this publication may be reproduced, distributed or transmitted in any form or by any means, including photocopying, recording, or other electronic or mechanical methods, without the prior written permission of the publisher, except in the case of brief quotations embodied in critical reviews and certain other noncommercial uses permitted by copyright law. For permission requests, write to the publisher, addressed "Attention: Permissions Coordinator," at the address below.

J. M. R. Gaines
17 North Pointe Dr.
Fredericksburg, Virginia 22405
www.jmrgaines.com

Publisher's Note: This is a work of fiction. Names, characters, places, and incidents are a product of the author's imagination. Locales and public names are sometimes used for atmospheric purposes. Any resemblance to actual people, living or dead, or to businesses, companies, events, institutions, or locales is completely coincidental.

Book Layout & Design ©2013 - BookDesignTemplates.com

Ordering Information:
Quantity sales. Special discounts are available on quantity purchases by corporations, associations, and others. For details, contact the "Special Sales Department" at the address above.

Life Sentence/ J. M. R Gaines -- 1st ed.
ISBN 978-0-9981721-1-8

To Jo, the Entara of this Earth

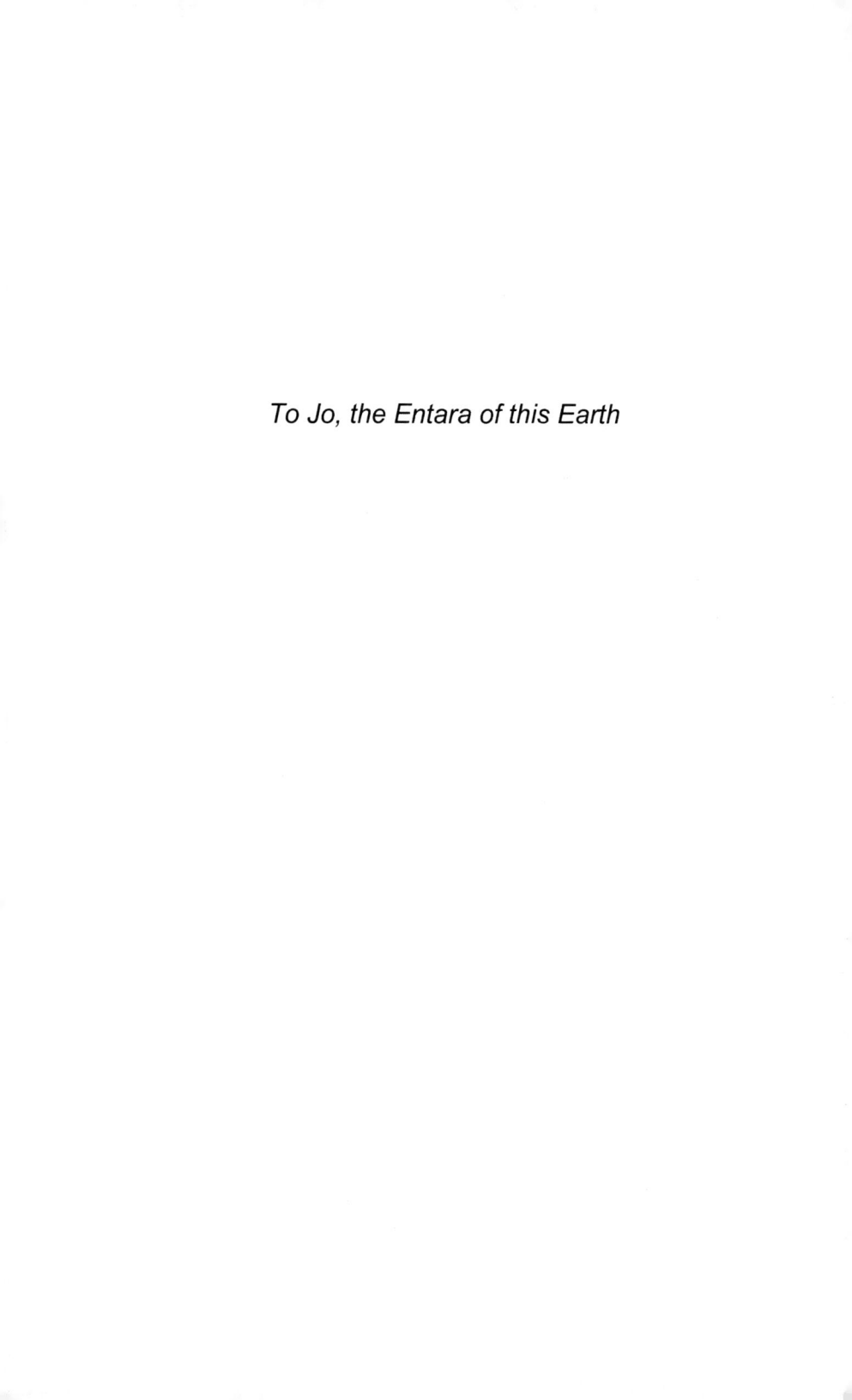

1

The judge wriggled uncomfortably in his robes as he read the scrap of paper, then passed it back to the bailiff and said, "Foreman of the jury, in the case of the state against Wilhelm Klein for first degree murder of Feldwebel Schmidt, Kommissar Lebov, and Inspector Ciccolini, how find you the defendant?

"Guilty!"

"Defendant, have you anything to say before sentence is pronounced?"

"I was framed," answered Klein in a deadpan delivery.

"Mr. Klein, really! We have satellite photos of 1 to 35 resolution showing you pulling the trigger on two of the three auxiliary security personnel who periodically served as contractors to the government. If you hadn't decided to murder the third one in a lavatory, we'd have a photo of that, too. In that, DNA proves your presence. It's true all three were off duty, but their contracts afford them the same protection as full-time servants of the state. How can you possibly say with a straight face that you were framed?"

"What can I say? Do you always trust a camera a hundred miles up in the sky? You asked me if I had anything to say, and I say I was framed."

"Since there are no mitigating circumstances, I shall pass directly on to sentencing," said the judge, smoothing his moustache and ignoring the argumentative prisoner. "The court of the United Nations, District 12, Circuit C, Region 35, sitting in the city of Athens has found you guilty of murder. This is a capital crime and calls in principle for the death penalty."

Suddenly the walls of the courtroom erupted with protestors waving signs and chanting "Save a life! Save a life!" and "No more Justice with bloody hands!" The contrast between the projected images and the relative tranquility of the little court chambers was acute. Inside the room sat only the judge, the bailiff, and the robotically restrained prisoner. Even the foreman of the jury was only holographic, attending the trial from his home hundreds of miles away. But the streets around the Palace of Justice were filled with angry activists.

"This is Kent Phillips reporting from Athens where yet another death penalty has set off demonstrations around the Acropolis in protest to capital punishment.

As might be expected, the majority of the protestors are Greeks and Turks who have been here all week for this session of the assizes. But there is also a sprinkling of Brits, Poles, Germans, and French, since this batch of hearings includes an overflow from the courts all over Circuit C. Our psychometric reaction scale shows a reading of 67, which makes this one of the livelier responses of the week and may portend the outbreak of some minor looting and the torching of automobiles in the nearby neighborhoods. Now over to our analyst Demetrios Palamenides!" The screens shifted from the blond, Californian traits of the announcer in the streets to the darker, more elegant face of a man clad in a designer suit.

"Kent, we see this as a very controversial verdict. Before we cut away to commercials, I can tell you that our viewer audience rates confidence in the judge at only 22.7%, lowest of the past three weeks. And now a word from Müllerwurst, the fine old-world sausage founded in 2075." Dancers in *lederhosen* filled the screens, weaving their way through the happy chaos of Oktoberfest, while in a little corner window, the producer counted down to cue in the magistrate.

Judge Brock whispered "Shit!" away from the microphone and then turned back to his most dignified courtroom manner. "As I was saying, the death penalty is mandatory IN PRINCIPLE in these cases, but I am willing to indulge the public abhorrence for further violence and commute the prisoner's sentence to life if any authorized body will claim him for a prisoner. Is any authorized agent in the audience willing to make a clemency bid?" There was suspense on the view screens and the digital display of Judge Brock's approval rating shot up 10% on the courtroom master console. The public loved this moment almost as much as the crowds in the Coliseum must have loved waiting to see what the emperor's thumb would do. But none of the incoming data sources lit up. The bailiff, who was off camera and off audio, sneered in Klein's face and said, "Nobody wants to take a chance on a con with your rap sheet!" Watching the approval points erode from his digital display, Judge Brock suddenly added, "Since we are too close to dinnertime to evaluate all the offers coming into our studios, I have to say tune in tomorrow to find out the results of this sentencing, followed by the fantastic details of the LoBello rape case. This is John Gabriel Brock saying that's all for this issue of Criminal Court Drama!"

Klein slouched against the wall of his cell. He would not turn on the view screens, and he was tired of reading. He set his antique first edition of *As I Lay Dying* on the table next to the bunk. He had stolen it from a merchant in Colonial Williamsburg several years ago and never had a chance to really get into it before he was incarcerated. Rossellini the trustee rolled up the prison library cart outside the bars.

"That's pretty depressing crap to be reading in your cell," he remarked. "How about this to cheer you up? Two Tibetan girls and an orangutan?" He held up one of the generic black holodisks that were loaded with prison porno.

"Unlike you, I don't fancy sex with animals."

"Huh, you'll be lucky to get an animal where you are going" pouted Rossellini. "You'll be happy to get an orangutan. Or even a mangy monkey!"

"What do you mean where I'm going?" Klein knew that the trustees were often privy to all sorts of news that the cons could not normally get.

"I mean you have been claimed!"

"No shit! Where?" Klein's mind raced. Maybe one of the platforms in the Arctic or Antarctic. He could face that. They said Kerguelen Island wasn't so bad if you had warm clothes. Even the moon. That would take some adjustment, but he could take the moon. Just no asteroid duty. An endless spinning of stars in the black void would get to him in a matter of weeks. Anything but asteroid duty.

"Domremy"

"What?"

"I said Domremy. You are about to become a proud citizen of the colony of Domremy."

"Where the hell is that?"

Rossellini started to chuckle. "Wellll, they say you tie your ass to an ion accelerator, take a deep breath, fly out to Way, Way the Hell Out There, then turn left and go as far as you can till you run out of fuel!"

"Funny man. I'm going to recommend you for a merit badge in geography."

"No kidding Klein," said the trustee, turning serious for a minute, "You have any final desires, you better try to hook up now. They gonna ice you down for a good many months to send you out to Domremy. I know because I seen the requisitions for the suit. You're facing one hell of a long nap, man."

"Nuts," said Klein, looking at the floor. "In that case, give me the damn holodisk."

It was worse than Rossellini had predicted. The next day they put him on the Jet-Cat for the trip across to Alexandria. Klein had hoped they would launch him up to the platforms from Woomera so that he could experience the exhilaration of lifting off from Earth. But it was not to be. They were treating him strictly as cargo. He would be iced down on Earth and launched in a container with a hundred other stiffs from the big mass driver that Olivetti had just built in the desert down near Mogadishu, almost exactly on the Equator for minimum orbital thrust. He would have liked to look out on the Mediterranean whisking by at 80 knots, but he was to be locked in a windowless biologicals hold with an armed robotic guard and case after case of the latest Ebola serum. He shuffled down the gangplank at Alexandria, right onto a bus for Port Said. There, in a ratty little lab, they handed him over to a pair of sadistic technicians who didn't give him enough tranquilizer to put him to sleep. They laughed and laughed as his panic grew. Few people who have not been iced can imagine the feelings that go through you as your body systems shut down one by one and paralysis creeps up from your toes to your head in an almost discernible line until it reaches the face. The mouth shuts down first, as you gag on your last attempts to articulate a word, any word, before you can speak no longer, then your nose, as you frantically dilate, gulping for a last breath of air, then, last of all, the organs of sight, slowly numbing and dying while you strain until it feels like your eyeballs are going to pop out of your head as you grasp at the last few twinkles of light.

He became vaguely conscious of still being alive when he was somewhere out in space, cramped onto a shelf in a transport compartment, still in his shipping suit. After a while he began to panic again, as it seemed that he would soon exhaust whatever air was slowly pumped into the suit, asphyxiating before he could move his arms and legs. Shouting did no good, but just as he thought he would go mad, a crew member came into the room, turned on the light, and nonchalantly went down the shelf unzipping suits, quickly passing by Klein to finish the row. The man had already opened the hatch to head for other chores when Klein was able go croak out, "Is this, is this Domremy?"

"Where?" said the puzzled mate. "I got no idea where you carcasses are going, but this is the spaceport at Tau Ceti. You'll be reprocessed and sent out again from here."

Klein felt a wave of nausea sweep over him as he realized he would have to go through the icing process all over again, maybe more than once, before he got to wherever Domremy was. He must have fainted after that.

There were gentle hands, wiping his face with a wet cloth. "If I'm dead, they must have sent me to the wrong place," Klein thought to himself. The face of the woman bending over him was not exactly angelic, but Klein could have believed it. As he strained to talk, the woman hushed him. "You must keep quiet, Herr Klein. Your vocal chords are damaged. You must have scr... It must have been a most difficult trip."

His eyes drifted to her nametag. Helga Pedersen. "I see you want to know who I am. No, I am not German, but a Dane. But we have a lot in common. I was commuted to Tau Ceti fifteen years ago. Yes, I was just a girl, but old enough to be tried as an adult. No matter what for. Don't ask, don't tell, as the Americans say."

Klein's face settled into a calm expression as Helga continued to clean him up. He could feel pins and needles in his hands and knew that meant he soon would be able to move them. In fact, he could twitch them a little already. Helga noticed his efforts. "Yes, your neurologicals seem good and you should have full body functions. Reproductives they will know about later. You know that you were shot out through the Van Allen Belts in a freight container, so nothing is guaranteed. But there doesn't seem to be any reason why you can't assume your new job out on Domremy."

Klein tried to form a question mark with his face. He must have succeeded. "What is your job? I'm afraid I can't discuss that with you. Obviously, it has nothing to do with family life, or they wouldn't have shipped you out like a sack of potatoes. All I can tell you is that you need all the sleep you can get, because your new life will be very, very tough. So take advantage and rest now."

Even after he could speak and move again, there was little more information that he could obtain from Helga, or from the sad-faced physician who eventually pronounced him fit. He got two weeks of workouts in the gym with lots of time off for reading and what seemed like surprisingly good food. No wonder -- Tau Ceti's planets were beautiful places, like Earth without the plagues and pollution. He never got to see them, except in holotours. At the end of the fortnight the sad doctor very gently anaesthetized him and started the re-icing process. Whatever he gave him, it kept away the nightmares that had plagued him on the stage out from Earth.

His second reawakening was quite different. The crew of the freighter Nahant was a ribald collection of space sailors who favored old-fashioned heavy metal music from the twentieth century and toasted their revived "passengers" with ice-cold vodka. A simple pledge to obey ship's rules was enough for them, though they warned Klein that, at the first infraction he might be clamped in irons or even flushed out the garbage port. They knew precious little of what went on surface-side on Domremy, but seemed to have an electronic acquaintance with most of the inhabitants. They assured Klein that he would certainly be attached to the militia under the command of one Marshall Stafford and that he would see plenty of fighting against indigenous species. Every man they dropped off on Domremy was a top-quality fighting man, they assured him, except for a bunch of stupid pacifist farmers, but the crew all disputed among each other what the possible chores for a triple cop-killer would be like. So it was that several days later they came in view of a blotchy orange-colored planet, gave him a final toast, and shuttled him down in a lighter to surface coordinates called in by the gruff voice of Marshall Stafford. Klein was the only passenger to debark at Domremy, the others all going on to the next colony at Dahlgren. That didn't make him feel any better.

As he squinted into the powerful, pervasive light of Domremy's binary suns, Klein heard someone call his name. In front of him gradually emerged the shape of a tall, wizened man dressed in loose white robes and a flowing silver cape and broad-rimmed silver hat. A 6-round Kikkonnen multi-rocket launcher was propped on the side of his saddle. He was astride an animal Klein had never seen before, but which looked like a cross between a horse and an alpaca, with the curly fleece, short limbs and erect ears of the latter, but the mane and tail of the former.

"I'm Willie Klein. You must be Marshall Stafford."

"Best if you just call me Marshall. You ready to be sworn in?"

"Guess so."

"Raise your right hand." It was raised. "You swear to uphold the laws of Domremy Colony and to make no exceptions to any orders given you by a colonist?"

"I do."

"Got any money?" barked another man urgently, as he loaded boxes onto a mechanical rover.

"What?"

"Money, money! You got any on you? Not that spacescript shit but real dollars?"

"Sorry, pal," answered Klein with a shrug of his shoulders, as the fellow turned grimly back to his work.

The Marshall rode a few steps closer to Klein. "Amos has a sister on Dahlgren and he's trying to buy her fare back here. We're all pitching in, because there are damn few Earth women on this planet, as you'll learn soon enough. Here, better take this." The Marshall reached back to pull a long bundle from his saddlebag and passed it to the new recruit. Klein unwrapped it to find an M221 sniper's rifle with scope, well-oiled and beautifully maintained. "You're familiar with the weapon." It was more a statement than a question.

"Trained on one in the Marines."

"So I noticed on your rap sheet. That was one of the reasons we claimed you. You feel comfortable sitting a thallop, we brought one for you. Otherwise you can ride in the wagon with Amos and the boys." He hadn't even noticed that the lighter had almost noiselessly ascended back into the atmosphere and was now no more than a baseball-sized shape in the sky. The wagon looked very crowded.

"I suppose I'll see what it's like to ride."

The thallop's gait took some getting used to. It was stiff-legged, somewhere between a Tennessee Walker and a trotting horse. He noticed that its ears nervously scanned and twitched to various points of the horizon, like antennae. It must have something to do with these Locals the sailors had mentioned. Everyone in the detachment was armed as though they expected some kind of violence. "How come I have this instead of a Kikkonnen like you've got? You afraid I'd shoot a few of you and make a break for it?"

The Marshall spat on the ground and said, "What would be the point of that? You got your own ship to take you back to Tau Ceti?"

"I don't know, these prairies don't look too inhospitable. A man could do pretty well out here on his own."

"A man could get pretty dead out here on his own, only not fast enough!"

That puzzling remark made Klein ponder a bit. "You still haven't explained why everybody but me has a weapon that can flatten a few tanks, while mine will only fire old-fashioned bullets."

"It only makes sense, since our target's so much different from yours. What did they tell you up there, anyway? Or not tell you?"

"They told me almost nothing."

"Damn, damn, damn them administrators! They didn't tell you you were coming here to be a mankiller?"

"A mankiller? What man do you need killed? And why can't you do it yourselves?"

"We need you to kill any one of us, if necessary, and we can't do it ourselves because if you get ready to shoot us, we're already worse than doomed."

That is when Klein learned about the Locals and about why a copkiller from Bremen was claimed by a farming colony billions of miles away from Earth. The Marshall explained that every man in a detachment was armed with Kikkonnens except the mankiller. Kikkonnens were the only weapon effective when a Local weighing about 500 pounds came bounding two or three hundred yards through the air to snatch a host. One round from a Kikkonnen would blow it to pieces, or at least shred it so badly with shrapnel that it would fall short of its target and be dispatched by a grenade or laser handgun. Locals most often attacked alone, although they had been known to gather at times in small groups. Coming in through the air at eighty-five miles an hour, they were a pretty frightening adversary. They landed with pin-point accuracy and needed only a couple of seconds to fasten a human being to their underside with several pairs of claws sharp as steel, then, with one bound, they were almost out of range again. The adults were strictly vegetarians and didn't finish off the host. Instead, they stabbed through the spinal column with their ovipositor and laid four sausage-sized eggs in the host's innards, then buried it up to the head in the soft sand. Those sausages were hungry little devils, but often the host was still alive – for a little while – when they emerged a week later. The mankiller had only a few seconds to sight up when it looked like a man might be seized, and at best could get off only two or three shots. With an effective range of almost 2 miles, the M221 was best suited to dispatching any host before the Local got out of range.

Klein had barely digested all this incredible information when he was called upon to use it.

The Marshall had just radioed up ahead to the next settlement and turned to the newcomer. "Still about 15 klicks to go. The shadows are getting long and they tend to attack then, if they haven't already. They're torpid at night and never bother anybody. Watch your thallop's ears. They sense something out there. There could be one over by those low hills, or hunkered down in a gulley below the grass line. You just stay back in a safe place and resist the urge to shoot at them. You waste rounds on them Locals and I'll waste you myself right here and now!"

Just then there were shouts of "Incoming! Eleven o'clock!" An ominously big shape bounded up at what appeared to be an impossible range and halved the distance to the detachment before coming to the ground again. Amos and the others in the wagon leaped down and snapped the safety off their rocket launchers. The Marshall and the others who were mounted formed a neat protective chevron in front of Klein.

"Here it comes!" someone yelled, and the shape again hurtled towards them, drawing fire from all the Kikkonnens. As Klein was drawing a bead on the man closest to where he judged the Local might land, he saw out of the corner of his eye as the Marshall waited a split second longer than the others to fire, carefully leading the target as it dropped out of the sky. His rocket caught it square in the thorax and blew off the head from the rest of the body. It toppled wildly in a straight free-fall, landing in the grass, where Amos and the others on foot swarmed toward it. It looked like a huge grasshopper that had been grossly mangled. Amos tossed an incendiary grenade onto the corpse, but immediately the foot soldiers ran back, yelling,

"Mated pair! Watch out for the female!" at the top of their lungs.

The second attack came at only half the distance of the first, from a point about 20 degrees further to the left. Unfortunately, one of the riders had gotten a little out of position, drawn by curiosity that proved fatal. He only got off a couple of rockets that fell well behind the zooming creature, while those of the rest of the detachment, fired obliquely, went short or long. In an instant, the man was knocked to the ground and pinned beneath the huge creature. It was over twelve feet long. Klein could see it tensing its enormous hind legs to spring away with the prey. He aimed at the cavalryman's heart and pulled off several rounds as the Local began to get airborne. Fountains of blood on the man's white uniform showed that he had not missed.

Klein looked around proudly, expecting some sign of applause or at least stoic encouragement from the detachment. They only stared glumly after the disappearing Local, casting quick, nasty glances at the mankiller before resuming their duties.

"Don't everyone say thanks at once!"

"Listen, mankiller, no one is going to like what you do," the Marshall explained. "This is a small colony and everyone gets pretty attached to their neighbors. There is not a man here who would not hesitate a nanosecond too long if he had to shoot another militiaman. That's why we need a cold-blooded murderer who will be reliable when it counts. Everybody on Domremy is going to give you whatever you want. Nobody is ever going to deny you or get in your way. But nobody is ever going to feel any kind of sympathy or kindness to you, because we all know who you are and why you are here. I'm just telling you the way it is."

And so it was. As the detachment rode into the settlement, the farmers emerged from their adobe dwellings and Quonset huts to look curiously at the newcomer, but there were no smiles. The detachment broke up with few words. A fattish colonist stumped up to Klein's thallop and held the reins.

"Howdy, mankiller," he said matter-of-factly. "The name's Peebo. You'll be staying in my extra room. Eat in any of the commissaries, your choice."

"The name's Klein."

"Yes, sir. No harm intended...sir," Peebo blurted awkwardly, leading the animal away.

Detachments went on patrol around the perimeter of the farming community every other day. Every few nights a group of the colonists gathered in the square with searchlights, flame throwers, and grenades and went out looking for dozing Locals. The only ones who abstained were a group of farmers, including his new landlord, Peebo, who seemed to have some kind of devotion to non-violence and didn't mix much with the other colonists, who were employed by the corporation that held the planetary patent. The violent ones reminded Klein of the peasants in the old movie "Frankenstein," though they had a lot more firepower. They were just as determined to free their village from the terror of the monsters. In fact, they were pretty effective, because no Locals had been spotted in the immediate vicinity of the settlement for over two years, much less bounding in on the attack, as they so often had during the bloody formative months of the colony. They had plenty of scores to settle with the Locals over dead comrades, more than enough raw hatred to drive them for decades. The only thing they feared was the prospect of a hopeless, lingering death, a death from within that at the same time would spawn another generation of attackers. That was why the job of the mankiller was so crucial. He tried to get to know people in the settlement, but it was almost impossible. The few women and even rarer children fled long before he got near enough to hail them. The doctors had still failed to lick the problem of sterilization that resulted from both trans-light space travel and radiation in many planetary systems, so few male colonists could find women willing to accompany them, even if it were permitted, and repro was always chancy. As for the men, they maintained a highly respectful, but icy tone whenever they answered his questions. No one ever addressed him first if they could avoid it. One day, as Klein was walking down the main street, he saw a group of figures alight from thallops and took them at first for men with an oddly purplish tan. Then, on closer examination, he found that, despite the fact that every one of them was as bald as a Swedish wrestler, they were all very definitely female.

Klein saw the sheriff walking across the street and went to join him. "What's with the bald girls?" he asked, jerking his head towards the newcomers.

Marshall Stafford pulled a pair of binoculars from a pocket, passed them to Klein, and simply said, "Check out their eyes."

They were a bright scarlet color. When Klein appeared confused, the Marshall added, "They're Forlani, been visiting some of their kind in the next settlement. Females outnumber the males about twenty to one or more. They got some hair where we don't, and vice versa, but they're the closest thing around to a lady's company, unless you're lucky enough to pay to bring in an Earth woman, and you never will be. They're mighty free with their favors, too. Pay you to get to know them better."

"I don't need any aliens for that," snuffed Klein as he strode back to his rooms.

The settlement was getting a name. It now had a big enough population, no thanks to Klein's sharpshooting, to cease to be merely Site 35 and to claim its own identity. At a meeting, where Klein stood silently in the back row, the inhabitants proposed the names of various former hometowns out of competitive nostalgia, until someone suggested they choose the name "Stafford Station," and everyone quickly agreed. There was to be a parade and a barbecue, thallop races, a pie-eating contest sponsored by the wimpy farmers, and a little concert given by a musical group from the colonial capital, some two hundred miles away. People from some of the neighboring settlements came in for the day on their transports. The day started badly for Klein. Peebo was shuffling around behind the adobe house early in the morning, setting up a table and a small cooker, along with some other things. Eventually, he knocked discreetly on Klein's door and said, "Sir, would you like to come outside and see what I've set up for you?"

"I've put a nice comfortable chaise out here for you under the tree," he explained, as Klein followed him outdoors. "Last night I went over and got some of Purdy's very best barbecue meat and I've got a great big batch cooking for you here over the coals. This is a nice spot where you'll be able to hear the band, just like you were right next to them. And I've got lemonade, and a whole berry pie, and there's another one in the refrigerator inside, and there's a cooler of "Colony Light" beer in the cooler, and…"

"Why are you doing all this just for me?" snapped Klein, cutting off Peebo's enumeration of goodies.

"Well, sir, you understand. It's a celebration today. People come in to feel good and forget about their troubles. Forget about the Locals for a few hours. See old friends and not have to worry about what's going to happen next week or the week after. I know you understand, sir. It's not that anyone wants to disrespect you in any way, but if you were out there on the street, mixing with the folks, well, it would make them think... Don't you understand?"

"Damn right I do," Klein barked, ripping the top off a can of Colony Light. "No day to see the mankiller out in public."

"Please don't get mad. It ain't my fault. Those Forlani will come over if you want them to. Just take your pick. If there's anything I can get to make you happy, anything at all..."

"You can get your ass out of my sight, Peebo. Go mingle with your own kind."

"No offense, sir, but you should be with one of them Forlani. Don't be mad at me, it wasn't my idea, Mister..."

"Go ahead, say it, call me Mankiller!"

Peebo, totally upset and ashamed, simply withdrew backwards, making little bows on the way, afraid to turn his back completely on his enraged houseguest.

Klein spent several hours in the chaise, drinking the contents of the cooler, can after can. He tried a little of the barbecue, but had no appetite, and fed most of it to Peebo's dog, out of spite. From time to time he glanced over to the Forlani house, which doubled as the settlement's bordello. Every once and a while a few of them would come out in the doorway to watch the proceedings and laugh at the quaint ways of the

Earthlings. He quickly grew tired of the bouncy music and retired to his room, taking most of the remaining beer from Peebo's refrigerator on the way. He drank and smoked and read a novel by Tahar ben Jelloun, but it was hard to concentrate, so he put on earphones and played albums by the late 21st century metal band Thunderchild on the sound system until he got a headache. As he walked back and forth with a throbbing skull, he stopped to look out the window at the Forlani house. Then he took several pills and fell asleep for a while, dreaming of a labyrinth of cells with bars of ice where he searched and searched for an elusive girl with long, dark hair and an Empire gown, who appeared for a few seconds and then vanished just as he got close to her. When he awoke, it was getting dark and the doorway lights were on in the Forlani house. He glared at it through the window. Suddenly, he grabbed a hat and stuffed it down on his head to hide his features. Jamming his knotted fists into his pockets, he strode rapidly across the street. He pushed the door open, like a cop invading a drug den. Entering the central room, he ran his eyes over the inhabitants. Several of the purplish, bald females had been laughing with male visitors or chatting on the sofas. They had all stopped talking when he burst in the doorway. All at once, one of the Forlani came through a beaded doorway holding a couple of drinks and gave a little peep of surprise when she found herself bumping into the intruder. He grabbed her brutally by the upper arm, which was covered with short, light brown fur. "You, you're coming with me. Don't think about resisting. And you," he snarled, looking at the others in the room, "Don't you dare try to interfere if you want to go on living."

"Of course, sir," agreed the one he had seized. Putting down the drinks and taking his hand from her arm and holding it, she added, "You needn't have taken the trouble to come over. I was waiting for you to call on the communicator." She smiled and led him back through the front door and across the street to Peebo's house.

He hadn't paused to think about the differences in anatomy. In this case, getting some tail literally meant what it said. He had wasted no time when he got back to his room, slinging the purple creature onto the bed face down, but when that tail wrapped itself around his leg in a playful way, Klein's mind almost went blank. He would have lost all interest had his partner not demonstrated very convincingly that she had certainly not lost hers. The Forlani were built almost like humans, with organs in pretty much the same places, but, oh, what those "girls" could do with them! No human female Klein had ever been with, from the Reeperbahn to the Vegas Strip to Pushkinskaya, could have the unbelievable muscular control of this Forlani wench. It was an erotic experience he had never dreamed of before. But the more he tried to oblige her by giving her a climax to remember, the more he was perplexed by her. She giggled, she laughed, she teased, and she seemed to enjoy herself enormously, but she definitely did not react like a female from Earth. When she finally relaxed and began to rest, it struck Klein that she seemed more like a football striker who had played all the way through a World Cup match with extra time and shootouts and was most satisfied with her play than a human woman who had felt the ultimate sensual release.

The next morning Peebo left a tray with two servings of breakfast next to Klein's bedroom door before he went off to tend his fields. Entara, the Forlani, had smelled it and gone to fetch it and brought it back to bed for Klein. She gnawed on a triangle of toast and said to him, "I hope you slept well last night. You seemed very restless."

"I wouldn't have been 'restless' if you weren't here," he retorted.

"You like to boink more than you like to sleep," she observed.

"Boink, huh? It's been a long time, but yeah, I suppose I do."

"Boinking is nice, but it's not as good for you as a good night's sleep." When she spoke, she made a giggling noise that annoyed Klein, though he eventually realized that it wasn't the same as a human giggle, but just part of the process of communication.

"You better be prepared to spend most of the night awake when you come over here."

"Of course," she said. "Would you like me to send someone else tomorrow? I don't want to be what you Earth people call….greedy. You can ask for any one you want. Though perhaps we don't seem all that different to you."

"You'll do just fine. I want you to spend the night with me and only with me, understand? But I want you to know it's nothing serious. It's only for the fucking."

"Oh, please, mankiller," she laughed uproariously, falling off the bed, "Do not say it that way! In our language it is just too …silly! If you knew what it meant in Forlan. It's like…. It's too funny to explain. Hahahahahahaha!"

Klein could not help smiling at the way Entara was incapacitated with laughter. "All right, then, do you understand, it's only for the boinking, nothing more, nothing sentimental."

"Oh, yes," she sobbed, stifling the last few chuckles, "We Forlani are not nostalgic about these things the way Earthlings are. You will see in time."

He did. She became his regular companion, and he often congratulated himself that he was not becoming sentimental about his furry little squeeze. But every so often, he occasionally pronounced the f-word anyway, just to see her reaction. She was, he realized with some Schadenfreude, a more perfect playmate that Hugh Heffner could ever have enjoyed.

One night, as Entara eagerly settled in next to him in bed and prepared to caress him, Klein made a request. "Listen, Entara, I've decided I like the way you feel, all by itself. Tonight I want you to curl up next to me and just sleep and let me enjoy your being there without any boinking."

She sat up and looked alarmed. "Klein, are you sick? Wait, I am sure I can find something for you in the medicine chest."

"No, I feel fine. It's just a whim." Seeing her puzzlement, he explained further. "It's a kind of irrational impulse we Earth men and especially Earth women get from time to time."

She looked self-consciously at her own body. "Have I been too vigorous for you? That's it, isn't it? Don't worry, I can be very, very soft and gentle…"

"No, Entara, you have already been so gentle I can hardly stand it sometimes. And you're just right on the vigor, too. It's that… I want to try to understand you in a sort of non-professional way."

Entara mulled it over and concluded, "So you're saying you feel a fondness for me which is not related to our arranged boinking. Klein that's never happened to me before, and I'm not sure if it's happened to any other Forlani companion before. Oh, Klein," she purred, giving him a kiss on the lips that finished with a little lick to his eyelid, "You are making me extremely special, extremely contented. I will never forget it and I want you to know that everything between us, from this moment on, is strictly because I want to. It is free from all duty and consideration. It is just an expression of me."

She curled up with her head on his chest and rested with a look of absolute peace and harmony. Klein thought to himself that was better than any climax he could probably ever provoke in a woman of any species. *Some people used to call that love. But forgive me for not saying the word to you. Would you understand what I meant? In any case, I would have to make promises to you that I think I could never possibly keep.*

Before the year was out, Klein had killed a man from nearly every house in the settlement. He kept track on a little map he had made. It was his perverse, professional amusement. Sometimes, if he managed to dispatch a target very neatly, with a single round, he found a little gift by the back door to Peebo's house that led into his room. Usually it was some item of the dead man's clothing or tools. But no one ever left a note or thanked him face to face. He had only missed three times, despite emptying his clip at the vanishing Local and its grim prey. Each time, the Marshall immediately mentioned that he had shot well and tried his best, but that a bad angle of fire, or the sunlight, or some other natural factor had made the shot impossible. Occasionally, their detachment would stop at a neighboring settlement. All the people there seemed to know in advance who he was and to shun him almost as much as they shunned their own mankillers. He got to have a nodding acquaintance with some of his counterparts, usually to borrow ammunition or consult on some technical, weapons-related matter. Most had grown even more taciturn than he in their unchosen profession. He did learn in his visits to these "foreign" places that he enjoyed a secret esteem that his own townspeople never expressed to him, but sometimes shared with their neighbors. Partly because he worked with the famous Marshall Stafford, who could have been elected president if the colony had been authorized to have one. But partly, too, on his own account. He also learned that there were more than a few Forlani who envied Entara for being his companion. He had been the object of several blatant attempts at seduction while away from home. Though flattered, he had never succumbed, considering Entara to be his unexpected little treasure, his Schatz. Like a careful Chinese Confucian, he made it a point never to brag about her to anyone and to compliment her as little as possible, as though the gods would become aware of his good fortune and take her away. He even searched for ways to disparage her.

"Bad enough to be boinking one fuzzy alien," he thought to himself. "God only knows what I could catch if I got promiscuous with the likes of them. They'll hop in the sack with anything that's vaguely male. Entara only stays because she knows what I'd do to her if she didn't."

However, despite such defamation of Forlani in general and his in particular, he could not help knowing that the Forlani saw nothing wrong or even special with interspecies sex. They regarded it as a mere trifle, a humorous attempt to oblige the blustering Earthlings who ran the colony and showered them with money in exchange for a few nightly contortions. Reproduction with their own was an entirely different matter, however. Entara had explained that procreation within the Forlani race was regarded as absolutely holy and that the chance to mate with one of the relatively few fertile males was an imperative that few Forlani females would pass up, even if their families did not insist with the strongest of threats and rewards. A Forlani who was pregnant or caring for a minor child was treated almost as a goddess and could demand virtually anything from any of her kind without any need for remuneration. The honors of motherhood continued all the way through old age and even, to some extent, after death in matriarchal rites that Klein only dimly comprehended. Apart from this fetish with motherhood, the Forlani were extremely hardheaded and sensible, rather like worker bees that think little of their own glorification.

One morning when Peebo had already gone to the fields, Klein amused himself by commanding Entara to make him some breakfast. Usually she complied without taking umbrage, but today she pertly answered, "Do it yourself! I am expecting a call from my family that may have good news about one of my sisters." Just after she had snapped on her meager clothes and dashed outside, Klein was astonished to hear a knock and see a human face at his door. Marshall Stafford simply said, "Boots and saddles!"

Grabbing his rifle and bandoleer, Klein asked, "What's up? There's no patrol scheduled today."

"Got an aid call from the new outlying settlement down south, number 66."

"Don't they have their own specialists?" Klein complained.

"Not anymore."

"You mean their whole detachment was wiped out?"

"Looks like it. At any rate, they're all gone. And several Locals were spotted bunched together. Looks like we may be facing a whole nest of them."

The detachment rode hard most of the way and they could tell right away when they got to No. 66 that plenty of things were wrong. There was no sign of any perimeter, but a ditch had hastily been gouged out around the town and filled with all the fuel available. The flames and smoke would usually repel any Local attack. A gap only a few meters wide was left open, facing the road to Stafford Station. The thallops reared and bleated at the fire and smoke. On the inside there were signs that, in spite of the makeshift defenses, the line had been breached and individual houses had been attacked. As the Marshall ordered Amos and some others to deploy sensors at strategic points, a few weary defenders emerged from behind their barricades to tell their story of several days of terror. First the detachment had failed to return. Then the remains of a relief column had come racing back to town to recount their spotting of the Locals and their own deadly skirmish. Then, even before the ditch had been completed, the first attacks had come. People had been pulled right from their homes. Klein looked around and saw some dead bodies in the streets. Forlani. The Locals had killed them instead of carrying them off, because for some subtle biological reason they were unsuited to be hosts for the Local larvae. Normally a Local would not even bother to approach a Forlani. Perhaps they were dealing with a mutant strain of Local that was not only more numerous, but less finicky about whom they killed. The Marshall even made sure they kept a vigilant watch during the night, worrying that the normal sluggishness of the creatures might not still be a factor. Fortunately, there were no new developments while it was dark.

Well before dawn the detachment were out of their bedrolls, uncoiling heavy-gauge copper wire in a spiral in the center of the settlement. There was a five-meter opening in the middle. Marshall Stafford took his mankiller aside as the others worked feverishly. "It's been years since we've had a perimeter breach like this, where the Locals attack the settlement instead of attacking in open country. It has its advantages and drawbacks. These wires, tapped into the town's main generator, should be enough to fry any Local that lands on them. They can't see the layout in the square here until they're nearly on top of it, so they don't have too much room to maneuver. On the other hand, neither do we. We have one man near each end of the main street with a free fire corridor outwards. Two stand back to back in the middle to cover the ones that come in over the houses. The rest find cover facing outward from the houses and try to hit any that take off with rockets.

"I volunteer for the middle," said Klein.

"No way," answered the Marshall. "We need you covering the four men on the main street. And I'm damn firm about that, because I'm the best shot with a Kikkonnen, so I'll be in the center."

"You can't. We need you to give orders."

"You all need my shooting eye more than you need my orders right now. If anything happens, Amos is second in command."

They didn't have long to wait. The sun was up barely a half-hour when the first Local came right out of it, bounding toward the village center.

With the sun in their eyes, the shooters in the center missed, but one of the creature's legs landed on the grid and it was quickly electrocuted, searing with an evil smell. The Marshall bulls-eyed the second before it could land. The third came down the street from the north end and was wasted by two rockets. The fourth came over the houses from the other side at the Marshall's back, where a militiaman named Wiggins winged it. It landed on the grid, but managed to reach out with its mantis-like arms to grab Wiggins so that he was fried along with his target. The fifth tried the other end of the street and caught rockets from both the man at the end and the Marshall. The sixth got the man at the opposite end of the street and Klein hit him with a head shot as the Local took off. A barrage of shots from the men on the outside of the houses brought both of them down. People were just breathing a little easier and the Marshall was reloading when the seventh came in, low over the houses, and grabbed him.

"No, damn you!" exclaimed Klein. With one shot he shattered part of the joint of a leg. Then he started to shoot off the claws that already held Stafford firm. But there were four sets and he couldn't get them all.

"Shoot me! Shoot me!" shrieked the Marshall, as the Local struggled into the sky.

Klein jammed a second clip into his rifle and tried to shoot off another claw, unsuccessfully. Already the distance was becoming critical. He shot off part of another leg joint, slowing the beast further, and managed to shoot off one more claw. Then the red one-mile warning light on the scope was flashing and he realized he would have only one more sure chance to take Stafford's life. Already the men outside the houses were bracketing the Local with their rockets. He drew a bead on the Marshall's chest, not risking a head shot, sighed, and fired into his heart. Some men were already dashing toward their thallops to try a pursuit, but Amos shouted for them to maintain their stations and made a point of telling Klein at the top of his voice to kill any man that didn't. It was almost noon before Amos was satisfied that the attack was finished and ordered all but the sentries to stand down and clean up the mess. He glowered at Klein as he ordered, "Get some rest. You take the point tonight when we go out and whack that thing." He couldn't have been any harder on Klein than Klein was on himself – not because he had disobeyed orders and procedure on how a mankiller had to behave, but because he had had to kill the one man he had come to care about, and almost hadn't been able to do it.

Entara's smile vanished from her face when she saw Klein scowling as he came back from the mission. She did not miss the fact that Amos now rode in command. Nevertheless, she approached Klein as soon as he strode away from the detachment. "I'm very sorry. But we need to talk."

"Not now."

"It's important. The message from home. Something has gone wrong."

"Beat it! I said leave me alone!"

"But you don't understand, things are not what I expected."

"Aren't you listening? Maybe this will teach you," he snarled, as he let a backhand go across her face. She yelped loudly as she fell away, her hand going to the deepening purple welt on her face. Then she turned and ran across the street to the Forlani house.

Klein walked back and forth sulking in Peebo's back yard, then went inside and raided his host's whiskey. He was halfway through the bottle before he began to think more clearly. He had known what he did to Entara was wrong as soon as he did it, but like many violent men, he had an almost pathological opposition to making any excuse for it. "Tomorrow she won't make a big deal about it," he assured himself. "I need more time to decide how to tell her. Damn, damn, damn!!!" he shouted, taking out his frustration on Peebo's furniture. He splintered the table with a single chop and kicked a chair through the little mantelpiece where the farmer had arranged a few souvenirs and trinkets. Then he grabbed all Peebo's remaining alcohol and locked himself in his room.

Klein had only a slight hangover when he awoke the next morning, gradually realizing that the sun was already high, yet Peebo had not gone to the fields. He was poking discreetly about in the house repairing the damage to his belongings. "Another apology to make," grumbled Klein. "And the worst is, I already know that it has to be accepted."

Looking toward his door, he was surprised to see in silhouette the shadow of a female in a cape. "I knew she wouldn't hold it against me," he whispered in a hopeful tone. But when he opened the door, he saw that Entara's face was uncharacteristically glum and that she faced the ground.

"I couldn't go without saying goodbye."

"Oh, come on, Entara! I didn't mean it. You're not going to walk out because I gave you a little slap? No, that's wrong. I never should have done it. And I deserve for you to walk out. But just give me another chance."

"It's not about your hitting me."

"What?"

"I tried to explain but you were grieving too much for the Marshall to listen to me. The message from home. I have to go. It wasn't my sister they chose to go to Firilh Ghati, it was me."

"What are you talking about?"

"I have to go have children. It's my sacred duty -- in our language, we call it *avesti*. I wish I didn't have to, but I must."

"How can you just walk out to procreate with someone you never even met? You're crazy! I need you here. Now more than ever."

"It doesn't mean the same thing to you. Your people cannot understand. If it were just for me, I would happily stay, but they are the family's children, too. My duty is to keep life going."

"I would never leave you. You can't do this to me."

"I am so sorry. I have spoken with Ragatti and she will stay with you. She has wanted to for a long time and offered me money and gifts if I would let her. I'm sure she will do everything she can to make you happy. You will probably enjoy her more than me."

"No, no, listen to me, listen to me!" he gasped as he grabbed her neck in his hands. "I'll kill you before I let you go. I want you, not anybody else. If I can't have you, no one else is either." He had begun to shake her violently. She offered no protest, but went limp in his grip, almost welcoming the prospect of death from the jealous murderer. Suddenly he felt a sharp metallic blow on his head. Turning, he saw Peebo wildly swinging at him with a skillet.

"Shame on you! Shame on you!" yelled the fat little farmer. "Let her go. Let her go right now."

Klein let her drop to the ground. Peebo rushed past him and picked her up, trotting over to the Forlani house, where the other females had gathered in a whispering knot at the doorstep. Klein lumbered back into Peebo's house, snatched up his rifle, and sat with it on his knees as he waited for the man to return.

When Peebo opened the door, he saw the gun and started to take off his hat in his usual deferential way, but then stiffened his lip, jammed the hat back down, and walked forward. "You can shoot me if you want. I won't say I ain't afraid, but you're going to hear me out first. That girl feels about as much as one of her kind can feel toward the likes of you. You should never, never have treated her like that. It ain't decent. She was always the better part of you, and that's for sure. Now she can't stay with you. It ain't her fault. They have a duty to life that none of us can understand. Especially if we make our living taking it away. But you got to try. She cares for you so much, that she'd rather die now than go and start her family. That's right. They already had to stop her once and two of them are going along with her to wherever this Gati fellow lives so she doesn't do it again. But they're worried. They think she'll find a way sooner or later, maybe even after she's pregnant, which would be worse. Unless you let her go. You got to find a way to let her take leave of you and still keep some shred of honor. That's all she'll have, because I think she already gave all her feelings to you. There, I'm done now, shoot if you're going to." Peebo crossed his arms across his chest defiantly, then uncrossed them, realizing he had covered up the target zone.

"I still feel like shooting you, but I'm not so dumb that I don't know I owe you something a lot better," said Klein dejectedly. "By the way, I thought you clodhoppers believed in non-violence, not in whacking people with steel pots. But you're right. Go over there and tell them I'll be over in a few minutes and make sure that Ragatti is around, too."

As Klein went in the door, he tried to put a proud look on his face, though he felt like his entrails were torn up inside. They were standing in a semicircle waiting for him. He held out his hand and said, "Ragatti, you come on over here." One of them stepped up and took his hand. He looked her over and said, "I think you'll do just fine." Then he turned to look Entara in the eyes. "You've never really seen me mad before, but I get like that a lot. One of those people on Earth I strangled just like that, because he looked at me the wrong way. You didn't do anything to deserve it, Entara, but I don't apologize for it, because it's part of my nature. If you didn't see it before, too bad for you. I always told you there was nothing sentimental in my wanting you. You are free to go. You really meant nothing more to me than a little pleasure, and I think … er … Ragatti here will be taking care of that in the future. If she knows what's good for her. So goodbye and bon voyage!"

A wan smile came across Entara's lips. "You lie so badly, Mankiller! But I want you to know that I will not forget you."

Physically, Ragatti resembled Entara in almost every detail Klein could think to examine. She had all the technical skills of pleasing an Earthling that her fellow Forlani had. And she would wind up having her way with Klein. But as much as Klein tried to live up to the reputation Entara had created for him and to show off his virility, he realized inside that the unique playfulness and the uncanny anticipation of his own feelings that characterized Entara would probably never be there with his new consort. Late at night when Ragatti had dozed off, Klein made his way out to the edge of Peebo's fields and walked for what seemed a very long time out into the tall prairie grasses. Then he fell on his knees and wept. He could hear the rustling of the grasses in the night breeze and didn't care if it was a Local sneaking up on him, hoping the damned locust would finish him off then and there. When his eyes were too dry to shed another tear, he rose slowly and staggered back to the house. Peebo, squatting in the grass cover where Klein could not see him, let him walk back a long distance before he rose, too, and followed as quietly as he had come, giving a little whistle from time to time as the third Domremy moon rose over the horizon.

Erica Duquesne had come to dislike her job as a Junior Executive overseeing the Domremy Colonization Project for Hyperion Corporation. She disliked having to fill out mountains of paperwork and forms to explain the smallest downturn in colonial productivity (which almost always stemmed from the actions of the alien life forms the colonists called "Locals"), as well as the fact that she constantly had the company Board of Directors questioning her as to when the colony, which was still clearly unsafe for any "decent" folk, would be opened up to wider immigration. But mostly she hated working with her supervisor, Senior Executive Bill Hollingsworth. A man whose career advancement had come from a combination of a degree from the Erickson Business

Institute when it was still considered prestigious, office politics, and sheer luck, Hollingsworth had become infamous within Hyperion for taking shortcuts to success that frequently sabotaged the careers of his subordinates. *I think I'm next*, thought Erica as Hollingsworth began to discuss the situation on Domremy.

"As you can see, the area around the former Site 35, now named 'Stafford Station' by the colonists, currently appears to be mostly secure. Attacks by the 'Locals' are down roughly 88.7 percent. Based on this, I recommend appointing a new marshall and moving the experienced defense forces to new sites further into the frontier," said Hollingsworth.

"Which candidate do you propose appointing to the position of Marshall? He'll have big shoes to fill in replacing Stafford. According to the polling data we obtained, he had the highest approval ratings of any marshall on Domremy, and his team was one of the most efficient in terms of Local eradication in their area…"

"And because of that, we have more flexibility in terms of who we can choose for the next marshall of Stafford Station. I'm going to have Sam Geller appointed marshall of Stafford Station and send that man killer -- what's his name, Klein? -- out to one of the more troublesome sites. Which would you recommend?"

Duquesne sighed. "I don't think we should begin the transition this early, and Sam Geller's testing scores for marksmanship, leadership capacity, and organizational capabilities are all among the lowest of the possible marshall candidates. Maybe we can throw a bone to the colonists there by allowing an election. They always love the illusion of self-determination. But if we must transition the old marshall's team out ASAP, I'd recommend sending Klein to Site 89. Lots of reported Local attacks, high mortality rates, a minimum of competent staff...if any site needs an effective mankiller, it's Site 89. But I strongly recommend a different candidate for the Stafford Station marshall, like Steven..."

"Site 89 sounds like an excellent choice," said Hollingsworth. "Get the paperwork filed so we can have him shipped out there and transitioned to the new site. As for Geller, I think he'll suffice for Stafford Station—that site is calm enough that we don't need to waste our stronger candidates there. Be sure to send all the necessary reports for Domremy to the Board of Visitors—they'll be very pleased to see the progress in the Domremy colonization project. I'm going to lunch now...try to get those flowcharts measuring Site 89's mortality rates on my desk by the time I'm back this afternoon." Then Hollingsworth left Duquesne alone in her office to wrestle with the problems of mortality flowcharts and incompetent marshalls.

Sometimes it feels like I'm the only one who does any work for this company, Duquesne thought as she filled in the stats on Site 89 and prepared the flowchart.

As she took a cursory glance at Klein's personal files, she corrected herself. *Although I know that's a lie.*

2

It feels naked to be a mankiller without a gun, Klein thought as he sat in the cramped train seat awaiting arrival at Site 89. After Jim Stafford's death and his unceremonious departure from Stafford Station -- hustled out the door with a "good riddance!" from Stafford's replacement and an order to relinquish his M221 before leaving on the train -- he felt like he had left behind everything he could possibly trust on Domremy. Peebo had given him his contact for emergencies, and…

"Does Earth truly look like it does in these…'shows', Klein? It looks so wonderful, with great trees, and castles, and wild lands, and…"

And I guess there's Ragatti here, if I'm really desperate, Klein reasoned. "I don't think your favorite drama, *Heroes of Jamestown,* was ever an accurate guide to life on Earth. Historians have pretty much disproven the hypothesis that the Jamestown colonists were wiped out by Indian shamans who could summon zombies," Klein said with a cynical snicker.

"But surely it looks at least *something* like this, Klein. Mountains, lakes, forests...it would be so much better to live there than this dreary, endless plain of wind and dust. Do people still visit the old places like Jamestown?"

"Oh, you can still visit Jamestown...if you have enough money to pay for the submarine ride to go there. Rich folks tell me it's quite beautiful. A lot of those places you enjoyed watching on those TV shows are under water now...all of New Orleans, most of New York except the Floating Theatre of Broadway, what used to be the gambling area of Macau, and even the District of Columbia, the old capitol of the United States. Most of the low-lying and coastal areas of Earth got flooded around the beginning of the 22nd Century."

"How could the Earth have changed so rapidly?" Ragatti asked. "The Forlani History Keepers, the *xartivash*, say that nothing has changed in our weather and land for the equivalent of thousands of Earth years. What happened to Earth?"

Klein sighed. "This train we're riding on runs only on electric power. Most Earth transportation now is either electric powered or natural gas --eventually it'll all be electric. But before then, up to the end of the 21st Century, we used mainly petrol-based fuel. It made the

Earth's climate much warmer, and the seas rose, flooding the continental coasts and low-lying islands. Huge areas that had been covered in deep ice melted. We used petrol because it was cheap, and we stopped using it too late to save many of our coastal cities. Much of Earth's farmland became too arid and dry for agriculture, and that's one reason why we're here to colonize."

"Well, why are *you* here? Peebo and his religious friends are farmers, all right, but what about you?" Ragatti said with an inquisitive flash in her eyes.

"I don't want to talk about that."

"Will you ever tell me?"

"Probably not."

As Ragatti turned away with a crestfallen look on her face, Klein looked out the window and watched the endless waves of bluish green Domremy grass pass by. It was soothing, like watching the waves of Earth's oceans. Klein put on some headphones to blot out the sound of the inane Earth shows Ragatti was watching on the overhead monitors. He listened to slow instrumental music and watched the rolling waves of grass until, in spite of the bumpy train track and the horribly cramped seat that crushed his knees into his chest, he fell asleep.

He awoke to the sound of the announcer's harsh, scratchy voice. "Last stop, Site 89, everybody out!" As Klein walked out of the train with Ragatti, they saw a group of heavily armed men standing underneath the train stop shelter. In the center of the group was a man in early middle age with straw colored hair and sunken eyes. "Welcome to Site 89, mankiller," the man said. "My name's Cashman. Yours?"

"I'm Klein, former mankiller from Stafford Station."

"We got your reports from over there. Seems like you have a damn fine record of doing your job. That record of yours better stay top notch, because we don't care much for mankillers around here otherwise," Cashman said. The men surrounding him stared at Klein, looking for signs of weakness and incompetence in their new mankiller, any excuse to be rid of the untrustworthy outsider.

Klein defused the situation the only way he knew how. "I can't be a mankiller without a gun. Where's mine?"

"You'll find some stock M221's in the armory. Only the best for our man killers. A good gun is the only perk they'll get here. Tarkington will escort you to the armory, and you can pick the one you want there." Tarkington, a tall, muscular man with a shaved head, stepped forward, prepared to guide Klein to the armory. Klein nodded at him.

"One question," Klein asked Cashman. "Housing. At Stafford Station I lived at a farmer's place. Where's the mankiller supposed to live here?"

The crowd of men snickered at Klein's question. After an awkward pause, Cashman said, "You'll sleep in the room above the bar, because nobody in this town'll take a damn mankiller into their home after what our last mankiller did! Billy Frederiksen, aka 'Billy Sin.' Couldn't quite stop his murderous ways here on Domremy, even with all those people he got to shoot as part of his job! Killed the man he was lodging with. Once we heard about that, we formed a posse, shot him dead, sent out the order for a new mankiller, and got you. This is a law and order town, and I intend to keep it that way."

And Klein began his service as the mankiller of Site 89. Some things were familiar – the precise aim and range of an M221, the ominous droning noises of the Locals, and riding into the wilderness on thallops at the crack of dawn and the dim twilight. His housing, however, was nothing like Peebo's farm. The room above the bar was cramped, poorly ventilated, and most of all *noisy*. Every single drunken profanity, slurred greeting, and drinking song wafted its way up to torment Klein as he struggled to sleep, especially on the dreaded "Wild Fridays" where the bar would serve drinks until 2AM. Klein was sorely tempted to live with Ragatti in Site 89's communal Forlani housing until she explained that the rooms in the housing were just as small, and the Forlani as noisy as the barflies below him. So he abandoned that plan and began taking a Somega pill each night to knock himself out and sleep as smoothly as possible.

Klein tried to distract himself once a day by sending a message in code to Peebo. Before he had left Stafford Station, his landlord had seemed intent to give him a quick education in the ways of the pacifist farmers, on the pretext that there were many more of them on the outskirts of Site 89 and that they could give Klein a hand if the rest of the residents were as stand-offish as their reputation indicated. Peebo had explained that he belonged to a closely organized group that outsiders usually called the Religious Dissenters, but who usually referred to themselves as The Circle. They had undergone various types of harassment and persecution on Earth because of their refusal to participate in corporate agriculture and had taken refuge first in rural countries away from the corporate centers and eventually on the colony planets. The corporations with planetary patents were eager for anyone who could grow anything out-of-system and they felt that the dissenters' odd ways and views would simply wither and disappear eventually in the wave of colonial prosperity. All the more so because they had to leave their beloved wives and children behind. Their strong traditional ideas about reproduction, in an age when more and more "civilized" women were using non-coital procedures, if they chose to have children at all, were checked by the biological dangers of space travel and planetary settlement. The WEF had already pronounced the dissenters doomed at their latest Davos meeting and instructed the UN government to behave accordingly.

But according to Peebo, the Dissenters considered space as a salvation rather than an extinction. Confident that they could overcome the medical problems of extraterrestrial breeding, they communicated secretly with each other all over the colonial planets, and even beyond into some alien systems that had accepted them, through a code they called Crop Talk. It seemed to an outsider like a lot of boring farm jargon. To a sophisticate, all farmers ever discussed was the crops and the weather. And that was exactly what Crop Talk consisted of, but with its own phonology, morphology, and syntax, as well as body language. Besides basic Low English, it included a lot of foreign elements the dissenters had picked up during their diaspora from the First World. Spanish, Creole, Gujarati, and South Vietnamese bits went side by side with more familiar expressions. Vegetables, farm procedures, agro-marketing, and animal husbandry could be made to express all sorts of things. But Peebo had limited Klein's instruction so far to a variety of messages involving danger, communication, and matters of health. Without any immediate danger, Klein's messages for the time being confined themselves to dull statements about his physical well-being and closed with the Crop Talk equivalent of "Write again soon."

The townspeople of Site 89 were a different breed than those of Stafford Station. He could rarely get any of them to say more than a few words to him, and even months later, they still looked at him like a leper. In Stafford Station, men hated a mankiller because he might take one of their loved ones, but in Site 89, hating a mankiller was the closest thing they had to an official sport. People even seemed to make a show of it, going on about how horrible it was for a great man like Cashman to have to rely on scum like Billy Sin and "that new mankiller I can't remember." Only Tarkington slowly began to talk more openly with him, and even his conversations tended to rely on some alcohol to loosen his tongue. One of the few sources of amusement to Klein was that there seemed to be relatively few brawls in the barroom; Klein reckoned that this wasn't so much because Site 89 was "a law and order town" as Cashman claimed, but because people were scared shitless that a sociopathic mankiller would put a bullet in them at the first sign of conflict. *At least the owner of the bar thinks I'm worth something*, Klein often thought as he enjoyed a discounted beer on those long nights.

Klein made sure not to drink so many discounted beers that it would interfere with his romping with Ragatti almost every night. He had to admit that Entara had chosen him a new girlfriend who offered enough physical excitement for any man and who was extremely well skilled, if a bit too "technical" perhaps, at the maneuvers of sex. She reminded him a bit of a Romanian figure skater years ago who whirled across the ice with stunning expertise, but never seemed to share the emotional thrill she gave to her fans in the arena.

One night after a notably lusty interlude, he was about to fall asleep when he noticed that, unlike

Entara, Ragatti made a sort of regular noise as she slept, a sort of light buzzing. He must have laughed a little too loudly, because she woke up with a start. "What's wrong? Are you unhappy with me? Is there any danger?"

"None of the above, Ragatti. I just realized that you snore."

"Snore? What is that?"

"Well, I can't demonstrate because if I tried it, it would make a noise that doesn't resemble you at all. You just make a pleasant little noise as you breathe in your sleep."

"Oh!" she exclaimed, sitting up. "I suppose Entara didn't do that. Well, she was raised with privilege. I am just a very ordinary girl. I've made my way the best I could."

"Of course you have," Klein assured her. "Ragatti, you are a very expert and wise companion. So indulge me and tell me how boinking with me compares to your experiences with males of your own kind."

"How in the cosmos would I know? I've never mated. I'm still *ehpliah,* a pre-mater."

"Does that mean you consider yourself a virgin?" Klein said with a chuckle.

"Absolutely. Klein, for a partner whom Entara has bragged about and who is now a legend in every Forlani house of pleasure, you are sometimes astonishingly dumb. Don't they teach you anything about biology on Earth? We have to study twenty or thirty major types of partners in our training."

"You can help me now. I gathered from Entara that you do not consider boinking to be the equivalent of mating, but why not? Don't Forlani males settle down with their females at night just as we do?"

"You must be joking! Once they shake out of their post-coital stupor, they're usually scared by all the blood and rush off to cleanse themselves!"

"Blood!"

"Klein, pay attention now. The organ of the Forlani male is nothing like yours, it's sharp, long and jagged and it pierces right into our tissue and can sometimes even damage organs. The *plieh,* the mated partner, almost always loses liters of blood and requires immediate attention from a team of sister attendants after the mating. Sometimes it takes many, many days to recover, while she is fed special juices that keep her alive. Meanwhile, her body changes. We change so much after mating. If we are fortunate enough to mate and survive, the fertilized cells in our bodies change our whole chemistry forever."

"My god!" Klein exclaimed. "Why would you consent to go through that? It sounds like torture."

"In a way it is, but without mating, there can be no birth. And birth… I'm not even going to try to describe it. Our own males don't begin to grasp it and I doubt you can, even if you try. It is the ecstasy. It is what every one of the Forlani yearns for."

Klein could hear the staccato *clack clack clack* of the drenching summer rain on the roof as he sat on his flimsy bed at night. His supply of Somega had run out and he had forgotten to go to the drugstore to get some more, leaving him trapped between the din of the bar below and the hammering of the rain above. His nonsleeping stupor was interrupted by a loud banging on the door, and he stumbled over to respond. As he opened it, he saw a bleary-eyed Tarkington waiting for him. "Mission time. Boss found a whole bunch of Locals standing in one place for a long time on the radar. We don't know what they're doing, but he says it's a good opportunity to take 'em out before they move."

"Locals at 3AM? Seems strange…they usually don't show up after 11. Are they sure the thunderstorm isn't making the scanners malfunction again?"

"Too many heat signatures for another malfunction. Boots and saddles, we gotta go."

Klein cursed under his breath and lumbered out of his room down to the thallop stables. He noticed that the thallops were excited, bleating and snorting, their usually stoic demeanor transformed by the storm. Rain was not a common occurrence on Domremy and the thallops had evolved to survive for long periods on little water, but Klein was still surprised at the dramatic emotional change it brought in them. *At least someone out here is enjoying this*, Klein thought as he rode with the rest of Cashman's crew to the area where the Locals were congregating. The farther the seven-man crew rode from town, the taller the native Domremy grasses grew, until the prairie reached its maximum height of about seven feet. The colonists' defense forces generally didn't venture this far from town, as the tall grasses obscured their vision and made it harder to get an accurate shot on the Locals. Most of the men in the crew were nervous; only Cashman kept his icy focus, undisturbed and calm in the unfamiliar environment.

"We're coming up on the Local site. If we can catch them by surprise, we should be able to kill several in the initial barrage, then the rest when they flee -- and Locals usually do flee when they get hit by focus fire. Be prepared for them to bound off in all directions. We'll have to dismount and walk through the grass as softly as possible to ensure a successful ambush. The damn rain is making the thallops too jumpy, and there's a good chance they'll give our position away. Our mankiller will dispose of any hosts we find already onsite. Dismount and prepare to move in!"

As the men moved forwards towards the Local gathering, Klein realized that Cashman's instinct had been correct; the thallops were nervously pacing around and snorting, and they likely would have fled the area if not for their control collars preventing them from running far from their riders. Through the sounds of thunder and rain, Klein could hear the rhythmic droning of the Locals growing louder as the kill team inched closer and closer. Most of the sounds tended to blend together, like an insect's buzzing call, but Klein could distinctly make out two recurring phrases in the Locals' cries that sounded almost like words -- *mahorshuvash*. The words seemed to come either at the end or the beginning of crying sequences, and increased in volume and clarity each time the Locals spoke them. The rhythm and structure of the cries reminded Klein of a religious ceremony, and he began to wonder if the Locals were merely creatures driven solely by instinct or if they possessed some unknown level of sentience, even sapient intelligence. The thought of interrupting a religious ceremony briefly sent a chill down Klein's spine, but he reassured himself with the knowledge that the Locals had never before shown any capacity for anything resembling language or sentient behavior. *Maybe it's just a mass mating, like some types of insects have*, Klein though as they crouched down prior to attack.

The men were standing in two horizontal rows, one behind the other. Cashman was standing behind them and would make a chopping motion with his hand to tell them to fire at will. He raised his hand into the air, beginning the motion.

Mahorshuvash....

His arm was in a vertical position over his head now.

Mahorshuvash...

His hand wavered for a second, then began to fall.

MAHOR SHUVASH!

Cashman's hand silently slashed through the air in a fraction of a second, and the men poked their weapons through the grass and opened fire.

Klein first realized that something was very wrong when he saw no hosts -- human, thallop, or any other life form the Locals typically utilized, amidst the assembly of insects. In the split second he saw the site before the first shot was fired, he was able to make out a few other details. The Locals were standing in a circular pattern. There was a particularly large Local with red hind legs at the farthest point away from where they were breaking through, and in the center of the circle, there were three ancient Locals lying on their backs, with ossified joints and glaucous eyes. The chanting and droning stopped immediately as the colonists crashed through the grass and opened fire, replaced with a stunned silence of horror.

The first rocket, judging from the trajectory -- Klein guessed it came from Tarkington's Kikkonnen -- smashed into the large Local with red hind legs, reducing it to a burning, screaming ruin. Another rocket slammed into one of the ancient Locals in the center of the circle. The creature died making a guttural noise that sounded to Klein like some kind of barbaric curse. More rockets from the initial barrage smashed through the circle, flinging the Locals in multiple directions.

Then, in a fraction of a second, the *screeching* began.

After all his time on Domremy, Klein had never heard a Local screech before. He had only heard the typical buzzing noises that the made for the most part, along with the droning rhythms of the ceremony his crew had just interrupted. A Local's screech did not sound anything like these more typical noises. It was like a combination of metal shearing on metal and a cat's nails scraping against a chalkboard. It was a sound to provoke agony and fear in the listener, a Mobius strip of sonic pain that seemed to come out of nowhere and continue endlessly. It was not a sound of hunger, mating, pleasure, or any everyday aspect of existence an organism could feel. It was a sound that meant one thing.

War.

The counterattack was as swift as it was deadly. Most of the men had barely had time to reload before the Locals charged their formation. Schaller, one of Cashman's most trusted men, was one of the first to go down, first tackled to the ground and then shredded into a gory mass of flesh by an enraged Local. Mutombo, a veteran of the Pan-Central African wars, died in the blink of an eye, decapitated by a Local's forelimb. Bulgakov, former inmate of the Russian Federation's most dreaded prison, died in agony as a Local speared through his stomach and lifted him off the ground.

The surprise attack had not scattered the Locals, making them the easy prey Cashman had planned. Instead, it had resulted in a massive, swarming attack, uniting the Locals into one brutal charge that overwhelmed the first row of humans. Cashman realized that his remaining men, one of them only a mankiller with a gun too low-caliber to hurt a Local, could not possibly drive off the Local assault. It was time to give the order to run.

"Cease fire and retreat! Get back to the thallops and get out of here ASAP!" Cashman yelled as he began running. The remaining four men's retreat was a disorganized rout with no covering fire, no clear view through the tall grass, and no semblance of tactics other than running as fast as possible. Driven by the maddest animal fear, their responses to the situation varied wildly. Tarkington held up his heavy Kikkonnen, tried to see if he could protect himself during his dash, whereas Klein immediately threw down his M221 and raced to the thallops as fast as he possibly could. Cashman's façade of supreme control had cracked, his face marked by rage and fear as he threw down his Kikkonnen and adopted Klein's tactics. The three men heard another agonized scream behind them, informing them that Radford, one of their men from the second row, had been caught and ripped to shreds by the Locals.

"We're nearly there," Cashman yelled to Tarkington. "Just drop your damn gun and run for it!"

A Local leapt out of the grass and slashed deep into Klein's leg. He fell to the ground, defiantly roaring at the Local even as it prepared to butcher him with its forelimbs. A rocket from Tarkington's Kikkonnen sent the Local careening to the ground to die in a pool of its own blood. As Klein tried to stagger to his feet, wincing in pain, he watched as another Local flew up over the top of the grass and leapt onto Tarkington, pinning him to the ground. Cashman ran to Klein, propping him up by the shoulder.

Klein could barely tell what was happening around him, as he felt pain shudder through his body. He tried to move his remaining good leg in sync with Cashman's, but could feel himself growing weak with blood loss. Adrenaline and fear surged through him, eclipsing any sadness he felt over the death of Tarkington. Finally, they reached the area where the thallops had been left. Cashman jerked on his thallop's reigns, ordering it down onto its knees, and slumped Klein across its back. Then he mounted another thallop and galloped away, leading Klein's animal, as fast as the thallops could carry them. Klein fell into unconsciousness as his thallop fled across the plains.

When his eyes opened again, he was in a dimly lit cave, and he saw Cashman crouched near him holding a flashlight and a medkit. He could feel a liquid, burning pain and his injured leg could barely move.

"Pretty bad wound you got there. Might get infected if it doesn't get treated," Cashman said in a monotone. "I got a medkit here if you need it...but you'll have to tell me a few things."

Shit...Cashman, what do you want to know? You have my files from Stafford Station, you have my conviction record from Earth...what else do you need? I'm a mankiller. None of us get picked for this position because we have a clean record. Just use the medkit on this wound and be done with it."

"I'm not interested in your court case or your record here, Klein. I'm interested in what you did *before* you got into the criminal justice system. Every time I've asked I've always gotten a 'not now' or 'I don't want to talk about it'. You're gonna tell me *exactly* why you're here *now*, or you ain't gettin' anything from the medkit."

Klein held out as long as he possibly could. The dull, throbbing pain in his wounded leg grew worse and worse as time passed and Cashman patiently waited. Cashman gave him everything he needed – food, rations, water, even a Somega when he tried to sleep the pain away – but not the medkit. To his chagrin, Klein found himself developing a splitting headache, a possible side effect of his wound's infection. After suffering for what seemed like an eternity, Klein finally called Cashman over to him.

"Cashman...I'm willing to talk. I'll tell everything. Just give me the medkit."

And Klein explained how he fell into the criminal justice system.

Klein's job as a career civil service worker for the Treasury department of Düsseldorf always seemed an ill match for him. It consisted of day after day of hunching over a keyboard and peering over endless stats and flow charts depicting how public works projects, public/private partnerships and corporate ventures impacted the city's finances. Most of the time very little was revealed in terms of new information; for the most part, his job was to double check analyses that had already happened and verify their accuracy, passing the reports on to his superiors. Sometimes, Klein even felt nostalgic for his grueling years in the German Marines that got him the job in the first place; at least in that job, it felt like things were actually *happening*. He was nearly finished with his afternoon shift and was drinking a cup of coffee in his cubicle, when he saw an unusual project appear on the list of approved programs…

"Project Kinderaugen." Listed as a "project to better verify the security and well-being of Germany's children," Klein could find no details on what the project actually *did* or what it was supposed to accomplish. Even stranger, the project seemed to have no recommended budget. Its budget was simply whatever the city put into it, with no warnings of going over budget or notifications of surpluses. Buried near the end of the report, Project Kinderaugen seemed to have been strategically positioned to be passed over by and forgotten about by a weary employee. Klein's curiosity gnawed at him and he went to ask his boss, Mr. Achenbach, about why this particular project had such unique accounting standards.

"Achenbach, there's something I think you need to see here…"

"Okay, but make it quick. Only 15 minutes left till the end of our shift."

"I found something strange near the end of this list…it's listed as a corporate project called 'Kinderaugen'. I don't think I've ever seen anything come through the Treasury that has no recommended budget or specified limits. I don't think I can approve this in good faith unless I have more specifics."

Achenbach sighed. "Oh, the Kinderaugen thing. Someone must not have entered the full data in for that one correctly. I'll just finish that one myself, since I have access to all the files. You've nearly finished the rest of this set of projects and then you can go home. Tie it all up done by the end of shift."

Although Klein still had his reservations about Kinderaugen, he also knew how important punctuality was on his job reviews. "Sure. I'll go finish the rest," he said as he left Achenbach's room and went back to his cubicle. The remains of the assignment were uneventful, with nothing eye-catching to distract Klein from finishing it on time. Once the last fifteen minutes were up, Klein left the office and got on a bus to go back to his apartment. He slowly became more relaxed on the bus ride, the bizarre discovery of Kinderaugen receding into the distance of his memories as the street lights and shops of Düsseldorf passed by. As the bus stopped near his apartment,

Klein quickly walked out amidst the crowd leaving at the stop.

An old man walking next to Klein suddenly fell to the ground, clutching his shoulder in agony. There was no sound of gunfire, but Klein's military expertise had taught him that snipers often used silencers for their rifles. Klein's mind, dulled by the rhythms of civilian life mere seconds ago, transformed back into the mind of a soldier as adrenaline surged through it. As the other people in the crowd leaving the bus began to become panicked and disoriented from fear, scattering in an ungainly mob, Klein sprinted for the door to his apartment complex. He had no weapon and no idea where the sniper was shooting from, and could only hope to be safe in his room. He rushed into the building and ran up the stairs to his one room apartment. Klein felt a very slight sense of relief that there was no one at the door or inside the room waiting to shoot him, as he had been worried that the assassin had an accomplice waiting to kill him. After an hour crouched behind the couch with a gun in his hand, Klein began to relax slightly and sat down, turning the TV on to the regional news. A report about the shooting at the bus stop was currently airing.

"Michael Schneider, a retired banker and resident of Düsseldorf, was shot in the shoulder today as he and a crowd of passengers were exiting from a bus. He is currently at a city hospital in stable condition. No suspects have yet been identified."

As the news shifted from coverage of the shooting to discussions on the weather and celebrity fashions, Klein began to think over the events in his head. *There was one shot, and it hit Snyder in the shoulder. He could've been aiming for that man or me -- I can't be sure, since we were standing so close together. I'll take a couple days of sick leave and then report back to work. But I'm not going to make the mistake of going unarmed while I think the sniper is still out there.*

After two uneventful days of watching the news closely to see if Schneider or anyone else was targeted by the sniper, Klein returned to his job, but his former boredom was replaced by a gnawing paranoia about the continued threat of violence and the true nature of Kinderaugen. Even as he worked on the mundane duties of his normal job, information on Kinderaugen remained frustratingly out of reach in any of the databases he was generally allowed to utilize. After a week of finding nothing on Kinderaugen, he decided to ask Achenbach if he had finished filling out the Kinderaugen forms.

"Hello, Achenbach," Klein said as he walked into Achenbach's office. "About that Project Kinderaugen…it's been a week, and I still haven't found out whether it got finished or not. I can't find any further information on it in the database. I feel responsible, since it was assigned to me. What happened to it?"

"I told you I'd finish Kinderaugen for you, and I did. I did it on Wednesday, while you were out on sick leave. There's no need for you to be preoccupied with it any further."

Klein began to grow frustrated with Achenbach's obfuscation. "But there wasn't even a record of it in the expenditures column! Usually, projects are listed there after we finish processing them…"

Achenbach had an irritated look on his face as he answered Klein. "Look, Project Kinderaugen is a very important priority to us. It's research that will protect and enrich the lives of children around the world! You have no idea how much this project means to the city of Düsseldorf—not just in terms of the potential employment and financial windfall, but in terms of *prestige!* This city needs a program like this, and it's a very high priority that we get it, even if it means not dotting every "I" if it makes our corporate partners happy. So please, stop worrying about Kinderaugen. It's all been handled. We won't hold the fact that you didn't finish this one assignment because you were sick against you."

"Thank you for doing this for me. I don't get sick very often, but when I do, it's good to know that my superiors won't hold it against me," Klein forced himself to say as convincingly as he could. He walked out of Achenbach's office knowing he could count on no further help from Achenbach in understanding Project Kinderaugen, and considered what to do next as he finished his remaining assignments and decided to stop at a bar on the way home.

One beer led to another as Klein pondered what to do next about Kinderaugen. He thought about quitting. He thought about re-enlisting in the Marines. He thought about getting a flight back to Las Vegas and working as a mercenary in America. The secret war was still going on in Central America and he knew he could hook up with a recruiter who worked around the big Pyramid. A dozen futures, equally bad, ran into each other and blended like cheap paint. It was time to head for the gent's.

The lavatory could have served a rifle platoon, but it was empty when Klein went in to enjoy the pause that refreshes. His bladder felt like he had consumed at least a gallon of beer. After a few seconds another fellow came in and strolled up to a urinal a few places away from Klein. He was a tall, lanky guy with an aquiline nose who could easily serve as a model for the adjective "swarthy." He unzipped loudly and made a big deal about unfurling his private business. Klein decided he felt uneasy about this newcomer and zipped up to make a speedy exit. As the fellow ostentatiously reeled in his extensive privates, he actually blew a kiss at Klein. Klein was about to remark to him that he must be barking up the wrong tree when he noticed what all the machismo was meant to cover up -- a bulge under his jacket. Knowing that as soon as decency had done its duty, the guy would next whip out a pistol, Klein preemptively stepped up and took a swing at him. But he was too slow. The other fellow executed a neat side-step and used a judo move to sling Klein down on the tiles. He was really smiling now, as he had apparently decided to kill Klein without gunfire and slowly advanced to finish him off. *Italian,* thought Klein*, graceful on their feet, deadly in the water, and the commandos all get years of very effective judo training. But I bet he didn't sit in with the Spatznaz as I did.* Recalling what his instructor Voroschenko had taught him during the Herat action, where most duels were fought down on the dusty ground, Klein brought the assassin down with a variation of the old Russian leg drop and then, still spinning on his butt, slipped a knee around his neck and locked in the triangle choke hold. The Italian wasn't thinking about his package now, as he struggled in vain to breathe and to pump oxygen into his failing brain. In thirty seconds he wasn't thinking any more at all. Before slipping out and leaving in a hurry, Klein checked to see that he hadn't just murdered a man strictly on instinct, but the gun was right there under the Italian's jacket, along with what passed for a badge in the secret police. He walked home as normally as possible, played Scarlatti to calm his nerves and soon fell into a surprisingly deep sleep.

It seemed for some reason important to act casual for the next few days, so Klein went through the motions at work, rode the bus home, went back to his apartment and had dinner, but he felt too nervous to watch TV or really take a rest. Finally he decided to take a twilight walk on the Rhein.

Klein looked at the orange setting sun slipping below the horizon as he walked down the riverfront, passing by cafes, electronics shops, and stores selling novelty gifts to tourists. As he walked down the riverfront, he thought he could hear the sound of footsteps close behind him; turning his head, he saw a man in a thick coat with reddish hair following him on foot. Klein nervously turned into an alley and began to walk quicker. The red-haired man picked up his pace and followed him. Klein looked over his shoulder again and saw the man reaching into the pocket of his coat. He could see the man clutching the butt of a gun in his hand.

Klein had only a few seconds to respond. He drew his own pistol from his coat pocket and shot the man directly in the heart. He examined the man's body, looking for ID cards or dog tags, and found a police badge. *Oh shit. Whoever is after me must be either rich, or in a position of real authority if they can use cops as assassins. I'd better not stay here too long if someone else in the force is out here searching for me. Touching the body would incriminate me via DNA evidence, so I'd better leave it lying here and get back to my apartment. I'll be safer in the confines of my apartment than out here, where I'm sniper bait if I'm out in the open too long*, Klein reasoned in his mind.

Klein briskly jogged back to his apartment, his heart pounding in his chest. He opened the door and slowly began to become more relaxed, but was too nervous to think straight. Thinking about his would-be assassin, Klein reasoned that, if the men sent after him were policemen, they would try to avoid killing him in such a way that would incriminate themselves, which meant the preferred tactics would likely be another sniper attack like at the bus stop, or a kill in a darkened alley with no witnesses. Finally able to relax, Klein took a Somega and fell asleep.

There was no word from Achenbach or anyone else at the office about Kinderaugen during the remainder of the work week. Klein had decided to take a trip away from the city, to a forested area along the banks of the Ruhr, to clear his head and give him some time to think of how to proceed with his search for Kinderaugen information. He hoped that a good, long walk through the woods would relax his mind enough that he could come up with an effective means of obtaining the Kinderaugen information. Pondering his potential future after blowing the whistle on Kinderaugen, he stared out over the river valley, taking time to savor the details of the landscape in the setting sun.

Klein heard a rustling noise in the bushes behind him. He turned and saw the barrel of a rifle pointed at him. Immediately he rolled for cover, anticipating the shot. *At least it's not a sniper rifle*, Klein briefly thought as he charged through the trees in search of a defensible position where he could get the rifleman in range of his pistol. He crouched behind a fallen tree and lined up a shot at his pursuer, only to see *another* rifle poking through the leaves of the trees above him. Klein scuttled through the underbrush as the shooter opened fire. He heard a snap behind him as he crawled through the thorny branches of a bush, but he felt no pain or difficulty moving, and reasoned that the shot must have hit a branch rather than his body. He knew that if he was trapped in the bush for too long, the sniper would hit him eventually, so he had to quickly improvise a counterattack. He turned his body through the bush, feeling the thorns slash through his face and hands, and fired his pistol into the clump of leaves the rifle was protruding from. He heard a yell of agony and saw the shooter fall to the ground with a sickening thud. Klein shot the fallen gunman in the head and killed him instantly, only taking a few seconds to glance at the blood oozing from the man's still corpse. He heard the noisy chatting of a hiking group coming from further up the trail and knew he had to get clear of the bush and away from the area before they arrived. He finally tore his way free of the bush and bolted in the direction of the parking lot to escape the woods and evade his remaining pursuer. As he ran for his car, he could hear accusatory yelling from behind him; it sounded like the remaining gunman had been blamed for his partner's murder by the hikers. Klein breathed a sigh of relief as he sat down in his car and turned the key, knowing that if the second assassin was arrested and accused of the shooting, he would be temporarily safe.

Klein had difficulty concentrating and thinking about the mundane duties of his job during the next week. His evaluations were slower, his analytical mind disoriented, and his attention fractured as he remained preoccupied with trying to find information on Kinderaugen. Luckily for Klein, this was the last week before the office would close to allow its employees two weeks of summer vacation, and Achenbach and the higher-ranking staff seemed just as mentally preoccupied with their coming vacation plans as he was with possible conspiracies. Klein could see the other employees staring at images of beaches, concerts, and mountains on their computer monitors as he struggled to finish his daily assignments. He overheard Achenbach having a conversation with Erich, one of his coworkers.

"Achenbach, I think I may have filled out some of the figures wrong on the forms for SRI. Is there anything I can do to correct them?" Erich was not normally the type to admit a mistake, but seemed more honest and straightforward than usual, as if he anticipated that Achenbach would be more forgiving than usual prior to vacation time.

"Go to the Data Reclamation Department and get the codes to fix it there," Achenbach said. "Get it fixed up before the end of the day, so we can include it with the other forms we submit for this quarter. Prioritize fixing that over the assignments you haven't started on yet."

As Erich briskly walked out and left for Data Reclamation, Klein seized the opportunity and followed him into the elevator. Erich was a rather shy person and rarely talked to Klein, or anyone else at the office, when he didn't have to, and he wasn't any more talkative the day before his vacation than on any other day at the office. Erich and Klein walked together into Data Reclamation, and saw why the supervisors tried to keep the staff from using the room as much as possible. The place was filled with a dizzying array of printed forms and files, and computer screens packed with spreadsheets and lines of text. It was such a flood of information that it seemed impossible to make sense of it, yet there was only one employee there to help organize it all: Fritz, Director of Data Recovery. Fritz was a rail-thin man with horn-rimmed glasses and spiky red hair. He rarely left the confines of Data Recovery during the workdays, and this was the first time Klein had ever seen him. After ten interminable minutes of looking at his watch and tapping his finger while Fritz helped Erich find the necessary forms and correct his mistake, Klein was called in.

"So, you in here to correct some accounting mistakes too?" Fritz asked. "Seems like a lot of people from Achenbach's division have been having problems today. You guys are going on vacation before we even let out!"

"You know how it is," Klein said. "For my vacation this time, I'm going down to the Reeperbahn to check out the...nightlife. I've rarely been there before, and I'm feeling especially curious this time."

"That's a pretty rough place for a vacation. If I was ever in a place like that, I'd be so worried that I wouldn't be able to enjoy myself."

"Couldn't be any worse than most of the places I went on furlough while I was still in the military. Now, about this problem...I made a critical error on accounting for something called Project Kinderaugen a couple of weeks ago, and Achenbach told me I'd better fix it before we go on vacation at the end of this quarter. Could you please bring up the Kinderaugen files for me?"

"Seems a little late to be fixing something from a couple of weeks ago, but I guess it's okay if your supervisor insists. Just a minute while I search the files to bring it up for you...sorry if this takes a little longer than usual, I usually don't get requests from this far back..."

Klein was able to maintain his patience for two more minutes while Fritz searched through the database for Kinderaugen. He felt a manic sense of excitement surging through his mind as he waited for Fritz to finally locate the information that had brought him close to death several times. "Here's the Kinderaugen file! I made sure to make as much of it accessible as possible to you, but there's some weird security protocols that prevented me from accessing the entire file. I'm sure you'll be able to fix all the mathematical aspects, however...none of that was encrypted or protected."

Klein walked over to the computer terminal and began to study the Kinderaugen file...

**PROJECT KINDERAUGEN
LEAD RESEARCHER- S. Dorfman
DATE 2152 11/7**

RESEARCH BEGINS. HAVE SUCCESSFULLY PERSUADED OFFICIALS IN DUESSELDORF TO PROVIDE FINANCIAL SUPPORT INTO "KINDERAUGEN." PROJECT WILL UTILIZE NEURAL IMPLANTS INTO CHILDREN AGES 5-14 TO MONITOR MENTAL ACTIVITY AND SOCIAL DEVELOPMENT DURING CRUCIAL DEVELOPMENTAL PERIOD

**DATE 2153 4/1
NEURAL IMPLANTS IN INITIAL TEST SUBJECTS NOT SUCCESSFUL IN TRANSMITTING ADEQUATE DATA AMOUNTS. REQUIRE NEW TEST GROUP AND MORE EXTENSIVE NEURAL IMPLANT ARRAY. TEST SUBJECTS WILL BE DISMISSED TO THEIR FAMILIES AND GIVEN COMPENSATION**

DATE 2153 15/4

SECOND NEURAL IMPLANT DESIGN HAS BEEN FINALIZED. ALLOWS FOR MORE MONITORING OF ENDORPHIN AND SERATONIN LEVELS IN TEST SUBJECTS, AND EMOTIONAL TRACKING PROTOCOLS (I.E. MONITORING TRANSITIONS TOWARDS INTENSE ANGER, PLEASURE, ETC.) CHANGES TO KINDERAUGEN REQUIRE RE-SUBMITTING FINANCIAL APPROVAL FORMS THROUGH DUESSELDORF TREASURY DEPARTMENT-V2 KINDERAUGEN WILL BE MORE EXPENSIVE THAN V1.

DATE 2153 20/5

FINANCIAL APPROVAL PENDING FOR PROJECT IN DUESSELDORF TREASURY DEPARTMENT. TEST SUBJECTS CURRENTLY BEING SELECTED FROM PROSPECTIVE RECRUIT POOL. EXPECT TO COMMENCE KINDERAUGEN IN FALL.

DATE 2153 25/5

MANAGER AT TREASURY DEPARTMENT REPORTS UNNECCESSARY INTEREST IN KINDERAUGEN BY LOW-LEVEL TREASURY EMPLOYEE DURING APPROVAL PROCESS. PROJECT IS OTHERWISE PROCEEDING AS PLANNED.

DATE 2153 30/5

KINDERAUGEN APPROVED BY DUESSELDORF TREASURY DEPARTMENT. NEURAL IMPLANT V2 PASSED ALL PRELIMINARY TESTS AND IS USABLE AS OF THIS DATE. START DATE OF KINDERAUGEN CURRENTLY BEING FINALIZED.

Klein inserted a memcard, an inch-long portable flash memory device, into the computer so he could store the Kinderaugen information that was not encrypted. It only took half a minute for Klein to discreetly put the memcard into the computer's port, copy the information onto it, and shove it back into his pocket. Fritz was playing with a paper clip and looking impatiently at the clock on the wall while Klein copied the Kinderaugen data. He typed in a few meaningless lines of numbers to give the impression he was actually working on editing the accounting on Kinderaugen. Then, he deleted the superfluous lines and told Fritz he was finished.

"Well, that was pretty quick," Fritz observed. "I wish everyone here was able to fix their mistakes as fast as you, Klein. You really have an eye for detail."

Sometimes I wish I didn't, thought Klein as he left the room. There was little time left before the end of the workday and Klein needed to complete as much as he could to give the illusion to Achenbach that he was still busy with finishing his assignments. Luckily, none of the remaining assignments were very difficult, and Achenbach was too preoccupied with reading emails from his superiors to have paid much notice to Klein's brief trip to Data Reclamation. The remaining work session passed quickly and before long, the office closed for the day, sending Klein and his fellow employees off to their two-week vacations.

In his apartment, Klein considered which steps he should take next. He needed a suitably credible newspaper or magazine that he could leak the Kinderaugen information to, and decided on *Der Spiegel*, which was still one of the most credible magazines in Germany, long after it had lost its print component over a century ago. He emailed the Kinderaugen data to one of its news editors, a fellow he had briefly known during his studies, then began to plan the second phase of his scheme to expose the Kinderaugen project. Even with the information in the hands of *Der Spiegel*, he had to do something radical and dangerous to convince the public that Kinderaugen was truly a threat to public safety. He needed to show that the hitmen sent to kill those who sought the truth about Kinderaugen not only existed, but were a true threat to society. To do that, he needed to stop hiding in the shadows and seeking safety from the assassins, and to expose them in a method as scandalous and newsworthy as possible to catch the public's eye.

He decided on a showdown at the Reeperbahn, the infamous "sinful mile" of Hamburg.

The Reeperbahn was a hallucinatory, intoxicating place, a strange stretch of cheap and not-so-cheap bars, discos with blaring neon lights, and gilt-edged strip clubs with innuendo-laden names. It had taken over 50 years since the 2007 ban on weapons in the Reeperbahn for authorities to finally become convinced that the ban could be relaxed. Even in the middle of the 22nd Century, certain aspects of the old ban had been retained -- the prohibition of assault weapons, rifles, and "any type of explosive" (effectively even large firecrackers!) was still in force along the Reeperbahn. Klein's plan was to exploit this law to his advantage, since the weapons restrictions made another sniper attack less likely, and he would have a better chance against an assassin armed only with a pistol than one armed with heavy weaponry.

He stopped in front of a bar with a flashing violet electric sign that read "Cathay." The sign was written in a strangely elegant script that was reminiscent of ancient Chinese calligraphy, which contrasted sharply with the harsh, blaring electronic music echoing from within. Klein felt a sense of tension and anxiety that reminded him of how he had felt before the prior assassination attempts. He saw a short man with black hair standing close to him, and the man was reaching into his pockets, as if he was trying to grab a gun. Sweat poured down Klein's face as he rushed into the bar.

The main Asian influence in the Cathay bar, other than two stylized lions on each side of the entrance, were some scantily clad baristas wearing little more than the thinnest possible bikinis and panties. They all seemed to have perpetual smiles fixed on their faces as they walked around taking drink orders. One of the baristas came over to Klein.

"Welcome to Cathay. What is your pleasure?"

"One Heineken, please," Klein answered.

"Two drink minimum."

Klein gave a sigh of frustration. He always hated having to spend more money than he absolutely had to, and he had only gone into the bar to avoid a possible assassin anyway. "Okay, *two* Heinekens please," he requested.

"Thank you," the barista said and walked off to get his beer.

Klein took a look around him and saw a huskily built man laughing loudly from across the bar at a table. He had deep brown hair and a thin beard, and seemed to be having a great time as he laughed and joked with the other customers and the staff. At the speed of a striking viper, the man threw his table down and pulled out a pistol, firing at Klein.

Klein crashed his own table to the ground and began firing at the assassin in retaliation. The blaring of the music was drowned out by the screams of the customers as they began to bolt for the exit. The bar's bouncer started yelling at them from behind the cover of a desk near the tap. "Take this shit outside or I'll shoot you dead!" Both Klein and the assassin ignored the bouncer, firing at each other and ducking behind their capsized tables, until the bouncer brought out his own pistol and started shooting.

Squatting close to the ground to minimize his target area, Klein ran behind a booth that he hoped would offer better cover from the two men shooting at him. He felt a sharp pain in his left leg as he ran, and fell onto his belly, writhing in pain as the assassin walked over to him. He frantically tried to reload his pistol, but the assassin stamped down on his hand, forcing him to drop the gun. Klein could see the assassin's gun pointed at him and heard his voice…

"You're under arrest!"

"So the last guy that was after me wasn't an assassin at all," Klein said as he finished explaining how he had come to Domremy. "He was just a regular cop sent out to get me. The Düsseldorf police had been monitoring my internet usage and saw all the things I had been looking up on the Reeperbahn, and alerted the Hamburg police. The one assassin I didn't kill -- the one I *thought* had been accused of killing the rifleman -- identified me as the killer of the other cops, and the two departments had been working together to get me. If I hadn't run into the cop in Cathay, I probably would've run into a different cop at another bar or nightclub on the Reeperbahn. They had the whole place staked out."

"Pretty lucky to get away with your life after killing three cops, even if they were dirty," Cashman said. "What happened to the reports you sent to *Der Spiegel*? The media would have reacted differently to the trial if they knew that those cops were assassins sent to kill you."

"That's the damnedest thing," Klein laughed bitterly. "The news editor from *Der Spiegel* received the email with the data on Kinderaugen, but they couldn't make any sense of it! Apparently the data was encrypted in some way that means that it couldn't be 'read' except on machines given verified clearance by the Düsseldorf Treasury Department. *Der Spiegel* couldn't access the data unless Treasury allowed it, and they weren't about to put their asses on the line to try to save a cop killer."

Klein watched as a cruel smile spread across Cashman's face. "That's good to know, because it means you haven't got any leverage over my boss." Klein could only listen to Cashman as a sickening realization dawned in his mind. "You didn't think that Dorfman had only cops *on Earth* working for him, do you? He pays a shitload more than any marshall staying clean on this rock ever got, even Jim Stafford. And after you found out about Kinderaugen, he's been offering good money to see you dead. Of course, I'm not going to kill you now. You told me everything about the dirt you had on Dorfman, and I made you a *promise* to give you the antibiotics in exchange for that information. Of course, bringing a man back alive from that debacle with the Locals looks better on *my* permanent record, and I didn't make you a promise that you'd live forever…"

Klein finally blacked out from pain and exhaustion as Cashman leaned in to give him the injection from the medkit.

Two days later, Klein had only a nasty scar on his leg and an occasional tingling pain to remind him of his encounter with the Locals. His mind, however, was considerably less healthy after learning that he had not escaped the reach of Dorfman and the Kinderaugen conspiracies on Domremy. He had called Ragatti into his room, and was preparing to make an important call back to Peebo. Ragatti had noticed his nervousness and paranoia, and was feeling unusually anxious herself as a result.

"Klein…why have you been so nervous since you returned two days ago? Have I done something that frustrated you? Is there something about this settlement that you dislike?"

"As a matter of fact, there *is* something about Site 89 that's pissing me off, but it's not anything you did – or.anything you can control. I really need to talk to Peebo now, and I'll tell you what I can after I talk with him. But right now you need to start packing your things." Klein got his phone out and called up Peebo, who was stretched out on his couch after a hard day's work on the farm.

"Peebo, this is Klein. I've called to find out how your tomatoes are doing. The tomatoes around here are all rotten." Ragatti thought Klein must have actually lost his mind to waste time talking about the garden with his old landlord, but she didn't realize that the Religious Dissenters had developed their own code language, Crop Talk, and that Klein had been permitted to learn bits of it. Rule One of Exile Life: all communications are monitored, recorded, and compu-analyzed. He had just told Peebo that an emergency had arisen.

"I wish I could send you some of these crummy tomatoes to see if you could find out how to make it better. I bet if you looked at just one, you'd know what to do."

"Well," replied Peebo, "I'd certainly like to have a look at one of them tomatoes. Of course, I might have to keep it around for a while before I figured it out."

"That's exactly what I want you to do. But you might have to send it along somewhere else, too, if that doesn't work out. You and the boys might have to decide where to go next with it."

Peebo could hear Ragatti's indignant yelling in the background as she threw clothes into her travelling bag. He knew exactly which "tomato" Klein was referring to, but couldn't guess what had broken up their domestic arrangement. "Why should that fruit go bad all of a sudden, Klein? It never gave anyone trouble as long as I've known about it!"

"Peebo, it's maybe not about the fruit, it's about what's happening to my own digestion. I can't talk about it over the phone, because it's a bit disgusting and I don't want you to get indigestion, too, but it's best you just don't waste any time talking with me and see to the harvests yourself. I don't want to pass on any rotten fruit to anybody because I'm too stupid to grow anything right." *It's best that no innocents suffer because of something I've done.*

"I know why you're a mankiller and no gardener, dammit! But you can count on me and you don't have to fancify any details about using the outhouse where I'm concerned. Shit is shit!" *You're my friend, you don't have to hide anything else from me!* That's what Peebo is saying.

"You may know I have no green thumb, but you don't know why, and it's better if you don't pick up any of my bad personal toilet habits." *In other words, for your own safety, it's best you don't know more.* "Please, take care of them tomatoes for me, because I'm sending a jar of them out of this settlement by regular mail." *Peebo will meet her discreetly at the station first thing tomorrow.*

"I'll do it, Klein," Peebo said with sadness and confusion in his voice. "I hope you get over those toilet problems okay. Domremy needs more mankillers like you."

Klein tried to reassure Peebo. "I'll be fine. I know what I'm doing. Talk with you soon," and hung up. He looked at Ragatti's face and saw an expression of anger and disgust at what she perceived as Klein's betrayal of her. Her hands were trembling with rage, and she was barely holding back a desire to let loose a loud scream.

"Ragatti, this isn't what it looks like. My feelings for you haven't changed. It's just that if you stay here, things will be worse for you than you could possibly imagine."

"How could it possibly be worse?" Ragatti yelled indignantly. "Do you even know what it means to be a Forlani woman rejected by a male? To be -- what do humans call it—"turned away" -- that is one of the *greatest* insults you can possibly give us in our culture! Did you even think what the other Forlani here or in Stafford Station would say about me, how quickly the rumors would spread? I would be considered lower than the most pathetic, low-born female from…"

"No, Ragatti. I don't know, and I don't pretend to understand Forlani culture from what little experience I have of it yet. What I do know is the people I'm up against here in Site 89, and I know that if you stay here, you'll be dead sooner or later. If you value your life, you'll get out of here on the train first thing tomorrow and go back to Peebo's farm. But whatever you do, you can't stay with me any longer. I'm not safe anymore-for you, for Peebo, or for anyone else who knows me."

Ragatti angrily stormed out of Klein's room, leaving him alone with a nagging pain in his leg and the dangerous uncertainties of a future working for a man who was conspiring to kill him. Klein decided to go down to the bar and squander his paycheck on some cheap Site 89 Special beer. The skunky stuff was so intensely vile and sour that Klein avoided it whenever he possibly could, but now was the right time for libations and Site 89 Special was all he could afford. *It's gonna be a rotten night*, Klein thought as he sat down at the bar and ordered the first of four glasses of Site 89 Special.

What Klein didn't know was that a good measure of Ragatti's distress was coming from the fact that she would have to report what had happened to a certain someone back on her home planet. It would take a lot of tact and trouble to redact and send the report through secure channels and she was already expecting a blistering reply, since she had failed in such an important mission.

Ragatti herself could not have been more astounded when she received the coded answer a few months later through a new consort sent out to the communal house where she was then living. "Praise to you, wise and competent Ragatti, for your faithful service. Do you not realize that your Like-Male did the only possible thing under adverse circumstances, and that you could not help him more? Prepare yourself in physical and spiritual beauty, for you will soon be called to the court of a very eminent lady, where you will rejoice with some of your sisters and where you will be preferred." Ragatti couldn't believe she would soon become exalted and perhaps even someday become a Minor Wife herself, which often happed at court. She could not have guessed that Entara would become so powerful so quickly, to be able to offer her such a reward. She wished she could apologize to Klein for her ungracious scene, though she knew she must never communicate with him again on her own initiative.

Erica Duquesne was looking over some stats on the grain harvest yields on Domremy when she was greeted by the unwelcome sight of a smirking, self-absorbed Bill Hollingsworth standing in the door to her office. "Hello Bill," Duquesne greeted him. "You're looking happy today. How are things going for you?"

"Excellent, Erica, excellent," Hollingsworth responded. "I've just gotten the Board of Directors to approve my special request for Domremy. It will make this division immensely more profitable once it's been carried out. I have big plans for Domremy once this goes through."

"What is this special project you've been planning?" Duquesne asked. "You've been going on about this project for several weeks now, but I still have no idea what it is. Since it's been approved and we're going to be doing it anyway, I think we'd benefit if you made it public now."

Hollingsworth's face had the self-conscious smirk of a man who felt he was on top of the world. Duquesne felt herself practically gagging on the fumes of Hollingsworth's sense of empowerment, as if the weasely executive was a ferret in heat. "Erica, this is our new project. *Frontier Heroes of Domremy*! We send out a film crew to Domremy, and we use them to capture the colonists as they go about their ordinary jobs – farming, ranching, fighting these 'Local' creatures. Put some slick editing into it, use it to assemble a narrative with compelling characters, and we'll not only have a massive ratings success, but also a tool to fuel tourism and immigration to Domremy! We can use this program to finally get a decent class of people to immigrate to Domremy, and we'll finally monetize the planet better than using it as a simple penal colony!"

"Bill, this planet is barely subsistent as it is. 94 percent of the population is still convicts, many of them there as a result of violent crimes, the rest for some form of Dissenter activity. Do you really think people like that want to be filmed, especially if all the money from it goes to the corporation rather than giving them a cut? They'll see a bunch of film crews and interns there with a life that looks great compared to theirs, and they'll start feeling envious, maybe even murderous. And that's not even mentioning the fact that this planet is still crawling with Locals, and has weather patterns that are unpredictable to us, and…"

"Of course there's a risk," Hollingsworth said. "All business has a certain amount of risk, business involving dangerous alien worlds more than others. But think of the potential upside! The *Heroes* franchise has been trending downwards for years. That last installment – what was it, *Heroes of Jamestown* – that barely made back its budget, even with all those OptiCon sales and promotional partners. By turning it into an Actuality program and making it about current events, rather than about some event in the past that isn't relevant to our audience anymore, we could revitalize the franchise at only a fraction of the budget *Jamestown* had!"

Duquesne had seen this before. Hollingsworth had entered the state he so eloquently called "the Zone," in which became so intoxicated by his theories for success and the seeming infallibility of his hypothetical schemes that nothing could possibly dissuade him. She could only listen to the rising crescendo of excitement in his voice as he described commercial tie-ins with clothing and firearm companies about "The Domremy Experience," leaving the task of actually managing the risk of the project to her. *He won't listen*, Duquesne thought. *This project is his baby, and whenever he gets it into his head that a project is a sure thing that he can shepherd through like this, he won't listen to criticism. Until it's too late, of course.*

3

Before the sun rose over the horizon in Site 89, Cashman had called a meeting of his crew to order. Since the events that had become known as the "Great Storm Massacre," Cashman had sent a request for more men to fill the ranks of his crew. Some of the men were fresh off the transport ships, and though they had been debriefed and instructed in the proper methods of protocol and respect for rank on Domremy, Klein could hear the sounds of men grumbling and cursing under their breath, unhappy that they had been called into a meeting at the crack of dawn. "I'd better not be hearing that shit, people," Cashman said. "You've all been called here because something important is about to happen here in Site 89. A film crew from Earth has been sent by Hyperion Corporation. They will walk with you, and they will record events around town that are, in their mission statement's words, 'both mundane and extraordinary'. That means if the Locals make a raid on the town, the film crew will be there, trying to shoot every minute." Cashman could hear a solitary muttered curse from the back of the room.

"Doing everything within your power to help this film crew is mandatory," Cashman continued. "Not only is it good for our PR, but we'll be getting a considerable stipend for doing this. And the more helpful you are to the crew, the more generous the stipend. They'll only be here a couple of months before they leave to go film at the other sites, so you'd better be on your best behavior. Any violations and you'll be doing night watch for as long as I want to assign it to you." The grumbling abruptly ended.

"Anyway, they start setting up equipment around town tomorrow. They expect to film mainly in town, so we won't have to go far out into the wilderness." Klein could hear several of the men breathing sighs of relief, no doubt at the fact that they wouldn't have to risk a repeat of the Great Storm Massacre. "They'll need armed guards for their filming sessions, and you'll be paid well *if* you volunteer. If I don't get volunteers, I'll choose armed guards by lottery, and those chosen won't get any extra money. Mark my words, this show will get filmed, no matter what you think of it. Got it?" The men nodded their heads, dreading the "welcome" they would have to give the newcomers the following day.

The film crew arrived at 8AM, coming in on the train that had dropped Klein off months ago, before its schedule had inexplicably been reduced. Now, for the moment, everything was back on time. All of Cashman's men were there to be introduced to the film crew, including Klein. The men stood at attention as Klein called out their names and described their duties. Klein noticed that Cashman introduced him to the film crew last, as if he was ashamed to work with him. "And this is Klein, he's our mankiller," Cashman said unenthusiastically, and then whispered something to the director of the crew that was inaudible to Klein. The director then introduced himself.

"Howdy y'all, my name's Spenser Eckhart!"

The men in Cashman's crew stood in total silence at the director's cheery introduction. What felt like half a minute passed by in silence. Cashman finally turned and glowered at his men expectantly. They squeezed out a stumbling and poorly synchronized "Howdy Spenser!" in response. Spenser continued with his introduction, "Me and my crew are gonna be filmin' the new program, *Heroes of Domremy,* in this town, which is…"

"Site 89," Guzman, one of Cashman's new recruits who was standing next to Klein said in a bored monotone.

"Site 89, eh?" Spenser continued. "Well, we will just have to give this little ol' town a name by the time we're through! But I'm getting ahead of myself. We're gonna need some help setting up recording equipment. Anyone want to volunteer, take a step forward." For a solid minute, no man stepped forward. Then Cashman turned on his withering glare again, and one man stepped forward first. It was Mark Hyams, a tall, blond, blue-eyed man who was one of Cashman's new crew. "Sure, I'll do it," Hyams said, his face twisted into a smile even more awkward than Spenser's. Four additional men from Cashman's crew – Harris, Aleksandrov, Byrne, and Guzman – stepped forward to volunteer for Spenser's request. No one else came forward, much to the chagrin of Cashman, who wanted the introduction over with as quickly as possible. Cashman decided to vent his frustration on the man who had become his favorite target. "Klein will be your sixth worker from my team. That should be enough to help get you set up." Klein sighed at the task that awaited him, knowing that on a deep psychological level, his mind was better suited to handling the sudden adrenaline rush of a Local attack than the boring physical grind of moving heavy equipment around.

Klein had been setting up the filming equipment over the course of the morning and the afternoon. During this time, he had come to know the personality of Spenser Eckhart quite well. Spenser always went out of his way to *seem* like a folksy, relaxed "good ol' boy," but his affected performance did a poor job of disguising his true nature. The man was a slave driver who could put even Cashman to shame -- he made his crew work continuously through the blazing heat of the Domremy afternoon with no lunch break, and would obsessively focus on the smallest, most irrelevant details of the filming equipment's condition. Klein winced at the fate of Aleksandrov today, who had been chewed out for 10 minutes for the unforgiveable sin of scuffing the paint on the bottom of one of the "tower cameras," stationary cameras mounted on a tripod that could swivel around on remote control and offer a panoramic view of the town. The man's one redeeming feature was that he was *not* a hypocrite—absolutely no one was safe from Spenser's incredible drive, not even Spenser himself, who had not taken a second to eat or relax during the installation of the filming equipment. This knowledge offered little comfort to Klein, whose previously injured leg had begun to feel strained once more after carrying a particularly heavy tripod into the center of town. Klein could hear Spenser going off on another tirade to one of the workers, and the anger he had accumulated over the course of the morning and afternoon finally overwhelmed his patience. *I've had it with this sawed-off little asshole of a film director coming down to this planet and treating us like shit*, he thought as he walked in the direction of the noise. *If I pull this off right, I might even get something of benefit out of this...*

At five foot four inches in height, Spenser was a relatively short man, but his booming voice more than made up for his size in terms of his abilities to intimidate his underlings. His musical Southern drawl could shift into a raging yell at a moment's notice, and made him an expert at manipulating people with a sense of fear or anxiety about their job. His latest victim was Guzman, the last of the five men who had volunteered to help set up the filming equipment. Guzman had muscular arms, but his beer gut and pudgy round face betrayed his overall lack of athleticism to Klein. "C'mon man, I need that money!" Guzman pleaded. "You have no idea how hard it is to get decent pay out here, this place is a penal colony! Cashman pays us the lowest amount the corporation legally allows. You said we'd get that extra money if we volunteered for you…"

"First of all, my name is not 'man'. It's 'Spenser.' Secondly, your boss, Cashman, told me I could pay any volunteer that I took from his men 'at my satisfaction,' meaning that I only have to pay you if I'm satisfied with your performance. And I'm certainly *not* satisfied with your performance after you sneezed all over that precious lens. Thirdly, I…"

"Thirdly, you're a smug little shit and I'm fucking sick of listening to you. Want me to fix that lens for you? Here you go, princess," Klein said and grabbed the camera lens, wiping Guzman's snot off it with his sleeve. Outraged, Spenser yelled back at Klein, "What the hell's got into you, talking to me like that? I'll take away every red cent from your paycheck for this job!"

Klein responded, a knowing smile on his face, "You were never going to pay me anyway. I never 'volunteered' for this 'job,' Cashman forced me to do it. You honestly think Cashman would tell you to pay me when you don't have to? He hates me worse than anybody else on Domremy."

Klein's forceful response and smiling face fanned the flames of Spenser's rage. "I can make you lose more than a paycheck. I can make you lose your job! I'll get you busted down so far you'll be lucky if you can get a job as a janitor in this town!"

Klein was still smiling as he responded to Spenser, "Sure you will, princess. I'm sure Cashman will be chomping at the bit to fire his one mankiller, and go through another waiting period, maybe a couple of weeks if he's lucky, maybe a couple of *months* if he's unlucky, in the hope that he can get another mankiller who's stable enough not to start murdering townsfolk in their sleep. And I'm sure your bosses will be happy that most of the first season of whatever the hell kind of program you're trying to film won't have a 'real' mankiller, just whichever member of Cashman's crew is unlucky enough not to carry a Kikkonnen anymore and try to pull off nearly impossible shots that they're not trained for. Great plan you got there."

Shocked at the prospect of a foe he couldn't threaten, fire, or reassign, Spenser could only sputter out a feeble attempt at intimidating Klein into obedience. "I'll file this in my report to Cashman! You haven't heard the end of this!" Spenser looked down at his watch and noticed that only five minutes remained of the time Cashman had allotted him to use his volunteers. Embarrassed by Klein's insubordination, he decided to end the work session now and pretend the incident with Guzman -- and Klein -- never happened. "All volunteers did a great job today, so I'll let everybody out 5 minutes early. Anyone who *volunteered* can pick up their paycheck from this job in a week from Cashman. See y'all tomorrow!" *I might hear the end of this sooner than you think,* Klein thought as he walked away. *But if I do, it'll be from Cashman, not from a blustering blowhard like you.*

Guzman caught up with Klein as he was walking back to the bar. "Uh, Klein...thanks for saving my ass back there, man. I would've lost all the money I would've gotten from this job if you hadn't done that."

"No problem," Klein replied. "Princess there was giving me a giant goddamn headache with all his whining. I was waiting for a chance to shut him up." *That, and the small fact that I felt like my leg muscle was about to give out, but I'm not to tell newbie here which parts of my body are injured*, he thought.

"You'd better not be callin' him 'Princess' anymore, man. He might try to get revenge somehow, or get you fired or somethin'," Guzman told Klein.

"What, by complaining to Cashman? You must not know much about us mankillers, Guzman. It takes a special kind of person to shoot dead an unarmed man who's done nothing against you, when the time calls for it. People, especially the kind of people in *this* town, may hate us, but they know they still *need* us, and they can't replace us easily. Being a mankiller is the best kind of job security you can get on Domremy."

"Um...Klein?"

"Yeah, you got another question?"

"That thing you told Spenser about mankillers murdering people in their sleep...you just made that up 'cause he was an Earther and he'd believe anything, right?"

Klein shook his head. "Absolutely not. That mankiller who murdered people in his sleep was Billy "Sin" Fredericksen, the mankiller here before me."

Klein watched as Guzman stood wavering, fear clashing with gratitude towards the man who had saved him. After an awkward pause, Guzman thrust out his hand for Klein to shake. "I won't forget what you did for me, man," Guzman said. "Wanna go get some drinks at the bar?" Klein smiled at him and said, "Sure. I'll tell you more about the history of Site 89 and what you have to do to watch your ass around here. It can get pretty complicated..."

Klein had drunk a couple of beers -- just enough to help dull the pain from the ache in his leg -- and had gone up to his room. When he opened the door, he found his new Forlani girlfriend, Ixtara, waiting for him. Ixtara had been with him only a brief time, and Klein didn't know much about her character, but he thought she had much less ambition than Ragatti did. Ragatti used to chatter about her dreams of going to the Forlani equivalent of medical school. Ixtara talked about her family life long ago or asked about Klein's background or what Earth was like, only giving brief responses whenever Klein asked her a more current question. She was obedient to Klein and didn't try to pry for sensitive information, but Klein found the extent of how reserved she was disconcerting. "Ixtara, could you put that leg brace on me? This leg's been bothering me today, and I'll need to work tomorrow, so the brace will help keep it from getting injured."

"Oh, really? How did it get injured? Is there anything else I can do for you, Klein?" Ixtara said.

"Just a nagging injury that's been bothering me," Klein said, giving the most non-descriptive answer he could think of. "And the only thing else I need for the day is one Somega for a good, clear sleep."

"So, you won't be needing any other...form of service tonight, Klein?" Ixtara responded. On a personal level, Klein disliked how businesslike the terminology Ixtara used to define sex with a human male was. No more innocent cuddling up with her as he often used to do with Entara, nor even enjoying Ragatti's rhythmic snoring. "No, Ixtara...not tonight," Klein sighed. "Just a Somega. And if the Somega is too potent and makes me oversleep as sometimes happens, be sure to punch me in the shoulder really hard so I can wake up and go to work. Physical pain seems to be the only thing that can knock me out of the effects of the Somega, and even that only works in about the last hour or so the Somega's in my system.

"So, about...six thirty, then?" Ixtara asked.

"Make it six forty five," Klein replied as Ixtara went to the medicine cabinet to get the Somega. *She may have a terrible personality, but at least she's good at technical details. That goes for keeping me awake at night and waking me up when I do fall asleep. I enjoy the staying awake part a good deal more.*

Two weeks into the shoot, Klein had adjusted to working around the filming of *Heroes of Domremy*. Cashman, worried about a repeat of the Great Storm Massacre, had forbidden expeditions into the wilderness, so *Heroes* was shot exclusively in the town and surrounding farms. Spenser's "creative vision" of Site 89 mandated that everyone act in a friendly, inviting, "folksy" manner that Klein utterly despised. Spenser considered Klein one of the most "difficult" of the town's residents to work with, which suited Klein well, because it meant less time on camera being forced to choke out Howdy's and Y'alls in a terribly forced attempt to make his existence on Domremy look happy and hospitable. Most other people in town were not as lucky as Klein; the bartender, Erskine, was a frequent target for Spenser's film shoots, and hated his on-camera persona so much that he was constantly looking for an opportunity to vent his anger about it whenever he was off camera.

"You're lucky he hates you so much, Klein. He's put me on camera for interviews eight times, and he keeps complaining that I don't sound enough like a 'cowboy'! Does he even realize what our old lives were like, before we all got sent off to this rock? I was a chemistry teacher back in Arlington then, with a real career..."

"Was that Arlington, Texas by any chance?" Klein asked.

"Does it really matter?" Erskine said.

"Well, no, but there's an Arlington, Texas, an Arlington, Massachusetts, and an Arlington, Virginia. You Americans seem to have a fascination for reusing the same name for cities in different states. I suppose you're excused, since we've had a couple of Stolbergs and Frankfurts for over fifteen hundred years. You never talked like a person from Texas – before Spenser made you talk that way, anyway – but maybe you had parents from a different state, or you moved from another state to Texas before you started your teaching career, or..."

"If you must know, it's Arlington, *Virginia*," Erskine said. "Not that it really matters much, a middle school chemistry teacher is a lousy paying career pretty much anywhere, even in Deutschland now. In fact, it paid so poorly that I ended up committing the crime that got me sent here."

"Financial fraud?" Klein asked.

Erskine nodded. "Got a bunch of people in my church into a Ponzi scheme. Once they figured out what was going on, my old life was over. Even if I had finished my sentence in a prison on Earth, my career as a teacher would have been ruined with that on my criminal record. So I decided to volunteer to get sent to a penal colony instead—it doesn't have the amenities of life on Earth, but it's a hell of a lot cheaper, and I figured the best job I possibly could have gotten after my arrest was as a bartender anyway. Things worked out pretty well until Spenser showed up and forced me to be 'Good ol' Sam Erskine'. At least today I'm off the hook, though, since he's working on outdoors footage today."

"He's gonna be shadowing us again," Klein groaned.

"I don't know if that's what he's planning to do. He might go pester the farmers for interviews this time," Erskine said.

"Let him try! They'll just talk manure to him and laugh because he won't understand he's being insulted."

"I'm just glad I don't have to put up with him today, and I hope you don't have to, either. Good luck!"

"When it comes to Spenser, my luck is anything but good," Klein said as he left the bar to go to his daily patrols of the perimeter of Site 89.

When he reported to his patrol duties, Klein received the news he had been dreading to hear: that Spenser would be shadowing his patrol for the day.

Cashman had worked out an agreement with Spenser that the amount of time the recruits would be filmed would be more limited than the time he could film the farmers and shopkeepers in town. Spenser agreed, believing that all the colonists could be considered "Heroes of Domremy," but also because he found it difficult to work with the Local-fighting recruits. They had little patience for retakes, were constantly on edge worrying about Local attacks, and many were suspicious of any form of camera surveillance and recording, a holdover from their pre-colonial criminal backgrounds. It seemed to Klein that there was always at least one altercation between the film crew and Cashman's men during the days they were filmed; usually it was fairly minor, like two men cursing at each other or someone threatening to bust a camera or fry a hard drive. However, there had already been one fistfight that had resulted in cameraman's nose getting broken, and rumors of other grudges passed around the bar in the nights after the filming sessions. Klein thought it was mostly hot air and a waste of everyone's time, but he was still wary of the potential for violence, knowing the hostility, frustration, and resentment that the inmates of Domremy felt.

"C'mon, say somethin' funny, Alek," Guzman asked.

"No. I am not feeling 'funny' today," Aleksandrov replied.

"Spenser's not letting us go until you at least *try* to tell a joke. You've gotta have *something*, man. At least tell one of those 'In Soviet Russia...'one-liners. Anything to get us out of here!" Guzman whined.

"Those haven't been funny in at least ninety years. I will not be made an object of ridicule," Alek said.

"Y'know Alek, you're right," Spenser said. "Those are clichéd. Why don't you tell us about how your time on Domremy has turned you from a convict...into a hero. Something inspirational and life-affirming."

"I was a man of respect and honor on Earth. On this world, I tell stories for idiots who want to make a TV show. There is nothing heroic about this," Alek growled.

"You'd best shut up and do what the man tells you to do!" Hyams yelled. "I was one of the first to sign up to help Spenser, and I did it for the exact same reason you did—making money. Unlike you, I intend to work with Spenser, not against him, because if I get popular from this show, the company will be back to work with me again and make me more money. So say the damn thing he wants you to and get this over with!"

Alek snorted. "So, your glorious future is begging for scraps at a table like a little dog. You can have it. I want no part of this humiliation."

"Do what I say, or you'll be eating through a tube in the infirmary!"

Aleksandrov rolled up his sleeves to reveal his arms and shoulders. They were covered in tattoos, and Klein could see two eight-pointed stars near his shoulders. "Do you know what theses tattoos mean?" he asked Hyams.

Hyams clenched his hands into fists. "You start a fight with me Alek, you'll regret it. I'll get Cashman to make your life a living hell..."

Hyams' sentence was interrupted by a stiff jab in the face by Alek. The force of the blow rocked Hyams' head backwards, but did not knock him over, and he countered with a blow to Alek's chest. Alek gasped for air but was already swinging his fist around for another blow. The punch hit Hyams hard in the shoulder, but Alek was unable to follow it up; Hyams quickly tripped him, sending him sprawling to the ground on his back. Hyams seized the opportunity and got on top of Alek, delivering a flurry of jabs to his face. But his offensive was short-lived as the stronger, bulkier Alek flipped him over on his back and hammered him with vicious punches to his temples, alternating his left and right hands in a violent blur. An ugly gash opened up above his right eye, and Hyams' struggles quickly weakened. Sensing his victory, Alek got up off Hyams and spat on his prostrate body. "Go tell your boyfriend Cashman how well you fared against me," Alek said as he sneered.

Blood pouring into his eye from the cut, Hyams staggered to his feet, still swooning from the force of Alek's blows. "You..." he managed to gasp out as he drew his fist back and lunged at Alek in a desperate attempt at retribution. Hyams' offensive was slow and badly telegraphed, and Alek had anticipated it before Hyams had even gotten back to his feet. Alek sidestepped Hyams' clumsy lunge and shoved him from the side, sending him sprawling into a clump of grass. Klein heard a loud cry of pain come out of the clump of grass, a sound far too sharp and agonized to be someone simply landing the wrong way. Klein wondered if the Locals had staged a surprise attack and carried Hyams off in the tall grass, but the continued moaning and broken English coming from the clump of tall grass suggested Hyams was still there. "Spenser, call in Cashman *now*! Guzman, Byrne, help me carry Hyams out of the bush. If Hyams is still alive, we have to get him to the infirmary *now*!"

Klein had become numb to the sight of men being carried off by Locals; such horrors were burned into his mind so thoroughly that they seemed as much a part of his job as the brutality of wars on Earth were when he was a soldier. He had begun to think of the Locals not as simple monsters, but as an enemy army, with its own tactics and methods of engagement. Doing so gave them a sense of familiarity to Klein, who had learned to anticipate their methods of movement and draw an accurate shot on his targets as they tried to escape. As much fear and anxiety as the Locals could still inspire in him, it was the rational fear of a soldier in combat, not the irrational terror of a child quaking in fear of some imagined eldritch abomination. It seemed so long that he had even begun to forget that raw sense of shock the first time he had seen a Local leap down and carry a man off.

What he saw next ripped back the veil of time and experience and opened his eyes to the raw horrors of Domremy once more.

Hyams had fallen on his chest. He had landed on a strange creature that bore a strong resemblance to a toad, with a squat four-legged body, large eyes, and a long tongue. It was large beyond the size of any earthly toad Klein had ever seen though, roughly the size of a medium-size cat, and had a jarring coloration of black with yellow stripes that looked like no other animal on Domremy. The creature's back was covered in wicked two-inch long spines, and the spines had ripped through Hyams' jacket and shirt and punctured his chest at several points. Stuck to Hyams, the creature was flailing its limbs and issuing a distinctive, booming call that sounded like "VA-ron-EY, Va-RON-EY" over and over.

As disgusted as he was at the creature's repulsive appearance, Klein was moved by a desire to save Hyams. He took his M221, got a bead on the "toad's" chest, and shot the creature dead. Sickly yellow blood oozed out of the creature's chest wound as Klein yelled, "Somebody call Cashman, dammit! We gotta get this guy to the infirmary NOW! Guzman, Byrne, help me carry him!"

Klein rushed up to Hyams and ripped the creature's corpse off his chest. He could see Hyams' muscles involuntarily shaking and could hear Hyams trying to form a sentence about something. "Ff.. f.f.. A...

Llleexx… Bbbbbuuuurrrnnnnii," he stuttered out as his body shook.

"We need a trolley to wheel him into the infirmary! Harris, get that one and bring it over here!"

"But that's for the camera…" Spenser meekly protested as Harris casually brushed him aside and took the trolley. The camera fell off the trolley with a sickening crunch as Harris raced over to where Hyams had fallen.

"On three, lift and put him on there!" Klein yelled. "One…two…three!" They quickly lifted the shuddering Hyams on top of the trolley as he continued to attempt to form sentences. "Ssss…trrreeeee…" Hyams wheezed out as he was placed on the trolley.

"Guzman, other end of the trolley! To the infirmary!" Guzman and Klein moved the trolley as fast as they could, and for once Klein was surprised at the speed Guzman could muster in an emergency.

Almost immediately after they had left, the other men could hear the sound of Cashman's approach. "What the hell just happened?" Cashman yelled as he arrived. "I leave you people alone to film a program that's supposed to enhance the value of this place, make us all some good money, and you manage to completely FUBAR everything in a manner of hours! Why did I just get an emergency call?"

The shock of the event had caused Spenser to completely lose his nerve. In a normal frame of mind, he might have avoided instantly incriminating the individuals involved, respecting the convicts' propensity for violence, if not their concepts of honor and *omerta*. In panic and confusion, his rational sense of self-preservation was lost. "It was Aleksandrov! He's been giving me trouble all day, insubordination, being unreasonable, until Hyams finally called him out on it! Hyams challenged him, and fought like a *lion*!" Spenser exclaimed. "But that...that *bastard* Alek fought dirty, and knocked him onto some kind of weird alien toad monster! He probably put it there too, and was just waiting to put Hyams into that trap! That evil twisted *bastard...*"

"Shut up! Alek, is what he says true?"

Alek's face was so hard and unmoving that it could have been a piece of iron. "He is lying. The man attacked me. I defended myself. I had no idea that toads lived on Domremy. All men should defend themselves," he said succinctly.

"You know what that sounds like to me, Alek? That sounds like a bald-faced lie. Anyone here gonna tell me who threw the first punch, and why?" Cashman yelled. None of the men spoke. *Omerta* was based on fear far more than honor, and the men were more terrified of Aleksandrov than they were of Cashman, that distant schemer who had come to spend more time playing mental chess games and worrying about filming rights since Spenser had arrived. Spenser was horrified at the men's response, and finally realized that his poorly planned tirade had actually made *Alek* look stronger. *Before, he might have just seemed like a dim thug to them. After what I said about him planting the toad, he'll seem like a much smarter strategic genius, and a much greater threat than Cashman*, he realized as the rational aspect of his mind finally regained control.

"So, you want to play it that way? 'Snitches get stitches', huh? Well, this is what you're gonna get from me! No more filming bonuses. And halved pay for six months! No more alcohol in the bar until I say so! And if I ever hear any of you so much as grumble while this man is filming, I will personally shoot you in your goddamn head myself! Understood?"

The men all nodded.

"Now get onto patrol! Filming today is over, because I said so! And Alek, if Hyams dies from whatever that toad put into him, so do you!"

As he left with the other men to go on patrol with Cashman, Aleksandrov stared at Spenser with his hard, steely eyes. There were no words spoken; Alek remembered Spenser's command. But to Spenser, the harsh glare of Alek was scarier than any verbal threat could possibly be. Under the stare, Spenser felt the last of his courage and resolve melt away, replaced by a lurking persistent fear. Aleksandrov was angered. And as long as Spenser remained at the settlement, he was in danger of paying a terrible price for his mistake.

It had been a long, hard, unrewarding day. Cashman sat on his bed in his room sighing, taking a breather after the exhausting march he had forced his men – and himself – to perform as punishment for what had happened to Hyams. When he had stopped by the infirmary after the patrol, the Medrobo had told him that Hyams was in "critical, but stable" condition; the actual doctor, being shared between several settlements, was "not available to speak with currently." *Goddamn Medrobos with their flat voices, trying to play at emotion*, Cashman thought. *Only there 'cause it's so rare to get a real doc signed up for this colony...*

His most loyal man, Hyams, had been severely injured and would probably die due to that undisciplined, savage thug Aleksandrov. Cashman knew that the man was guilty, but none of Alek's peers would dare rat on him right to his face. Thanks to Spenser's moronic rant, they'd probably be unlikely to incriminate him behind his back, either. Luckily for Cashman, Alek did have a major weakness: regardless of whether the men believed him to be a superman capable of brilliant premeditated revenge schemes, Cashman still knew he was nothing but a dim Slavic ox, a clod with no leadership potential and no grasp of strategy, who could be easily dispatched with enough cunning. Cashman had more pressing concerns at the moment, a different enemy who *did* have a grasp of strategic thought, and someone he had already let live far too long. To defeat such an enemy, he needed a means of monitoring their plans and learning what more information he could out of them before he could arrange a clean kill, a convenient accident that wouldn't leave a mess that could implicate him. He picked up his phone...

"Hello there. I'd like to play a chess game soon. Maybe a few days, couple of weeks at most?" Though Cashman had no contact with the Religious Dissenters, he too knew that all calls on Domremy were monitored, and so had been forced to create his own crude code language so that he and his accomplice could communicate. It was far cruder than Crop Talk and could only convey a very limited set of meanings and ideas in comparison to the code language of the Dissenters, but it suited Cashman's purposes well.

"Certainly. A week and a half sound good to you?" The voice on the phone was soft, feminine, whispered. It reeked of guile and scheming, and Cashman hated it, for it represented someone devious, intelligent, and most of all, *unpredictable.* Cashman hated intelligence, hated randomness, and despised underlings who possessed ambition. He preferred loyal, unwavering, predictable folk like Hyams.

"Quicker's better. I'm really itching for a game." Cashman hoped he wasn't betraying his urgency *too* much. Seeming too anxious in his tone of voice wouldn't only make him look cowardly to her, it would make him look suspicious to the people who were doubtless monitoring the conversation even now."

"Don't worry," the voice giggled. "I'm sure we're not talking Bobby Fisher."

"All the same, you should tell me how it's played. That way, I'll be sure to win big in our wagered game."

A sense of greedy urgency crept into the feminine voice. "We *will* split the winnings just like you said, won't we?"

It'll be a snowy day in Hell before I split it with you like I promised, you manipulative bitch, Cashman thought. "Yes, just like I promised. I'm always willing to reward anyone who helps me win a big game. Be it football when I was back in high school, or chess now."

"Which kind of football was that again?" The voice seemed puzzled, as if the concept was entirely alien to her. Cashman sighed. "The kind only Americans play, honey. The one where you use your hands more than your feet and everybody kicked that weird way until the 1970s, when they started kicking like everybody else."

The voice became unexpectedly enthusiastic. "But I heard the Canadians and Australians play that way too…"

"Bye, darlin'." Cashman ended the call. *My "great football" career consisted of sitting on a bench until my junior year of high school. I'm not sitting on a bench ever again. Now I play to win.*

Klein was sitting in the bar thinking over the day's events. He had little patience for conversation and small talk, especially after he had seen Hyams sent to the infirmary. But Guzman had decided to sit next to him, and was prattling on anyway, oblivious to the fact that Klein was not in a talking mood.

"Biggest damn frog I've ever seen, Klein! I swear that thing was the size of a cat! And it probably killed Hyams, too! Worse than chupacabra. We should kill every one of those goddamn things before anybody else dies! You agree with me, right?"

Klein tried his best to hide how tiresome he found the conversation by not sighing. "Hyams is still alive. I saw him in the infirmary. The Medrobo said his vitals were critical but stable, and no internal organs were ruptured. There was only the spine wounds and the venom. I think he'll get better in time. We got him into the infirmary pretty quick."

"Hope you're right, Klein, but who knows how many of those toads are still out there? There's probably dozens of 'em past the town perimeter!"

"Well, if its anything like an Earth toad in terms of diet or lifestyle, there can't be too many that big," Klein said. *I know as little as anybody else about the biology of these "toads," but if it gives you any peace of mind, I'll lie to make you feel better -- until my patience runs out.* "For all we know, it could be a rare or endangered species, like the King Cobra on Earth. Big and scary, but rarely seen."

Guzman took a huge swig of beer, as if he was unconvinced by Klein's explanation and needed further persuasion. Klein was rapidly losing interest in the conversation and decided to go up to his room to get ready to sleep. He shrugged his shoulders. "You probably won't see another one for a long time, if ever," he said as he headed for the stairs. Before he went up, Klein could see Erskine motioning for him to come up to the bar. Klein wearily trudged over, wondering if there was some discrepancy on his bar tab.

"Got somethin' I need to see you about. Come into the room behind the bar," Erskine muttered, trying to be as low-key as possible. Klein followed him into the back room. It was a messy, disheveled place, with papers and mementos strewn about, and a dartboard with a picture of an old, white-haired judge on the wall adjacent to the door. It was a room seemingly reflective of carelessness and apathy, in sharp contrast to the anxious tone in Erskine's voice.

"This afternoon, I heard a very interesting conversation coming from your room. There was this female voice coming out of your room..."

"Ixtara? I let her crash there this week. She claims she can't find another place to stay, the other Forlani don't like her much for some reason..."

"I couldn't make out most of it, but I overheard something about football. I was gonna just ignore it, but something about it rubbed me the wrong way. When the hell did Forlani women start playing football? Nothing about it makes sense. Have you been talking to her about football lately?"

A nagging sense of anxiety began to form in the back of Klein's mind. "Can't say that I have, either

American football or what you Americans call soccer, but I'm sure she has other clients."

"That's another thing," Erskine said. "I've never seen her with another 'client' from the moment you brought her in. Most of the other Forlani women seem perfectly willing and able to go from man to man, but her—she only seems to spend time with you. There's something really suspicious about her, she acts like no other Forlani woman I've seen or heard about in my time here."

"You think she might be a spy from Hyperion?" Klein asked. He, too, was beginning to become unnerved by the sudden change in Ixtara's behavior. Klein had never heard of the Corporation using Forlani as spies, but his short time on Domremy had convinced him that virtually anything could happen in the colony.

"I don't think so, and that makes me even more anxious. Why would Hyperion go through all the trouble of recruiting a Forlani spy and sticking her in some crappy bar in the middle of nowhere? I don't know what she's doing, and that makes me even more anxious. I need you to send her away. *Now.*" Erskine's sense of anxiety became more palpable to Klein as he became more emphatic. "You've been a big help keeping the local thugs from acting up, so Cashman stays off my back, but if you're harboring people involved in some kind of *weird conspiracy*, I can't let you have that room above the bar anymore!"

Klein responded, "I have no idea what she's doing. I'll make sure she's gone by the end of the week, so you don't have to worry about anything."

"I'd better not hear about any suspicious goings on even after she leaves," said Erskine. "This bar has a reputation to maintain, with you or without."

As Klein went up to bed, he considered the potential reasons behind Ixtara's strange behavior. Maybe Erskine was just being paranoid—running a business in Cashman's "law and order town" would be a miserable experience for just about anyone, and if it ever got out that the place was a den of spies from Hyperion or anywhere else, customers would no longer see the bar as a place where they could safely complain with impunity about the misery of their personal lives. Business would be as good as dead if that happened. But Erskine did have a point...Ixtara had never demonstrated much interest in Earthly customs while she had been with him, and certainly *nothing* in sports. And if she did have another client, why would she be chatting with him in the afternoon, when most of the convicts on Domremy were still hard at work in the fields and the towns? Klein tried to reassure himself that it was just his nasty old habit of jealousy, his imposing of human customs and notions of morality onto the Forlani, but his mind wasn't dominated by *anger* towards her; instead he felt a deep suspicion of her motivations. Erskine's paranoia about a *weird conspiracy* began to seem less like a silly tinfoil hat fantasy and more an illustration of a potential threat.

He decided to give Ixtara a simple test as he came into his room. She was stretched out on his bed, smiling at him in an attempt to seduce him. Klein had other plans. "Hello, Klein," she called to him softly. "Hi, Ixtara," he said back in a tired voice, feigning apathy. "Not interested tonight?" she asked him, a crestfallen look on her face. "Maybe I should get you a nice Somega for sleep tonight."

"No, I'll get it myself tonight. I'm not *that* tired." Klein thought he could see a flicker of uncertainty in her eyes for half a second, but it was gone before he blinked. *Gonna need a little bit more of a test than that.* "You know, I've always wondered," Klein said as he stretched out on the bed, "why I've never seen a Forlani male. What exactly is it that they *do*?"

Ixtara had a questioning look on her face, as if she was puzzled by the notion that Forlani males had to *do* anything. Then she smiled and gave a musical giggle. "Forlani males aren't like human males. They don't have to *do* much of anything, certainly nothing that could compare to what you do, Klein. They are the Seed Bearers, the ones who anoint the females for the gift of *Avesti*, the Exquisite Moment that is the sacred duty of all women. For this gift, they are to be respected, protected, and cared for."

"I've heard women describe pregnancy as a lot of things, but never 'exquisite'," Klein said.

"Ah, but it is, it *is*! The only thing that can compare with that is the day that a Forlani woman is Chosen as a man's First Wife – if she is Chosen." Klein sensed a very slight but palpable tension in her voice on the word *if*, as if there was some sort of ancient frustration buried deep within Ixtara's memories. "But of course, you are also very valuable and precious to me, Klein."

"I hope I'm not just valuable in the financial sense," Klein said sarcastically.

"Oh, no! Certainly not, Klein! You very proficient in the pleasure-making arts as well and I enjoy our time together!"

Guess Forlani don't have much room for romantic sweet talk in their culture, Klein thought. *At least the women certainly don't. Enough beating around the bush, time for the test.* "Ixtara, I've been on this world for what feels to me, at least, like a long time. I've been with a lot of Forlani women, but I feel like I've never truly understood them or their culture. On this Friday, would it be okay if, instead of just sleeping here and screwing each other with no real understanding, what if we went to the Forlani enclave and had a date there? You know, drink, talk about things, learn about each other, and *then* have sex instead of the other way around?"

Klein could sense Ixtara's shock at his request. "W-well, Klein, I'm not sure if I've kept up the relationships I needed to in the Forlani community…"

Boom. Now I know Ixtara's trying to pull something, even if I still don't know exactly what it is. "I'll be the one arranging the trip. I'm sure the Forlani will take my money just as willingly as anybody else's. Maybe we can even charm your way back into their good graces! I'll make the arrangements so we can leave two days from now, on Friday night, and get back around Saturday afternoon. It'll be great!"

Ixtara sat apart from him on the other end of the bed, silent and aloof. She didn't even bother to look at Klein's face. Klein saw only back of her head as he turned the lamp off. He stared at her shapely figure silhouetted in the darkness, but for once judged the lithe Forlani shape with a new objectivity. "Not giving me any tonight, sweetie?" Klein called to her. Ixtara said nothing. "Suit yourself, but I might just decide to dock your pay for tonight," he told her. Still no response. *Yep, something's definitely up. Come Friday, I'll figure out what that is.*

On Thursday afternoon, Klein decided to check in on Hyams in the infirmary. It was far more poorly equipped than most hospitals on Earth, with only a few beds and an overall philosophy designed to get patients out as quickly as possible. There was no doctor permanently assigned to the facility, because Hyperion Corporation found it difficult to find doctors who would willingly sign up to get shot across the galaxy to work in a dismal penal colony and sever ties to all their friends and family on Earth. Domremy did have a few doctors, but they were far too scarce for each settlement to have one on permanent assignment. Instead, each infirmary had a Medrobo to perform basic medical tasks and look after the patients, and doctors were only called in when absolutely necessary. The doctor who had stopped by to perform the toxicology report on Hyams was already long gone to another settlement, leaving only the Medrobo to look after the bedridden victim. Noticing Klein's entry, it swiveled its head around and greeted him with a flat, placid, "Hello, Willie Klein."

The Medrobo had been deliberately designed not to look human to avoid the "uncanny valley" in design. Hyperion's designers had determined that designing an almost completely human android was impossible; they could create a shape that appeared human to the naked eye, synthetic "hair" and "skin" that were very convincing, and even emulate the basic sound of a human vocal tract almost perfectly. Yet the closer they came to the human form *in theory*, the *actual* reactions of customers became more and more unnerved. Maybe it was the strange flatness in that "perfectly emulated" human voice, the odd lack of muscle movement in the humanesque face, or a stare from those beautiful RealEyes that seemed a bit too glazed and zombielike, but the goal of creating a perfectly human android remained a lost cause. Instead, Hyperion Robotics designed the Medrobo; a squat 5 foot tall, heavily built, and decidedly nonhuman robot that spoke with a thick, mechanical voice. It had two arms to lift with and two legs to walk on, allowing it a humanlike range of motion, but its proportions and build were much bulkier than those of most humans, allowing it to lift and move heavy patients and objects when necessary. It was painted white and had a cylindrical head with two large, round glass eyes, and a smiley sticker someone had put in the middle of its forehead. "How can I help you today?" the machine calmly asked.

"Just checking on Hyams' condition. I was worried because that venom messed him up pretty bad."

"Hyams is doing considerably better, as you can see," the Medrobo said in its uniquely serene, unemotional tone. "The swelling in the inflamed areas has gone down, and he is now conscious and able to eat. However, he still suffers from severe hallucinations that impair his mental capabilities, and is therefore not recommended to leave the facility at this time."

"But the venom doesn't appear to have done any permanent damage to his brain or nervous system, has it?"

"No. It appears there is no permanent damage, yet the venom causes extreme physical discomfort, followed by hallucinations. There is a possibility of a temporary coma if the venom is absorbed in large quantities."

Klein nodded at the robot's explanation. An idea had begun to form in his head. Hyams was feebly reaching up off the bed and waving his hand in the air, trying to comprehend the world around him. "Look at the streaks...beautiful light streaks..." he feebly muttered while he waved his hand around. Klein turned and headed for the door. "Hope you get better, Hyams," he said and left the infirmary. Hyams said nothing in response, his mind still lost in venom-induced delusion.

That night, Klein stealthily moved out past the settlement perimeter to put his plan into action. He carried with him his M221, but for once, he doubted he'd need to use it on this mission. The rifle was slung over his shoulder, and the tool most essential to his mission was in his backpack – a large sponge that he had taken from his shower. He could not see the brilliant spiraling constellations of the Domremy night sky through the heavy storm clouds, and the humidity and heat of the air made him almost as sweaty and tired as he would be on patrol during the day. Standing alone in the darkness, Klein listened for the sounds that would guide him to his goal.

He heard the deep, croaking sound he remembered from the day Hyams was poisoned echo across the plain. *Va-ron-ey, Va-RON-ey*, the deep gurgling sound repeated at quickening intervals. Klein warily moved away from the settlement, through the tall grass, in the direction of the sound. The closer he got, the louder and more booming the sound became. There was a rhythmic, almost hypnotic quality to the croaking that drowned out the distant noises from the settlement, and it came to dominate the air the closer Klein got.

As the sounds of the croaking filled the air, Klein could see a rustling motion in a clump of tall grass. He pushed open the clump of vegetation and saw two of the spiny toad like creatures locked together; a large yellow and black one was lying on its belly, while slightly smaller yellow and green one was groping it enthusiastically. The *Va-ron-ey* croaks were becoming faster and faster as the creatures became more aroused. Klein took his sponge out of his backpack and put it on the ground close to the creatures. Then, he slowly lined up the butt of his rifle like a putter, and knocked the top toad onto the sponge. The creature frantically thrashed, its spines ripping deep into the sponge as it pulsed its back, pumping in its oily white venom. Klein looked down at the creature in disgust and prepared to shoot it in the chest with his rifle. "Damn Varoneys," Klein said, as he thought in the back of his mind, *Has that damn sound they make left such a big impression on me that I've started to call them that by reflex?* As he yanked the body off the sponge, the black and yellow Varoney got to its feet and stared at him contemptuously. When he pointed his rifle at it again, the Varoney gave one last defiant croak and hopped off.

Donning gloves, Klein squeezed the sponge hard, dripping the venom from it into the back of an open syringe. He now had the weapon he needed to put

Ixtara out of commission, which he hoped would buy him the time he needed to kill Cashman and end the Kinderaugen connection on Domremy for good. He didn't want to kill Ixtara, and he figured he had taken only enough venom to incapacitate her while he executed his plan. As he walked back to the bar, he planned out his moves for the "date" with her tomorrow.

Ixtara had a nervous look on her face as she walked into the Forlani enclave with Klein. Once they opened the door, Klein could see why. The greeter Forlani at the door lost her well-practiced smile at the site of Ixtara, and she did her best to disguise her shock at the site of the unwelcome new guest. "W-well, what would you like, customer?" Klein knew that *he*, rather than Ixtara, would have to be the one to handle negotiations with the Forlani working at the enclave. "We'd like an overnight room here. We'll be spending the rest of our money at the bar, so nothing too fancy, please." The greeter Forlani brought up a chart on her computer and checked over a map of the enclave's available rooms. "We have an Economy room available in the Waterfall suite that I think should meet your needs," the Forlani said, although the look on her face told Klein that she was thinking *that room's too good for one of you two.* "We'll take it," Klein said, and he and Ixtara walked to the bar.

Klein noticed the reactions of the other Forlani as he and Ixtara walked together. There were angry looks on their faces, and Klein heard the phrase "*Ashta!*" murmured a couple of times as they walked into the bar. Klein sat down at the bar and ordered a couple of martinis from the bartender. He began to talk with Ixtara as they waited for their drinks.

"You know, on Earth, they say a martini's a man's drink," Klein said.

"Really? I've heard human males say differently. Many of them prefer other drinks such as whiskey sour, bourbon, sake..."

``Neither Entara nor Ragatti ever gave a damn about drinking or alcohol of any kind. You'd only know what a "man's drink" was if someone coached you*, Klein thought. "Well, if it's good enough for James Bond, it's good enough for me. You've seen a Bond film, haven't you? Guys bring them over from Earth as files on the video players all the time."

"As a matter of fact, no. I'm not really interested in that sort of entertainment."

The bartender gave them their two martinis. Ixtara took some time to sip on hers. Finally she answered, "I like to play card games. Poker, blackjack...I enjoy games of skill. You?"

Klein casually took a drink from his martini glass. "I prefer sports, especially football. I was quite the footballer when I was younger. I was just watching Manchester United play against Real Madrid last

Sunday. You should've seen the touchdown Sanchez scored in that game!"

Ixtara maintained a poker face as best she could, but Klein could see her eyelids tighten in frustration. *Forlani may be better at emotional control than many humans, but they're not perfect.* "Yes, that was a spectacular game! Sanchez really...made an excellent play!" She started to drink from the martini glass rapidly, as if she was about to bolt and run for the exit. Klein asked her, "Wasn't he carrying the ball with his hands when he made that touchdown?" He watched her movement closely and saw her quickly getting up to leave her seat. Klein roughly grabbed Ixtara's arm, told the bartender, "We're going to our room now," and rushed off with her, his drink half-finished.

The room was as barren and dull as its "Economy" designation suggested. It had no pictures hanging on the walls, no video equipment for watching or playing programs, just a sound hologram of a waterfall. It had the barest, cheapest looking bed Klein had ever seen in a bordello. Klein shoved Ixtara into it and angrily yelled, "You've been spying for Cashman, haven't you? I don't know what shit he's been feeding you to coach you in Earth culture, but even the most ignorant sap knows that Real Madrid's "footballers" don't play with their hands, and they don't score touchdowns, but goals! Cashman's an American, and for them, football is a completely different sport where they *do* play with their hands and score touchdowns! You have two options now; get on that train and *get the hell out of this town*, or I'll stab you with this syringe," Klein said as he quickly pulled out the needle, "and you won't get up for a month!"

Ixtara reached into her pocket, and in the blindingly quick motion, Klein could see the glint of gunmetal. Klein grabbed her right arm and thrust the syringe hard into the flesh. "Hope you like a long sleep, you bit…"

But Ixtara's reaction to the venom was far more severe than Hyams'. She shook as violently as he had, but her face turned red. A horrible red swelling quickly appeared all over her body. She released an incoherent scream of pain and fell to the ground. Her shaking abruptly stopped.

Two young Forlani females, both carrying formidable knives, flung open the door and brandished them at Klein. A much older Forlani female, her face wizened with wrinkles, stood behind them. "Hands up, against the wall!" she screamed in heavily accented English. Klein stood still against the wall as the old Forlani laid her hand on the chest of Ixtara, feeling for a heartbeat.

"She's dead." The words came out of her mouth without a trace of compassion or sadness for the fallen Ixtara. It was as if a tool had been broken, a mere declarative statement. Klein found her next words even more disconcerting; the old Forlani simply asked him "Why was this woman with you?" as if *she* was somehow guilty of something, not him. Klein was too confused and disturbed by her bizarre emotional reaction to think up a convincing lie, so he told the truth of his first meeting with her. "She was my...what word do you Forlani prefer...*concubine*. She came into the bar at Site 89 where I work. Back then, I thought she was just another Forlani looking for work in the sex trade. I didn't realize that she was a spy for a man who wanted me dead."

The old Forlani asked him, "How did you discover she was a spy?" There was a sense of disgust in the words, as if she was not shocked that a person such as Ixtara could stoop to such a low. "I am the House Matriarch, the actions of all Forlani here concern me, no matter how dark a path they walk."

"One of my friends overheard a conversation between her and someone else coming from my room. She was talking about a bunch of strange topics that I haven't heard any Forlani interested in yet -- football, American football, 'playing to win.' It didn't sound like something a Forlani would say. So I brought her here and gave her an ultimatum that she either had to leave and quit working for Cashman or I'd stick her with that needle," Cashman said as he pointed at the needle, still stuck in Ixtara's arm.

"What type of venom did you use?" There was an amused, almost mirthful tone to the Matriarch's question, even though her face remained rigid and the blades of the other Forlani still aimed at his chest.

"The Varoneys. Those big, ugly toad things that make that goddamn annoying croak. I swear I'm gonna hear that noise in my dreams forever now, it was so loud"

"Ah, you used the venom of the Vile Ones," the Matriarch said with a dismissive wave of her hand. "A poor choice. It is usually not fatal, and in the rare event that it is, the death is extremely quick. The syringe only had enough to put her out for perhaps a week at most, had she not been allergic."

Klein undiplomatically blurted out the question that it had been on his mind ever since the Matriarch had pronounced Ixtara dead. "Why do you hate Ixtara so much? What had she done to you?"

The Matriarch sucked in air through her teeth, making a pronounced *sa* sound. Then she took Klein's arm. "It is not what this *Ashta* has done to me. It is what she has done in violation of our culture and our law. Do you understand the significance of the Second Wife to the Forlani marriage?"

"I've never seen a second wife," Klein responded. "I knew a Forlani who *wanted* to be a First Wife, but never a second."

The Matriarch continued, "The Second Wife is, in many ways, even more important to the family's happiness than the First Wife. Forlani males often choose their First Wife based on criteria other than what your kind calls sexual attraction and pleasure. Social standing, career, wealth...all these are extremely important in the choosing of the First Wife. Provided a male has the power to afford a Second Wife, it is her duty to make the man truly happy by flattering his ego. And Rohal, her husband, certainly could afford it. He showered her with rich gifts and affection, but nothing could win her attentions unless he divorced his First Wife and let *her* take the place of honor! A *divorce*! Such a thing is forbidden for any marriage among the Forlani! Like any honest male, he refused her request. So she left him one night to 'make her own way,' as she said it, and never returned. Rohal told me this from behind the bars of his cell, for in desperation he has Taken the White and can no longer walk among those who are sane."

Klein struggled to understand the psychology of Rohal and the other Forlani males. "He went insane because he couldn't have *her*?"

The Matriarch nodded. "Forlani males are not like the men of Earth. When they lose their wives, if they truly value them, they go completely mad. They are dependent on us, precious things to be treasured. Ixtara did not honor her husband, she only loved power and wealth. She could not be a part of our society. She was *Ashta*, to be shunned, driven out, and hated forever by our people. And the only reason I have not had you stabbed to death is because the life of *Ashta* is worth less than nothing; many of us would have tried to kill her, too, if we had the chance."

Klein told her, "Cut into the back of her neck and you'll find out what she did with her life after she left Rohal." Still curious, the Matriarch motioned for one of the other Forlani to bring forth her knife. The Matriarch sliced into the back of Ixtara's neck delicately and brought out a tiny computer chip, its metallic sheen glinting amid the blood.

"This is the proof that she was a spy, correct?" the Matriarch asked.

"Yes, that's the Kinderaugen chip," Klein said. "She was working for the man who wanted me dead. He's the only person I know who might have access to this tech on Domremy."

The Matriarch's face turned as hard as stone as she looked into his eyes. "This woman was *Ashta*, and that is the only reason you still live. You did not kill her. She committed suicide in this enclave, and no one else was in this room when it happened. This does not change the fact that I *do not trust you*. You will leave this enclave, and kill the man who made a spy of her. You will never return or ask for the services of any of the Forlani who live here, and if you do, you will be slain. Understand?"

"You won't tell the other Forlani enclaves what happened here tonight, will you?"

"No. This enclave will not be known as a place of death *unless* you return. Get out of my sight. **NOW,**" the Matriarch insisted. Klein nodded and quickly left the room. He wanted to leave this place, the site of disturbing revelations about the nature of Forlani sexual politics and Ixtara's earlier days, as soon as possible. As he walked out the front door, Klein realized that he wasn't as disturbed at the truth about Ixtara and the Forlani as he was at the truth about himself. All his earlier killings he had rationalized as self-defense, but for the first time, he had truly engaged in premeditated murder. *I finally belong on this rock*, he thought as he walked off into the dark in the direction of the train station.

Cashman paced around his office, waiting for his meeting with Spenser. Ixtara's Kinderaugen implant had stopped transmitting Friday night, and although he had not recovered her body yet, the audio files prior to her death left little doubt as to what had happened to her. *Klein knows I'll be able to assemble evidence against him quickly, no matter how much the Forlani stonewall my attempts to get the corpse. I'd better make my move to get rid of him soon—I won't be getting any more info out of him now.* Cashman sat down in his chair and began to think through his options for liquidating Klein.

His attempt to find a way to dispose of Klein was interrupted when Spenser barged through the door into his office. "Howdy Cashman, how's it going? I got a great proposal for ya!" *Like hell you do, Mr. "I'm trying to be a Southern gentlemen yet I can't remember to knock before I enter" Eckhart*, Cashman thought. "What's your idea?" Cashman asked Spenser.

"Well, I was thinking that we've shot plenty of great footage for *Heroes of Domremy*, but I haven't been able to shoot anything far from the town. Lots of folks watchin' our show are gonna want to see some real wilderness footage."

"Spenser, I've told you before, beyond the perimeter of the town it's very dangerous! We learned that the hard way, and we're not about to go out there again until we're damn sure the Locals are killed off in this area! The agreement we made..."

"Cashman, ol' boy, I've made *every effort* to keep to our agreement, but the fact is, Hyperion Corporation's contract for this program *mandates* that I have to shoot some footage beyond Site 89's perimeter. And today, I'm gonna do just that."

"You seriously want to go wandering across the perimeter into Local-infested territory on a *Monday*? The men are pissed off enough on Mondays when they don't have any special duties assigned, and you're expecting me to break it to them that they have to play nice for the camera in territory where they can get killed in the blink of an eye so that you can finish this goddamn series you've been needling me about for weeks? You, Spenser Eckhart, are a *fucking idiot*!"

"No need to get all testy, Cashman. If the good people of Site 89 won't assist us in finishing up this documentary, we'll just have to move it to another settlement that will. And of course, in doing so, we won't be paying y'all for the work you did, since you chose to cut our filming here short..."

"Fine. We'll get out there and film whatever garbage you want tomorrow. But this is the only time I'm letting you film beyond the perimeter, and afterwards, you're outta here. No conditions, you give us the money you owe us. And *you* have to be the one to explain it to them tomorrow morning, because I am not going to be blamed for *anything* that goes wrong out there. Understood?"

"Certainly. And I'd just like to say it's been a pleasure workin' with y'all." Spenser tipped his hat and walked out of Cashman's office. *Like hell it has, you stupid bastard*, Cashman thought. *The day your ass is out of here and I can get rid of Klein will be the best day of my life on this planet. Because from then on, I can start counting down till I lift off for better places.*

The men had gathered at the town's entrance early in the morning. Sullen faced and bleary eyed, they had been pulled out of bed early to listen to Spenser's announcement. They had no idea and no desire to know what Spenser was about to tell them. Even Klein, normally one of the more alert men among the group in the early morning, felt like a corpse, his Sunday night wasted in a nervous drinking binge. Spenser stood in the entryway to the town and began to speak to the unwilling assembly.

"Howdy again, y'all! This is our very last day filming in this town, so we're gonna be doin' something very special today! We're going to film outside the perimeter. It'll be a long march and take us most of the day, and we want most of you to go with us, so you're gonna be drawing straws. A long straw means you have to come with us on our final filming session, and a short straw means you get to stay here to guard the town. So, get in line, come up here, and draw your straw! No cheating!" Cashman, who was standing next to Spenser, stiffly elbowed him in the shoulder. Spenser winced and said, "This special day is my gift to y'all, so have fun!"

The glares of the men as they walked up to draw straws informed Spenser what they thought of his "gift" to them. One of the last men in line, Klein watched as many of the men he knew drew straws before him. Guzman got lucky and drew a short one; Alek drew a long straw and muttered a muffled curse. When Klein finally got up to the box and drew a straw, he took a look at Cashman and noticed he seemed agitated and tense; his body seemed more rigid than usual, and he was nervously drumming his fingers on his hips. *Cashman's probably figured out what I did by now. He'll arrange my death sooner or later, but he seemed pissed at Spenser during his speech. Maybe Spenser's expedition threw off his plans somehow?* Alone among the men, Klein was relieved when he drew a long straw; he reasoned that his last, best chance to kill Cashman would come on the expedition, which had thrown off his enemy's plans.

For once in the humid summer months of Site 89, there was a clear sky above, and the air was free of the oppressive mugginess that Klein had come to despise. He could still hear occasional croaks of "VA-ron-EY" echoing across the plain to remind him that today was only a respite from the usual weather pattern, and that the Varoneys, which Klein had come to associate with the stormy weather, were still active. The men anxiously looked at the ground as they marched, keeping a watchful eye out for the spiny toads in the nearby tall grasses. A screen of thallop riders moved ahead of the larger group on foot, providing a modicum of scouting. In contrast to most of the men, Spenser showed little concern as he charged about the group, making sure filming was going according to his plan and badgering the convicts unlucky enough to be in front of the cameras to "look nice." Other than Spenser, there was surprisingly little noise on the march from either the convicts or Spenser's film crew; it seemed particularly odd to Klein, who remembered many marching songs back from his days in the army. The silence even seemed odd in comparison to the strange chant of the Locals he heard on that earlier, fateful expedition beyond the perimeter...

We killed the Locals when we interrupted that chant. Maybe if I could get this group to sing loud enough, they'll show up for revenge! Maybe I'll still have to kill Cashman myself, maybe the Locals'll get him, but I still stand a better chance against him in the chaos of a Local attack than with all his supporters' guns trained on me. I'd better think up something...

Klein began to think up a marching song quickly and began to sing:

> Got an ache up in my head
> Walkin' round 'till I feel dead
> March right here for an hour or two
> Then fall back into my bed

A few of the convicts and one of Spenser's crew began to sing along with him. He began to sing a second verse:

> Haul this shit around all day
> Can't stop where I want to stay
> March right here for an hour or four
> Then I get drunk until I sway

Most of the convicts and many of Spenser's crew were singing along now. Klein began his third verse:

> Walk across this rock so far
> Damn, I wish I had a car
> March right here for an hour or ten
> Then head straight for Whiskey Bar

Almost everyone was singing now, leaving Spenser to desperately rush about the group and encourage the convicts to act "in character" as he wanted them to. The louder the singing got, the more frustrated Spenser became, yelling loudly in a desperate attempt to assert his authority as his face turned beet-red. The dour mood of the march finally began to lift as the men paid no heed to Spenser's repeated cries of "Shut up! Shut up!" No one seemed to notice that Klein, the man who had started the marching song, had stopped singing and was anxiously watching the surrounding grass, as if he was waiting for something to happen.

The attack came just as suddenly as it always did. The only sign was a brief rustling from the tall grass, which most of the men were oblivious to as they sung. Klein counted four shadows as he crouched low to avoid the arms of the Locals. He saw an intern scream as a Local grabbed him, but Klein got off a headshot on the poor student, saving him from weeks of agonizing suffering as a Local host. He watched as Byrne was impaled through the chest by a Local's forearm, dropping his Kikkonnen as it lifted him high off the ground. Klein glanced around the battle, looking for Cashman so he could get a shot off from his rifle before the convicts organized for a counterattack on the Locals. He heard Cashman's scream and turned around, prepared to shoot his hated foe dead.

He found Cashman screaming in the arms of a Local. He was desperately trying to use the butt of his Kikkonnen to bash the Local's head in, but he was unable to bring his arms around for a powerful enough swing. The Local bit into his shoulder with its bladelike mandibles and Cashman dropped the Kikkonnen, howling in agony. The Local was preparing to lift off and leap away with Cashman in its arms. Cashman yelled at Klein in pain and fury, "Kill me! Take me out, you bastard! No man deserves this!" Klein raised his rifle, prepared to shoot Cashman right between the eyes...

The bullet went wide, deliberately missing Cashman's head. Cashman was shocked as the bullet flew past his right ear, not even touching him or the Local. There was look of absolute horror on his face as Cashman suddenly realized his fate. "Klein, you son of a bitch!" he screamed in impotent rage as the Local lifted off, carrying him with it. The convicts had finally begun to mount a defense, firing on the Locals with their massive Kikkonnens. When one of the Locals was slain by a rocket, the attack ended as quickly as it had begun. As Klein surveyed the scene of the attack, he noticed that most of the kills from this attack had not been carried off, but had been killed on the spot, ripped apart the by the Locals' massive forearms. *This wasn't an attack to obtain food for the larvae, this was an attack for revenge. They're trying to show us that they can do to us what we can do to them, and they thought that marching song was our equivalent of their chant*, Klein thought. Relatively few of the kills had been among the convicts, who were becoming progressively better at responding to the Locals' surprise attacks; most of the kills were in Spenser's crew. Spenser himself was lying on the ground, his leg broken but with no life-threatening injuries.

"You IDIOTS!" he screamed. "You got nearly got us all killed with that goddamn song! I should have never signed on to make this documentary on this stupid fucking penal planet! I'll make sure not one of you gets one red cent from this miserable documentary! When I get back to headquarters I'll make sure this goddamn village gets *nothing* from Hyperion for this conduct!

An ominous shape loomed over Spenser and stamped down hard on his arm. Spenser screamed, thinking for half a second in his outraged delirium that the Locals had returned, before he realized that the being standing on his arm was indeed human. Through the glare of the sun overhead, he squinted and could see that it was his old enemy Aleksandrov.

"No, you won't be doing that," Alek said as his boot fell heavily on Spenser's arm. "Here is what you will do. You will give us the shares you said you would. If you do so, I will allow you to return and shoot another documentary on Hyams—he wanted to be on camera so much more than I did. If you do not give us the money, I will break your arms. Then your other leg. Then I will leave you here, and the Locals will take care of you from now on. Do we have a deal, my friend?"

For the first time Klein had ever seen him, Alek was smiling broadly as he gradually applied more and more pressure to Spenser's arm. There was a sense of cruel mirth in Alek, like a cat torturing a captive mouse, as he watched Spenser suffer. Spenser's agony was brief—Klein thought it lasted less than a minute—but it seemed like ages to Spenser. Spenser yelled, "Anything you want! Just get off my arm!" He breathed a sigh of relief as Alek stepped off his arm. "I am glad you see things my way. Of course, you will keep our deal, yes?"

Spenser nodded, too overwhelmed with pain and fear of Alek to resist. He called for the surviving members of his film crew to help carry him as men prepared to go back to town.

Aleksandrov sat in Cashman's former office, putting files together to mail to Hyperion's headquarters on Domremy. There were records of some of Cashman's communications with his handlers at Kinderaugen; Alek cared little about whatever Kinderaugen might be and what they were trying to accomplish on Domremy, but he knew that something so clandestine was potentially dangerous to Hyperion. *Perhaps, once I send these documents and computer files to Hyperion, they will favor me. If I'm lucky, they will appoint me Marshall, as Cashman was.*

Alek thought about Cashman, the pathetic excuse for a man who had run the town until very recently. He had been an abject creature, content to serve as a cat's paw for the intrigues of some covert group on distant Earth. He never had the ambition to truly *rule*, to make a new life for *himself* on Domremy. A man like him would never be a true leader of men, only one that people served unwillingly under threat. And with his intrigues broken, his power melted away like an ice sculpture in the desert.

Alek would not be a leader like him. Unlike Cashman, he was a man of *vision*, of *strength*. The two stars tattooed on his shoulders reminded him of where he came from; he had risen up from the misery and poverty of Russia's underclass to become *vor y zakone*, a lieutenant within one of the Mafya families. He had killed many men who were enemies of his organization, and his superiors had granted him the eight-pointed stars on his shoulders as proof of his loyalty and status. The government of the Russian Federation had agreed to ship him off to Domremy as a form of banishment; no matter how many times they caught him and locked him up, his connections within the organization were so strong that he was never truly alone. Only on another planet would Aleksandrov be truly alone, unable to threaten them anymore.

Alek scoffed at their weakness. *On this world, I shall be stronger than I ever was when I walked on Russian soil. For here, I can rule without the constraints the organization once imposed on me.* He only needed a pathway to gain control of Site 89; then he would begin his ascent…

4

Klein watched Peebo approaching with his usual unhurried gait, slouching along the farm rows as he returned from the far ends of his garden. He supposed Peebo must market all this produce somehow, because there was far too much for him to eat, or even to distribute in the village. There were rows and rows of something growing on poles that formed little teepees, perhaps some kind of bean? That was not all, since bushes and tufts and tussocks of green stuff sprouted all over the place. He pondered how he would broach the topic of Cashman, the one thing he wanted most to discuss with Peebo. No! – the second most important thing. For he really wanted to find out if Peebo's contacts in the Crop Talk network had found out anything about Entara. There was no reason they should. After all, what did a Forlani wife matter to these rubes who seemed to spend all their waking hours jabbering about seeds and planting depths and days till harvest. Still, they often seemed to be uncannily well informed. Peebo was finally within earshot, though Klein somehow suspected that he had been aware of his presence even before his arrival and had been listening silently all the time.

"They been lookin' for ya," blurted out the farmer, before Klein could speak.

"They, who?"

"Fella named Dorfman."

Klein's mind slipped back to Germany. Dorfman. He recognized the name. Back when they had him in custody in Hamburg, before sending him to the high court in Athens. The jailers had spoken in hushed tones about a Dorfman. A kind of scientist enforcer or enforcer scientist linked somehow to Kinderaugen. In on the most secret experiments. Someone who cleaned up. For whom? Nobody seemed to know. The jailers had been wondering if he might show up and take Klein off their hands before he could be sent to Athens. They didn't want to be anywhere close if he showed up. This Dorfman apparently left no witnesses. Klein was suddenly worried for Peebo.

"You mustn't talk with him, Peebo, understand? On any circumstances. Don't worry about me, but you need to stay completely below the horizon where this guy is concerned. He could be, no he definitely is extremely dangerous. Promise me you won't get anywhere near him."

"Sorry, pal. Too late." The "sir" of their earliest days together had long disappeared, when Peebo began to initiate him to Crop Talk and switched to "pal" or "bub" most of the time.

"What did he ask you?"

"A lot of nonsense. Stuff he said was related to your record back on Earth. Except he seemed a whole lot more interested in what kind of weaponry you were toting. Strange geezer. He obviously had a very quick mind, incisive you might say, but not a whit interested in anything important. I tried to ask him about the failures of those genetically altered soybeans back there and he just brushed me off. To tell you the truth, I lost interest in conversing with him then and there."

Klein breathed a little easier. "You were lucky, Peebo. That was a close call, you may never realize how close." Before he could ask any further questions about what Dorfman might be up to right now, Peebo sauntered over to some sprawling cucumbers.

"Just take a look at these cukes! Biggest plant in the garden, and they're mighty juicy. Ain't they beautiful? Make you a fine salad in just a while."

"Fine, my friend, but just now…"

Before he could finish the explanation, the farmer was off again. "Now you look at how strong this plant is right here. It's an exception. Doesn't get any more or less sun than the others, but it has twice as many cukes on it. Maybe it's the lack of bugs."

"But Dorfman…"

"You know, it's a peculiar thing. Some folks say bugs are funny, and you never know which ones might do the most harm." And then Peebo looked him square in the eye. "Wouldn't you say there was something just a little bit unusual about that?"

Klein realized that Peebo was Crop Talking. He had finally picked up the alert words and knew that a message was coming through.

Peebo picked a long, spotless fruit from the plant. "They say a man can be worried to distraction about a little gnat, when all the time a nasty wasp is just waiting to sting him. People can be strange, nicht wahr? Well, you just study this beautiful vegetable and study that plant and tell me if I don't get results, even with one that was planted later than all the others."

Klein now really did study the ground. The soil around the plant seemed less firm than the surrounding patch. The color of the plant and the fruits was a more vigorous green. Special fertilizer? Klein now realized what had happened to Dorfman. "But how did you manage…?"

"Nothin' to it, my boy, nothin' to it. You just put that potato rake in there real solid and give it a few good shakes and the job is done."

Klein imagined the dreaded Dorfman impaled on Peebo's farm tool. He remembered then that farmers in the Middle Ages could turn a flail, a pitchfork, an ox yoke, any everyday implement into a lethal weapon against bandits or marauding ex-soldiers. Was this something the Religious Dissenters included in their training? Another puzzle inside a mystery inside a conundrum.

"I thought you couldn't do that kind of ... planting without talking it over with the boys?"

"No time. They would all agree that thing had to be planted and fast. Weeds can spread before you know it, so sometimes you just need to up and act."

"I really have to congratulate you on those cucumbers, but maybe I will appreciate them more after they've been pickled. There was something else I wanted to ask you about. It has to do with a bull and a heifer."

"Well, you came to the right place and that's a fact. Nothin' I like to talk about more than the neighborhood livestock. I bet you want to know something about that one got shipped out of here some time back."

"Yeah, that's right."

"Well, you better sit down because the news is not too good."

In a combination of Crop Talk and low, precise sentences, Peebo told Klein that his former "girlfriend" (Entara's little joke) had fallen on difficult times. Klein had already learned from the Forlani at the nearest brothel that one of Entara's female relatives had died just before she left and she had been called home urgently to marry an important male who had been the intended spouse. Klein had already suspected that Entara would not enjoy being a stand-in mate, no matter how much the family would benefit from the alliance. However, Peebo was now telling him that the situation was much worse than he had feared. Entara had found that the new husband, Tays'she, was a particularly bad example, even for the Forlani male gender, which was not known its brains, its courage, or its gentility. Tays'she was an especially spoiled and dronish creature. Despite this, she had taken her family duties very seriously and already had a trio of beautiful daughters to care for, with more on the way. Klein was not surprised, since Entara had shown hints of a powerful maternal streak that neither of his more recent consorts had shared. She had discovered, furthermore, that her husband was involved in some corruption, but refused to expose him, rejecting the advice of her own mother. Word was that Tays'she was threatening to demote her to the status of second wife by taking a younger and socially ambitious bride. Right then and there, Klein felt a sudden urge to wring Tays'she's purple neck. His blood surged in his veins in a way that happens only in mankillers, so the colonists say.

Peebo let Klein chew silently on the bitter truth for a while as he regained his calm. He had been worried about this sit-down for weeks and was glad the message was now passed on.

For his part, when Klein had cooled his temper, he marveled at how much the Dissenters had been able to find out about domestic politics on far-off Forlan.

They had no farms there, as far as he knew, and it was a planet for which it was notoriously hard to obtain travel passes and transportation. The consorts in the local Forlani house could not possibly have known so much. He had always thought the Crop Talk network was a kind of quirk limited to a string of remote farms, but he now realized it might be capable of intelligence operations on a scale that surpassed both the Corporation and the Military. As the sun was heading for the horizon, he accompanied Peebo into the "cottage," which in reality now resembled something closer to a cruciform Quonset hut. He was hoping that no cucumbers were on the menu that night.

Fortunately, they weren't. But all sorts of other vegetables were, and he stuffed himself with lots of fresh treats. This led Klein into a deep sleep as soon as he had slumped down in the recliner in his old room in the original adobe wing of the cottage. That night he dreamed of Entara, surrounded by a herd of little purplish muskrat-like things. She was skipping with them through grass the color of white asparagus. She was speaking French and leading them in a little song…

En allant par la Lorraine avec mes sabots

En allant par la Lorraine avec mes sabots

En allant par la Lorraine, j'ai vu un capitaine dondaine…

The Forlani kits were chirping along like human kids back in the days when they still had *écoles maternelles* and *Kindergärten*, before they started pumping near-infants up with drugs and hooking them up to subliminal computer programs. When he woke up, he wondered what it all meant. He got as far as associating the pale grass and the song with a trip he'd made to Metz years ago, when he'd eaten white asparagus for the first and only time because it was on a *menu touristique et gastronomique* and been amazed at the difference in taste and texture from the freeze-dried type obtainable in the ubiquitous Aldi supermarkets.

Entara was still on his mind in innumerable, unfathomable ways when he came out to breakfast, so he decided to change the subject to jog his consciousness a little, and he told Peebo about the *Heroes* movie and Hyams and the Varoneys. Peebo listened intently as he leaned back, sipping on his colonial coffee made of scorched wheat and chicory.

"Varoneys, huh?" he chuckled. "Yes, indeed, that's a pretty good name for those critters 'cause that's just what they sound like." He gave Klein a little wink and invited him to the corridor leading to the new wings. "Follow me and I'll show you a little something."

As they passed the doors to the two transverse wings, Klein tried to catch a peek. They had started as little more than sheds and had always been pretty much empty, except for spare crates and packing material, but now, he noted, things had changed. One seemed to be filled with a lot of scientific equipment and boxes of what appeared to be old paper books.

Was Peebo developing a literary hobby in his spare time? Domremy was far too remote to try to hawk antiques like those. The other wing also had lots of boxes, mostly quite big, of varying shapes and sizes – not like the old produce packs that had been there during his residency. When they came to the remaining wing, Klein was astounded to see it filled with cages, chemicals, and specimens of Domremy wildlife.

They walked up to one very neat cage and Peebo exclaimed, "Voilà!" A Varoney squatted in it, looking at them expectantly. Klein could perceive it had a kind of splint affixed to one of the hind legs.

"What do you think? Oh, that isn't my first. She's number five. My own little rehabilitation ward for fractured Domremians. You see, these toads aren't really very fast or very smart – at least by most accounts. So when a crawler or another vehicle shows up, they're more than likely to just try to face it down and get themselves partly squashed. So I bring them back here to patch them up and study them a little."

"You know they're poisonous. How do you avoid those spines?"

"Easy. I just grip 'em with one of these harvesting arms of mine. See?"

Peebo demonstrated the articulated metal arm that had rested on a nearby barrel and showed how it clipped onto the desired object to allow safe lifting, even of a venomous toad.

"They're right interesting creatures. I had one that didn't make it, so I didn't figure he'd mind being dissected a bit before a proper burial. One very adaptive type of little animal. That's how they were able to survive after we came and changed their atmosphere."

"WHAT?" yelled the mankiller. "You mean Domremy was different from this?"

"Look it up. It's in the old records if you dig deep enough. The company semi-terraformed the planet before setting up the colony. It originally had trace gasses that would have interfered with human habitation. Unfortunately, when we changed the atmosphere, we made a lot of the wildlife instantly extinct. Including some pretty important parts I'll tell you about when I have more time someday. But the Locals and these little guys and some other stuff didn't depend on any of those trace gasses, so they evolved a little bit and fit right in with our simple nitrogen/oxygen mix. Except an ecosystem is an ecosystem and you can't just knock out part of it and expect no problems, just like you couldn't do without the brakes or the transmission on one of our vehicles. Like I say, it's a little complicated and I'll explain more some other time. Need to know only right now, ain't that right?" he chuckled, giving Klein a little slap on the back as he ended his joke.

"So did you find out anything useful about them?"

"Sure did. I found out how to keep them out of my garden so I won't step on one by mistake. A vine called goya. They're allergic to it and they won't cross a row of it, so I just plant it like a wall all around the garden area. You can eat it too, the goya, that is, if you cook it in some sauce – 'cause by itself it isn't all that wonderful."

"Anything else?"

"Yup, one other thing. The madam over at the Forlani house asked me to check out why these critters seem to be more toxic to the girls than to us. One of the girls just tried to pick one up out of curiosity and got sick without even being stung. It seems that, besides the spine venom, they actually have multiple toxins in the skin that are potentially harmful to Forlani physiology. They can result in a kind of neurological shock. I finally found the minimum fatal dose, which is mighty small, but I haven't been able to work out an antidote yet. I did get them to promise not to try to pick up any more of them, though."

Klein had to wait a couple more days for transport back to Site 89 because the surface trains were only running on an ever more reduced schedule. Supposed to be temporary, due to a parts shortage, they said, but temporary had stretched now to include indefinite, or so it seemed. As he lolled around the farm, he noticed that Peebo spent most of the time out in his crop-rows walking on stilts to avoid the Varoneys out beyond the garden. Klein would watch him go on out until he couldn't see him anymore. He would be gone so long that surely he must have gone to the limit of the crops and beyond. Unarmed. Without any patrol. Or even any tracking device (none of the Dissenters could abide wearing tracking anklets under any circumstances). What could he be doing out there all that time? Wasn't he afraid of being snatched by a Local? Could Peebo have found some way of managing with those creatures? Could other Dissenters, too? Need to know only, he repeated to himself. Better I don't ask too many questions till they want me to know – if there is anything to know. What was the Crop Talk signal, something about don't upset an apple cart? Apple cart? What the hell was that? His imagination in a whirl, he would go inside and punch up a football match, see how Borussia Dortmund or Monchengladbach were doing, but still found that his mind would find its way back to Entara sooner or later.

Entara sighed as she entered her marriage house, provided by her husband's Brotherhood connections. She never succeeded in completely relaxing when she returned to the small living space she shared with her mate, and sometimes the children, though by now it should have been familiar and comforting. Typical of most Forlani homes, the house was very compact and designed to provide a maximum amount of interior storage space at the expense of what humans would consider aesthetic appeal; the building was a simple, unadorned dome on the outside, with a door opening to what humans would consider to be a "living room." The living room contained a low couch, seats, and communications devices, which Entara rarely used. Like most Forlani females, she typically spent most of their time working with her extended sisters or socializing at the *mahäme* and relatively little inside the private home. Her new mate's bad disposition only increased the tendency to stay away. Nonetheless, Entara had obtained a new multiband receptor as a wedding present for her Tays'she, knowing that he enjoyed the human media programs that Hyperion Corporation had begun broadcasting on Forlan. Perhaps it might improve his moods. True to form, he was sprawled out in his recliner, watching some Earthly melodrama with rapt attention. Entara heard the cacophonous yelling of an angry woman coming from the holoscreen as Tays'she swiveled his recliner around to face her.

"Hello, wife," Tays'she said lazily to Entara. He was about a foot shorter than his spouse, and had a slender build with spindly limbs, typical of Forlani males. His eyes were a deep jade shade of green, and Entara had once been enthralled by their beauty, when he had given her the honor of becoming his First-Wife-in-Standing. As the years of their marriage had passed by, she found herself less attracted by his physical beauty and unhappy with his shiftless, arrogant nature. It seemed that he never tried to keep the living quarters in good order unless she nagged him, and he often let bills go unpaid, languidly drifting through life with the barest minimum of effort. Entara remembered Klein, who for all his vulgar, violent human emotion, possessed a single-minded drive and sense of purpose she had never seen in any Forlani male.

"Good day, honored Tays'she," Entara said as she touched his left hand in the traditional Forlani greeting. Tays'she nodded and asked her how her day's work at the Interstellar Passport Center had gone. "Oh, pretty much a normal day. Just screening some prospective workers for the Forlani enclaves on human colonial worlds."

"Any interesting prospects?" Tays'she asked, as he stabbed at the screen of his tablet.

"No, that is, none of the ones today had a troubled childhood or adolescence. None of the applicants from this group were rejected," Entara answered.

"How disappointing," Tays'she said. "I was hoping for another mandatory rejection like that one fleeing her family. The histrionics you described from her in the evaluation were...quite entertaining."

Entara gave an exasperated sigh. "Not all workers in the enclaves outside Forlan would have the advantages I had. A wealthy, supportive family, contacts that guaranteed me an excellent job with the Passport Center when I returned...what kind of a runaway or exile would have that? If Domremy is an example, many of the humans that went to the enclaves were dangerous and violent men. I would not trust an emotionally damaged young woman with them."

"Might make for an entertaining show," Tays'she said languidly as he turned his attention back to the holoscreen. He was fixated on watching the angry woman screaming at her children as they revolved around her, firing back insults. Realizing that the chances of having an intelligent conversation with her husband had just dropped to zero, Entara walked downstairs to the lower level where the bedrooms were located. She saw stains remaining from an alcoholic beverage Tays'she had spilled a couple of weeks ago.

"I asked you to have this spill cleaned up yesterday! How long before I must ask you again?"

"The servant was late today and was not paying attention. It'll get done when it gets done," Tays'she replied from upstairs, not bothering to come down to look at the stains. Entara gave a frustrated snort and went to take a look at the room her three daughters shared on the rare occasions when they did not spend the night with her or their friends at the mahäme.

Entara was startled to see her eldest daughter, Ayan'we, sitting on her bed in the room. "What are you doing here at home, Ayan'we? You are still supposed to be at the Leadership Academy!"

"The teacher suspended me," Ayan'we replied. Her eyes were downcast, and she was fully anticipating her mother's frustration. "It's not as bad as it sounds,"

Ayan'we continued. "Only a week-long suspension, not a year like Volana got a couple of months ago."

Ayan'we had predicted her mother's response well; Entara was furious with her. "How can you have such an arrogant disregard for your future? You were always the best student among your sisters, the one with the greatest hope for social advancement, and you choose to sabotage your own academic record for the sake of some sophistic argument with your Instructors? Even the smallest infractions at the Leadership Academy will stay on your academic record *forever*! After all we've done for you…"

"After all *you've* done for me," Ayan'we said. "Father hasn't done anything and I doubt he ever will. Not that he's been good to you – I heard him threaten to make you a Second Wife last month, he makes you do all the work – he …" she paused as though she was going to say something more, but stopped herself abruptly when she saw the sudden look of embarrassment and shame on Entara's face. Finally she blurted out, "He doesn't care about *any* of us."

"I will not hear you talk that way about your father," Entara snapped, as she collected herself. "He has…many issues on his mind that trouble him. His clique is very wealthy and perhaps the Brotherhood forced him into our marriage a bit too early…even if he were to take a new First Wife in my place, it is still his right to do so as husband, according to our ways.

However, he would lose so much standing, I'm sure he'd never do that."

"And our laws also say that *he* has to be the one to maintain this private house, as the husband and owner, while you go out and do your job. He has those gelding servants, after all. I've been paying attention in class, Mom, even if it looks like I haven't. I just don't agree with all the teachings. Look at you. You've done everything the laws tell us to do for Father, and he still gets to threaten to reduce you to Second Wife, even when he lounges around all day and contributes nothing? It's not fair to anyone, and I'shan and Tolowe know it too, even if they're too shy to tell it to you in person like I will."

Ayan'we's speech only served to further fan the flames of Entara's rage. Her feelings mixed with anxiety as she wondered if the two younger daughters really shared Ayan'we's attitude. On Earth, the three would still be considered rugrats, like the screaming brats in Tays'she's melodramas, but children matured so rapidly on Forlan. "You *must* start writing the Letter of Atonement to your Instructor *right now*. Perhaps if you do a good enough job, the Overseer at the Academy may pressure your Instructor into letting you back early."

"Can I clean up that beverage stain on the rug first?" Ayan'we asked. "It'll just stay there until Dad gets sick of looking at it and whines for you to clean it up otherwise."

"As you wish," Entara said. "But be sure to have your Letter of Atonement in before the end of the day, or else the school might…"

"I'll have plenty of time to get it in before then, Mother," Ayan'we said. Entara couldn't help but be pleased that her daughter referred to her with the *proper* honorific "Mother," as opposed to the casual "Dad" she always used to refer to Tays'she. Entara nodded to her daughter and angrily stalked off to the bedroom she shared with Tays'she.

She passively fell onto the massive brown mating bed in the center of the room, the only place in the house that Tays'she cared enough to keep in proper order. After all she did to keep her family in harmony, it seemed to fall further into chaos with each passing day. Seemingly her only reward -- and the only memory of the genuine passion Tays'she had shared with her -- was this lusciously furnished room where they bedded together, and for the past year, only on the too-frequent occasions when Tays'she insisted on mating. When her mate was building up to a lusty rage, she would send the girls off to the care of her near-sisters at the mahäme and they would not have to send more than two attendants to help Entara through the following day. She had discovered that she was remarkably resilient and recovered from mating injuries much more rapidly than most Forlani wives. Perhaps the attendants from her matriline were not really necessary any more for her health. That did not prevent her, though, from enjoying their company and compassion. It helped dispel the disgust of pleasing her self-absorbed mate and the tendency to get lost in reverie about the fun she had had with Klein when she was technically no more than a pleasure worker.

The shelves of the mating bedroom were filled with elaborate geometric woodcarving from Tays'she's days as a young artist. There was a stunning painting depicting the Great Spiral of Being on the left wall, and a beautiful ceiling fan imported from Earth spun above the bed. Entara stared at the gold and silver fan, hypnotized by the dance of its luscious colors as it whirled around endlessly. She had concentrated on it during the first mating, the most excruciating, as the passing of each blade promised it would all be over very soon. Except it was not soon at all, and when her husband had eventually pulled himself away from her with a grimace and called the attendants to come in and care for the bride, she had lost so much blood that she was in a deep coma for three days. But since the *plieh* changes had rearranged her physiology, she'd learned to minimize the shock from piercing and the blood loss. It was worse psychologically. The pain of the fundamental emptiness of her relationship with Tays'she contrasted with a dim passing memory of the few early days after the marriage rituals, when they had first moved into the house and she had seen the beautiful room he had prepared for her, little realizing, despite her bride's training, what an ordeal faced her, or how often she would fantasize at the mahäme about her innocent bedtime games with Klein back on Domremy.

Entara thought back to Ayan'we's words; though her daughter was uncharacteristically blunt for a Forlani, she spoke out of a sense of justice for her mother, not out of maliciousness. If Tays'she divorced her, she would be banished from this room except for the times when he asked her to come in; she would be cast off to the *mahäme* or into some small alcove, only allowed in when Tays'she *and* his new First Wife permitted it. The past few months, she wondered more and more about the female *she* had replaced, for in her case First Wife meant only first for the moment. Even her own matriline would tell her little of the one whom Tays'she had rejected immediately after a first mating and who had subsequently disappeared from the area. Entara realized she didn't even know her predecessor's name, only that she was from the Picks-the-Fruit people. She had a strange feeling that perhaps her daughter knew more about this than she and was holding something back. Almost as if she were a child of Klein rather than Tays'she – poor Klein who always held back so much. *Perhaps I've been too harsh to Ayan'we*, Entara reasoned. *She does not act un-Forlani because she does not care about her education. She behaves as she does because she cares too much about me, and will not restrain herself as custom demands. Perhaps it is good that some do not behave "properly" in society.* But Entara did not want her daughter to see her in her moment of doubt—she would have to be a disciplined, resolute mother to maintain order in her family, for the good of all of them. *Ayan'we must still be disciplined, for she must realize that our laws are not for the good of the individual or the immediate family, but for the good of all.*

After his visit with Peebo, Klein returned to Site 89 and found the settlement celebrating a new holiday. He had stayed on at Stafford Station as long as possible, alleging all sorts of aches and pains, in hopes of learning more about Entara, but to no avail. Now all the buildings in Site 89 were festooned with red, blue, and gold streamers, the colors of the Hyperion corporative logo, and he saw men wandering through the streets drunk in the afternoon, when they normally would have been working. A man who had clearly had one too many Domremy Specials slowly lurched towards Klein, and he yelled out "Better get your ass to the Town Center, mankiller! Big meetin' in ten minutes!"

"Why the meeting and the sudden celebration? Nobody told me about this when I left on the train last month," Klein asked.

"Didn't you see the fliers they put up this mornin'? It's Government Day, the day we citizens of Site 89 get to choose the candidates for Marshall!" The man was violently swaying in his drunken excitement and stretching his arms out to try to keep balance.

"Free two beers for everybody, just go the th' meetin' and see the candidates!"

This guy's gone way over those "free two beers" by now, Klein thought.

"Best day since I been shipped off here," bellowed the reveler. "I'd go too, if I was…presentable."

Klein had no idea who the prospective "candidates" for Marshall were, but the speed at which the political development had been announced shocked him. He rushed off to the Town Center, aware that a momentous occasion in the development of Site 89 might be occurring. As he dashed through the town, Klein took a glance at Erskine's bar, seeing that it had a giant cardboard sign proclaiming the "First Annual Government Day" that had been put up hastily; many of the other buildings had similar billboards announcing that they were honoring Government Day by taking off work. Once Klein reached the Town Center, he quickly learned why.

There was a massive assembly of men in the central square, standing in disorganized clumps rather than the orderly rows the company usually expected. Like Klein's acquaintance from the alley, many of them had gone far past the point of the two free beers and were stumbling around in a drunken haze. There was a fat man on stage whose uniform identified him as an employee of Hyperion Corporation who was pontificating about the "great future and growth of this settlement" in such a long-winded style that drunken hecklers were jeering him from the front row. Klein heard the familiar voice of Guzman yell to him, "Hey, get over here! They're about to announce the candidates." Klein moved in the direction of the voice, slogging through the milling crowd to find him.

Although not nearly as drunk as the man from the alley, Guzman had clearly been enjoying himself during the First Annual Government Day. "Hey man, where were you? We heard you was sick," he inquired, almost slapping Klein on the shoulder, but thinking better of it at the last second. Klein had been secretive about lining up a temporary replacement for himself after a few chaotic months in the post-Cashman era.

"Playing hooky. I was off visiting with my old landlord at Stafford Station for a little while. This all came as kind of a surprise to me when I came back," Klein confessed.

"Don't worry, nothing important happened so far. This guy up here has just been gassing off about a bunch of crap about progress and hope for the future. Nothing important got announced yet."

The man on stage was finally preparing to end his speech. "And with prosperity and anticipation for the coming years, indeed the coming centuries, it brings me great pleasure to announce the candidates for Marshall of Site 89. Your first candidate…," the man briefly fumbled with an envelope, "is a man who has uncovered a conspiracy involving the enemies of Hyperion Corporation amidst this settlement, through his own grit and brilliant analysis. The name of this man is…Aleksandrov."

Klein recoiled in disgust at the thought of the brutal Alek becoming Marshall of Site 89.

The man on stage yelled out, "Aleksandrov is the only man who has declared his candidacy for Marshall so far. Anyone else who wishes to declare their candidacy should step forward now!"

Klein felt a hard shove from behind push him forward. Guzman whispered to him, "Get up there, you can't let that asshole win!"

The momentum had thrust him in front of the crowd, and he tentatively began to walk forward, becoming less hesitant with each step, until he reached the stage. He'd be damned if he was going to let himself become a laughing stock because of this mob of drunks!

"What's your name, sir? "the fat man asked him.

"Wilhel…Willie Klein," Klein said. *Gotta make the name sound as informal as possible if I'm going to preserve any pride. I'm not anxious to start telling tales of old home week when nobody in this town even knows where I come from. Willie will have to do, for now*, he thought.

"Of course, of course. And your second candidate for Marshall, the town's newly returned Mankiller, Willie Klein!" The two candidates, Alek and Willie, stood together on stage, facing outward towards the audience. The crowd was no longer expressing itself through jeers and cursing, as it had during the fat man's long-winded speech; instead, there were loud hoots and yells of the candidates' names as the settlers awakened to the prospect of some kind of truly democratic government in Site 89. But the joy of democracy was far from Klein's mind; his thoughts were ruled by uncertainty and fear of retribution from Alek for opposing him. Still waving confidently to the crowd, Alek had given Klein no angry glare or other outward sign that he would be targeted for retribution, but Klein knew that Alek was the kind of man who would *always* respond to a challenge with violence. It was only of matter of when it would come, and in what form.

Ayan'we's mind had not stayed idle for long. Even though she was confined to the parents' home or the matriline's mahäme during her suspension from the Academy, she had not been denied communication access, and therefore could still exchange messages with the few virtual friends who made her feel comfortable -- the online group that called themselves Echidna's Children. Ayan'we had never met any of them face to face -- or at least she didn't think she had, since they all communicated by codenames. They chose their personal codenames of mythological monsters that they had studied during an *Earthly Religion and Mythology* class at the Academy, never revealing their true identities or residences. The group met in chatrooms on ForlanScape, the most widely used social networking site on the planet.

The leader of the group, Chimaera, was organizing a vote among the membership to determine which site to attack next. *We've been getting lax lately, and we're losing our sense of ambition. Taking down the Academy's Registry of Scholastic Awards for an hour? Pathetic. We need to make a big splash, take out an important government site*, Chimaera typed. Nemean Lion answered, *Why not take down the Passport Center for a while? The Instructors constantly brag about the Interstellar Passport System, let's see how they react if their glorious program gets knocked offline for a few hours.*

Ayan'we felt a lump rise in her throat at the thought of attacking a government site, especially the one where Entara was an important personality. The Academy would instantly expel her if she was discovered, denying her any productive future and condemning her to the life of a Menial, scrubbing floors and windows all her life for minimum wage. *I don't want this. We could be ruining our futures if we attack the Passport Center. I joined this group to make fun of Instructors flailing around when we took down their web pages overnight, not to have the Network Enforcers come after us when we anger the highest level of government!*, she responded.

Nonsense, the Lion replied. *We won't take any vital information from the site on the attack. We're just going to attack the Network Time Protocol using our botnet to flood the time synchronization servers with false requests from the site. We may not be able to take it down correctly, but it'll be hours before they know what's going on!*

Smart, Chimaera responded. *I read that kind of attack was common on Earth's primitive Internet for a time, but nobody here has tried it yet. The results should be amusing, if nothing else.*

Ayan'we was horrified at the direction of the conversation. *I want nothing to do with this attack. If this is the future direction of our group, count me out*, she typed.

Then you won't be missed, the Lion responded. *If you don't have the courage and ambition needed to be one of Echidna's Children, then you will have no place in our glorious future.*

Goodbye, Ayan'we ended the conversation and powered off her computer. There was nothing she could do to prevent the attack, and she believed the only thing she could do was to be offline when the attack occurred so the Network Enforcers wouldn't trace the attack to her machine. She could only sit on the bed in her room and wait for the after effects of the attack to make themselves apparent.

Ten minutes later, she heard Tays'she bellowing in frustration from the living room, "*Meh'tra!* Ayan'we, *get in here now!*" Ayan'we bolted at her father's command. *He barely ever raises his voice, let alone curses.*

Something must be seriously frustrating him, she thought.

When she reached the living room, she saw Tays'she standing next to the couch, his face red with anger. He roared, "*Just* when I was filling out the Brotherhood Tax forms through the Revenue Center, *the site crashes!* I had been working on the forms for hours, just about to submit it, and *this* happens! *Meh'tra!*"

They must have spread the attack farther than the Passport Center if they hobbled the Revenue Center, too. Better try to prevent him from getting any angrier, Tays'she thought. "Um, Father…is there anything I can do for you?" she asked.

Tays'she's voice began to become more measured, although Ayan'we could tell he was still exasperated, ready to explode into rage at a moment's notice. "Work on some of these tax forms for me. I know it would be just an approximation, without the aid of the Revenue Center…but you are studying mathematics at the Academy, and you might as well put your skills to use, even while you are suspended."

Ayan'we saw the huge box filled with folders that contained the household's tax forms, as well as other forms related to her father's contacts with the planetary society of males, the Brotherhood. She barely suppressed a groan at the site of her workload. "Certainly Father," she meekly responded, flattering him with an honorific for a change. 'I'll get to work on it right now."

"Excellent," Tays'she said. "It's not as bad as it looks—the only forms you need to work with are in the yellow folders. Do not touch anything in the blue ones—it's not relevant to your work on the taxes. I'll be relaxing with a drama."

"Certainly," Ayan'we answered, and carried the massive box to her room. She put the box down next to the desk and began to sort through the folders, removing the yellow oness so she could work on them. As she reached for the last yellow folder, she accidentally grasped a blue folder with it, and it fell open as she tried to pick it up. She shuffled through the papers that had fallen out of the blue folder as she tried to put them back in order, but saw a small, seemingly innocuous phrase on the bottom of one:

FastTrack.

Ayan'we had never heard of "FastTrack" before, and was intrigued by the seemingly innocuous name. Why had something as apparently everyday as FastTrack been filed in the blue folders? But Tays'she, lazy as he was, could also be remarkably impatient if things he requested were not completed expediently. *Mother learned that the hard way*, Ayan'we thought as she sighed and put the paper back into the blue folder and prepared to work on the vast assortment of yellow folders that contained the family's tax forms. Taxes, like other facets of wealth, were largely a matter of abstraction on Forlan, where everyday economics were minimal and simple. The main reason for meticulous care was that this particular abstraction had a good deal to do with the way the Brotherhood arranged matters of marriage and male education. *If I ever do have any brothers, I hope they appreciate the trouble I'm going through for them, the lazy slugs!* Ayan'we smiled at her own impolite thoughts.

Klein surveyed his ramshackle campaign office as he sat across the table from Guzman. There were freshly printed campaign posters with the words KLEIN FOR PROGRESS in giant red letters on the walls, an "artist's rendering" of Klein that was much more clean-shaven and handsome than Klein had ever envisioned himself, and a reasonably professional-looking desk for the candidate to conduct his campaign from. Despite this, Klein felt almost no sense of progress or achievement in his campaign; his biggest forward momentum had been simply setting up his office on the second day of the first week. He was nervously spinning a pencil while Guzman explained the latest woes of the campaign to him.

"Alek got an 11 point lead on us in the early polling," Guzman said, riffling through his notes like a cub reporter. "He's got posters everywhere, people supporting him going door to door, and what do we have? A couple of posters in Erskine's bar? We've gotta get better organized, man! We need our posters up, we need more supporters going around getting our message out, we got to get people on our side! It's been almost two weeks and we haven't stepped our game up, what's with you, man?"

Guzman told me he had never been involved in politics back on Earth, but after these last few weeks, I don't buy that anymore. He's got such passion for this election, I feel I can never live up to it, Klein thought. "I've tried getting those campaign posters for us up, but the business owners on the north side of town won't even give me the time of day! When I tried going up there to put 'em up a couple of days ago, all I saw was endless ALEK signs posted all over that part of town. I recruited a couple more people to campaign for us, but they'll only work in the south side or near the bar, and I spent all last night trying to tell people about the campaign myself! What the hell else am I supposed to do if Alek's got one whole part of town locked down like that?" Klein said, exasperated.

"I hear Alek's not gettin' that kind of support by playing fair," Guzman said. "Some people say he's been sending out hired thugs to threaten people into supporting him, or offering money under the table to his supporters after he's elected...I remember what that shit was like back on Earth. I don't want it gettin' started here."

"How do you expect us to compete with that? None of us have the connections or whatever the hell kind of secret accounts Alek is using, and the only way to compete with money is more money, so I don't think we're gonna outspend him...."

"You don't have to *outspend* him to *outcompete* him," Guzman said. "We got allies of our own. Didn't you say you were friends with some guy who was involved with those religious folks...what was their name..."

"Dissenters," Klein said.

"Yeah, Dissenters. Anyway, I don't think religious people would like their Promised Land being taken over by Russian Mafia guys. If we went to 'em and explained what was going on and why they should help us out, maybe we could get their support in the election and they'd give us the numbers we need to win."

"It's not that easy to get their support," said Klein. "I don't know the Dissenters that well, other than Peebo and a few of his relatives, but even though they don't like the crime and corruption of Earth, they don't seem to me like the types who would get involved in a political campaign that might involve hostility and violence. Why ruin their attempt to make a fresh start of things by forcing them into politics when they're practically fresh off the ships from Earth?"

Guzman was becoming more and more excited as the conversation went on. "They may not *want* to be involved, but they *will* be involved soon enough! I know how this shit goes down on Earth, a guy like Alek doesn't take *no* for an answer, he'll come after anyone who doesn't support him..."

Klein heard a loud banging noise coming from the door. He got up out of his seat and walked over to the door, and opened it to see Erskine standing in the doorway. Erskine had a slightly agitated look on his face, but otherwise appeared as he usually did, with no visibly different body language that Klein could see. "I need to talk with you inside your office, Klein," he said. He followed Klein in and sat down next to Klein's desk.

Erskine sighed, as if he had thought long and hard about what he was about to say. "Klein, I...you're gonna have to get a new place to sleep. All the campaign posters, all this political stuff in my bar...I've been getting complaints from some of the customers. They don't want to have to look at or think about all these depressing things or worry about their futures, they just want to come in, have a brew, have a laugh, and this campaign makes it really hard. I can't have you using my bar as a campaigning place, you're gonna have to leave now."

Erskine's words triggered a sudden flood of anger in Klein's mind. His voice erupted in a rage-filled shout, the rational aspect of his mind lost to an elemental force he could no longer control. "We made that goddamn agreement in the beginning of the campaign!" he shouted at Erskine. "I was counting on that fucking bar as a place I could use to recruit people, and all of a sudden, you just kick me out?! After all I did to help keep this town safe, this is the thanks I get?! Did Alek beat the shit out you to get him to kick me out?"

Immediately after he said it, Klein realized the error of his words. Erskine had no noticeable scars or bruises, and did not seem upset about the prospect of Klein leaving him. *Damn my rage,* he thought as his anger subsided. *Alek probably didn't need to use a beating on the guy, just a little bribe. Should've remembered a lot of guys will sell each other out at the drop of a hat on a penal planet.*

Erskine looked angry but maintained his composure. "You have to get all your stuff out of your room *today*. Do it or I'll have it all thrown out into the street. You don't have a room above the bar anymore. That's the end of it," he said and walked out of Klein's campaign office.

Something about the indignity of having a man he had thought was his friend abruptly sell him out had trigged tremendous anger in Klein. After the initial explosion of rage had worn off, he was still left with painful resentment and a gnawing craving for revenge on Alek. He'd show that bastard who could play hardball politics on this planet!

"Guzman, that idea you had about the contacting the Dissenters for help…that sounds like a great idea now. I'm gonna get to work on that. After I finish hauling all my stuff back from the bar, that's the first thing I'm looking into."

Over the course of the last several weeks, Tays'she had become increasingly hostile to Entara for reasons she didn't understand. One day her husband had screamed at her for an eternity because she had come home late and had gotten some cheap takeout instead of a "proper" meal. Another day he had chosen a more passive-aggressive method of venting his anger at her, choosing to lock her out of their shared bedroom because she had forgotten to get him a batch of paint he had requested. Just as mysterious as Tays'she's anger towards her was his odd reaction on the day Ayan'we had returned to the Academy; when Ayan'we had returned the box with the family's tax forms to him, he had nervously gone through it, as if he were concerned that *something* important might have been missing. Entara pondered; did Ayan'we know something that Tays'she had kept from her? Or was she just becoming paranoid because of Tays'she's increasing irritability? She couldn't make up her mind, but the nagging suspicion didn't leave her.

    This particular day, Tays'she's behavior was even odder than it had been over the past few weeks. Instead of being frustrated and irritable, he seemed to be in a state of euphoria, walking about the home with a secretive smile on his face, politely answering all her requests, and even taking the trouble to call her at the Passport Center to tell her that he had a "big surprise" waiting for her when she got home. After finishing her day's work, Entara took the monorail back to her private home, a sense of inescapable anxiety lodged in her mind about the nature of what the "surprise" was.

She opened the door to her house and saw Tays'she standing in the middle of the living room. He had a glowing smile on his face, and there was a female Entara had never seen before reclining on the couch. The newcomer was wearing an expensive looking blue dress that accentuated her tall, slim figure; though Entara did not know the woman's exact age, she appeared several years younger than Entara. The mystery woman looked at Entara with a cold expression on her face, as if she was trying to determine whether Entara was a rival or merely a bystander.

Confused by the sight of the stranger in her living room, Entara asked Tays'she, "What is the meaning of this? Who is this stranger, and what is she doing in our house?" The anxiety that she had suppressed all day gave a forceful edge to her voice as her negative emotions rose to the surface.

The smile left Tays'she's face, replaced by an expression of wavering uncertainty. Did Entara, his First Wife, still have a strong enough will to challenge her fate? *I can't hold back my decision from her any longer*, he thought, and began to explain to her. "Entara, you are no longer my First Wife. This is Ha'maya, who shall take your place. I shall allow you to continue living with us as my Second Wife, as you have pleased me greatly in technical and ... other matters."

"After all I have done for us, *this* is how you reward me and our children? By condemning me to a dishonor that most Forlani would not wish upon their worst enemy? Do you think so little of me that I am trash to be cast out? " Entara responded.

"Our children will have the same rights and entitlements they had when you were my First Wife," Tays'she said, "and no one shall be 'cast out'. This decision will simply allow you to focus on your duties at the Passport Center. Your earnings there will continue to strengthen our family…"

"Is that all I am to you? Some miserable *kar'ya*, a beast of burden to earn for you?! *Meh'tra, Tays'she! Meh'tra!* You've stuck that organ of yours inside me and torn me up so many times I couldn't think you wanted more, but I'm not enough for you. Even after I was impregnated for life, you kept at it again and again just for yourself. I wish I didn't have to go on having your children, I wish I could just spew everything from you out of myself. I… I…" Entara stopped herself only when she realized that she did love her own children, the ones born and the ones to be born, despite what she had suffered through the mating, despite the rottenness of her husband, despite the insult to her and all her line.

She was so violently upset with Tays'she, so outraged with his brazen dishonoring of her status as First Wife, that the only way she could restrain herself from attacking him was to rush to the room her daughters shared on their rare nights at home. She could barely hear Tays'she saying that it was his legal right to make this decision and that he would not change his mind as she left the room in frustration. When she reached the room of her daughters, she punched the desk in a fit of rage, yelling *"Meh'tra!"* again and again as she vented her disgust with the situation. The man she had agreed to marry for the benefit of her family, who had claimed according to the ancient marriage rites of the Forlani that he would *"cherish and honor"* her forever, only cared about her as an instrument of wealth, a thing of earning potential! She was no more than a carcass to him.

Even in her fury, she realized that this was not the *absolute* worst case scenario she had dreaded. Tays'she had said she would not be cast out; presumably that meant she would be afforded some puny room in the house with a sleeping bag, and her children would not lose their inherited status as Tays'she's children. *Pity they'll legally be considered Ha'maya's children as Tays'she's 'Children of the first bed' from now on*, she thought to her chagrin. As for those yet to be born, they would only have the matriline to provide for them, with little chance for marriage or advancement. It was one comfort to know that Ayan'we, at least, would always consider her Mother. She again remembered the strange, awkward exchange as Ayan'we returned the box full of folders to Tays'she. *What does Ayan'we know that I do not?* She pondered.

The meeting with the Dissenters had taken about a week and a half to set up, and Klein knew it would have taken longer if his friend Peebo hadn't somehow requesting that the process be expedited. The Dissenters typically didn't have a mindset of hair-trigger responses, but Klein had told Peebo that the campaign would be over soon, and Peebo had assured him the Dissenters would oblige as best they could.

It took place in a barn outside of Site 89's town center. Klein noticed the barn was well-used, with bales of hay piled up and a bleating thallop in a stable against the left wall. The only visual cue that the barn was a place of importance was a small circle of ash with a cross inside. This ephemeral symbol, used by the Dissenters to mark their temporary "churches" and meeting places alike, was chosen because it could be so easily erased after the end of the meeting, insuring that none of Hyperion's representatives would find a record of the massed Dissenters in the place. Klein and Guzman sat down on one side of the ash circle; on the other side, Peebo and a man Klein didn't recognize were seated. The man who was new to Klein appeared to be a middle-aged black man, his hair just starting to turn white. The man turned his face to Klein.

"Welcome, Klein, friend of Peebo. To a farmer, a day ends at sunset," the man said.

"To Klein, a day ends at sunset," Klein repeated. *One of the first things Peebo explained to me was that 'a day ends at sunset' is their way of saying that this conversation never leaves these walls. Maybe that's why the Dissenters never like to schedule their meetings at any time other than twilight*, he thought.

"I am the man the Council has sent to speak with you," he told Klein. "I am sorry, but our true names are not to be told to people not of our faith. My name to you will be Trevor, though it is not the name God gave me."

"It's always good to find a friend on the road at night," Klein said, repeating the last part of the Crop Talk code Peebo had taught him for speaking to the Dissenters. "Glad to meet you, Trevor."

"It's good to find a man who needs a guide at night," Trevor said. "I have been told that your town faces the threat of corruption and violence. Please explain to me why you need our help."

Klein struggled to find a way to phrase his problems with Alek so that they didn't *just* sound like a personal struggle, mulling his words over before he spoke. "There's a man running against me named Alek for Marshall of Site 89. I'm not going to lie to you, he's leading me in the polls right now, but he's not the type of person who would run a fair election. I think he may be using threats of violence and property destruction to make people support him, but I *know* he's been using bribes. What I need are dependable supporters, the kind of people who won't be swayed by money under the table and have strong moral convictions."

"What you are saying," Trevor asked, "is that you want the Council to encourage those of our faith to support you in this confrontation, correct?"

"Yes," Klein responded. *This guy really cuts to the chase, he makes me feel like my responses to his questions are inarticulate and wouldn't convince an idiot*, Klein thought.

"It is good that you are a friend of people of our faith," Trevor said. "If the people of our faith welcomed the concept of political engagement, we would likely be inclined to support you. But perhaps you don't fully understand our history yet, or the notion of *why* the Dissenters chose to leave the Earth. Do you remember what had happened to other religious groups before the Dissenters had formed?"

Dammit! I knew there was some kind of trick question involved somehow, and I have almost no religious education, Klein thought. *I may not be able to con this guy into thinking I'm some kind of religious genius, but at least I can't let him know how frustrating this campaign—and this conversation—is for me.* "I'm sorry, I don't know too much about the history of religious movements in the 21st Century," Klein answered, giving a response that was as honest as possible.

Trevor had a sad, almost wistful, look on his face. "So many of those movements, those churches, had once started out with genuine *good* in their souls and *truth* in their minds. But they almost invariably became eaten, *consumed* by the Sin of the world around them. They believed they could master, and ultimately vanquish, Sin by controlling the great political engines of their times. In some cases, they could even win a brief victory over Sin, banishing some obscene aspect of the world around them for a brief time. But that taste of politics always led to *worldliness*, and it would always gain possession of their souls, no matter if it be slowly and secretly or abruptly and dramatically. They would always become bound to the Sinful Earth, another aspect of Sin within themselves, as much as they claimed they hated it—building gilded halls they claimed were "churches," saying that a man poorer than them was not loved by God, spreading hatred and bile and filth to their enemies as the Enemy of All does to Man. Do you understand why we came here, Klein?"

"You wanted a New Earth, like it says at the end of Revelations," Klein said. "A new world, where you could teach people to live without the sins of the old."

Trevor smiled. "Exactly! We, who are called Dissenters, took that name because we want to leave the Sinful Earth behind, for it—and the great powers that govern it—are so drenched in Sin that they will corrupt all. We do not want to conquer other men's souls by violence, though we will defend ourselves if we are attacked. We will not build gilded halls like those of the Sinful Earth do, but meet in secret places, like the Old Christians did, with only this mark to guide us," he said, pointing at the ash circle. "We will not tell others that God does not love them because of the misery of their mortal life, but teach them the glories of God, so they may turn to God and live for a better tomorrow. The technology, wealth, and worldliness of the Sinful Earth we wish to leave behind so that we may have a chance of cleansing our souls to see Him. How would interceding in your election accomplish this?"

"Because," Klein said, "If you don't declare for me in this election, Alek will almost certainly *win*. And, unlike me, he won't take a *maybe* for a positive response. He'll come after anyone who doesn't emphatically support him in this election. Also, I don't know exactly where that money of his is coming from, but I can bet it's nowhere good, and he'll be sure to cause a lot of trouble with it after his election."

Trevor had a thoughtful expression on his face. Klein didn't get a sense of antagonism from the man, despite the fact that he had felt frustrated during his questioning. But Klein's hypothesis that the Dissenters were not a group who enjoyed political engagement was proving difficult to overcome. "I, and the Council, will consider further what you have said. But know that we do not make decisions quickly or act quickly as a group. It may take us many months to decide what we will do."

"But the election's less than a month from now!" Guzman blurted out.

"A good vintage gets better with age," Trevor told Guzman, and swept his hand through the ash circle. It was a sign that the meeting was over, and the place's value to the Dissenters had been reduced to being just another barn. Klein turned around and left with Guzman.

"Damnit, I really blew it back there!" Guzman whispered to Klein once they were out of earshot.

"I don't think *you* blew anything," Klein said as he responded to Guzman. "I think the response he gave us was what he, and the Council, had planned out *before* the meeting had even occurred. Those questions weren't about our campaign so much as they were about studying *us* and our concepts of faith and sin. Don't you remember what he said about teaching the glories of God?"

"So they were *never* gonna help us in the election?" Guzman asked.

Klein sighed. "No, they weren't. They were studying us to see what we'll be able to do for them or with them later on, but I don't think they were ever interested in *this* election."

"That sure as hell ain't gonna help us out now!" said Guzman.

"Damn straight," said Klein.

Later, when he spoke again with Peebo, he asked his old landlord if there was anything else that perhaps couldn't be spoken of. Peebo simply frowned and shook his head. Whatever it was, it was not time for Klein to know.

Ha'maya had begun to exploit her newfound power quickly in Tays'she's household. She had immediately moved into the mating bedroom Entara had once shared with Tays'she, forcing Entara into a dingy little storeroom originally intended to hold wood and other materials for Tays'she's artistic pursuits. Entara had begun to realize that there was an upside to Tays'she's decision to end his career as an artist; although the room was cramped and tight, there was still enough room for her to stretch out and lie down in a sleeping bag. She knew that the meager amount of space she had would have been non-existent if the room was still be using to hold wood for Tays'she's carvings. Despite her urge to leave completely and stay at the matriline compound in the warmth of her own sisters, she spitefully spent at least a couple of evenings every so often in the detested little room, mainly as a sign she was not renouncing all claims. This was all the more difficult and lonely because her daughters had taken already to spending their nights at the compound, scorning the place their father and his new female considered home.

Unfortunately for Entara, there was no upside for her to living with Ha'maya. Tays'she's new First Wife took delight in asserting her superior rank at every turn, belittling Entara in private conversations with Tays'she, and always regarding her with a smug, haughty attitude. *Tays'she casting me out would've been the more merciful path*, she thought, *but I must try to maintain my status as a member of this household for the sake of my three daughters.* Entara knew that if her husband cast her out, her children could easily be disowned in the eyes of the Brotherhood, and she would have no legal means other than the matriline to protect their inheritance and financial status. *Did this also happen to the children of Tays'she's First Wife before me,* she wondered.

"Entara," Ha'maya called from the dining room, "Could you please come and make some drinks for us? We're discussing Ayan'we's academic performance – *or lack thereof* – at the Academy, and I think I need a good, stiff drink to help absorb the shock of these reports! Come get me something to drink, Second Wife of Tays'she."

Oh, I'll give you something to drink, you olata, Entara thought as she hurried to the kitchen from the living room, where she had been resting briefly. As she mixed the materials Ha'maya had requested for the drink – some expensive vodka and orange juice from Earth, both of which, since imported, cost a nasty chunk of her monthly salary from the Passport Center –.she put a few small drops of extract from the ishtapa plant into the drink. The ishtapa plant was a rare shrub which grew in the wetter parts of the caverns of Forlan. It was traditionally used as a cure for incontinence among the Forlani, but it wreaked such havoc on the digestive system − typically over the course of a day or two after taken − that some viewed the cure as worse than the ailment itself. Entara silently wondered what Ha'maya's opinion on the matter would be as three droplets fell into the drink mixture.

When she entered the dining room, she was not surprised to find that Ayan'we and Ha'maya were loudly arguing about Ayan'we's grades at the Academy and what they meant for her future. Entara had urged Ayan'we to return home for a few days so the youngster could participate in Daughters Day and observe her work at the Passport Center, and she had thought that the first meeting between her daughter and Tays'she's new mate would go more smoothly if she was there to supervise it. Unfortunately, her demotion had left her with no leverage over Ha'maya, who continued to viciously berate Ayan'we.

"Look at these grades, Ayan'we. *Look* at them. 'Insufficient' in Cultural Studies of Ancient Forlan? I could easily get a 'Superior' rank in a class like that when I was coming up through the Academy! Pathetic! No girl in my walls walks away with an 'Insufficient'! What is your explanation for this poor performance?" It was a major insult: a girl in the walls could be a placeless servant, only admitted to the home for labor. Ha'maya was preparing for a total rift with Entara's children.

Entara could see that it was taking all of Ayan'we's emotional self-control to keep from yelling at Ha'maya. "My explanation," Ayan'we calmly responded, "is that I did not get an Insufficient rank in that class. I only got a Substandard. Tays'she didn't read the report very clearly. He should check it again."

Tays'she, clearly bored with the argument between them and already inclined to regard Ayan'we as a lost cause, flipped through the pages of the report again. "I was wrong because the report uses imprecise organization," he admitted. "Only a Substandard. The Instructor worded the criticism as if she had assigned an Insufficient, though. I really wish they would report the rank *before* the argument."

The correction did nothing to change Ha'maya's attitude towards Ayan'we. "Insufficient... Substandard... what kind of a difference is that? Still too pathetic a performance by a member of this family! Tays'she tells me that your sister Tolowe got an Exemplary in Ancient Forlan! Pity I didn't get to meet her instead of a...a *slacker* like you!"

Ha'maya's use of the word *slacker* struck Entara as curious. Most Forlani wouldn't have used Earth slang to describe a child with substandard academic credentials. Her awkwardness using the alien phrase was palpable; Entara noticed that even Tays'she, uninterested in the conversation as he was, had raised an eyebrow. *Does Ha'maya have some knowledge of Earth culture that she's kept secret from us?* Entara wondered as she walked over to table to offer Ha'maya the drink.

The effect, typical of ishtapa extract, was very rapid. A minute after she had taken a drink from the glass, Ha'maya clutched her gut in pain. "What...what did you do to me? Did you...*poison* me? Trying to keep *your* worthless daughter from me, you....you *olata!* Tays'she, she poisoned me!" Ha'maya screamed.

Dense as he sometimes was, even Tays'she knew what the "poison" was from Ha'maya's physical reaction. "I think you should go to seek relief right now, my First Wife," he said. "I will get you some medicine for your upset stomach. I hope this did not happen *intentionally*." Entara noticed the angry emphasis on the word *intentionally*, and realized she had made a terrible mistake.

"Throw this *olata* out of this house! I demand it!" Ha'maya screamed in rage. "I will have justice!"

"You will go to calm yourself, *now*. The situation will be *resolved*," Tays'she said, shooting Entara an angry glare. Ha'maya followed his instructions and hurried away. "She will make you pay for this," Tays'she hissed at Entara before he followed his First Wife.

Once Tays'she was gone, Ayan'we turned to her mother. "That, even for a beloved mother," Ayan'we said with a sigh in a low voice, "was a very stupid thing to do."

"I know," Entara said, "but this situation is horrible for me—and for all of us! I could be cast out, you could be disowned...that horrible woman has ruined this household!"

Ayan'we shrugged. "Keep your voice low...I've got something important to tell you. Tays'she ruined this household long before she came in, and you won't be cast out. I have an...*arrangement* with Tays'she that prevents that."

Entara's eyes opened wide in shock. "What kind of an arrangement do you mean? Is it an arrangement that will save you from being disowned through her plotting?"

"Yes, Mother," Ayan'we said. "Do you recall when I gave the box back to Tays'she? As it turns out, I found a blue folder in it that said something about a program called FastTrack. One of the days I was working on the tax forms for him, I mentioned that I had found it, and told him the name FastTrack."

"And how did he react?" Entara questioned her daughter. She was starting to wonder about the nature of Ayan'we's supposed leverage over Tays'she. *Could my husband...lazy, oblivious Tays'she, actually be involved in something strictly illegal?* She wondered.

"He became very apprehensive and nervous. Once that happened, I realized that just the fact that I knew the name 'FastTrack' was somehow a threat to him. On the day I had finished, he was ranting at me that I had taken too long doing the taxes, so I threatened to tell everyone at the Academy that he was involved in it!"

"Ayan'we, you can't do that! Tays'she is still your Father, and being involved in scandal would destroy this family's standing if it was exposed! I could never work at the Passport Center again, and you would never be permitted to return to the Academy!"

"I know," Ayan'we said. "But the Fifth Axiom of Negotiations teaches that the threat of destruction is superior to the act of destruction, for threat ensures that you will stay intact. Dad's always been selfish, and he knows being exposed will destroy *him*. So as long as I...*we* know this, then he won't disown or cast out anyone for fear we'll tell everyone that he's involved in this FastTrack somehow. And this is the real reason I agreed to come home this week, not to observe you."

"So, I see you *have* been studying Culture of Ancient Forlan much harder these days," Entara said, impressed with her daughter's grasp of Forlani logic.

"After you told me to," Ayan'we said. "My Instructor told me I was very close to bringing my grade up to Sufficient. Of course, I still prefer Science."

Entara was relieved but still depressed at having to share a house with the loathsome Ha'maya. Her daughter had proven more than "Sufficient" at Forlani logic, and her curious nature had likely saved her—and all her daughters. But she would still be subject to abuse and belittlement by Ha'maya that would likely become even worse after her ishtapa "poisoning" incident. "I'd like to go do some writing now," she told her daughter.

"What kind of writing?" Ayan'we asked, ever curious.

"Oh, just a letter to an Earthman I met back on Domremy explaining my problems. There's no way a paper letter will reach him from here—I'll burn it after I write it—but it will feel good just to write down how I feel, as if I could still speak to him."

"Klein! You're writing to Klein. Oh, Mother, good, I know he will not refuse to help us," Ayan'we said rather dreamily. Then she suddenly switched to an urgent, practical whisper. "No need to burn it. I know some people at the Academy who will be able to get it smuggled aboard a freighter to Domremy. Just make sure it's only paper...I'm certain our government here on Forlan would intercept any electronic communication."

Entara was elated. "Thank you, daughter, for all you have done for me!" she said as she embraced Ayan'we. For the first time in what had seemed to her like an epoch, she smiled in true gladness.

However, as Entara was leaving the house in happy anticipation of hugging her sisters at the matriline, for only there could she be safe writing what she had decided to write, she saw something out of the corner of her eye that froze her in her tracks. A group of females was chatting near a fruit-and-insect stand a short distance from the doorway. Entara recognized them from her work with the Passport Office – they were top level security police! She realized she had better gather her wits and walk away with apparent carelessness, though all three lobes of her main heart were beating frantically. She turned into a leafy bower on the way to the matriline chapter house and quickly ducked behind a large orange shrub. She stayed there long enough to ensure that she hadn't been followed. That seemed at first like good news, but as she reflected on it, it turned much worse. Since there were at least four officers, and they had not thought she was important enough to tail, they must be watching the home and Tays'she. Ayan'we's partial revelations about FastTrack echoed in her head. She realized she would have to talk again with her daughter and find out what kind of threat it posed to the family. Whatever it was, the presence of a whole patrol of secret security police – the kind who normally dealt not with individual matters, but with important threats to the planetary order – meant that she and her offspring were now in danger of something far more grave than merely the disruption of a marriage. The letter to Klein had just become an entirely different affair -- a plea for help that might involve his special talents.

The election was finally, mercifully, over and done with. It had been an even worse rout than Klein expected. In the end results, Alek had won the vote by a margin of 25 percent. Not just the north side of the town, but a substantial majority of the south side, had turned out for Alek. Some high-profile citizens ended up supporting Klein's campaign, but in most cases it was long after the support could have helped, and he and Guzman were left tearing down posters and banners in the relocated campaign office with nothing to show for their effort.

"Damn, that was depressing," said Guzman. "One of those polls claimed we were closing on Alek…"

"Even the closest poll had a gap of seven percentage points in Alek's favor," Klein said, sighing. "I don't think we had much of a chance even in the best case scenario. Our last hope was getting the Dissenters' support, *that* would've been the miracle we needed. But nothing short of a miracle would've saved this campaign."

"With all the support he had in the election, Alek's gonna *own* this place. What the hell can we do here if nobody will even give us the time of day?" Guzman said.

"I'm thinking I should go back to Stafford Station and try to work as a handy man or maybe a farmer. Being a mankiller on Domremy is the most miserable work imaginable. I've ended up being driven out of two towns now because of who got chosen to be marshall! I'm sick of the politics of this position, and I'm fed up with being blamed whenever I have to kill a decent man because the Locals are carrying him off. I think the Dissenters were right, Guzman. I think we should just try to get along on this world and live an honest, hardworking life."

"*You* as a Dissenter?" laughed Guzman. "You're one of the few friends I have on this planet, but your mind is geared to violence as much as any man I know. You may not enjoy the fact that people treat you like dirt because you're a Mankiller, but you *need* an enemy, an adversary to define yourself against. If all you had in life was trying to help people and listening to sermons about the Sinful Earth, you'd die of boredom. Maybe you should wander across Domremy fighting Locals all by yourself like Rambo in the old digitals, I don't know. But I do know that you'll never be a Dissenter."

Hyams sauntered in the open door. He had served the Klein campaign with loyalty and dedication for all of the last week and a half. "Hey guys, can I come in and help clean up?"

"Sure," said Klein.

Guzman grunted and shot a resentful look at Hyams as he walked in and started putting some posters into the trash bin.

"Hey! Sorry I couldn't help you guys out earlier, but I was just too busy filming my show, *A Hero of Domremy*. I wanted to get that bastard just as much as you guys. So, what're you planning to do now that the election's over? "Hyams said.

"I think I'm gonna go try something new, maybe go be a farmer or a tinkerer in Stafford Station. You want to come along? Staying here might be dangerous—Alek's not likely to get any more forgiving now that he has actual political power," said Klein.

"Oh, I'm not really worried about Alek. I don't think he wants to piss the people in charge of my show off by doing anything to me. They say I'm making loads of money for the Corporation from it, so protecting me is a top priority!"

"Good to see we've got our priorities straight," grumbled Guzman.

"If that's the kind of treatment I get from supporting you guys, I'm not doing jack for you!" whined Hyams as he walked out.

"Great job, Guzman. You cost us our last political supporter," Klein growled.

Guzman shrugged. "If you really want to go be a clodhopper, can I go with you? I got a feeling that Alek's not forgetting the fact that I was your campaign manager. I'll probably be safer there than I'd be staying here."

"Sure. But don't be surprised if you have to listen to a lot of those lectures you hate so much about the 'Sinful Earth'. Think you can take that?" said Klein.

"Can't be any worse than campaigning!" Guzman laughed.

But as they left the office to see if their two-faced Local bartender would sell them a few beers, they were stopped by a messenger from the Site 89 com office. He pulled up to them breathlessly and gasped, "Boots and saddles, both of you. Grab your weapons and tactical gear and head for the launch site pronto. You're both needed off-planet and it's not a request. Lift in three hours – you've just got time if you hurry!"

Klein and Guzman spun on their heels and ran to get their arms. They knew a military order when they heard it. "Beer will have to wait!" Guzman panted. "Farming, too!" muttered Klein.

5

Images flitted across Klein's mind in that strange half-sleep of an iced space traveler. He had a hazy memory of being herded into a shuttle and meeting a "Sergeant Bradford," a man that the soldiers called "Brad" behind his back. He had a loud, abrasive voice and a no-nonsense attitude, but seemed to be an honest, straightforward man, which was more than he could say for many of the people of Domremy. A vague recollection of Bradford's last words to him – "You've been through this part before, this is the easy part" – flitted through his mind as he tried to recall the events of his life on Domremy prior to being recalled into space for this mission. He remembered relinquishing his M221 sniper rifle at the orders of a Marine on board the shuttle, and the sense of insecurity that gnawed at his subconscious as the gun that had served him so well disappeared into a gray plastic bin. The anxiety of being unarmed was so strong that it only vanished once the massive amount of icing drugs he had been given prior to space travel started to take effect.

Through most of the shuttle's flight, Klein's sleep was a thoughtless void, a state of unconsciousness so deep that both dreams and nightmares were denied him. Occasionally images would form—an odd insect-like creature carrying him off in his arms, victory over a Russian man in a small town's election, a series of strange, inhuman women with shifting faces and names he couldn't remember. Occasionally memories began to slowly congeal and names returned to the images: *Locals* to the bizarre insects, *Entara* to the alien woman who appeared most frequently. But just as a sense of time and place began to reassemble, Klein would hear a soft hissing noise coming from one of the pipes attached to his suit and another dose of the chemicals entering his lungs, returning his mind to the unconscious abyss and ripping his recollections away from him again.

The effects of the icing drugs finally began to fade away, and sensation and memory began to return to Klein. He was vaguely aware of the tingling in his shoulders and sleepily dismissed the feeling, but when it crept across his chest and down onto his belly, heading south, his eyes sprang open and he leaped from his bunk yelling, "Shit!" He brushed the alarm stinger off his body.

With a loud metallic *click*, the door to Klein's room swung open. His vision was still a bit blurry, but he could still identify the man standing in doorway as Sergeant Bradford. "Up and at 'em, Klein! You and the other apes on this shuttle got a meetin' with Major Chaudhury, so get your ass into the meeting room for the briefing!"

Klein saw several other residents of the Domremy penal colony moving down the hallway in varying states of awareness. There weren't many -- Klein thought he glimpsed eleven, maybe twelve at most – and he couldn't recognize most of them. He heard a loud shout of "Como estas, amigo!" from in front of him, and saw Guzman high-fiving a man unfamiliar to him. A Marine was motioning the men to enter the open doorway to a small room. Klein moved with the group of somnambulant bodies into the doorway, his mind still dull from the effects of the icing.

The room was very bare, with unadorned grey walls that made it look like some sort of storage compartment and cheap metal folding chairs and a wall-mounted computer that had hastily been put in. Guzman, who was sitting next to a guy Klein recognized as a fellow Mankiller named Rodriguez, waved from his bench. Rodriguez nodded at him and was about to speak when a Marine officer came into their compartment. He was typically no-nonsense. "I am Major Chaudhury and you can all consider yourselves auxiliary conscripts in the Marine Force until you are discharged. You will obey my orders and those of any other Marine officer or be flushed out the hatch immediately, understood?" The mankillers and convicts silently nodded.

Chaudhury produced a stylus from his pocket and tapped the monitor. A multi-dimensional map of a space station appeared. "You have been activated to help deal with a situation that has developed at Transfer Clavius, the next station on the way to Dahlgren. All that you need to know is that a transport infested with Spondean parasites docked there several days ago, and by the time they were detected it was too late. Fortunately, the crew were able to seal and quarantine the station before they were overcome. Two ships had already departed before the danger was recognized. Their personnel were also overcome and the ships have been neutralized by military action." So dozens and perhaps even hundreds of humans had already been snuffed so that the parasites could not spread farther. SOP.

Chaudhury continued, "When we reach Transfer Clavius, my men will take care of the parasites. Your job, similar to what you do on Domremy, is to deal with the infested. Let's not call them survivors, because they won't be, for long."

"*Mierda*," blurted Rodriguez. "You're going to ice us and thaw us out just in time to spare you the trouble of killing our own kind."

Chaudhury glared at Rodriguez as he said, "You and the others would not have been selected for this mission had you not already demonstrated an aptitude for violence. Though not all of you were designated mankillers on Domremy, every single one of you has some prior history of aggression that marks you as having the *potential* to kill your fellow man. Don't insinuate that you are somehow 'above' the tasks you have been commissioned to do, or I *will* have you jettisoned. Understood?"

Rodriguez had a disgusted look on his face, but offered no retort to Chaudhury. He nodded silently in response.

"Excellent. I trust there are no more objections." Chaudhury continued. "We will soon be docking not with a transport, but an attack vessel." Klein had spotted the set of rings around the hull of the ship they were approaching against the black backdrop of space in the viewer screen. "This means we will be travelling in live mode at many times the speed you have experienced before. So you will not be iced, but juiced." A murmur ran around the gaggle of convicts. It made sense. Icing takes a couple of days to process completely and a couple of days to come down. These boys needed to jump out of their ship combat ready. Spondean parasites were supposed to give no more than forty seconds reaction time at close quarters, and a space station is very close quarters. It was not combat that was bothering the men, but the idea of juicing. They all knew that, unlike icing, juicing had a 10-15% failure rate. Major Chaudhury scanned them over one last time. "Any questions?"

"Do we get breakfast?" Rodriguez snarled. They felt a bump through their shuttle bulkheads.

"Sorry. Disembark now. Processing will begin as soon as you are boarded on the *Kearsarge*. That is all."

There was little to remember of juicing but more bits of weird dreams and sensations. Not painful, but strangely incongruous. The juice wore off as they were slowing for landing at the station. The mankillers were issued some combat fatigues, but they waited weaponless as they heard portals opening for the Marines to rush onto the station decks and vaporize the parasites off the necks of their human hosts. The "survivors" would be left to stumble around almost brainless until the mankillers were summoned. This kind of thing happened any time humans had to be neutralized. Rumor had it that the military was working on robots who might be able to do the job, but so far programmers had been reluctant to go so far as to enable AI entities for homicide. Who knew if it could be effectively controlled? Convicts with commuted murder sentences, like Klein, were a cheaper and more reliable alternative.

Finally the "Go" signal flashed in the compartment and as the mankillers were rushed out the hatch onto the station, they were given a handgun and a belt of full magazines. Klein, like the others, was a bit shocked at first. They were old percussive pistols, Taurus 9mm. Most folks had not handled anything like that for a long time, but they were more convenient for up-close execution than M221s that had an effetive range of nearly 2 miles. Again, it made sense, in a company-military kind of way. Before being sent up to Domremy, Klein had shot detectives with a weapon not too dissimilar. He held it up and showed the others, in case they hadn't. Switch to single shot and cock back the action. With a finger on the other hand, he pointed to the spot next to the ear where the round should go. They moved out and quickly started putting down the zombie-like inhabitants of the station, changing magazines as they ran along.

Even without the parasites attached to their necks, the "survivors" were instantly distinguishable from healthy humans. They always had a glassy look to their eyes, staring straight ahead with no expression. The hands of the survivors had a tremor to them, and there was a twitchiness to their mouths, as if the dim remnants of their minds were still trying to recall how to form words. Killing them was easy as long as Klein could convince himself that they had completely lost their humanity, but he had his doubts. One of the ones Klein slew was an old man with a long white beard and thick glasses over his eyes. There was an almost professorial pompousness to this once-human, its mouth constantly opening and closing as if trying to recall some lecture, its shaking hands still outstretched like it wanted to make some grand gesture. Out of a mix of pity for the man he used to be and morbid curiosity as to the exact nature of the "survivors," Klein let the once-human thing linger too long, staring a few seconds at the creature as it shambled towards him. A loud bark of "Shoot it now!" in Bradford's brusque voice came out of his com, and Klein fired his Taurus at the creature's head. The bullet passed directly between its eyes, ripping through whatever remained of the thing's cerebral lobes, and the "survivor" expired within a fraction of a second. Klein felt a twinge of remorse looking down at the disheveled heap in front of him, wondering how much memory the creature had retained of the man he had once been before he had blown its brains out.

When Klein found himself at the end of a long corridor with no other targets to shoot and a Marine guard facing him who was shaking his head, he thought he was done and prepared to hand over the pistol. Sergeant Bradford shouted into Klein's com, "Not yet. Go over to sector 6, deck B. Your friend Rodriguez needs some help, it seems." Klein assumed Rodriguez had just run out of ammo and ran to his location to give him an assist. He found Rodriguez hunched over next to a closed bulkhead, with the bodies of several survivors splayed around him. Klein noticed that they looked like members of an extended family: he noticed a woman in late middle age, a young man who looked about nineteen, and an old man, all dead from massive head and chest wounds.

"What's wrong, amigo?"

Rodriguez faced Klein with a sick look. "Niños. Todos ellos son niños."

As desensitized to killing as his time on Domremy had made Klein, the thought of killing a child filled even him with revulsion. Latins always had trouble with the young ones, and Klein wondered how much Rodriguez had suffered back on-planet if he ever sighted on a kid in the clutches of a Local.

"Està bien. Espera aqui." He opened the bulkhead and stepped into the compartment to take care of it himself. He choked down his disgust as he looked into the compartment and saw the children inside. Though the parasites that once sat on their necks had been carefully removed by the Marines, they still had the blissful look of angels that roused a sense of sin out of the dark recesses of Klein's atheistic conscience. Only one thing to do: pick the prettiest little blonde girl and start with her. Shut off the old mind and think only of the individual little blonde hairs where you are aiming.

Suddenly, Klein heard a pained yell from behind him! As he turned, he heard the sound of a nine-mil barking out. He saw a small child dead on the floor and Rodriguez frozen, with an anguished look of shock on his face. There were bite marks on Rodriguez's leg, indicating the survivor had attacked him and drew blood before he had killed it. Klein had been told that the survivors were dangerous and possibly infectious even after the parasites had been removed, but was startled that they retained some alien instinct to actively attack the uninfected. With grim resolve, he realized what he had to do to the other children.

His fingers clenched up and he felt a surge of vomit coming, when all at once a soft hand touched his shoulder and a voice said, "Stand down, Mankiller. This is something I know how to do better."

He turned around to see a woman with light brown hair in a medical uniform. "I've seen you before, haven't I?"

"Yes. At Tau Ceti station on your way out."

"Helga Pedersen."

"Yes. I was the nurse who prepped you for your second icing. I'm glad you remembered. You may not want to remember this, so you'd better leave."

He turned and had almost stepped out of the compartment when he turned to watch her. She had cuddled the little blonde girl in her lap and was stroking her hair, singing a nursery rhyme in Danish while an assistant behind her readied a syringe. Helga's gentle coaxing had lessened the girl survivor's aggression, somehow recalling a dimming memory of when she was a beloved child. The shaking in the girl's hands stopped, and her mouth closed and relaxed. Helga kissed the girl on the forehead when she injected her.

Rodriguez had been sitting in a detention room and dreading his debriefing for about an hour. He knew that Chaudhury would not take it lightly if he ever found out that the child had bitten him and drawn blood.

Chaudhury had it in for him ever since he had interrupted him during the briefing and if he found out that Rodriguez was potentially contaminated, his chances of returning to Domremy alive were slim indeed. The fear of death burning inside his mind, he turned to the religion the *Disidentes* on Domremy had taught him. He pulled a chalk stick and a small piece of paper out of his pocket, hastily drew a circle with a cross inside it on the paper, and started praying

Padre nuestro, que estas en el cielo...

Sergeant Bradford swung open the door to the detention room. "What is the meaning of this?" he roared at Rodriguez. "You were given a very specific objective to complete, and you completely FUBAR'd it! Klein had to clean up the mess your sorry ass left behind! Tell me, you incompetent piece of shit. What do you have to say for yourself?"

"Can't do this anymore!" Rodriguez yelled. "Killing all those people, then the niños…it's killing my soul! I can't sleep or think without their faces in front of me anymore! I can't be a mankiller no more, I want out!"

"You're not a good soldier," sneered Bradford. "You're not even a good mankiller anymore. I should have you thrown out the airlock now, before Chaudhury gets around to doing it. Instead I'm gonna give you a chance to prove you aren't the worthless, cowardly puke you've been on this assignment. Take a swing at me, I dare you."

Rodriguez wavered. *Is he trying to trick me into getting court martialed?* He thought to himself. Hesitantly, he raised his fists to defend himself.

"You heard me, you pussy! *You* throw the first punch! Don't do it and I'll drag you off this goddamn ship myself!"

"Maldito hijo de puta!" Rodriguez yelled, putting all his rage and force into a haymaker aimed at Bradford's head. Bradford quickly brought his left arm up to block the punch and countered with a strike to Rodriguez's nose. Bradford watched as Rodriguez winced in pain as blood trickled from his nose.

"Looks like an ugly nosebleed you got there," Bradford said. "Not as nasty as that bite the survivor gave you, of course. First 48 hours after contact, we have about 85 percent chance of clearing the infection, but it starts to plummet after that—that's what Helga says anyway. Lucky for you I found out before Chaudhury, he'd have had you liquidated immediately if he discovered it. You'd best get to sick bay and ask for her ASAP."

Rodriguez nodded, his bloodied face smiling for once. He quickly left the detention room and hurried in the direction of the sick bay. *A good sergeant always fights for his men*, Bradford thought. *Even if he has to hurt them do it.* He pulled a cigarette lighter out of his pocket and used it to burn the paper with the chalk circle that Rodriguez had carelessly left on the floor. When dealing with God, don't ask, don't tell.

Klein was disarmed, sitting idly on a chair in the canteen of the *Kearsarge*, when Helga Pedersen came through the door, looking sad and exhausted. She sat down across from him. "They have to wait a few hours before decontamination clears the ships for departure. I'll be returning to Tau Ceti, of course."

"Is Rodriguez doing any better?"

"Oh, his condition is improving quickly. He should be cleared for return to Domremy in about two weeks. He was very lucky to have Bradford find out about his exposure before Chaudhury did—I doubt Chaudhury would've given him the option to come to us. Rodriguez's body may be free of the Spondean parasites, but his mind—I think he'd been exposed to the psychological trauma of killing for far too long, and the experiences of this mission made him finally snap. He should never be a mankiller again."

"About Bradford discovering the wound before Chaudhury...you don't know anyone who might have clued him in on that, do you?" Klein asked.

Helga briefly smiled at him. "If I can save even one person from the parasites, I feel like my job is still meaningful. Sometimes I think the times I'm able to save lives are the only things keeping me sane. I've seen so much death here on this one station, I'm starting to feel like a mankiller myself."

"I'm glad you don't have to live at Site 89 like I did. So many of the colonists from the days when Cashman was still in charge there ended up dead."

"Who was Cashman?"

"Guy I used to know. Worst boss I ever had. I've been on Domremy so long that I can't remember the official business-speak for a firing...what is it that the HR people say?" he asked.

"I think the term they prefer is 'amicable severance' these days," she answered.

"Well, my severance from him definitely wasn't 'amicable' in the least!" Klein said with a chuckle.

Her hand made its way across the plastic table and took his. "Can you come and lie down with me for a while? I know it's officially forbidden for you, but I've arranged for no one to be looking and I suspect you have a nasty back injury from your recent engagement that needs my medical attention."

He looked her straight in the eye. "Are you sure you want this? You could get into a lot more trouble than it's probably worth."

"I know it sounds stupid," she answered. "But after saying goodbye to all those little souls, I can't help but think that some of them may still be around. Maybe looking for some place to live. I want to try to get pregnant again."

"You can probably find a man at Tau Ceti who can actually see you again afterwards, or at least send you a digital. I don't know if I can be any good for you. I've been iced twice, juiced once, and exposed to a Class 9 binary's radiation for years now. I'm probably shooting nothing but blanks."

"Other men were not there where we just were. I have a feeling about you. Let's try."

Try they did. On and off for quite a long time. Afterwards Klein felt exhausted but couldn't seem to fall asleep. He just lay back with Helga's head on his shoulder and his left hand cupped around her right breast. There are things I must remember about this, he told himself. Let's see, her hair is thinning, decidedly. She has a weak chin. The skin on her elbows is chafed and scaly. She could smell better. He wracked his brain trying to fill it with negative things so that he would not be haunted too much by memories of his first sex with a human female in over half a decade and – who knows? – maybe his last? He even felt guilty, despite himself, because there were moments during their coupling when he had lost focus on Helga and thought about Entara instead. Certainly Helga might not be happy if she knew that during their passionate embraces he had imagined himself in the limbs of an alien prostitute. This was not working out.

"You must really like breasts," her heard Helga whisper.

"Sorry, I thought you were asleep."

"I can't seem to open my eyes. You really hit the spot, and I have to tell you, that doesn't always happen with me, so you can write it down in your little book if you have one. You're as good as the very best boys back home."

"Where's home?" he asked, to make polite pillow talk.

"Right now, under water somewhere. I came from one of the last of the polderized Frisian islands. My family raised pigs and had an orchard – luxury foods now. Finally the cost of keeping the sea out was just too much and the government closed us down and moved us to Jutland, where I studied medicine."

"I'm from Bremen. Once my dad took me on a boat ride to see Old Bremen. After the sub was down a couple of meters, you could see the plan of the streets, and further down, you could still read the signs on some of the shops. Except the only customers were eels and plaice. To see the cathedral down there was really something. Made me think of that music by Debussy."

"There's probably a mussel ranch on top of the fields were I used to play."

"What the hell did you do to get up here?"

"Didn't you realize?" she laughed. "I'm in the same line of work as you really. I killed a man. I could have taken my degree and moved to Greenland and become rich. Instead I broke the law and was commuted to Tau Ceti."

"You're just full of surprises. Sorry, Helga, but you don't seem like much of a gunman to me."

"That's not how. I killed a fellow with a fork lift."

"A fork lift? That's original!"

"Spur of the moment. The bastard had molested my niece. Actually, he had molested me, too, and lots of other girls in the neighborhood, over the years. I got over it pretty soon, but my niece and sister were absolutely overwhelmed, so I took it on myself to do something. I knew complaints were no good, since there had already been plenty and nothing meaningful had happened. So I went to the plant where I knew he worked, full of rage and without any organized plan. When I saw him next to a big wall of crates laughing with some other workers, I couldn't help think he had just told them about screwing me and my niece. There was a fork lift right next to me and any girl brought up on a pig farm knows how to use one, so I climbed on and accelerated right at him. He turned around when he heard the noise and just stared at me like a dolt for a few seconds. At the last minute he tried to leap away, but I followed him and skewered him right through the guts with one of the blades of the lift. I felt very proud of myself. "

"You actually killed somebody for justice. I just sort of fell into it without thinking," Klein said, wary of telling her about Kinderaugen and Dorfman. "I've had so many enemies over the years I have trouble remembering them all—except Cashman. The time I was on Earth on the run from the cops seems so alien to me now, like fragments of another man's life. Domremy does that to you."

"Nice talk. Let's get back to something else. Tell me how nice my breasts are."

"That's easy, because they're round and delicious."

"You lie. They're starting to get droopy. You know, I already have two teenage sons down on Tau Ceti. How old do you think I am?"

"I couldn't possibly say. You know, I'm not used to having partners with breasts."

"Of course, there aren't many women on Domremy. You must sleep with aliens! Which ones?"

"Only Forlani, and not many of them."

"I thought they had breasts. Several in fact."

"Only when they've had children. Before that, it's just a row of little nubs in the brown hair."

"How erotic." She sat up straight. "That's probably why you tolerated the fact that I hadn't shaved. I hear pubic hair is very out of fashion again back home."

"Forlani have all kinds of hair in places we don't," he chuckled, stroking her head, "And no hair in places where we usually do."

Helga became quiet and hugged him a little closer. Klein hoped she wouldn't get too sentimental. Mankillers were not allowed to receive calls from off-world, and he didn't want to think of her being unhappy because she couldn't speak with him again. He realized that he couldn't really forget either. It was true that a couple of hours of Helga was not much compared to the bond he had forged with his courtesan Entara, regardless of the futility of a human coupling with a Forlani, from the point of view of procreation. Yet he couldn't help admiring this woman's innate kindness, her instinctive gentleness, and – he had to admit – her shear bravery for thinking of having a child with a convict like him in the confines of penal servitude. No matter how her chin receded or how many scaly spots she had on her skin, he knew she was going to stay with him for more than a little while. It was not impossible that the next time he cuddled up to his newest Forlani girlfriend, he might think of Helga at some point. Life is such sweet shit, he thought. It's a good thing we have somebody to order us around most days.

"What time is it?" Helga finally asked.

"Soon six bells ship time."

"Damn. My ship has to leave soon. And I still have to pack up some of the medical supplies. I'd better get moving. You'd better leave while I'm in the shower."

That sometimes scaly, sometimes heavenly smooth epidermis was moving away from him for good. Yes, it was better if he got dressed and went to have a long drink or two before they started to think of juicing him for the ride back to Domremy.

Just as she was stepping into the shower she turned and faced him. "I have to ask before you go. Do you want to know? I would feel better if you did. I don't exactly know why. I promise not to bother you, whatever happens, but it would feel better if you knew."

"Well," Klein drawled, staring at the deck, "There may be a way. I have friends in a special group and they have their own way of communicating without using digital. Could you write me a letter?"

"That's really retro," she chortled. "Would you like a clay tablet or would pen and ink do, if I can find them?"

"They would do fine. Send it inside a parcel of some kind of agricultural stuff, well wrapped. Here's the address." He grabbed her phone and tapped in the delivery coordinates for his old landlord Peebo, who would give an extra degree of secrecy from the prying eyes of the authorities.

"That should work, Klein. Please don't get in trouble by sending me anything, understand?"

She suddenly trotted over and kissed him on the lips, quickly, before turning and saying, "Please get on your way, now."

Ayan'we's discovery of the "FastTrack" program her father was involved in had frustrated her natural sense of curiosity. She knew that Tays'she was involved in *something* he would never disclose willingly, but she didn't have a sense of what it was. Did it have something to with gambling debts he had racked up on a brief but eventful trip to the Laguna Casino three years ago? Could it be grade inflation in certain Academy courses to graduate more Forlani candidates for interstellar travel before they were truly ready? Ayan'we remembered how her father had reacted to a description of a young Forlani woman who was so desperate to get an off-world passport that she had become mentally unstable. Tays'she had casually dismissed the poor woman's suffering with a flippant

"She should have tried harder," showing no more compassion or empathy than one would show for a crushed insect. It was Tays'she's un-empathetic, dismissive attitude towards everyone but his new First Wife Ha'maya that had caused resentment to fester into hatred in Ayan'we's mind. Her mother had been treated with injustice, and she wanted to see just how low her father could sink! She pulled out her tablet computer and began to hack into Tays'she's files and secure data – he wouldn't allow anyone else to use his laptop, but she had become an advanced enough hacker from her time in the Echidna's Children group to learn how to remotely activate his computer and access his files. It was extremely common among the Forlani, who often traveled to far-flung places in their lives and careers, to utilize a code that would allow them to activate their home computers regardless of location and to access local files.

With the help of some code breaking software she had acquired courtesy of her past hacking career, Ayan'we began to bore through Tays'she's computer security. The remote activation code was relatively easy; her software managed to crack it in 10 minutes. The true challenge was trying to navigate the sprawling mountains of data in Tays'she's computer to find what she wanted. There were seemingly endless photo files of the dullest vacations, leftover essays and diagrams from Tays'she's career as an artist, copies of letters Tays'she had written in response to ezine articles, and much more. Making her search even more bewildering was Tays'she's incredibly lazy system of organizing his computer's data; many of his folders were organized by date, rather than by content, forcing her to search through dozens of folders with bland names like "Projects December" and "Letters Fall." Finally, in a folder unassumingly titled "Tax Calculations May," Ayan'we found the main file labeled *FastTrack*.

Ayan'we was not surprised that her father had encrypted the FastTrack info; the information on the file was obviously something he wanted to conceal at all costs, and that only served to spur her curiosity. However, she was shocked by the nature of the encryption – instead of a simple alphanumeric password that could be cracked by automated software, the input screen mandated that she trace the answer on the computer screen in the glyph script of Ancient Forlan. She gave a hiss of displeasure at her realization that she would have to use knowledge from her absolute least favorite class at the Academy to crack the code. Ayan'we began to doubt whether Tays'she was as careless and airheaded as he had seemed to her for so long.

The first puzzle was relatively simple, the clue being "The First Council." Most graduates of the Academy – at least those who kept their Ancient History classes fresh in their minds – remembered the date of the First Matriarch Council, when the matrilines were originally established and Forlani culture truly began. Ayan'we's progress was hindered only by her difficulty at forming the number glyphs. The intricate flowing script confounding her hands after a lifetime of simple typing and touch gestures. Once she finished the first puzzle, she anxiously waited for the screen to display the next puzzle as a green disc spun to indicate the encryption program was still running. The second clue was the phrase "Walk the Path," which was far less specific than the clue to the first password. There were many descriptions of "paths" and "roads" in the religious and philosophical literature of Ancient Forlan that Ayan'we had muddled her way through in writing papers and reports for her class. *Just what path was Tays'she thinking about,* Ayan'we wondered.

Ayan'we took a guess based on Tays'she's penchant for narcissism and self-interest. *The Value of the Men of Forlan*, a philosophical book written by the philosopher Tash'An to proclaim the glories of Self, seemed like the "path" that Tays'she would be most interested in. She entered the opening passage from the book, "As I sat under the tree in the falling rain, I realized my greatness," and breathed a sigh of relief as the green disc spun again and the encryption program generated the final puzzle. When the hint to the final puzzle was displayed onscreen, her relief quickly turned to dread; the hint was "Beyond the horizon of tomorrow," a phrase that sounded *nothing* like what either her instructors or the philosophy books she had read for her courses had described. *Meh'tra! How can I possibly solve this*, she thought as she frantically attempted to recall any references to "horizons" in the Academy courses she had completed. She heard a loud knock on the door as she tried to stifle her frustration with the unsolvable puzzle. She shoved her computer into a drawer in her desk as she saw her mother enter through the doorway.

"Ayan'we, what have you been doing alone in here? You said you finished your work for the Academy an hour ago!" Entara exclaimed.

"I did. Mom, I know this is going to sound dangerous to you, but…"

"*What* have you done, Ayan'we? Did you do something that could get you thrown out of the Academy again?"

"No, Mother, not this time. I did nothing…but I think Tays'she did. Remember when I told you that Tays'she was involved in something called 'FastTrack'?"

Entara nodded. There was a look of anxiety and dread on her face. Her irritation with Ayan'we had been quickly silenced, replaced by fear of her daughter's coming announcement.

"Well, I think I found out exactly what 'FastTrack' is. I hacked into his computer remotely, but I can't get through the security program without your help. The last question is something I never went over in my classes. I need your help solving it."

Entara felt a sense of relief at her daughter's confession, although she didn't show it on her face.

"Yes, I will help you. A few days ago, I saw security police outside our house. I think they were looking for info on whatever Tays'she is involved in through this 'FastTrack.' It may be so severe that it could affect our matriline if they find out. Show me what this security program is, and I'll try to solve the puzzle."

Ayan'we gave a brief, nervous smile as she reached into the drawer and pulled out her tablet. Entara glanced at the hint onscreen and began slowly tracing an intricate pattern with her left hand. After finishing the pattern, she put the tablet back down on the desk. Ayan'we could see the familiar spinning green disc again, indicating that Entara had entered the correct response. Her mother had ensured they would finally understand what FastTrack was!

"I can see why you couldn't solve the final puzzle," Entara explained. "The hint about 'the horizon of tomorrow' was a reference to a book called *Beyond the Great Spiral*, a philosophical text which was judged heretical by the Culture Ministers long ago. In the time when my generation was going through the Academy, it was possible to take elective courses which included a few brief fragments of the book. By the time your generation went through the Academy, the Culture Ministry had changed the curriculum and eliminated all references to *Beyond the Great Spiral*."

"Dad chose a password that I couldn't solve!" said Ayan'we.

"Yes, I think that was his intention," said Entara. "He always knew you were rebellious and strong-willed, even before you found out that FastTrack existed. I think he had always tailored his passwords for protection against you, rather than me. He doesn't consider me a threat to his plans—or at least he won't until he realizes that it was me who cracked the code."

"I have a spoofing program installed," Ayan'we said. "It creates a false IP address for my device, so he won't be able to trace the hack back to this machine..."

"Even if he doesn't know the exact address, he'll be suspicious. If he's as clever as the strategy of devising a password system that you couldn't solve indicates, I doubt he'll make the same mistake twice. We'll have to be very careful."

The tablet gave a high-pitched beeping noise to indicate all the security had been successfully passed. Entara picked up the tablet and began reading about the FastTrack program that Tays'she had tried to conceal.

As she read over the details of the mysterious FastTrack, Entara realized what it was, and why Tays'she had tried to keep it secret—it was a program to export young Forlani women, most of whom would have failed the Psychological Stability tests the Passport Office gave, out into the human colonies without official passports. Any Forlani who left the planet without an official passport could never return to Forlan, and would have to live forever on another world making a living any way they could—or as a slave to humans and other races that dominated the other worlds. To be in a family that invests in the *slave trade* was a crime so grave that the family's matriline could be utterly destroyed. Her line sisters might be disenfranchised, impoverished, and dispersed into menial roles. Entara's disgust that her husband was so morally weak that he would invest in slavery mixed with her fear of her own daughters being forced to beg in the crowded city, with no mahäme, no matriline, and no future.

"Ayan'we, about delivering that message to Klein through your contacts at the Academy. I'm going to finish that message tonight, and I need you to deliver it as soon as possible. It may be the only way to save this family from what Tays'she has done."

"Mom, what's FastTrack about? What exactly is it that Tays'she did that's so dangerous to us?"

Entara sat down next to her daughter and took a deep breath, preparing to explain to her daughter the horrors of FastTrack that she had just discovered.

The next icing did nothing at all to clear Klein's mind from the dizzying experience of the massacre at Clavius and the subsequent tryst with Helga. In his jumbled dreams during the return trip, he could barely tell if he was making love to a human or an alien or to both at once. The visions were incredibly exciting and at the same time strangely humbling, as though his own body was just part of some higher process he could never manage to grasp.

After the descent to Domremy's surface in the shuttle, the group of homicidal deputies broke up within a few minutes, each heading off in a different direction, though Klein wished he could have spoken longer to Guzman and Rodriguez, perhaps to share something of his perplexity or at worst to have a friendly beer. Yet he was in no hurry to return to Site 89, feeling in his gut that Alexandrov could not possibly have made the place any better in his absence. He decided to try to call on Peebo and found him at his farm outside Stafford Station in the midst of a rapidly growing family of Dissenters. When they all lined up to welcome him into the house, he could not help thinking they looked like the family of Charlie Chan in the old 20th century classic movies. A new wife (or perhaps not really so new, judging from the group of children that swarmed around her) shuttled back and forth from the kitchen to the living room. Klein couldn't remember her name as Peebo reeled off all the new relatives, so he just called her "Ma'am." Apparently Peebo's brood had just reassembled after stays in several different Forlani facilities between Earth and Domremy. The Forlani had given them passes as cleaning contractors to disguise the move from Hyperion's intelligence agents. *Just like Hyperion to ignore child labor laws while trying to break up Dissenter families. The Forlani, treated like chattel themselves, must have gotten a kick out of using Hyperion's own greed against them,* Klein mused. Peebo was very concerned that Klein might be suffering from some kind of PTSD after the massacre and insisted on hearing the gory details, although Klein knew how distressing all this bloodshed must be for a devout Dissenter. His old landlord dealt with it pretty well, but seemed much more interested when, in private, Klein related to him the encounter with Helga. Peebo made him repeat a lot of details about the medic and Klein had the impression that the farmer intended to check into her through the uncanny network of Dissenter intelligence.

As the conversation appeared to be trailing off, Peebo's face took on un uncharacteristic scowl as he announced, "A letter came for you. I didn't know if I should tell you now. You might not like the contents. Sorry I had to poke into it, but it came in Croptalk and encrypted to boot, so I couldn't avoid finding out. "

"What kind of letter?" Klein exclaimed. It was much too early to be news from Helga, unless she had had some kind of tragedy.

"It's from Forlan. From Entara. I'll at least let you read it by yourself."

When Peebo had stalked out of the guest bedroom, Klein unfolded the letter, written on scrap paper so that it could be easily burned up in Dissenter fashion. Entara's original must have had to be destroyed along the way as a precaution against discovery by the Corporation. His brows furrowed deeper and deeper as he read of the threat to Entara and her family. She had done a good job of communicating the severity of the situation without disclosing details of FastTrack, which she simply called, "the plot." It didn't take much for the wild visions of his icing dreams to return to his head, nor did it take long for him to resolve that he had to find a way to get to Forlan immediately to help her.

"Peebo, I've got to get off planet again."

"A big difference between leaving the barn with the farmer's herd and sneaking out on your own."

"You must have contacts with Forlan just to get this letter. Isn't there a way?"

"A way for revenge? You know that's not our creed. Blood for blood is not within the Circle. And now I've got the family to think about. I know you mean to do well in your own way, but do you even trust yourself to do well? It's not really your row to hoe."

"Just transport, friend, that's all I ask."

"You won't have a weapon. Security in Forlan customs is airtight. Plus, Forlani males can be tougher to overcome than you think."

"I'll use my bare hands if I have to."

Peebo mused a minute before responding. "Well, maybe if you can control yourself and promise not to kill, I may be able to help, but it won't be easy. The transit I can probably arrange on my own, but for other things we need a little help. I'll send for the vet and he'll be here tomorrow evening. Until then, think over if you really feel you need to risk this. I'm going to see the missus."

Klein had already been back at Site 89 for several weeks, chaffing at his daily patrols as his mind turned constantly to Entara. He was upset by a weird mixture of arousal, fear, anxiety, and curiosity. He could kick himself for the way flashbacks to past love-making with her popped back into his head, despite his efforts to control them. Ever since his childhood, since the time the family broke up, he had prided himself on his ability to focus and control, to worship at the idol of progress, no matter how tarnished it might be. Now he was victim to floods of what could only be rank sentimentality – and what was worse, he liked it. To be honest, he cherished it. It was way beyond ordinary Schadenfreude and seemed to be becoming an obsession. Moreover, it distracted him from the rotten feeling that he was becoming an unwilling accomplice in Alek's scheming management of Site 89. His emotions were in turmoil. He longed for the ability to move, to act, maybe to kill, if that would restore what passed for sanity in his psyche.

Finally he got a Crop Talk sign from Peebo that he was to meet in the Circle. Luckily, a train was just due to leave. He shoved his thallop into the barn for someone else to take care of, snapped his M221 into its clips on the wall of the arms room, and sprinted to the station, actually leaping from the platform onto the end of the train as it pulled out, and forced his way into the door at the tail end. The company men in the car snickered and made quiet remarks about how anxious he must be to get to the Forlani house at the end of the line, but the handful of Dissenters in the car merely looked up for a second, nodded his way, and went back to staring out the windows or reading their seed catalogs.

The sun was moving low towards the horizon when he reached Peebo's farm and his host hurried him along to the building where he had met with the Dissenters before. This time there was a bigger delegation, perhaps a dozen, including a man Peebo called Cousin Al, who had been on the train from Site 89, somewhere up ahead of Klein. Peebo and Klein stood at the foot of the cross. The others formed a crescent at the other end. Klein recognized Trevor in the center, with a bronze-colored fellow on his right and – to his surprise – Peebo's wife on the left!

"Greetings once again friend. The sun goes down as we speak. We understand you wish to leave?"

Klein tried to be as succinct and unemotional as he could in describing his desire to help Entara. He closed his speech by requesting, "I don't want to dig to the center of the Earth. If you put me in a wagon, I don't seek to hold the reins. But if you can meet the tailed ones at the fair, I would be your hand forever to be able to be among them." In Crop Talk, this meant Klein was not asking to be let in on any Dissenter secrets, that he was content to know as little as necessary in order to obtain what he desired.

Trevor looked around his group in the crescent and each nodded approval. "It's true we have an understanding with the purple critters. We play the fiddle for them and they dance for us. They're fluffing up the pillow for you now. Truth is, they're mighty fond of fruit, as you know. So from time to time we send a consignment of seeds and saplings. Helps them set things straight up there. Now, you've been a kind of a hand to Peebo once in a while, so you'll get sick at work and help out here again for a few days. The doc here," he nodded to the bronzed gentleman, "will fix things up. Then it's Route 66 for you, pal."

"I'm so grateful, I…"

"Felicia will speak now."

Peebo's wife took a step forward. "Before you peel the turnip, there are a few things to say about the knife. You know our ways. We will not tolerate any wanton killing. That purple bull up there has never gored you, nor has he ever touched us, though we know full well he cannot abide staying in his pasture. So you'll handle him as we handle the livestock, with this."

She held up a kind of glove with a metal boss in the palm that held a small retractable spike. Klein had seen Dissenters on the farms use them to inject sheep, goats, and especially skittish thallops with serums and vitamins.

Felicia went on. "It holds five doses. Dr. Patak will supervise."

"Yes," said the bronze-skinned doc, in an accent that might have been Punjabi, "I know something of the Forlani body and you will have five doses, in case you may miss the right place with some. I say the dose must be administered to the neck to be effective, just here." He pointed to a point beside his Adam's apple. "However, there you will actually inject one and one only dose, for an effect that will last several days. You will see me tomorrow for further details."

Trevor looked around both sides of the circle and asked, "Is that the last tune?" When everyone nodded, he started to erase the ashen symbol at their feet.

The next morning, just as Klein, Cousin Al and Peebo finished scything a field of barley ("Course I got a harvester, but we need some exercise for Route 66"), Klein saw Dr. Patak sauntering up the road. The doc beckoned to Klein, who followed him into the equipment wing of Peebo's settlement.

"I have brought all the necessary equipment for you," Patak chirped as he spread out a variety of beakers and bottles and other items on the lab table. "Of course, Peebo will furnish all the ag equipment you need to take care of the saplings in the shipment. You will be caring for them, but they will also be caring for you, because, you see, saplings are too fragile to ice, and will require daily tending, so you won't be iced either, and will travel in relative comfort with only light daily work. Here is your injector. I have checked it and sterilized it, so it will work perfectly. Here are vials with five doses of toad toxin, carefully measured and prepared, that Peebo will place among apparently identical vials of plant vitamins until you reach the destination. If you wish to practice injecting, which I recommend, borrow one of Peebo's needles and try it out with vitamins on some sheep. This one must be used only on the Forlani target and then given back to Peebo for disposal. Perhaps, if all goes well, you may not have to use anything so… intrusive, after all," he added with a little sigh.

"And here," he went on, "Are your papers as a member of the Farm Union. Naturally, you cannot use your mankiller ID on Route 66, and in fact, you'd better leave it completely behind.   Now, Wilhelm Klein, hmmm. Since I am a native speaker of the king's English, and god save his majesty Henry X, no longer emperor of India, I will anglicize your first name to William, which I trust will cause no objection. Klein will become a middle initial K. I hate to lie and find that it is sometimes best to use a mother's birth name in the manner of our South American friends. What is it, please?"

"Himmelreich, with two m's, one l, and -eich at the end."

"So, congratulations, William K. Himmelreich, new member of the Farm Union, but I think I will distress this card a bit to make it seem less suspicious and more like something a field worker might carry." Patak hummed a little tune as he smeared what looked like a few grains of turmeric and graphite on the card before lamination, then dipped it with tongs into several successive solutions that darkened the covering and made little blisters in places.

"Wonderful, now it looks like you could have been hoeing beets for twenty years. Additionally, I have used my veterinary credentials, which on Domremy are as good as any MD's, to report you sick with a badly strained back and agonizing pain. By the time they call to get you back to work, you will be long gone. Cousin Al will report you were lost on a trip into the savanna to prospect for a new field site, and Site 89 will assume for the time being that you are Local bait. Arrivederci e buon viaggio!"

Two days later, the cargo transport for the *Kagahashi Maru* floated up from the surface of Domremy with nearly a hundred saplings that Peebo had assembled, along with several boxes of ag seed and fertilizers, as well as the servile William K. to tend the plants, since it was now Peebo who had developed terrible back pain that necessitated delegating everything to a helper. Peebo had accessed some reading material about Forlan to help Klein comprehend the nature of the consignment. Certainly, he knew already that Forlani consumed mainly fruit and certain types of insects, despite Entara's private cravings for toast and jam. What astonished him in his reading, however, was to learn that Forlan had undergone a planetary environmental disaster ages ago, during something called the Time of Cities, which had led to the ominously named Time of Famines. At the end of these crises began the Modern Era, featuring the reorganization of Forlani society into the female matrilines and the male Brotherhood. It was the matrilines which oversaw the environmental and agricultural restoration of the planet, under the direction of the Council of Nine and various sub-agencies. This agricultural consignment of theirs was destined for the Eyes of Alertness matriline, the one Entara belonged to. In return, Klein surmised that the matrilines must be doing something to help the Dissenters, and he suspected it had something to do with the unheralded appearance of wives and children on Domremy. People on Earth characterized the Dissenters as having all sorts of retrograde ideas on reproduction, since they had totally rejected the in vitro methods that had become so popular in upper levels of human society. "Only the poor procreate, and the rich only fornicate" was the watchword on the teleprograms. When he had been shipped to Domremy, only adult men like Peebo and Cousin Al could be found at the Dissenter settlements, so it followed that during the intervening years, they had discovered some way to eliminate the physiological dangers space travel posed to the reproductive system, particularly for ovulating females and young males. They could then complete the colonizing process.

With little to do each day but feed the plants and little to talk about with Peebo that couldn't be monitored, Klein used his old computer skills learned at the ministry to do some discreet digging. His big discovery was that, as he guessed, Dr. Patak was more than met the eye. He bore a striking resemblance to a Dr. Sharma who had won the Albertson Prize for physiology by discovering a way to restore breeding ability to cloned rhinoceri and mastodons. Sharma had been reported dead in a tragic decompression accident on the Europa shuttle, but Klein wondered if his bronzed ally had not already learned how to change identities as easily as he had with Klein. It still remained for him to figure out just how the Forlani were aiding the Dissenter exodus from Earth, but he made a mental note to try to learn what he could on Forlan.

Space travel without the suspension of icing could be a tedious affair, but at the end of three weeks, the *Kagahashi Maru* had finally completed its intermediate stops and was hot, curved, and normal for Forlan. One day, after watering and feeding the plants as his act demanded, Klein returned to their cabin to find Peebo lounging in his bunk with a wistful look.

"You know, pal, I never would have believed it after all those years of separation without losing control of my emotions, I find myself missing Felicia an awful lot after only a matter of weeks. I guess the experience of being reunited gave me expectations I was able to keep under control earlier. It just shows how perverse the human mind can be. Feelings always seem to trump reason."

"I know what you were doing all that time, but what was she doing?"

"I must have a bubble of water in my ear. Can you repeat that?" Peebo replied, rubbing his ear a bit. This meant Klein had forgotten that all conversations could be monitored, even on a third-rate transport like the *Kagahashi Maru*.

"Oh, I was talking about that big grey ewe back on the farm. Did they deliver her straight from Kasimba's (one code word for Earth) or did you get her from some farmer in between? "

"Well, for a long time, she had to stay in a pen next to Kasimba's banana grove (Central Africa). But when the time came, they sold her off to Aunty Fox (the Forlani!). For a couple of long summer days (years), she just mostly helped calm the other critters down and keep things orderly (worked as a servant of some kind). Lived in a nice purple barn (a Forlani house). They put their brand on her, you see (furnished her with a new identity). But I figured that was a waste of good mutton chops, so when I got a chance to see her at the livestock auction at Grover's Corner (the transshipment station on Premidathra), I moved her on into my herd."

So the Forlani were helping the Dissenters move their wives and children off Earth and through various points in the colonies by hiring them as servants for the girls' houses. Klein recalled that on trips to the Stafford Station house with Entara and Ragatti, he had usually seen some females of other races cooking, cleaning, or doing other domestic tasks so that the girls could always be ready for a paying client. He had never guessed they might be refugees being moved about by the Forlani. However, it made sense, because as he thought back on it, he had seldom seen the same servants twice. He supposed this was why the Dissenters felt such an obligation to help restore the Forlani home planet's ecology, and perhaps even why they had agreed to this hare-brained scheme of Klein's.

Having satisfied his curiosity by digging to the root of the mystery of the link between Dissenters and Forlani, he realized it was dangerous information and he had to cover it up. Having had a fairly high security clearance in his days back in the BNATOR forces, he tried to remember the anti-interrogation techniques a wise old Serbian had taught him. First he mentally designed all the facts into a geometric solid in his mind. He reviewed it many times until he was sure how he visualized it. Next, to lock it. He picked as his password the name of a neighbor's cat back in Düsseldorf. He reviewed everything again before applying the mental lock. Of course, this little trick would not stand up to drugs and specifically directed electro-biological probing. Nothing would. But the subject matter was so obscure that he doubted any Hyperion interrogator would be able to get on the right track and know the right questions to ask in order to get at the truth.

Days later, as everyone was beginning to stow and strap for unloading, one of the mature Forlani females on board as a passenger summoned them all to the view screen. "Come see this! Our own patrol ships have started to protect the space near Forlan." They squeezed closer to the screen and saw a squadron of odd vessels that looked something like snowflakes in old Bavaria, hexagonal shapes arcing across the outer reaches of the Forlan solar system. "Of course, the hex interceptors separate for military action. Built by the Song Pai, who have protected our system under contract and furnished these vessels to make up our own defense force."

"Yeah," said the marine officer, "The damned Song Pai kept Hyperion out of this system twice when the company tried to grab it with a mercenary flotilla. And there's the bad boy that did it, Carrier 16." He pointed to an area of space that seemed at first to be black emptiness but as they approached took on the shape of what looked like a huge ovoid sieve. "Each of those holes is a launch chamber and when the Song Pai activate, an attack fighter emerges from each of them. The entire crew takes part, except for a few caretakers on the main ship. No escape or rescue apparatus because they don't expect to come back. Minimal life support because they don't expect to need it. Medical equally unnecessary. Just like the kamikaze in the old video legends. Their ships are designed as suicide vehicles that can take out the maximal target payload. They never conserve anything, just one big gambit designed to decimate the enemy. Their oath is inviolable and they relish the thought of dying to liberate the young souls, as they say. I've always thanked my lucky stars that the company didn't succeed in sending *us* in there and had to settle for a Blackwater task force that got the crap kicked out of it before retreating. Lost a few old comrades among those dead mercs. And old Carrier 16, with a few dents and a full crew complement, no doubt, is still out there prowling for now."

Klein didn't realize that he would soon have his own personal reason for holding a grudge against the Song Pai.

Even though the temperature in the office was set to 73 degrees, the level that Hyperion Corporation had calculated would provide the most stimulation for its employees, Bill Hollingsworth could feel sweat rolling down his brow. His supervisor, Mr. Samuels, had called him into his office for a meeting. Mr. Samuels was not a man given to small talk, and when he called a meeting, something important was likely to happen as a result. Hollingsworth had felt increasingly nervous as the day dragged on, anxiety over the reason for Samuels' meeting creeping through his mind. He had spent the day looking over dozens of online articles with contradictory advice on negotiating with supervisors, and his day had been very unproductive as a result. But Hollingsworth was not worried about the minor details of a single wasted day; he had become preoccupied with the fear that his boss had prepared to "release" him, and prepared himself for a stressful interview where any misstep could potentially result in his firing. Survival took priority over the more mundane tasks of his job. Finally, the time of the appointment arrived; a few seconds before his digital watch indicated it was four in the afternoon, Hollingsworth was waiting at the door to Mr. Samuels' office. He walked up to the door and gave a single, soft tap on it to indicate his presence. "Come in please," a friendly voice beckoned.

Mr. Samuels was roughly the same age as Hollingsworth. He had a peaceful, inviting expression on his face as he beckoned Hollingsworth to sit down. Hollingsworth began to feel slightly more relaxed as he sat down in the large, comfortable chair Mr. Samuels kept for his guests. "There's something we need to talk about," Mr. Samuels said.

"Well, if there's something that's displeased you about my performance, I'll make sure to correct it," Hollingsworth said. "I know that *A Hero of Domremy* isn't getting the kind of ratings it used to, but I've some ideas to make it fresh again."

"About that," Mr. Samuels said. "*A Hero of Domremy* had about what, three good seasons before the ratings started dropping?"

"Four," Hollingsworth corrected him.

"Well, the ratings and revenue stream from *A Hero of Domremy* have plummeted in this latest season.

You know our policy when a program's rating starts dropping."

Hollingsworth did his best to hide how nervous he felt, but Mr. Samuels could still see the beginnings of a frown on the corners of his mouth. "Well, I'm sorry if the higher-ups have decided our show shouldn't continue, but I have some other ideas."

Mr. Samuels' voice dropped an almost imperceptible degree lower and softer. "That's a part of what I'd like to discuss about your performance over the past few years, Bill. We've noticed you haven't had much in terms of ideas for monetizing the enterprise over the past few years. Other than *A Hero of Domremy*, most of the productive ideas for the colony have come from Erica, not you. We think that you may not be the best fit for your position in our company anymore."

The words Hollingsworth had been dreading came at the end of the sentence, although he had anticipated them since Mr. Samuels had referred to him by the informal *Bill* rather than the more formal *Mr. Hollingsworth*. Hyperion Human Resources had determined that using informal names put employees at ease and made it easier to "negotiate" with them in difficult situations. *By negotiate, they invariably mean getting their way with only the most puny of consolations to their employees,* Hollingsworth thought.

It took all of his emotional composure not to raise his voice at Mr. Samuels. "Is this about the fact I'm getting on in years? Because if it is, you'll be getting a call from my lawyer for age discrimination."

Mr. Samuels gave an irritated cough. "This decision has *nothing* to do with your age or how near retirement you are, it has everything to do with your *productivity*. You just haven't put in the effort that our other employees are in comparison. We've been analyzing your performance in your duties for some time, and we've made the decision that it's time to release you. Of course, you can discuss your temporary post-employment options with Human Resources."

At least the prick's not beating around the bush anymore, Hollingsworth thought. "Of course. I'll go discuss this with them first." Hollingsworth knew his attempt to intimidate Mr. Samuels into allowing him to keep his job was worthless; there was no way he could afford an advocate who could possibly compete with Hyperion's brilliant, expensive attorneys. It was the reptile part of his brain, the angry, atavistic voice screaming for a chance to make its rage felt. But it was as useless as any other individualistic effort within the monolithic Hyperion Corporation.

"Naturally, you'll be asked to stay on an additional two weeks as we finalize the details of your release. You'll oblige us, won't you?" Mr. Samuels asked.

"Certainly," Hollingsworth answered. "I'm going to get some things from my office to show to HR now."

"Oh, and here's an official printed statement on the matter of your job performance I prepared for you. You will read it, won't you? It's a very nice statement," Mr. Samuels said.

I wish I could tell you where you could shove that "nice statement" of yours, Hollingsworth thought. "Certainly. I'll be sure to read over it before I leave today."

"Good luck to you in all your future endeavors," Mr. Samuels said as Hollingsworth got up out of the seat and left the room.

As he briskly walked down the hallway to his office, Hollingsworth's mind churned with anguish and thoughts of opportunities lost. To be fired so quickly, with only four more years before retirement benefits! Maybe he shouldn't have counted on *A Hero of Domremy* lasting a couple more seasons, maybe he should have paid more attention to the spreadsheets of agricultural yields, but could he have truly done much more for the company, after his many years of loyal service? He reassured himself that he had indeed given it his all, and that Hyperion would always move to find some motivation to release its employees before they could officially retire and claim benefits. Had old Gunderson really deserved that firing over his inappropriate joke he had posted on the company's chat forum accidentally? And now to fail for a cause he had always secretly dreaded.

Ag! Ag! Ag! It had always been Hollingsworth's least favorite aspect of colonial activity. He was trained in Human Exploitation Management and should not be blamed for the failure of the Ag projects. Why, he could not even manage to keep a cactus alive on the shelf of his thin office window! Erica, who did not have a window in her cubicle, would bring him some green thing from time to time to try to encourage his interest, but it would be dead after only a few days. He was aware that his Hyperion Fields project had been a disaster, but he tried not to think about it. A few rare plantations actually produced good results for a season or two, but then withered. The fertilizers or the pollinators or the chlorophyll transfer went wrong and the Ag engineers in their offices in Iowa couldn't figure out a fix. He wished he could freeze a few of them and send them out to Domremy to be responsible, but that wasn't going to happen. As it was, the best they could manage were a crowd of Asiatic peons Erica signed on through her contacts in Delhi, Hanoi and Beijing. Those fools would let the machinery run down and then disappear from the HF facilities. He suspected a lot of them must be running off to the Dissenters. Ah, the damned Dissenters! The rare warm bodies Hyperion could beg, borrow, or steal to send to farm efficiently on Domremy – and only if the blockheads could be coaxed to accept a transit contract that granted them their own land and their own hours. No matter how large the bonuses he offered them to work overtime in the Hyperion Fields, they seemed to scorn them, preferring to putter around on their own plots. Of course, their plantings were apparently quite successful, for they managed to grow plenty of stuff for themselves and the other colonists, too. However, instead of lending a hand to HF, they were always tending their own gardens. He'd read somewhere long ago in one of the few college texts he had bothered to open that when the Soviet Union was collapsing back in the twentieth century, the people on the communal farms did the same thing with their little vegetable gardens, growing more than the state itself. He seemed to remember that Caribbean slaves had lived in the margins centuries earlier, although they were only permitted to till their own patches one day a week. These Dissenters were the same kind of riffraff, experimenting with all kinds of unauthorized things the company never encouraged, smuggling all kinds of things up through the Farm Union and various phantom transport outfits before Hyperion could stop them. And as soon as Hyperion closed down one of the conduits, they had already opened another. It was useless trying to talk to them or get them to explain because they would just chew on hay and jabber about potatoes. They had the connivance of the nearby authorities, too, since they supplied all the ingredients necessary to keep a thousand "artisanal" breweries and distilleries going on every site on the planet. All the non-Dissenter colonists seemed to be good at was consuming massive quantities of booze, drugs, and porn, and then going off to the Forlani houses to dip their wicks.

Damned Forlani! They were supposed to be Erica's problem and she always bragged about how efficiently they serviced the convicts that had been commuted up to Domremy. He had tried to explain the economic downside to her, but she always seemed uninterested and managed to change the subject. Would she ever realize that the Forlani managed to suck up a lot of capital at the expense of all that screwing? But did they invest it in the Local economy so Hyperion could reduce the subsidies? – No! Instead, when they weren't doing the horizontal dance, they lived as frugally as nuns and sent every credit back to their home planet. Hollingsworth had often wondered after a night in one of his favorite corporate bordellos if there was not some way he could lure human whores to his colony, but they always seemed to laugh at his proposal of being iced and then plunked down in a great sea of empty prairie. Damn! So much grass up there and yet why couldn't they manage to fill up his supply ships for the Earth trade? Just thinking about Ag made his temples start to throb.

Erica Duquesne walked up to Hollingsworth, interrupting his thoughts. "Hello," she said to him. "Is everything okay?"

"Yeah, just feeling kinda tired," Hollingsworth said. "I feel worn out from all the work I've been doing this year. I think I'll be taking a break in a couple of weeks."

"Really?" Erica asked, her eyebrows slightly raised in surprise. "You almost never take a vacation."

"Yeah," Hollingsworth said. "I think I need to think things over. Besides, my show, *A Hero of Domremy*, got cancelled, and I need some time to consider new directions."

"I'm sorry," Erica said. For once, she felt genuine concern for Hollingsworth. Although she hadn't experienced it happening to anyone close to yet, she had heard stories of what happened to older Hyperion employees once their "most valuable assets" had been terminated. She silently wondered if this was being used as an excuse to shove Hollingsworth out the door. "Is there anything I can do to help you?"

"Not really," Hollingsworth said. "I think I'm going home early today, I think I'm developing a headache. Just keep making sure things are running smoothly on Domremy."

"Certainly," Erica said. As she returned to her office, she remained tense and suspicious over Hollingsworth's fate. *Maybe he just got fired because he was getting lazy. But if that's the reason, why can't I feel secure in my position? How long until it happens to me, too?* Doubt and uncertainly clouded her mind as she returned to the work in her office.

6

"Continue moving forward and prepare to present your documents," repeated the gentle Forlani voice every minute or so as the line inched ahead. Customs had already been a breeze at the efficient new Processing Area where their transport had alighted a few hours ago. The Forlani inspectors had been happily enthusiastic about the saplings, asking all sorts of questions about the fruit as if they meant to devour some then and there. They had pretty routinely approved all the other material, including the injector and the vials of toad venom made to look like agricultural hormones. The Song Pai guard gliding about in the background on his lower tentacles had appeared to eye them from a distance, if "eye" is the right verb for a creature covered in an elaborate breathing helmet where nothing resembling a human eye was discernable. The Forlani females appeared to ignore their large and disgusting co-inspector, though they occasionally dabbed some cream below their noses, which Klein suspected was a perfume to cover up the Song Pai's overwhelming dead fish odor. The one finicky thing about Entara, Ragatti, and the other partners Klein had taken to bed was their delicate sense of smell, as they had all invariably insisted he had a precoital wash-up. He knew that the Forlani houses on Domremy were equipped with a room that resembled a decontamination chamber, through which naked clients of objectionable scent were made to pass before they got together with the girls. That the Forlani women who had to work with Song Pai could survive the olfactory experience was really proof of their seriousness in developing planetary security.

"William K. Himmelreich," said the inspector who took his ID, pronouncing the H in a sort of Slavic guttural way that was one of the several Forlani equivalents of the earthly letter. "Where do you come from?"

"Domremy, Stafford Station."

"And when did you join the Farm Union?"

He rattled off the date in G-time and was pleased that he remembered it exactly as on his form.

"Very well, next!" Klein shuffled ahead slowly so that he could eavesdrop on her questions for Peebo, who was right behind him.

"Floyd Arthur Pickens." Klein had to control himself so that he didn't burst out laughing, even though it was not the first time he had heard Peebo's real name.

She only asked Peebo a few perfunctory questions and sent him on up the line. Klein would have sworn there was some unspoken policy among the Forlani to give Farm Union arrivals a bit of preferential treatment, despite the formalities. "No problems, Flooooyd?" Klein drawled.

"Quit yer snickerin'" huffed his landlord.

"We done yet? I can't wait to get out of here and see Entara."

"You wish! Those buggers up there will probably insist on a cavity search," snarled Peebo, glancing at a couple of Song Pai toward the end of the immigration area.

"Been there, done that. We had them all the time when I was in stir. You wouldn't believe the stuff prisoners tried to cheek into the prison: drugs, butane, weapons, even some weird stuff like..."

"You ain't never had a search like this. I didn't want to tell you about it earlier because I didn't want you to get nervous, but these squids are mighty invasive. Whatever you do, don't lose your cool! If you do, we'll never get past the checkpoint."

Sure enough, they were passed into a clear plastic corridor and made to strip. Klein felt a little self-conscious, even though he knew perfectly well that nudity was not a concern for the Forlani, who only wore clothes for some sensible reason and often not at all. His prudishness turned to defensive tautness when one of the big chartreuse cephalopods loomed above him and forced him with powerful tentacles to assume the position. The tentacular thrust up his rectum and way into his bowels was more than anything he had ever experienced in the penal system, but the explosion of lukewarm material inside his intestine practically made him turn on the creature with murderous anger. It was a good thing Peebo had reminded him of the necessity to stifle his feelings.

Cursing under his breath, Klein cleaned himself off inside and outside as best he could with some towels from a convenient dispenser on the clear wall. "Tell me that wasn't what I thought it was!" he barked at Peebo.

"It was," said the farmer, as though a windstorm had just flattened his barns.

"I'm going to have some blood for that! I just got a big desire to cut that thing open and see what his insides look like."

"Don't let it get to you. You've got more important things to think about now."

"Right, and after that, maybe I'll think about him again, because I managed to pull this off while he was having his jollies." Klein opened his fist to show Peebo a metallic bar that might pass for a badge among the Song Pai guards. "I'll track him down if it's the last thing I do, I swear. That's one thing I can't tolerate for long, even if I have to tolerate it for now."

When they had gotten dressed again and reclaimed all their ag material, Peebo arranged transport with a red-caped Forlani in the main terminal and they took their load to what turned out to be a kind of agricultural experiment station on the outskirts of the sprawling city. When they had finished unloading and seeing to the saplings, Klein turned to Peebo and asked, "Where do we bunk? I need an extra-long bath to start with, before I go see Entara."

"Well, my bunk is in here," said Peebo, pointing over his shoulder, "But you're staying at the mahäme according to her directions."

"Why the hell do I want to go to a mahäme? I thought that was some sort of a nunnery. That's the last thing I need. I just want to be with Entara. Alone. For a long time. Understand?"

"Look, pardner, I have very little say here and she, apparently, does. I'm sure everything will be explained. Our transport driver has already got the coordinates by message and she will take you. I'll get word to you when I can, and don't forget your promises in the circle." Peebo turned away and started to open the door to the building, but then looked back at Klein. "And remember, take your time and be sure about things before you run off half-cocked. Maybe that's not the expression. But keep in that smoldering mind of yours that the future of a lot of people rests on your shoulders and you absolutely cannot act free-lance. Good luck."

Klein was in a foul mood when he got back into the passenger compartment of the transport as it started down an avenue. Eventually his ire and frustration calmed enough for him to notice that the driver was watching him with a sense of interest that he could only associate with Forlani back in the houses of Domremy. "Are you comfortable Mr. Klein?" she purred.

"My name is Himmelreich," replied Klein, suspicious of some deception.

"Oh, please don't worry. I am of the Eyes of Alertness and would never betray you. I am taking you to our mahäme and several people know you are coming. Everyone will be so excited when you get there, because there is not a single member of the matriline, I swear, who has not heard of you. I am so honored to be your driver." Then she added with a special emphasis, "If there is anything at all that I can do for you, please let me know. I really, really want to be a friend. My name is Canthli, by the way."

"Thank you, Canthli," Klein politely responded, not knowing exactly what to make of what seemed to be a proposition, as they say on Earth. Why had Entara leaked the news of his visit to so many people who didn't seem to have any reason for knowing about it? It seemed counter-intuitive and dangerous, unlike her naturally methodical train of thought. And why go to this stupid monastery anyway? There must be better ways to conceal their plans than to make it some kind of theological occasion. How were they supposed to renew their love when a whole sisterhood was spying on their intimacy? All he wanted now was to hold her again. He could feel his mind gravitating despite himself toward the delicious thought of their bodies enfolding once again, and perhaps forever.

Canthli interrupted his reverie. She passed a card through the little partition that divided the compartments. "Please accept this and never hesitate to call me. If you press the orange dot twice, it will instantly alert me and I will try not to be too far away." He must have looked so stupefied that she added after a few seconds, "Mr. Klein, perhaps I have made an error by being so bold. But you must excuse me. We all admire you so. The whole matriline, but others who have also heard, too. You are... a very special individual."

Klein would have liked to ask Canthli more questions to try to orient himself, but the truth was that he was so confused by the conflicting welcomes he had received on this planet, being buggered by a giant bully of an octopus and then offered whatever he wished by the first female he encountered, that he was having trouble articulating anything. Moreover, bashing at the doorways of his consciousness was the thought of Entara, a happiness that he had so long denied himself to contemplate and that now seemed just beyond his grasp, almost within the reality of his miserable life. He watched the leafy thoroughfares of the city of Plambo' slide by, but his thoughts were filled with images of his most cherished partner, projections of exactly how she would look now that she had given birth to children, stage rehearsals of how they would greet each other, the first words they would say, the first time in ages that they would again touch each other. When the transport began to slow and moved through a stone gateway, he realized that the huge structure they had been driving by for some time must be the mahäme. It was almost a city in itself. Once they had passed through the gateway, low buildings, mostly of stone, stretched away in several directions, alternating with tall Forlani lawns and flowering gardens. It was not like any monastery he had ever seen in Germany, but resembled in some ways a university or some kind of science center. And there were no nuns' habits, just luxurious purple Forlani flesh and honey-colored fur.

The vehicle stopped in front of a pavilion where three tall Forlani females, attired in yellow caftans and hats that looked like chefs' toques, awaited him. As Canthli watched him emerge from the door, she gave him a look that can only be described as a reverent smile and wished him a very happy stay. He guessed the three figures on the steps must be some kind of Mothers Superior and it turned out he was right. "Greetings friend Klein!" they said in chorus. The one in the middle then went on, "We are the mahäme-ki and we will be responsible for your service and your comfort, when you are not actually in the company of Entara-para."

Klein wondered what made Entara a para, but instead pursued another line. "What do you mean by service, exactly?"

"It is a natural question," answered the second of his greeters. "On this world, no visitors are accepted without some kind of service role. It is especially important that we respect this custom because to do otherwise might attract undue attention from the Brotherhood, which can be very nosey. You will be asked to serve in the Training Center. This mahäme, like all the others, has one, but we like to think ours is particularly fine. This will only occupy a small part of the day and in the intervals, we will arrange for you to speak with Entara-para and help her with certain matters."

"What kind of training do you think I can provide? My usual profession on Domremy is very… violent, and I understand that all but a few people on this planet are very disinclined to that sort of thing."

"That is certainly correct," responded the third of the leaders. "In fact, though, you can be very useful in the Training Center, which prepares young women, among other things, for off-planet work in a way that you are already familiar with."

"Do I understand that you want me to help prepare young Forlani to be companions for alien males?"

"Precisely. You see, Mr. Klein, you already have a rather unique status here. We have come to learn that natives of Earth for some reason seek to be very secretive about their most intimate contacts, but that is not the case among us. At least among females. In particular, if a woman has been pleased with an intimate encounter of any kind, whether or not it is what you would term sexual, it is essential and customary to share that experience. It is the basis of our song, which for our females is the highest and almost the unique form of art. Rest assured, Mr. Klein, that Entara was most extremely pleased by you and that the songs she has shared in the matriline have revealed to Forlani entirely new facets of intimate relationship and forms of happiness that were previously unimagined."

"I never would have thought she would kiss and tell," muttered Klein to himself.

But his first interlocutor quickly corrected him. "Yes, indeed. Kissing in fact is a large part of it. A whole chapter of the new epic. But by no means the only one. The way you and she were able to develop, without any apparent plan, a whole panoply of informal interaction – no, perhaps that is not the right expression – let's see, how did she put it in that ballad? Fun, yes, that's it."

"And playfulness," added the third Forlani. "Play is what you call this almost gratuitous quest for joy without shame, isn't it?"

"Yes," agreed Klein, "I suppose you can look at it that way. So permit me to ask, is it right to say that you want me to help these young women learn how to be happy with their customers?"

"Just so. But also to share the happy feeling with them. Perhaps that is the most important of all. Because, of course, you understand that for us Forlani there can be no happiness that can even compare with the happiness of birth. That is a supreme happiness that is reserved for only the fortunate few," she added wistfully. "Yet now we are facing very modern challenges and the matriline must develop the very best and most excellent interplanetary relations in order to improve things right here. The Training Center is the focus of our efforts. And Mr. Klein, in the near future, you are the focus of our training center."

"What you are asking me…" Klein paused as he saw the Forlani equivalent of raised eyebrows, "Perhaps requiring me to do is a bit unusual, particularly for human males. I certainly have no personal experience doing this kind of thing. There are feelings to consider…"

"Come, Mr. Klein," said the second speaker, "It is very obvious from the songs that you are an individual who does not allow himself to be pushed around by his own feelings. Just the opposite. That is one of the things that make you so special for Entara-para. The depth of sentiment that you are able to deal with, often to suppress, is now legendary. So is your generosity. We feel sure that you will not refuse. Now please follow us to your quarters, where you may rest."

There was no arguing with these women who were insisting that he perform a kind of work that would only be considered appropriate on Earth for a gigolo or a pimp. They obviously had a case for why it was important to them, even on a planetary scale. He would just have to soldier on in a way no soldier had ever done before. Well, not recently anyway, he mused, as he recalled bits of ancient history about Caesar and Alexander. *In boca al lupo*, as the Italians say.

Klein was relieved the next day when he had his first session in the Training Center that he was not expected to perform before crowds, like some interplanetary Chippendale dancer or porno king. Instead, his training was organized more along the lines of an Oxford tutorial. He would meet for a couple of hours with small groups of Forlani, from two to a half dozen, in what resembled a comfortable studio apartment from 20th century Earth. Furthermore, while all the students did not hesitate to touch him and even sometimes to fawn over him, he quickly discovered that they had already had theoretical and practical initiation into all the usual sexual positions and techniques. Though each of them insisted on some kind of coupling, they were mostly more curious about what is usually called foreplay and, later on, afterplay. Klein could see right away that he might have to organize a whole seminar he would call "Kissy-face and cuddling."

Of course, as he felt a lithe young body sidle up to him, he instantly pictured her mentally as Entara. Training was like lying with an unending succession of Entaras, each slightly different, but variations on the same loveliness. He caught himself before long using these trainees as sexual guinea pigs for what he hoped to accomplish when he was finally together with the one he longed for. This left him with a weird feeling of double infidelity, as though he was simultaneously cheating on Entara and on his students. Was he violating some kind of dimly-instilled professorial taboo? He quickly dismissed this impression when he realized that almost every conventional educator would be dying to trade places with him.

Despite this accommodation with his role as trainer, Klein could not help thinking from minute to minute, *Why hasn't she gotten in touch with me personally yet?* Was she in danger? Was she under constant surveillance? Was this training supposed to be some kind of blissful appetizer to their reunion? When Peebo called him on a private communicator from the ag station, he managed to give a Crop Talk explanation of what he was up to. It must have sounded like a humorous version of a stud report. To his astonishment, Peebo did not seem in the least bit surprised about this turn of events, nor about Entara's silence.

Finally, after several days, one of the trainees who had recently shared his bed arrived at his quarters in the striped skirt that Klein now knew signified a messenger and told him that the next day he would be escorted to a meeting with Entara in the Orchards of Fataarey. His puzzlement aside, Klein was brimming with excitement when a couple of older women from the mahäme walked him several kilometers to a huge enclosure filled with trees where he found Entara along with a few other females sitting on some stones. She was wearing a gauzy top garment that looked like a cross between a teddy and a very short apron, for it contained a row of pockets around the hem. Klein was amazed at her radiant beauty, apparent notwithstanding the changes in her body. The fur on her body and limbs had turned a darker, chocolaty brown, she had developed a slight belly, and her torso, which appeared to have bulked out a bit like a featherweight on steroids, definitely showed the contours of a double row of six mammaries. When he gazed at her face, he almost gasped because her eyes had turned from an almost scarlet red to a shade between brass and gold. Peebo had made him read some files about post-childbirth changes in the Forlani physiology, but he was taken aback and delighted just the same.

All these realizations actually took some time, because the first thing Entara did was to leap up, hug him tenderly, and kiss him on the lips. The others who were waiting with her watched them as though they were seeing the love scene from an opera. "Oh, Klein, darling, it's been so hard not to come running to you first thing, especially when you were right here in the city, in my own home mahäme, where I've slept so many nights. I hope you like your room because I picked it out for you myself to be right next to the fragrant kumugathria blossoms."

Klein didn't dare confess that his humble Earth nose had barely noticed a vague, sweet scent. "Then you can imagine how I've felt not being able to come to you."

When she had lingered a second time on his lips, she gave a little nod that might be the Forlani form of a blush. "These are my attendants and cousins Viga and Spomonthi. I needed to have some lookouts, even though this orchard is off limits to our males and is now closed to the public. I need a little exercise because I may be giving birth again before too long, and I thought we might have a refreshing run and pick some fruit. Would you like that?"

"As long as I can stay with you, I wouldn't mind mucking out a stable of cattle."

The girl attendants fanned out to either side of the couple as they trotted down a lane in the orchard. Klein had noticed that the two women from the mahäme were no longer nearby, and wondered if they were standing guard by the entry. Entara seemed to be very concerned about intruders. Klein was nothing if not well rested after his week of training and had long ago shaken off the aftereffects of prolonged space flight, but as he accelerated his pace, he was shocked when Entara seemed to be pulling steadily ahead of him without visibly picking up her stride. He had naturally observed that Forlani were quite agile in short bursts, but on Domremy they tended to stick near their houses. He had never suspected that in the open these creatures had such speed and stamina. What happened next bowled him over completely.

As they neared a tree, Entara suddenly yelled out, "Look, ripe fruit!" and with one bound soared up twenty feet into the air, grasping one branch with one arm and another with her tail.

Right. The tail. Evolution. It had to be more than a neat sex toy. He panted as he approached the tree trunk.

"Hop up! Aren't you hungry?" He didn't know what to answer. He could see out the corners of his eyes that the two attendants had stopped and were giggling a bit as they watched.

Suddenly Entara became aware of them herself and a look of recognition came over her face. "Oh no, I forgot. Here, catch." She tossed him a few apricot-like fruit one by one. Then she filled the pockets in her garment with more, before coming down to him as easily as a fireman descending a pole. She called something to the attendants and they went off in search of a snack of their own.

"Just like your females, pregnancy makes me hungry."

"But on my planet, it doesn't turn you into an Olympic athlete."

"Oh, I could jump at least that high before. That's what our ancestors did every day. Before the catastrophe. Forlan was more or less covered with trees then, the old scriptures say, and the scientists have proven it's true."

As she bit into the fruit a drop of juice collected on her lip and Klein impulsively leaned toward her and kissed it off.

"You've changed," she said with a wink. "You've gotten better. I bet the trainees are having the time of their lives. Soon my songs won't be the only ones heard about the lover Klein. Perhaps theirs will become more famous and mine will drift off where forgotten songs and memories go," she mused, stretching her arms to the sky. She turned to look him directly in the eyes. "I'll never forget, though."

"Entara, when can we be together? All the time on the *Kagahashi Maru* you were all I could think of. I know I have to confront your husband, but all I could do was imagine getting you in my arms again and never letting go."

She got very serious as she said, "Klein, schatz, the world has come around. We both have to change what we expect. Childbirth overthrows everything for us, and I don't mean just on the outside. The mating, the piercing, causes us to transform. Some organs actually move and others that were never there appear. If we spent the night together, it would not be the same, because I am not the same."

"I don't care about that. I don't care if you grew ten arms and you were covered with spines. You're so much more to me."

"But Klein, how can I explain so you'll understand? It's so different. Your females experience birth as pain, but for us it's a physical, palpable joy that surpasses everything. That's not all, because the birth feeling changes the entire way you look at the world. It's like when people become addicted to a pleasure drug, but it's all positive and it lasts. We cross a threshold that is permanent, and that's without even considering the children, the sense of duty, the vicarious pride."

She drew him toward her and kissed him again and settled her head next to his the way he always loved. "Klein, I know it's too much to grasp now, but I know some day you'll understand." She kissed him one more time and then they heard a series of whistles echo among the trees.

Entara sprang up and said, "The attendants have spotted something. We can't stay here any longer."

"I won't give up. I have to see you. I'm not leaving you." He grasped her arm, so much more muscular than when she came to him that first day on Domremy. She could have easily bent his back or pulled away, but instead she bowed her head in resignation and limply stood before him.

"If you insist on that, I don't know what I'll do," she said, more to herself than to him. She passed him a micro-memory device and added, as though reading from a prepared script, "Everything you need to know about the danger is here. I can arrange for you to meet Tays'she by appointment or by accident. I can talk with him beforehand if you want, but I don't think it would be a good idea. Remember that despite his flaws, he is clever, and potentially lethal."

She embraced him one more time and whispered in his ear. "What I'm most afraid of is that I've brought you here to die. That's the one thing I don't think I could survive."

Then she put his hand into the hand of one of the cousins, to whom she gave brief instructions. The girl led him away to the gate, where the two who had accompanied him earlier were ready to return to the mahäme. For a brief second, Klein had an urge to strangle both of them and return to bring Entara away with him, whether she wanted it or not. He grasped the micro-memory to remind himself not to.

The next day, Klein managed to muddle through his morning training hours without quite realizing how he did it. He had spent much of the night going over the files Entara had prepared for him on the micro-memory and constantly looking up references about various cultural details of Forlani life that were previously unknown to him, or indeed to most Earthlings. Fortunately, he had access to the vast mahäme library resources that contained things that were far more detailed than the best of earthly reports. Only after this painstaking scrutiny did he realize the enormity of the activities that Tays'she and his so far unidentified accomplices were planning. On his own planet it might have passed for an everyday scam or a clever piece of lucrative but relatively minor corruption. It was only in light of thousands of years of Forlani history and the considerable intellectual mass of their ethical system that the plot assumed its complete character of evil. Its eventual result might be – in fact, it seemed that this was the plan of some in the Brotherhood – the destruction of the great female solidarity of the matrilines that held together the fabric of their race's life.

He had finally come to understand how the seemingly scant revenues of the girls working in so many pleasure houses on far-flung colonies tied in with the over-arching enterprise of rescuing Forlan's damaged ecosystem, since the majority of income from each "trick" flowed back into the matriline's coffers to support not only the biological restructuring of their world, but also the network of hospitals and birthing clinics that cared for young and old Forlani, as well as a good part of their education. Though fewer than ten percent of the female population were approved for the idolized status of motherhood, all the females gave their efforts with selfless devotion to the mahäme system and the ninety percent who never enjoyed families of their own would sacrifice themselves in a heartbeat for those that carried on the genes for the matrilines. If untold numbers of the women were lured into poverty, isolation, and slavery on alien worlds under the auspices of FastTrack, for the unique profits of a segment of the Brotherhood, the entire delicate, hive-like system could soon begin to unravel and the ages of mass suffering would return.

These grim thoughts haunted Klein through the morning as he tried to serve the trainees with words and caresses that matched the affection they lavished on him. He had the feeling of having failed before he even started. Yet, you couldn't tell this from the rapt faces of the young women. Even when he was in his clumsiest and most distracted moments, they simply seemed to take that as an extra proof of his powers of intimacy and the superiority of his alleged feelings. He didn't have much appetite at lunch time, but when he thought he had said goodbye to the day's group, two of the girls took him by the arms and drew him along with them out the door.

"Teacher Klein, we see you eat by yourself each day in this apartment. You must be lonely. Please come along with us to the refectory to enjoy a little company. They say food is always better when reflected in another's eyes. Please! Please!"

In vain, he stammered a few lame excuses, but they wouldn't let go of him. When he finally gave up and let them lead him, they put their heads on his shoulders and beamed with happiness. They walked several hundred meters to a large domed building near the hospital complex. As they entered the atrium, Klein could hear a distinct rustling sound and as his little party came through the entry, he realized that the entire hall full of hundreds of young Forlani had stood to greet him. One stepped forward and began to sing in beautiful high notes. Soon the entire assembly had joined in, creating richly layered choruses that wove together. Klein realized that some of the highest notes were probably beyond the range of his human hearing, but he could not resist the allure of the beautiful melody.

When the song ended in a kind of coda, he told his little group, "What wonderful music! I would swear I recognize a few notes from compositions back on Earth."

"Of course, Teacher Klein. The song is about you, composed by Entara-para. It is called "Wind in the Prairie Grasses" and mentions the music the two of you listened to together. She blended some of this into this melody, which is famous all over the planet. That's why no one had trouble joining in once it started."

Klein's mind drifted back to his early months with Entara, when she had shown such curiosity about the recordings he had managed to scavenge in the communities of the settlement. She had seemed very moved by some of his favorites: Schumann, Mendelssohn, Brahms, Raderski. He often put them on to play while they were making love, which seemed to delight Entara particularly. He never would have guessed how much, or how lasting those impressions would be.

He noticed the people in the refectory were still standing and muttered a few words about how bad he was at speeches, when their heads suddenly turned to the other end of the hall and he realized they had been waiting for something more. A Forlani woman with a brilliant salmon-colored sash over a diaphanous pale yellow robe entered the room and strode confidently toward him. When she got closer, he saw with a start that his eyes were not deceiving him and that it was Ragatti. The young women at their tables saluted her with a series of whistles and chirps that voiced their approval for her.

As Ragatti came right up to Klein, she took his hands together in hers like a Hindu saying *Namaste* and kissed his fingers. He did the same for her.

"It's so good to see you again, Klein. I was disappointed that we were parted so abruptly. But I recovered quickly and the mahäme has given me great responsibilities. I have been named organizer of the birthing teams here at this hospital. Someone we know made me promise to come say hello and to apologize that she cannot be here herself. Now I must return and you have a meal to enjoy, but remember that you will always be in my thoughts."

Ragatti turned and made a gesture that told the assembly to be seated, waving to them as she left the room. Soon Klein was seated, too, and students from all his training sessions took turns bringing him delicacies to sample. He did his best to try a nibble of each, knowing that he would soon be inflated like a balloon if he ate much more. Seizing an opportune moment, he beat a retreat to his quarters and felt immense relief to collapse in a chair, no longer the center of attention.

He must have fallen asleep, because when he came to his senses again, it was well into the afternoon. He called Peebo on the com system and told him in Crop Talk that he should go ahead and make arrangements for his own return to Domremy, since he would be staying on indefinitely on Forlan. Peebo seemed upset at this announcement and peppered Klein with questions to make sure he had not already taken some rash action, but he reassured the landlord that he hadn't. He told Peebo he was sure he could change Entara's mind about renewing their relationship and that in any case, he had made up his mind to be close to her no matter what she chose to do. As soon as he put the com link down he began making plans to go right over to Entara's dwelling and sweep her up into his arms, even if he had to fight his way through a cordon of Forlani security. He was about to summon a transport driver when he heard a discreet tap on the door.

He opened it to find a small, silent Forlani female eyeing him curiously. "If this is for a training session, I'm afraid I've finished for the day and..."

"Don't worry, Teacher Klein. I'm sure you can tell I'm much too young and years away from *that* kind of training. Mother told me I should come and introduce myself because I couldn't come to the orchard earlier. My name is Ayan'we."

"Entara's oldest child," Klein whispered to himself. "Come inside and let me get a good look at you, young lady,"

"There's not much to look at, I'm afraid," she stated matter-of-factly. "I'm not beautiful like Mother or my aunts. I'm even plainer than my little sisters. I think I have inherited too much from my father," she added with a note of barely concealed disgust.

"You look very fine to me and I'm sure your mother treasures you a great deal if she sent you to see me."

She let this pass and strolled around the apartment, looking especially at his computer installation. "Not bad," she remarked. "I can see you've been reviewing the FastTrack files."

"You know about this?"

"I really found out about it before everybody else," she boasted. "But there were a lot of spooky things I didn't understand until Mother explained. The truth is I distrust Tays'she more than anyone else in the family." She turned and looked pointedly at him. "Are you going to kill him? I know about you, too. You kill lots of people. It would make me happy if you do. I should feel bad about that, and I would never say it in front of Mom, but something inside tells me he'll get us all if you don't. Will you kill him?"

"I've promised not to go that far."

"If you're worried about Mom, I know she'll forgive you. She can't love you the same way she did when she was a girl, but I know she won't blame you if you kill Tays'she."

"It's not to spare Entara's feelings. I've made a solemn promise to others who have always helped me. People who know a lot more about good and bad than I do. One thing your mother may have told you is that I do not like to break promises."

Noticing how Ayan'we seemed to know her way around computers, Klein decided he would try to change the subject. "Would you like to see some pictures of where I come from? I have some over here."

But as Klein rose to get his digital album, he felt a sudden wave of nausea. Way too many delicacies at lunch.

Ayan'we observed him as though she were staring at a bug under the microscope. "You look as though you need to fuck."

"What was that young lady?"

"You need to fuck. Sorry, my human languages are not so good. You know, fuck." She made a little gesture with her hand coming from her mouth that made Klein suddenly double up with laughter. *So that's what it means in Forlani. And all the time I thought Entara was being prudish. It does put a whole new spin on the word.*

"Are you all right?" queried Ayan'we, more concerned with this weird outburst of hilarity than with his nauseated expression.

"Perfectly OK now," he responded. "And by the way, the word in English is vomit and in German erbrechen. Fuck means something completely different that we will pass on for the moment. I'm just going to take a little fizzy pill and I'll be back to normal."

When he came out of the bathroom he saw that Ayan'we had opened the digital album herself and was rapidly going through the images. "These are really beautiful places. Is all the Earth like that?"

"Unfortunately not. And some of those places are no longer as terrific as they look in old pictures. This cathedral, for instance" he said, pointing to a soaring stone edifice, "was destroyed by an earthquake caused by a new kind of mining and no one ever replaced it. Too expensive, they said. That was before I left, which was also not so pleasant. Did your mother tell you about why I left Earth?"

"She said you were an exile. Sometimes I feel that way, too. I don't think I want to stay on Forlan my whole life. It's not that I hate it really, but I get this strange urge."

"We call it wanderlust. It's a bit of a blessing and a bit of a curse."

"We don't believe in curses."

"You should go on thinking that way. Can I get you a cold drink?"

"No. I'd better leave. I've got to go over to the lab for a health class."

"Well, it was a pleasure meeting you Ayan'we. I hope we get a chance to talk again. But you have to understand that when things begin to happen, they may happen very fast."

As she was about to walk away, Ayan'we glanced back at Klein and said, "I'm glad I got to meet you, too. It may not show, but I am. I was a little afraid of coming here. You're not what I expected. Not like any males I've ever met on this world. Thank you for coming all this way. And please don't stop loving my mom."

Days followed days and Klein's attitude deteriorated as his patience frayed. However, the enthusiasm of his trainees was a well that would never go dry. Each day they appeared with new questions that they asked as often with their bodies as with their voices. He suspected that they must be sharing their experiences somehow, because fresh faces would arrive and they would present comments and gestures that could only refer to something he had done at a previous session with different trainees. Perhaps they were able to sense his growing inner turmoil because "old" trainees began to come every day bearing gifts to cheer him up: an endless procession of flower arrangements and tidbits, but other mementoes, too, and even a little pet, a feathered, flightless lizard that gobbled insects. When he watched it in its cage, Klein had the feeling he was gazing into some distant eon of his own planet's past. This thing could be a cousin of ornithomimus or diatryma. It looked at him with an intense stare that seemed to pierce right into his head and often pecked at the cage to get his attention before uttering a collection of clicks, squeaks and gargles that might be a prehistoric version of "Chin up, sonny!" He dubbed it Quetzalcoatl.

But his restlessness only grew. His only contact with Entara was through a secure com link that a messenger brought one day. When he contacted her, he tried to bare his emotions, but she evaded him, insisting on giving details of her domestic life and the arrangement of the dwelling, for she had decided it was the only possible place he could confront Tays'she. To combat his funk, Klein began taking walks after lunch, soon mastering the path to the Orchards of Fataarey and to the Garden of Fulfillment, hoping for a glance of Entara. He spent one long evening going all the way to the Exit Center at the Spaceport and back, thinking that even though he himself never intended to leave, he might have to help Peebo to do so. After some hesitation, he plotted out the way to the home Entara shared with Tays'she. He found it in a pleasant neighborhood, across from what seemed to be a small park for children. Slipping back to his German days, he adopted his "you can't see me" stroll and his "I am nobody" expression. Before leaving the mahäme that day, he had borrowed a baggy coverall he had found in a closet near his rooms; it had been used at one time by alien construction workers and gave him a suitable disguise. He carried around some outdoor receptacles he found from one location to another, as though he knew what he was doing, in order to case the street for surveillance. Schoolgirls chatting on a bench, a vendor doling out some sweets, an elderly lady feeding fish in a pool, a transport delivering parcels. It seemed like the perfect residential street. Too perfect. His experience told him this was staged, and staged in an extremely proficient, professional way. Since his construction worker's facemask, meant to keep out dust and pollen no doubt, covered much of his face, he decided it was unlikely he would be recognized, and he ventured a little closer. Yes, the vendor's decorations contained mirrors aimed at Entara's dwelling, the elderly female's sunglasses contained reflectors, too, the delivery transport had an extra antenna, and the schoolgirls had com links that looked a bit too official for talking with classmates. Risking another little container replacement right in front of the dwelling, he could see there were figures in the shrubbery. They seemed grayish and bulky as they lurked among the leaves. Then another figure came out the door. Not Entara or Ayan'we, as he had secretly hoped, but a more wiry body with horny projections on the face and shoulders and a leathery skin with very little of the typical Forlani fur. He recognized it must be a breeding male. This was Tays'she. He was surprised that a gaudily dressed female soon emerged from the doorway and headed with the male out the side entrance and down a cross street that led to a market area. This was the new first wife, leading hubby out on a buying trip for more expensive clothes and jewelry. It was time to withdraw before his anonymity wore off and he began attracting attention, so Klein took a different route back to the mahäme.

His spying instincts fully reactivated, Klein began in the following days to get much more proactive about the upcoming confrontation. First of all, he reviewed the results of his visit to the Entara home. The "neighborhood people" were all females, but they were unlikely to be members of the matriline, who would have no reason to do surveillance, especially in such a professional manner. They could only be some sort of police or intel security representing the state. With a little research, he learned that the grey fellows in the bushes were probably castrated males, dobutu. They had failed to move up in the Brotherhood hierarchy and been gelded for use as stooges for the breeders. If the females were there to keep something in, the geldings were there to keep something out, and that probably was him. But it also occurred to him that they may be there to execute some aggression on behalf of Tays'she toward unwanted members of his family. He remembered what Ayan'we had said about distrusting her dad.

    Klein called Entara to ask her not to go back to the house. She insisted somewhat petulantly that she had no intention of abandoning her domestic rights. She seemed much more confused and distressed in the call, alternating between desperate recollections of the past on Domremy, turbulent confessions that she still desired him, and gloomy statements about seeing no way out of the dilemma. She flatly and angrily refused Klein's invitation to simply leave Plambo' and run off with him into the back country until they could escape off-planet. Then she hung up. Klein was about to storm out and begin some more spying when Peebo called on the open link. He was agitated and said Klein should abandon the mission and leave with him soon. There would be no more tramp ships like the *Kagahashi Maru* in the system for months to come and his backup plan of taking a Tugulean cargo freighter that regularly visited Forlan had fallen through because it had run into a nebular static discharge and was up for a long repair. That meant the only way off-planet was a Hyperion ship, and since the Brotherhood and Hyperion had grown quite chummy lately, Klein's chances of sneaking aboard after confronting Tays'she were virtually null. Klein repeated to Peebo that he should make his own arrangements, that he would dispose of any evidence himself, and that in any case he thought he would never be leaving Forlan. The call ended awkwardly, with neither of them really wanting to say goodbye.

Klein's first spying priority was to find out more about Entara's actual movements, so he walked to the Passport Administration and followed her when she left work. To his surprise, she went directly to the mahäme! Klein struggled with the idea that she had apparently been spending most of her nights at the same compound where he slept, concealing this information from him. The next day it was Ayan'we's turn to be followed. He followed her from her health lab to a series of buildings that turned out to be her public school, where she dropped off some materials and picked up others. From there, she went to the home, but her stopover there was very perfunctory, serving apparently to drop off books and pick up clothing. After a brief visit to a shop that served fruity drinks, where she chatted with a ragged group of friends who were all armed with some kind of computer device, she returned to the mahäme, where she talked for some time with her mother and then went to a dormitory area for girls her age. Neither had been harmed, approached, or followed by anyone but himself, as far as Klein could determine. The "neighborhood people" were still on watch, though this time it was an entirely different group. Likewise, the geldings were still posted around the house, and Klein was pretty sure that both Entara and Ayan'we had noticed them, while pretending to see nothing.

The next afternoon, Klein decided to trail Entara again, but to stop her for a talk before she got back to the mahäme. This time, though, things would be a bit different. She was quite late leaving work and Klein used his usual technique of trailing from a distance, but she surprised him by running up to a tram that arrived and hopping on in a direction he had not anticipated. He could see no more trams on the way, so he figured his only recourse was to wait at the stop and hope the next one followed the same route. By this time the Forlan twilight was thickening and, as often happened after sunset, a fog was beginning to rise. At the edges of the mist on either side of him, Klein soon detected furtive movements, not the limber, dancer-like movement of Forlani females, but a more sluggish and sinister variety.

Klein deduced he was soon to be visited by some dobutu, so he searched for a weapon. The schedule for the tram was on a pole with a hefty metal base that did not seem attached to the ground. He knew if he could wield it somehow it would have a considerable impact. After that, he would have to improvise, because the shadowy figures were drawing closer. As soon as the one to his right became distinct he latched onto the schedule post. Immediately sensing that it was too heavy to dead lift, he spun around with it as he had done with the hammer on his days on the Gymnasium track team and flung it straight into the attacker's midsection. Signpost and dobutu went sprawling down the sidewalk. One down. The one approaching from his left was not yet close enough for contact, but Klein could see he was carrying some sort of coiled weapon and raising his hand to use it. Before he could, Klein ran at him several steps, jumped as high as he could and landed a dropkick square in the gelding's face, making him collapse in a heap. *Maybe I can't leap into a tree, but I can still get it done*, he was congratulating himself, when he heard a sharp cry of "Klein, watch out, behind you!" and turned to see a coiled thing lashing out at him. Before he could move or withdraw another body dashed in front and took the blow. *Neutralize, neutralize.* Without even looking at his benefactor, Klein side-stepped, grasped the approaching arm of the gelding, twisted under it until he was behind the body, stretched it until it was an unmovable pinion, and smashing down on in, drove the dobutu's face into the pavement. Neutralize meant neutralize. He kept twisting the arm until a snap told him it was useless and dislocated.

He bent over to examine the dobutu's weapon when another voice warned him, "Be careful, Klein, it's a poison whip and you don't know how to handle it. Here, help me." It was a female Forlani who was trying to lift the one who had taken the blow meant for Klein. Up close to their faces, Klein could tell it was the cousins from the day in the Orchard with Entara.

"Spomonthi's badly hurt," said Viga. "We must get her to the hospital at the mahäme."

It was clear that the poison whip had not just immobilized Spomonthi, but had opened a nasty suppurating wound where it struck her torso. It reminded him of someone he'd seen long ago at a beach who had been stung by a Portuguese man o' war. He hefted her into a fireman's carry and told Viga to lead the way. When the mahäme was in sight he shouted to Viga to run ahead and get some hospital staff and the cousin sprinted off like a rocket. They were met at the entrance by a group of females who took charge and whisked Spomonthi away before he could ask many questions.

After a while, a girl wearing the red cape that stood for all sorts of organizing staff came down to talk with him. "We don't get many wounds like that. The Brotherhood is only supposed to use those whips for rituals in their own compounds and they are strictly illegal on the streets. Fortunately, you acted quickly and the wound had not spread to any vital organs. It would have been deadly if it had time to act, especially on your human body if it had hit you."

"Will you take good care of her?"

"Of course. Viga would thank you herself, but she wants to stay in the recovery room. Spomonthi will need much sedation. We will keep you informed." Then Red Cape got a sort of smirk on her face as she said, "Tell me, Teacher Klein, you have a reputation for... shall we say, thoroughness? Are there any corpses out there that we should take care of before they attract more attention? It's the law here."

"I think I hurt somebody's feelings, but there are no corpses." *Not yet.*

Having had enough cloak-and-dagger for a while, Klein rested the next day, confining his walks to a stroll through the nearby Gardens of Fulfillment. He felt so tired when he returned after dark that he thought about dropping right into bed, but his body suddenly grew taut as he realized he was not alone in the room. Quetzalcoatl was banging away on his cage and clicking like a demented Geiger counter. *Goons right here in the monastery?* But it was all right. The shape silhouetted against the window was female. "I've been to see Spomonthi," sighed Entara.

"It was your idea, spies trailing the spy?"

"The poor girls were being run ragged the last few days. And then this happened. My unfortunate cousin can be disfigured and once again, it is all my fault."

"You shouldn't blame yourself. It's doubly my fault, first for spotting the dobutu too late, then for not spotting the girls at all. I should have taken the poison."

"If you had, you wouldn't be over in the hospital, you'd be dead, wrapped in a shroud about to be shipped off-planet like a block of ice, and my worst nightmare would have become real."

"Entara, I…"

"Oh, I've been so wrong, so consistently. Thinking you could give up love without hating me, thinking I could give you up and act like such a little moral hero. I had to come tonight. Take off your clothes."

Klein quickly slipped them off and Entara pushed him gently down backward onto the bed. "Now you'll see how useless I am. Right there. You remember. No, it's not like before, but never mind, never mind. Tonight you'll see that at least I wasn't lying to you. Yes, just like that. Don't speak, don't try to say anything reassuring. If you feel like opening you mouth you just kiss me right here. Remember? And I will kiss you right here."

"I won't let you go away again ever."

She gasped as she kissed his eyelid. "Is that a tear?"

They lay together for a long time, neither of them having reached the shiver that douses the soul with joy. He wondered whether she was going to weep, too, but then remembered she couldn't. *OK, I'll cry a little for both of us.*

"Do you want me to go?" she finally murmured.

"No. I want to lie right here on me until the entire Milky Way falls from the sky. You realize this changes nothing. You're mine. You'll continue to be mine. And vice versa. There will be other nights. This kind of thing happens all the time among my folk. We've both been under a lot of stress. And frankly, I'm not sure I'm up to all this training."

"Oh, Klein, I can see what you're trying to do. I don't want you to just boink me for charity and kiss me as some kind of stupid penance. I'd rather that you just go crazy with ecstasy with all those girls every single day. I don't want to just sip tea with you and pretend neither of us misses what we had."

"It can be better, as great as it was before."

"I've got to go."

"Please tell me you'll come back tomorrow night. And every night after that."

"The day after tomorrow is when you need to confront Tays'she. If we wait any longer we won't be able to stop FastTrack. It has something to do with a Hyperion ship that's arriving. One ambush has already happened. Once you see Tays'she, there may be no more tomorrows for us. I have a bad feeling."

"That's why it has to be us. Tomorrow night. And if you come, I will prove to you that there will be no end. We will have lots of tomorrows. As many as we want."

"Wait for me tomorrow night," she muttered in an odd tone of voice.

Early in the morning, Klein attached a note to his door announcing there would be no training and grabbed a tram to the ag station to see Peebo to make important preparations. The farmer greeted him warmly, maybe because he had feared his friend might already have gotten into trouble, but he shared some very disturbing news. Peebo had been to the Spaceport to book passage on the Hyperion ship that had just arrived and talked with some disembarking passengers, who told him that the ship had a piggy-back attack craft with it. Very unusual and very dangerous, considering that the Song Pai had a ban on foreign military vessels in the system and they loved to shoot to kill. Peebo was worried that the Brotherhood planned to use their company allies to launch some kind of a strike to take out Entara. When Klein shared with him all that he had learned about FastTrack, just to insure documentation in case worst came to worst, Peebo was more positive than ever. He urged Klein to find a safe haven in the matriline properties for Entara and her children, but Klein came up with a little deceptive plan that he thought might ensure even better safety for them and they reviewed it carefully before parting.

Back at the mahäme, he found a packet of video tabs and a note from the three guardians of the institution telling him to view them and come see them if he had any questions. He quickly found that the tabs contained training sequences for the girls, but not of the type he had become familiar with. They were for the classes that dealt with mating and birth, obligatory for the entire matriline, since even non-mated women were almost always called to serve as post-mating or birth attendants. The mating videos shocked him with their goriness. The piercing of the female Forlani body by her aroused mate was more than any earthly woman could even endure. As the ventral diaphragms were ripped apart by the stiffened and knife-like male organ, there was an incredible loss of blood and tissue. As soon as the male had satisfied his rutting rage, an automatic sensor in the room summoned attendants to help the unconscious mother-to-be. The knowledge they needed to preserve her life went far beyond first aid and made human obstetrics look like a child's tea party. Lifelike animation showed how Forlani sperm was preserved almost indefinitely in a particular area of the wife's body and continued to be released to fertilize her ova through a periodic hormonal process that lasted for decades and decades. The number of pregnancies possible from a single mating reached into the hundreds. The birth videos were equally shocking, but in a different way. Instead of human delivery, with an Earthling woman grunting, pushing, screaming, and sometimes writhing in agony, the Forlani mother experienced an orgasmic thrill that could last the better part of a day, as the emerging fetus stimulated an entirely new nervous network that had formed, also through the silent miracle of hormonal change, as her body reorganized itself in the months after mating. Klein thought of a famous sculpture of the passion of St. Teresa of Avila, but the expression of rapture projected by that marble could not begin to capture the happiness of the Forlani delivering her child. The video explained that this nervous discharge had its biological function as it simultaneously ramped by lactic production in the mammaries and began the process of releasing another ovum for fertilization high up at the top of the birth organs. Not only that: the expression on the face of the birth mother indicated more than an orgasmic pleasure, for there was clearly some kind of psychic enlightenment that accompanied the physical transformation, a surprise that was also a confirmation, a liberation that was also a redemption. Klein groped for concepts to express what he saw but came to the frustrating conclusion that his own emotional vocabulary would always be too limited to translate it.

As a last resort, he decided he needed to get some advice from the mahäme-ki. They awaited him in their office, behind a typical Forlani crescent-shaped table, adorned in the glowing robes that indicated their rank and function.

"Your honors," he began in confusion, inwardly cursing himself for addressing them as though they were human judges, "Before I leave this place, I want to thank you for all you and the matriline have done for me, but I have one urgent question. You obviously know of my affection for a certain member of your lineage. But recently I have found it difficult to ... express that affection... in a way that I can consider adequate. Please tell me: for a woman, no, a wife among the Forlani, is there a way that I can please her so that I restore the joy we felt before she was mated?"

"You have reviewed the videos we sent?" asked the first speaker.

"Very carefully, but they do not seem to give my answer."

"Because you do not wish to hear it. You might as well ask if you could scoop up the Eastern Sea with a dessert spoon."

"Or capture the clouds in a bucket," remarked the second speaker. "Your own expectations cloud your vision. Can't you cease to be a slave to your own sensuality?"

"But I am not just talking about a physical reaction!" blustered Klein. "I don't seek anything for myself."

"Are you so sure of that?" retorted the third speaker. "Do you not recognize that this shiver of passion you seek is only a key, and also a cloak, for a deeper desire, an unquenched desire, that you have never truly faced?"

"There can't be anything deeper for me than Entara. With her I know I can be truly happy and demand nothing else."

"You create your own illusion, like our pets who play with a ball of fluff and imagine it is prey," explained the second. "That ball of fluff you wish to capture has a mind of its own, and that mind has now gone to a place where you cannot accompany it. You will drive yourself mad by trying, and whether you wish to or not, whether you know it or not, you will blame Entara for failing to be that which you desire, and which she has now surpassed. She is an extremely compassionate person. How do you think it will affect her when she senses this?"

"Because she will!" blurted the first speaker, striking the table with her fist. "In fact, I'm sure she already has. Do you want to destroy the very thing of beauty you want to hold?"

The third speaker paused a bit before intervening. "Make yourself grasp, Teacher Klein, that in order for you to truly cherish memory, you must allow it to dwell where it belongs, in the past, and not distort it by placing it in the prison of an imaginary future."

"I have trouble dealing with all this. Especially now."

"Then do now what you must," said the first speaker. "Live in your actions for the present and be mindful of all that you do. When you turn to your memories again, force yourself to understand what my colleague has just said, if you cannot come to those thoughts naturally. It is a discipline, a challenge, that I impose on you."

"You can't give me orders as though I was one of your members."

"Oh, but you are," the second speaker added softly. "Because the moment you touched Entara's heart, you became a part of this matriline, according to your intention or against it. You are now of us. You always will be until after your death. That is a promise, not an obligation."

The others nodded at what she said, and the first speaker gestured to Klein that he was free to leave the room.

"That cleared up absolutely nothing," muttered Klein to himself as he walked down the corridor. "Tonight Entara will come to my room as she promised and even if I am too stupid to come up with a solution, maybe fate will be kind and offer one herself." He hurried off to his room to see to some further details for the day of confrontation that would follow.

By nightfall, he had done all he could in the way of preparations. Waiting for Entara, he put some music on the sound system, a series of Schumann piano pieces he hoped would rouse his courage and somehow inspire him. Instead, it caused him to doze off from sheer mental exhaustion. The room was pitch black by the time Quetzalcoatl, his little sentinel, roused him once again from slumber and told him someone else had entered his quarters. Unable to see all the corners from his chair, the half-conscious Klein rose to survey the whole room. Then he felt the point of a blade behind his ribs, in just the right place to pierce his heart.

"Don't move. I know how to use this and I will if you even budge." It was a voice he recognized, Ayan'we's voice! Instinctively, Klein was about to move to Horse Position and disarm the intruder, but something stopped him. Was it curiosity, trust? No time to ponder.

"Now kneel down slowly."

"Ayan'we there's no need to worry. I won't harm you. Look, I'll do as you say."

"It's not me I'm worried about," she hissed, as she slipped the knife next to his throat. "I'm only doing this because I have to."

"Your mother may not approve."

Ayan'we began to breathe hard and then snapped, "Mom is going to kill herself if I don't kill you first!"

"My God, Ayan'we, that can't be true."

"I heard her talking to herself most of the day. She was pacing back and forth and moaning. I know she promised you one more night together, but then she plans to take poison. I saw her prepare it myself. I sneaked in and read the instructions she's left about caring for me and my sisters, and some legal stuff to make sure Tays'she didn't take all her credits and pensions." The knife was quivering in her hand. She was a very unwilling assassin, but as good as the next.

"OK, Ayan'we. I'd rather have you do this than some goon protecting your father. Stop and take a long breath. Believe me, I've done this before and it helps."

Ayan'we seemed to be sobbing. Klein took a deep breath himself and released it slowly, to show her. "And when you cut, do it deep and hard. I would consider that a favor."

Suddenly another shadow emerged from beside the door to the patio. "Ayan'we, don't you dare stir." It was Entara. "I've been listening to everything. I was even here before you came, waiting, because I had no idea what to say to Klein when I decided to wake him."

"This is the best thing, Mother, I've worked it all out. Don't try to stop me."

"Actually, you have worked it out, but murdering him is not the answer. It was you who showed me the way. Just now everything fell into place for me. I know what I have to do. How I have to take charge. Those thoughts of suicide were stupidity – seductive and powerful, but still stupidity."

"Mom, what are you saying?"

"What I am saying, daughter, is come stand by my side. And if you won't drop that weapon, prepare to use it to defend me, because together we will be facing some dangerous possibilities. Come to my room and help me with all the FastTrack evidence. We have to summon the mahäme-ki."

"Mother, I don't think it will solve anything just to prove it to them."

"No. I am also going to confess everything. Even all that has taken place between us," she added, turning to Klein. "What happens to me is now inseparable from what happens to all the sisters."

"Mother, even a confession in this compound won't solve much."

"It won't confess just to the mahäme. We're going with the mahäme-ki to the Council of Nine."

After a second of absorbing the shock, Ayan'we slid the knife into her waist belt and slowly stepped to her mother, who put an arm on her shoulders. "We're in this together from now on," Entara said softly. "I am invoking the Privilege of First Birth and keeping you by my side, though the Nine may well take away your sisters and all the other children I may bear."

"I understand, mom," said Ayan'we, hugging her close.

"And do you understand, Schatzi" she asked tenderly, turning to Klein. "Because this may be forever. I had so many apologies prepared for you tonight, for both before and after we came together. But Ayan'we's right. You would just have been embracing a corpse, and it was gruesome of me to try to steal a little joy, or a little pardon, before you understood that."

"This is better," Klein agreed, with a somewhat forced shrug. "Now everyone is in his place. And headed in the right direction. I know mine. Will the Council of Nine put you in a place of total safety?"

"I don't know."

"Then ask them to keep you here," said Klein, slipping her piece of paper. "Goodbye, darling. I will try to be in touch if I can."

Klein knew he had to try to manage some more sleep before he faced what he had to do the next morning, but before he did, he called Peebo on an open com link. "Entara and her daughter will be in hiding for a few days. If you need to reach them, they'll be at a place called the Sweet Plum Lodge, twenty-two kilometers northeast of Plambo'. It's normally closed in this season, but I rented Unit

Number Three as a hideout. Good luck on your ride back to Domremy."

As soon as he had returned Klein's wish, Peebo dialed another number, one that an agent of the Brotherhood had given him several days earlier, along with a large sum of Hyperion credits. He repeated very exactly the location Klein had just given him.

Early the next morning, Klein was strolling up the avenue towards Entara's home, clad in his workman's coverall and carrying a box that was nearly empty. The injector, fully loaded, was in his pocket. In the box was a stick he had found in the Garden of Fulfillment that he had fashioned into a formidable assault baton, along with some plastic bags and brushes. Verifying that the "neighborhood people" were in various places near the house, he went to a waste receptacle at the edge of the park, moving slowly like a reluctant chap who was paid by the hour, and took a long time replacing the trash bag with a new one. He had a good view of the house and yard and eventually spotted one dobutu. That was good news and bad. Good because it would mean he only had to get by one opponent to get in the door. Bad because he was sure others were lurking unseen elsewhere on the property. He couldn't see any security cameras on the outside, but that didn't mean they were not there. They were probably so well disguised that only the installers knew their location.

In his same lackadaisical, Willie-the-Workman pace, he turned the corner into the side street and quickly ascertained that there was only one state security person on that post, sipping a drink on the sidewalk farther up. Lazily, he drew a brush from his box and began to scrub the low stucco wall on that side of the house. After a moment, he glanced up the street and saw that his activities did not seem to have aroused the attention of the surveillant. Nor did he hear the dobutu shuffling his way. Transport traffic was picking up at the corner up the street and he only had to wait for a loud noise that might distract security for a second. It was not long in coming, as two transports scraped each other, starting a row between the drivers. Crouched low, Klein popped in the yard's side entrance, shoving his box noiselessly into the bushes. Now the goon. He was walking Klein's way and would be even with him in seconds. Klein thought of a way he could disable him without making any noise. *They don't seem too smart. Maybe I should walk up and say, "Your shoe's untied."* Instead, he found a big pebble on the ground and lofted it over to his the wall on the other side of the dobutu. When the unwitting victim turned around, Klein bashed him on the neck with a wicked blow of the baton. A quick glance at the neighborhood showed no reaction. He dashed to the door of the dwelling and breathed a sigh of relief to find it unlocked. There was no sign of anyone inside.

Crossing the living area, Klein entered the room that Tays'she and Entara had once shared. The light domes were dimmed, but Klein could still make out the brilliant blue and green hues of the painting of the Great Spiral of Being on the left wall. He could see Tays'she's darkened form standing in front of the bed, the glint of his yellow eyes shining in the darkened surroundings. *Forlani evolved from crepuscular creatures,* Klein thought. *He must know enough about humans to realize that we didn't. Entara had no idea how much she underestimated his guile.*

"You've come to kill me, Klein," Tays'she said. "Too bad, I have a gun trained on your heart right now." Klein could see it was a human Marine-issue sidearm, probably another thoughtful Company gift. The Forlani male voice had a calmly arrogant, self-assured quality to it. "I'm going to kill you in a minute. Don't make any moves, or I'll end your life a little early."

"You don't necessarily have to die. I'm just here to take you to people who will ask you some questions about FastTrack."

"Along with my dear Entara and her brat, no doubt. Too bad, Klein, there will be no corroborating witnesses, because my friends at Hyperion have a way of eliminating them and you, you fool, even supplied their coordinates. No, you're as good as dead. Why don't you tell me some details about how much you enjoyed slipping inside Entara's fresh little body? I know I did when we mated! An experience you'll never have, idiot."

He may have me in a bad position, but I bet I can still use his arrogance against him, Klein thought. "Before you kill me, tell me—how did you do it? How did you get involved in a conspiracy to sell your own people into slavery? Did you have connections with someone high up in the Forlani government?"

"Tell *you*, an off-world *ga'hor*, how I executed my plan? So you could tell others how much I profited from it, or steal the plans yourself? No, before you die I think I'll tell you *why* I did it. I've been a very, very bored man since I was married to my *true* First Wife, Ara'she. She was very hardworking, very religious."

Klein listened to the tone of Tays'she's voice. The concentration and focus in it wavered ever so slightly, as if he was slowly being distracted by the memories of his own life. Klein's muscles tensed, waiting for the opportune moment to strike.

"She was one of the Picks-the-Fruit people, from a poor matriline," Tays'she continued. "Loyal and honorable, like no other woman I've known. But even *she* grew curious of my side projects—how I *really* earned our money and strove to lift her out of poverty. When she learned the truth—that *olata*-- she couldn't put her honor aside! She would have revealed..."

Klein's attack came suddenly, just as Tays'she was becoming lost in the frustrations of his past. He brutally tackled Tays'she to the ground, jarring the gun from his hand and sending it flying across the room. He grabbed Tays'she's throat in his right hand, choking him out as he reached into in his pocket with his left and slipped on the injector, cocking the first dose into place. Klein had failed to pin either of Tays'she's arms, counting on his forceful tackle and choke to keep Tays'she immobile long enough to administer the dose. Klein saw Tays'she's left hand pull a slender metal object from his legging and stab it into Klein's right arm. Klein felt an immediate, horrible pain spreading through the limb, and released his choke on the opponent's throat, grabbing Tays'she's left arm by the wrist.

Klein could feel his right arm growing weaker by the second as it struggled to hold back Tays'she's knife-wielding hand. Tays'she butted his opponent twice with the horn-like bumps on his head, opening gushing lacerations, and forcefully kneed him in the ribs, making him grunt in pain as agony continued to flow through his body. Tays'she began to roar in profane rage as he hammered Klein's face with blows from his free right hand. *"Ga'hor! Meh'tra!"* he yelled as he bludgeoned the human with his fist. Klein could see yellow and white lights dancing across his vision as he struggled to position the syringe with his left hand. Tays'she gave a triumphant hiss as it seemed like Klein's right arm was about to give out, flexing his fingers as he prepared to stab with the knife...

With a berserk cry, Klein unleashed a lightning-fast left hook to Tays'she's face. Stunned by the force of the blow, Tays'she's knife-wielding arm slackened briefly. Klein grabbed it with as well as he could with his tortured right arm and brought his left around to position the injector at the neck. Klein could feel the surge of adrenaline that had powered his punch fading as Tays'she gripped him. The enemy's thrashing body felt hard as iron to Klein's weakened arm, and he yelled in agony. With Tays'she holding both his arms and the venom from the knife coursing through his veins, Klein knew time was not on his side as he was locked in combat.

As blood from the impact of Tays'she's head butts and punches trickled into his eyes, Klein felt a final, tremendous rush of adrenaline roar through his body. He drew his head back and put all his strength into a head butt of his own, smashing into Tays'she's nose like a meteor. He could feel Tays'she's grip on his injector-arm weakening, and finally wrestled it free. Blood and light blurring his vision, he stabbed the syringe into Tays'she's vulnerable neck, plunging it into his foe's artery with a force strengthened by rage and hatred. *For me, Entara, Ayan'we...and your true First Wife, the woman you murdered. Burn, fucker, burn.* Then he thought of an explosion engulfing Entara and Ayan'we. Ruthlessly, he clicked a second dose into the injector with his ring finger and rammed it home. *And this is for my little family.*

The horrific scream from Tays'she's lips sounded like beautiful music to Klein. Klein's terrible suffering mixed with euphoria at the sight and sound of his hated rival's utter defeat. He watched as Tays'she began to writhe and convulse, his screaming becoming more erratic. But the joy of victory faded quickly, replaced by a throbbing, burning pain that seemed to eat him from inside out.

Damn! That venom will be the death of me unless I make it to a medkit this instant! As Klein grabbed for his cell phone to call Entara, he watched as a change came over Tays'she's facial convulsions. The snide, hateful arrogance was replaced by a fearful, almost *subhuman* stare, as if Tays'she was losing his higher mental functions. Finally the convulsions and pain stopped, replaced by a soft quivering as Entara's mate lay in passive silence. Tays'she – if the twitching, animalistic *thing* he had been reduced to could still be called by that name – reacted nervously as Klein stepped away to scan the room for geldings. He had barely made two steps when they both came at him together, brandishing their poison whips. *Just what I need, more fucking poison!* Fortunately the Marine sidearm still lay on the floor, and with a rapid dive and roll it was in Klein's hands and two fragmentation rounds had took off most of the geldings' heads. He didn't need to know the "neighborhood people" would already be on their way after hearing the detonations, so he rushed for the side door and dove into the bushes. Seconds later, two female feet were visible only a meter or so away and a voice was saying into a comlink, "Agent four, west zone scanning." Damn, she was good, but then he had probably left a blood trail like a mountain stream.

"Up," she ordered, and Klein obeyed, thinking *Maybe this is the best way to go after all.* Facing him was a no-nonsense young woman with a stun weapon pointed directly where it would do the most good. But when she looked at him a different expression spread over her features, a kind of confused frown, and she lowered her stunner. *She recognizes me!* Making up her mind, she did a quick three-six-nine-twelve of the area and nodded towards the side yard entrance. "Go right," she hissed, "And walk, don't run." *I guess she didn't want to be the one to end the legend of Klein and Entara, even if it costs her a reprimand.* Then he asked himself how the hell he was supposed to saunter down the street with blood gushing from him. When he reached the corner drink shop, he saw it was providentially empty and the server was down behind the counter sorting something out. He spotted a washroom door and bolted for it, quickly rinsing off the blood and fastening makeshift bandages from a cloth towel. It was only then that his heart slowed down enough that he remembered and dared pull out a com card on a lanyard around his neck. The little purple light was still on, and he breathed a long sigh. Entara and Ayan'we were safe and sound in a room in the maternity wing of the mahäme hospital, under the watch of Ragatti, and Hyperion had just blown up a vacation unit on the far outskirts of Plambo' that was, unbeknownst to them, quite empty.

Peebo was already aboard the Hyperion ship that had undocked from orbit and hastily departed as it dispatched its little fighter to eliminate the witnesses. No need to worry about recovering it, because at that very second a single interceptor from Carrier 12 had just blown it to bits in the upper atmosphere of Forlan. The Song Pai pilot was cross, since this mission offered no prospects for a glorious self-immolation, or even a remotely worthy enemy, so he decided to engage in some helpful target practice, following the bits of Hyperion spacecraft and crew as they fell to the ground and blasting them into even smaller pieces. "If I can't seek a death that would release my seed, I'll just disintegrate every one of yours, you worms!" he snorted, before signalling "Out of ammo. Homebound."

Back on the more solid world, Klein still had the problem of getting away. The mahäme was out of the question, since it would certainly be under immediate surveillance, but he had written in his note to Entara that he would make it to the Orchards of Fataarey. Never having thought of how to actually get there in his current condition, he was dumbfounded until he noticed there was a second, forgotten card on his lanyard with an orange dot. He quickly pressed it twice. Before he knew it, there was a whirling sound outside the shop that indicated a transport had arrived for its fare and he dashed out the door and into Canthli's passenger compartment. "Mr. Klein, my goodness, let me get you to a hospital," she blurted out.

"No way. Please take me in an inconspicuous way to the Orchards and help me find an out-of-the-way place to rest."

Forgetting for a moment her infatuation with the stranger, Canthli did as directed and found a quiet grove with cover. She helped Klein from the transport, saw to his wounds as best she could with her first aid kit, covering him with kisses and caresses and insisting on comforting all parts of his body in such a way that Klein found it amazingly enjoyable. After he had fallen asleep, she drove off, but parked at the entrance of the Orchards to watch over her new friend and protect him from any threatening types that might arrive. *What am I going to do? Maybe I can set fire to the transport to cause a distraction?* She didn't have to entertain these noble but frivolous thoughts forever, because she, too, soon fell asleep.

Klein was eventually awakened by a young voice chirping out, "Teacher! Teacher!" When he replied in sotto voce, he found it was a schoolgirl. She gave a whistle and others appeared, with Ayan'we at their head. She took one look at him and frowned. "*Meh'tra,* are you a mess!"

"Thanks. Why are you here Ayan'we?"

"Who were you expecting, Joan of Arc?" This caused an explosion of giggling among the girls, an inside joke for their Earth history class. "Mom's officially confined to the hospital, when she's not with the Council of Nine. It's actually a good thing, since I'll have another sib within forty-eight hours. My sisters are visiting with Aunt Babatra, and you've managed to kill everybody else that was home. Too bad you didn't get my rotten stepmother, too, but she has run off with all the jewelry. Ragatti's watching over Mom and all the oh-so-responsible adults are confined to the mahäme, pending investigation, so we decided to have a little class trip. How can we help?"

"My arm is just about paralyzed from some poison you father was kind enough to stick me with, so an antidote would be good."

The girls huddled, whispering, and one ran off. "We think we know what it might be and my friend's bringing back something to help. What else?"

"I'll need some clothes that are not covered in blood, something that will disguise me, if possible."

"No problem. Anything more?"

"How about some food?"

"Duh, you're right in the middle of an orchard! Well, I suppose in your shape, you have a good excuse. We'll gather some for you. Wait here."

The schoolgirls fanned out and were soon bringing him handfuls of fruit so juicy that it slaked his thirst as well. While they were waiting, he asked Ayan'we if she could find him a way off-planet, for, as she reminded him, it was not just the Security forces he needed to worry about, but the Brotherhood, which was hopping mad and had mobilized their usually lazy ranks down to the last man to cover Plambo' and the rest of the planet, with orders to kill Klein on sight. The girls were soon tapping and commanding away at a variety of handheld computer pads and links, scouring the digisphere for a way for Klein to leave. In a while one returned with a vial of stuff that was supposed to counteract many poisons, a bottle of Forlani antibiotics, and numerous salves that the girls fought over as to who would get to apply them to the patient. Most of them paid absolutely no attention to Ayan'we's claim that "He's mine." Finally the clothes arrived and Klein was horrified when they were unfolded to see it was a kind of black bourka that an old woman might wear in the bazaar in Kabul if she were extremely devout.

"What the hell I am supposed to do with this?"

"What's the matter with you?" Ayan'we pouted. "It's a robe for engineering graduates and this is the right time of year, so no one should notice you as a human. Besides it's all we can find that's big enough. What, do you object to the color or something? Frankly, I don't think you should be so vain in your predicament."

"Fine, fine. So I'll be an engineer," Klein conceded, slipping the thing over him. He had to admit; it offered virtually complete concealment.

"People will offer you congratulations wherever you go, 'cause engineers are big shots, so just answer Plakka, plakka".

"Now what about a ticket home?"

One girl who had been organizing the digital search stepped forward and announced, "Bad news, teacher. There is only one ship docked and planning departure very soon, and no new arrivals are expected for about seven weeks. More bad news. It's a military ship. Even more bad news, it's Song Pai, and they're headed to the home planet. The only good news is that they have an ad out for indentures to do grunge jobs on the ship for almost no pay. Are you interested?" Her finger hovered above the response key.

"We have a saying, beggars can't be choosers."

"We have that, too," she chirped and she punched the key. "You have two hours to get to the Spaceport."

With that, the gaggle of girls began to break up, except for Ayan'we and two friends with late curfews. They accompanied Klein to a tram and went with him to the Spaceport. Anyone they crossed gave a respectful gesture to the engineering gown and offered congratulations, to which Klein responded with garbled plakka, plakkas. The only tense moment came at the entrance to the Spaceport, where a couple of security guards eyed the unlikely group curiously and some males stirred menacingly in the background.

Ayan'we disarmed the situation right away by prancing up to the guards and announcing, "Cousin Pinni's just got her degree and she's taking us on a vacation to the waterfalls on Flunie and we're going to make the reservations right now."

"Gosh, I wish I could go there, too," remarked the guard. "I've never been off-planet. Have you, Pu'una?" Congratulations and plakka-plakka's were exchanged and once in the port, the girls were in a hurry to head for their homes.

"I can never thank you enough for helping me, Ayan'we. I wish I could give you a message for your mother, but I don't think I'd ever have enough time. "

"Don't worry. You're stamped in Mother's memories forever as it is. As for me, I just might visit you again someday, maybe in a long time, but don't be surprised if I do."

"Nothing you do would surprise me. Goodbye."

When he had tossed his bourka and gone to the area where the indentures were being processed, he was relieved to see his disheveled underclothes were not much worse than the majority of bums that were signing up for this terrible job, mostly in hopes of scoring another hit of drugs in some off-world dive. He hardly noticed the documents he signed but as soon as he headed up the ramp to the lighter, he caught the overwhelming stench of Song Pai and knew that he would never get used to it.

7

Peebo sat alone in a booth in the flight lounge of the *Hyperion Duchess*, occasionally sipping a glass of cider without enjoying it and staring down at a thick envelope in front of him that was stuffed with company credits – his payoff from grateful executives for ratting out Entara and her children. Even though that was all a ruse devised by him and Klein to put them in safety, he still considered it blood money. People had been killed in exchange. It's true the pilots of the craft dispatched from the *Duchess* had planned to murder friends of the Circle, but they were still living beings. Though the company had already written them off as expendables, announcing in a bulletin that a "utility craft" from the liner had been unfortunately lost while attempting to retrieve space debris, Peebo felt compassion for them. It would just add to all the heavy burdens he would bring back to Domremy.

Ironically, the heaviest burden was something he wasn't bringing back, for he had no idea what had become of Klein. He obviously had not been apprehended, because the Brotherhood was fuming mad and doing everything to track him down. They had even contacted Peebo via deep space link and peppered him with questions on where he thought his former partner might be hiding. Peebo had given them the story that he believed Klein to be dead somewhere on Forlan, since he had expressed suicidal thoughts at being separated from Entara. He had accepted still more credits from them as a way of further deflecting any suspicions they might have. But deep down inside, Peebo felt Klein was alive somewhere, unlikely as it might be.

Of course, extracts from Entara's testimony before the Council of Nine had been big news while the *Duchess* was still picking up the transmissions in Forlan space. Her self-assurance was nothing if not inspirational, and it was clear the Council was treating her more as an equal than as a wrongdoer. She had skewered FastTrack so completely that no such scheme would ever be possible in the future. There were even a few views of her in the hospital nursing a new-born infant.

However, Peebo felt genuine grief and guilt when they broadcast reports of what had happened to

Tays'she. He would never be interrogated about his role in FastTrack because he had been reduced to a mindless, drooling zombie. It was clear that Klein had violated his oath and used more than one dose of venom, for which Peebo would rightly be considered equally responsible. Tays'she's cerebral cortex had been irreparably destroyed, leaving only a few of the lower brain functions in operation. He could breathe and be fed through a tube and led around by a handler, but he had no idea where he was, who he was, or even that he existed on more than a minute-by-minute basis. In many ways, it was worse than ordinary murder. It astonished him that, despite all that had happened, Entara refused to abandon him, as his official First Wife had abruptly done. Entara told the Council that she considered it her duty, as mother of Tays'she's offspring, to care for him and honor him as long as he may live. It seemed to Peebo to be a ghastly idea for a household, but if anyone could bring it off, it would be her.

Peebo also worried about details, like what had happened to the injector. Another missing piece of the puzzle he would have to explain back home. He hoped that Klein had had the presence of mind to destroy it. What Peebo didn't know was that between the confrontation and his hurried departure from Forlan, Klein had quite simply forgotten about the injector and the remaining shots of venom. They had actually been taken by the transport driver Canthli. Before making love to Klein in the Orchard of Fataarey, she had removed it from his hand. Afterwards, when he was asleep, she took it away along with his bloodstained coverall and left him to sleep in the clothes he was wearing underneath. They weren't exactly pristine, but she felt she would help by getting rid of as much evidence as she could, including this strange glove-like thing that might be a weapon. When she found that Klein had apparently left the Orchard, she brought the packet of incriminating stuff back to the transport barn and dissolved it all in battery acid. Had Peebo known that her kindness had taken this precaution, he would have had one less lapse to grieve over.

News on the telescreens still carried some reports of the ongoing investigation. The Brotherhood had immediately issued an official demand that Klein be prosecuted for murder, injury, and assault against several of their order. They had gotten their buddies in Hyperion to turn the *Duchess* upside-down in case he had stowed away, even though the time sequence for such an escape was illogical. The official statements of Forlani Planetary Security were much more cautious and discreet. They simply said Klein had been summoned to ask questions about possible immigration violations and violent incidents. They said that, as for Tays'she's horrible injuries, the cause had not been positively determined by the police examiner, and that the two dobutu had been "injured" by an unauthorized weapon that had been traced to Tays'she himself. While they acknowledged that Klein's blood had been found with all the others at the scene, it was unclear to them exactly who had been fighting whom, and that the guards might have been attacking both Klein and Tays'she with poison whips when the homeowner himself neutralized them. Interestingly, the little story of the bombing of a vacation unit at Sweet Plum Resort had been buried in small print as a gas explosion suspected of happening in the heating system. The Forlani patrol force and the Song Pai, who knew perfectly well about the Hyperion incursion, were obviously saying nothing.

Peebo was growing completely tired and irritated by the news when the screen thankfully changed to a sports event. He left the rest of his cider, took up the cursed envelope, and went to his cabin to sleep. Three more weeks of long sleeps before he could wake up to Felicia.

When he finally strode up to his old farm, Peebo felt a temporary flood of relief come over him. The whole brood was out in front of the house waiting for him, along with Cousin Al and a cheery Asian neighbor named Park who had overseen help for the family while Peebo was away. Children raced up to him and grabbed him by the legs and the waist, Park trotted up bowing to shake his hand, and Felicia just waited, beaming, as he approached to kiss her. It was a long kiss, and Peebo noticed that the usually stoical Al, who always reminded him a bit of the fellow in the painting

American Gothic, was chuckling away in amusement at his relative's homecoming and couldn't wait to tell long stories about it to the others in the Circle. After a meal that could only be likened to a banquet with all the favorites he had missed so much during his months away, Peebo retired to his bedroom to change, but Felicia had other ideas and followed him, closing and latching the door behind them. Peebo was overjoyed to find that her hunger for his body after this long separation equaled or exceeded his own.

They didn't emerge from the room until nearly noon the next day. The children, accustomed to adopting adult responsibilities during their years in Central Africa, had cleaned up after the previous evening's meal, finished the farm chores, bedded down without making a sound, risen the next morning, and prepared not only their own breakfast, but an exemplary lunch for their parents, complete with a bouquet of Domremy wildflowers in the center of the table.

It was that way for several weeks, for Felicia told him when they were next to each other in bed that she was not a woman to be satisfied with a simple one-night stand. In the afternoons, she accompanied him to the gardens and fields, boasting about all the improvements they had made during his absence. Once they even clasped each other in the middle of a patch of ripening barley and enjoyed each other al fresco, with the light breeze passing over their sweaty bodies.

Of course, Peebo delighted in his kids, too. They took turns on his lap at home or on the sofa beside him, showing him the books that they had read, their artwork, the new pets they had chosen among the livestock and farm animals, the little gadgets they had cobbled together while they had the run of his tool bench. He couldn't believe how lucky he was. But finally one day after nearly a month of this idyll, he woke up in the morning, pulled on his clothes, and walked over to Cousin Al's to request a meeting of the Circle the following night.

Although, soon after his homecoming, Peebo had turned the blood money over to Felicia to present to the Dissenters, as seemed appropriate to him, memories of his thoughts back on the space ship returned as he approached the barn chosen for the encounter. Facing him across the ashes were Trevor, Al, Park, Dr. Patak, and most of the members of the community, as well as a Hispanic-looking fellow who stayed in the background, perhaps a novice. Invited to speak his piece, Peebo laid out the whole lone story of the Forlan adventure, his own experiences and as much of Klein's as he could accurately recount. When he had finished this oral deposition, members of the group asked a few detailed questions before proceeding to the matter of his personal feelings. He told them he felt entirely guilty for the violence that had spilled over on Forlan. He should have intervened much earlier, he said, to persuade Klein to give up the whole enterprise. He should have stayed in closer contact with Entara and her family. He should have personally assured the destruction of the injector and venom. He should have found a way of staying longer on the planet, instead of letting Klein convince him to book on the *Hyperion Duchess*. Finally, he should have taken charge himself of Klein's removal from Domremy and brought him back to the Circle to explain things in person. Peebo also confessed to cowardice, for his haste to get away from Forlan was undoubtedly related to his horror of getting stranded there in a fiasco over which he had lost control, and which risked separating him from his family forever.

When his testimony was over, Trevor simply said, "Withdraw." Peebo knew this meant he should walk back to the far end of the barn and let them discuss his situation. It was quite a long conversation they had, with everyone but the newcomer taking part, and many opinions being brought out, reconsidered, dropped or polished up. Finally, a gesture from Trevor called him back.

"There is something you are leaving out. Perhaps you have not realized this yourself. Remember and reveal."

"There is more, Trevor. Sometime before we decided to leave Domremy, I had to take a life myself. It was unavoidable. A man named Dorfman came to my farm looking for Klein. He was a mutilator of children on the Evil Earth, someone whose plots Klein had tried to reveal. He came for vengeance and murder, to cover up more of his misdeeds. He defiled my fields. He was stalking a friend of the Circle. Had I allowed him to proceed, he would have brought misery everywhere. I did it quickly and hid the evidence. I have no regrets for killing that man."

"Are you sure, Peebo? Are you truly sure you have no regrets, or have you been hiding them from yourself? Probe deeply into your own horrors and confront them. Ask if they did not influence you in this cock-up on Forlan."

Peebo closed his eyes and soon came to grips with that very horror Trevor had just suggested. Peebo himself was responsible for a killing. Perhaps not a murder, but the violent taking of life just the same. He had known it as soon as he jabbed that fork into Dorfman's body and felt its convulsions through the wooden shaft. He had known he had gone to a dark place. A darkness he had tried to cover, just as the soil had covered Dorfman's corpse. Darkness he had tried to joke about and to turn to good, turning the rotten flesh into wholesome vegetables. He remembered a saying from his Dissenter studies: Matter changes all too easily, but the changes of the spirit are as slow to happen as the life of stars. Then it all came to him, the reality of Forlan.

"My god, you're right. My killing Dorfman caused me to neglect Klein. Deep within I knew it, but I tried to blame it on Klein, on the Forlani and their strange ways, but all the time I was hiding my guilt. I was afraid to be responsible for more killing, afraid others would know, but more so that I would know. I didn't want to sully myself with what Klein had to do because I was afraid of what it would make me. But what I wound up doing was worse. Klein acted only out of instinct and necessity, as well as out of passion and the need to protect Entara, but my way was the coward's way, unable to stand up to the terrible truth and making my friend the culprit in my place. Even though the revelation of it all seems so horrible, I feel strangely more peaceful now that I understand. I suppose the dread of responsibility is always greater than the actual weight of it."

"You hit the spike and drive it home. Don't you see how futile your words would have been without this breakthrough?"

"I do. Now I am ready to hear what the Circle has determined."

"We find that your actions were faulty in several ways. Indeed, your handling of the traveling arrangements was awkward, even given the mitigating circumstances. You were lax in not maintaining closer contact with a man whom you judged more on your hopes than on rational expectations. Klein always presented himself as a being with a double edge. We can't understand why you didn't try to find out more about this Tays'she and his actions, or to make sure Klein had more alternatives in dealing with him other than a fairly obvious physical brawl. However, other than the lack of precautions, we cannot find you responsible for Klein's bloodshed. You would certainly have been slaughtered yourself if you had tried to interfere. As for the injector, nothing more has been heard of it in the reports, so we can assume Klein properly disposed of it himself. Now what do you propose? Keep in mind that we will not accept any violence to yourself or any permanent separation from your loved ones, who are blameless in this event."

Peebo took a deep breath and said, "I propose shunning and lifelong isolation at my farm."

A huddle followed on the other side of the circle, and this time it was Park who answered, "Rejected. Your contacts with the Brotherhood and Hyperion may prove of great value to us in the future, as they did in averting Entara's death. The money you brought back has already helped us transport over twenty people to join us on this world, and we hope to bring more. This is too precious a benefit to forego. Propose again."

"I propose an end to the research activities I have conducted for the Circle and exclusion from all councils planning decisions for the future."

This was a shorter huddle and Patak spoke for the group. "We are aware of the pride you have taken in your research work, which makes the proposal worthy of consideration on your side. However, in the greater interest, your discoveries have already saved and improved many lives, both among humans and others, and your mind offers many opportunities for the future. On the other hand, your role in furnishing a weapon for Klein is at most incidental, since we are sure he would have done as much or more to Tays'she with his bare hands, if necessary. Therefore, it would be ridiculous to approve this proposal."

"Then I propose a retreat of two years in a remote location, without the privilege of communication."

This huddle was longer again, as many people seemed to be discussing particular points, though without any discernible disagreement. It was Cousin Al who came to the forefront this time.

"You know as well as we do that a retreat is always in order for anyone who feels the need. But two consecutive years is too darn long. You also know as well as we do that Felicia is showing the first signs of being pregnant. It is enough of an imposition on that woman to leave her for a while, without forcing her to be alone at such a crucial moment as birth. We will approve a retreat of no more than seven months at the Ecological Research Station on the southern continent, but only if you maintain communication with your family once each week. When you finish this period and providing that the assembly feels you have ensured that all possible responsibilities on the farm and to the Circle have been accomplished, we will approve resumption of the retreat for no more than three months at a time. Do you accept this?"

Peebo did, and thanked them for their understanding. He walked home with a lighter heart, knowing that now his only qualms concerned the fate of Klein, wherever he may be.

Klein's hands were at the controls of a powerful piece of construction machinery, but he could not help thinking he was still just the same as a member of an old-time chain gang. The chains on his legs were distance and isolation. Carrier 12 had been a cesspool, almost literally. The Song Pai are amphibious cephalopods, so the ship was divided into wet and dry compartments, with Klein and the indentures confined, naturally, to the latter. The Song Pai preferred the water most of the time and confined their dry activities to certain types of storage and to latrine time. Coarsely put, they didn't want to shit in the water because there was only so much water on board and the excrement fouled up the life support systems. Moreover, they had carried defecation to the level of a competitive sport or even an obscene art. They delighted in outdoing each other with the longest, loudest, hardest, softest, thinnest, and widest of shitting. The worst was target shitting, when they chose an indenture who was considered lazy or disrespectful and covered him with feces in marathons that would include as much of the off-duty crew as possible. Having quickly learned the jailhouse rules from his former experience, Klein had avoided this humiliation, and it was the worst of the addicts among the indentures who were usually bulls-eyed. The Song Pai made it a point of never cleaning up after themselves -- after all, that's what servants were for, and heroic interceptor pilots were entitled to their fun.

Every day it was a continual slopping out and Klein wished that he were Hercules and could release some torrent through this octopod stable that would once and for all wash everything away. But it was always there in its fetid abundance and the only relief he got was to haul around heavy containers in a cargo hold. The food was atrocious and seemed to be permanently infected with God knows what amphibious germs, the bunks were rock-hard shelves, the entertainment was non-existent, and the atmosphere stifling. To make things worse, the homebound voyage actually put the crew in a dangerous mood, since relaxed discipline encouraged the Song Pai to give vent to their naturally aggressive nature. Fights among them broke out over the most trifling matters and scores were often lethally settled, for two of their tentacles were armed with razor-sharp claws that were nearly a foot long. It was commonplace to see limbs lopped off or organs torn out without spectators being able to understand how or why. The only compensation was that indentures were protected from these sprees because of their contracts, which were inexplicably sacred to the squids. So violence to humans, though frequent, was low-grade, limited to shoving, tripping, and insults. This was an acceptable outlet among them because of the strict military discipline, since even a minor infraction of the Song Pai command structure became the occasion for public torture of the perpetrator, which often involved setting fire to a large part of his body. In the midst of this chaos, Klein searched as best he could for an individual to match the badge he concealed on the lanyard around his neck, but he could not find the one who had violated him in the Processing Center at the Plambo' space port.

During the drudgery of the long voyage to Song Pa, only one day stood out in Klein's memory, for it opened a new mystery that nagged at his analytical powers. It started at the midday feeding – you couldn't call it a meal. The crowded mess hall on Carrier 12 was filled with foul stenches that assaulted Klein's nose. There was a strong stink of ammonia coming from the walls, and the brownish glop that that the server robots were giving out to the line of humans smelled like some kind of rotten meat, even though the robot claimed that the substance was "edible and nutritious" on its text screen. Klein doubted that any food that could be most highly praised as being "edible" would taste very good, and was proven right the moment he took a small bite of the grotesque mash. Klein plugged his nose and shoveled the vile stuff down his throat as fast as he possibly could to get the experience over with quickly. "That bad, eh?" a skinny man sitting next to Klein asked.

The rusty door to the mess hall slammed open, and a large Song Pai guard squeezed through it. He stood near the entryway and held up his text screen so that all could see. "ATTENTION," he texted in caps. "ALL INDENTURES STAY TO ASSIGNED JOBS. THOSE WHO VIOLATE WILL BE PUNISHED. TOO MUCH

INSUBORDINATION LATELY. OBEY OR ELSE." The Song Pai then left as abruptly as he had entered, slamming the door behind him.

"What did the Song Pai mean by insubordination?" Klein asked the skinny man. "Everything looks pretty much the same as it always does to me."

"Ask Gordon over there. He got roughed up by one of the Song Pai guards pretty bad over something. Hasn't said much since," the skinny man told Klein.

Klein put his plate in the cleaner bin and moved over to Gordon's table. Gordon was a sullen giant, his face depressed and fearful, his once-confident demeanor shattered by the cruelty of the Song Pai. He was eating what remained of his food at a glacial pace. "Why was that Song Pai talking about insubordination?" Klein asked Gordon.

Gordon sat still, slowly chewing his food. After two minutes that seemed interminable to Klein, he finally began to talk slowly. "I was cleaning off the walls in Sector 3 as usual—some Song Pai must have decided to play a game of who could spray the most elaborate patterns on the walls again—and I heard this weird, scuttling sound. I thought it might be some weird kind of vermin, like a really big rat, or some kind of nasty alien. So I got my mop out, and I was moving in the direction of the sounds to go bash the brains out of whatever it was. The sounds were getting louder and louder, but just as I was closing in, one of the Song Pai guards grabbed me! He gave me these," rolling up his shirt to reveal a collection of ugly scars from a whip. "Then he used one of those computers to tell me 'DO NOT SEEK THE LOWLY ONE.' Don't ever look like you're not working when you should be, that's all I got out of it," Gordon shrugged and went back to sitting in silence.

"At least the squid didn't shit all over you," Klein said in a feeble attempt at humor. Gordon remained silent and had no reaction. A siren began to blare, the signal to the humans to end their meal and get back to work.

Near the end of his shift, Klein realized that Gordon's story about the "lowly one" had been distracting him all day. If the "lowly one" was just a simple vermin, why would the Song Pai be so insistent that Gordon not find and kill it? The Song Pai themselves were horrendously filthy and paid little heed to vermin, forcing the indentures to kill the rats and other creatures in the bunks themselves. Why would they care so much about a specific creature in the hallways, even coming up with a euphemism to name it? Even the punishment didn't fit the usual behavioral patterns of the Song Pai—they usually placed such a value on the contracts of the indentures that they would not dare inflict serious violence on them. Why did this one specific thing cause them to behave in such a radically different matter? Klein found himself drawn to the inexplicable mystery of the "lowly one" like a moth to a flame. He heard the sound of a creature scuffing across the floor, and picked up his mop to protect himself with. Maybe Gordon's vermin was something else altogether, he thought as he crept in the direction of the noises.

From his time on Domremy, Klein had become very experienced in concealing the sounds of his movement. He moved slowly and stealthily in the direction of the noises, his heart pumping faster and faster as they grew louder. At the end of the hallway, he smelled a strange, pungent scent he didn't recognize. He raised his mop in case it did turn out to be a rat, and made a final quick turn around the corner.

The creature was surprisingly large. It bore a resemblance to a Song Pai, but lacked the two bladed arms of all the Song Pai Klein had seen so far had. It was only about two thirds the size of the typical warrior. The creature's behavior was far more shocking than its appearance; instead of rearing up and brandishing its limbs as most Song Pai would upon seeing an intruder, this one seemed to be terrified; it flattened itself against the floor and tried to change its skin tone to the mottled grey of the ship. It quickly realized that Klein knew exactly where it was and made a hissing sound to try to ward off Klein as it backed away. Klein held up his data screen and told the creature, "Do not run -- I will not hurt you." But his attempt at reassurance did nothing to change the creature's behavior, and it let out a sodden yelp.

Klein suddenly felt a muscular cephalopod arm wrap around his chest. One of the Song Pai guards had seized him from behind! The smaller creature fled as Klein thrashed, frantically trying free himself from the Song Pai's hold. He could see the guard raising its arm to slash his head off, but suddenly the arm fell and the Song Pai's grip went slack. Klein pulled a limp Song Pai limb off his chest and turned around to see another Song Pai standing near the fallen body of his attempted assassin.

The new Song Pai held up a data screen. "Why are you here?" it asked Klein.

Too shocked to come up with a convincing lie, Klein decided to answer truthfully. "Another indenture told me he was punished because he heard a strange creature and got distracted from his work. It is not normal for Song Pai to whip their indentures."

The Song Pai flushed red at the sight of Klein's text. "The Lowly Ones are not accepted in our society. The Lowly Ones should all be exterminated, as should anyone who encourages them. Baku Ra, this one who tried to slay you, desired to keep this one's presence secret. He is dead and you have served me by aiding in his death."

"What are these things?" Klein texted the Song Pai. "Why would Baku Ra try to hide this thing and violate the Song Pai's behavioral code to protect it?"

The Song Pai flushed purple. "On Song Pa, you may find one who will tell you, but I will not speak of this shame. Go back to your quarters, and accept your punishment for disobeying a Song Pai."

"What punishment? You just said I served you against Baku Ra!" Klein angrily texted.

"You still disobeyed a Song Pai—Baku Ra told you not to seek the Lowly One. Obey the Song Pai," the creature texted as it sprayed its filth all over Klein.

Klein shuddered as the Song Pai's foul ordure slid over his bodysuit. He rushed back to the indentures' bunks, amazed at the cephalopods' seemingly infinite ability to find new ways to disgust and baffle him through their contradictory culture and behavioral codes. As he hosed himself off in the shower, he swore he would somehow find out exactly what the Lowly Ones were and their link to the Song Pai.

Once Klein disembarked on Song Pa, conditions improved a bit, but only because he was no longer in such a claustrophobic confinement. Along with the other indentured servants who had not succumbed to illness or OD'ed on Carrier 12, he was transferred to a construction crew. The planet had originally been about one third dry land, but over the eons the Song Pai were transforming that into a vast network of flats traced by canals. The majority of this work had long been delegated to cheap labor from off-planet. The dry lands contained ruins and vestiges from a non-aquatic species that had arisen long before the cephalopods , but which had managed to achieve its own extinction through mismanagement of genetic engineering – a not uncommon occurrence in universal history.

The intelligent Song Pai, previously a prey species of the Foregoers, had crawled out and discovered a whole advanced technology at their tentacle tips, including rudimentary space travel, which had boosted their advancement far beyond the normal evolutionary pace. Yet even though they were henceforth masters of both the wet and dry domains and found it convenient to establish some types of manufacturing facilities and mines on land, they tended to leave the water on a needs-only basis and assign the greater share of restructuring to the lesser species. On dry Song Pa, Klein joined a motley underclass of various biological origins marshalled by native supervisors, but left free during their rare hours off the clock to shift for themselves. Their camps resembled what Klein had read about slave quarters in the ancient South of the old USA: tacky houses where the workers huddled together, occasionally copulating and even marrying one another, devising their own music and games to conserve their morale, even cultivating a few vegetables to supplement the monotonous rations grudgingly doled out by their overlords. At the end of each project, the settlements emptied as workers were dispersed according to new priorities, with bowed heads and brief goodbyes. Almost no mementos, since the workers' heavy tools were nearly all they could manage to carry. Klein's lanyard, often replaced but still around his neck, still held a card with a little purple light whose illumination had given out long ago, another with an orange dot, a piece of wood hollowed out to contain a Song Pai identity badge, a fragment from an image of Entara that Ayan'we had passed to him as they parted in the Forlan spaceport, and the tooth of a fellow exile who had helped him during a difficult injury on an earlier project. He'd wished he had something from the Dissenters, but what? A vegetable that would have long since rotted away? A bit of ash that would have blown away in the wind? How could the people of the Circle cling to a God that left them so little to remember him by? Klein could not find a shred of faith in his dreary existence, only remnants of ridiculous hopes and dark urges.

Klein was on a job doing shoreline restoration where a maritime storm had damaged the vicinity of a hatchery, working in tandem with a crew of Talinians that were handling the underwater part. Talinians were alien amphibians like big, strong newts who handled a lot of subsurface work for the Song Pai. They had vocalization and a sophisticated language, but it all sounded like "slurrbb, slurrbb" to most land-dwellers, so Klein resorted to the ever-present texters to say what was needed. As he was using his loader to nudge a big rock into place, he got a text.

"You Clin?"

"What?" he responded, looking around. Ever since he had signed his indentures, he had gone by an anglicized version of his maternal great-grandfather's name and been known as Joe Miller.

An amphibian head emerged from the waves and the message on the machine repeated.

"Yes?"

"Me Fatty. Message for you off-planet. Friends seeking."

"Where you get?"

"Purple fur-thing home port. Give nice gift to deliver. Bigger gift if I can report. Where next work?"

"Uncertain. Dry land. More?"

"No."

"Thanks, Fatty. Clear waters you."

As a Song Pai supervisor was lumbering up, they both resumed their tasks. The super made no inquiry. These filthworms were probably just talking about how to position a rock. No worries.

The brief encounter with Fatty left Klein confused and disturbed. Someone from Forlan was apparently concerned enough to search for him, but who? Entara or one of the Eyes of Alertness? Forlan security? A minion of the Brotherhood? And how could he make contact to find out? He had never seen a Forlani on Song Pa and he knew they disdained the place. Indentured servants had no com rights, even on-planet. He had heard of elaborate schemes to obtain such coveted privileges, but had no idea how he could arrange it. If he succeeded, he might betray his own location to one of his enemies. Was it worth getting in touch with Entara at all? He had no inkling how she had reacted to Tays'she's injuries or death. Ayan'we was so independent that she was quite capable of hiding part of the truth from him; Entara had never voiced the same bitterness as the daughter had. Perhaps she had been blamed for the bloodbath and imprisoned or punished somehow. Plenty of reasons to blame Klein for his blundering. He was startled to think that in the years that had gone by she was sure to have given birth to numerous additional children. Was she a proud mother in the midst of a contented family that did not wish to relive old horrors, or a miserable drudge bereft of her offspring and itching to avenge her loneliness? Klein cursed himself for that last image, recalling that it was totally unworthy of the woman who had sacrificed herself in parting with him that night in the mahäme. *I really have become a wretched piece of crap! I owe it to her if not to myself to pull myself together and try to better things somehow.*

It had been several years since Bill Hollingsworth had been going back and forth between rare consulting jobs, so the glory of his old career at Hyperion Corporation felt like another lifetime to him. The days of monitoring and planning the Domremy colony were gone forever, replaced by the best possible gig he could find—at this moment, an "e-professor" for the Logos Corporation. The job was far less prestigious than it first appeared; in truth, Hollingsworth was a "professor" in name only, delivering recorded lectures on business strategies and administration from a preselected set of guidelines and lesson plans Logos approved for all its business teachers. He sometimes wondered why they didn't simply replace him with a software program, for all the good his "business acumen" was allowed to contribute to their scripted lesson plans, although he suspected the company was betting on the prestige of a former high-level Hyperion employee to boost their enrollment statistics. Hollingsworth did all his work by webinar and online interaction, and he had never seen his supervisor or his students face to face.

As the weeks passed by, Hollingsworth felt more and more distant from his old executive life. The prestige of managing a whole planetary colony (at least that which he didn't pawn off on Duquesne, he cynically conceded) seemed like a fading dream, replaced by the grinding reality of having to help confused students via webcam and managing his timesheets to make sure he never overbilled Logos for his services. The last evidence of his formerly exalted status was the aging Mercedes-Benz parked in his driveway. The Benz, bought at the height of his former glory, was an "enthusiast-minded" car that offered a rare luxury -- a manual driving function, complete with steering wheel and gear shift. Most cars had become "passenger only," relying on automated navigation and GPS to ferry their owners from place to place with no input from the owner. Hollingsworth had always harbored contempt for the "drone cars," as he called them, for they deprived him of one of the last unadulterated joys in his life – the sensation of actually *driving*.

After a particularly stressful week of administering midterms for his courses, Hollingsworth decided to head out of town, driving on country roads on Saturday to clear his mind. As he left the city, he slowly began to turn off the electronic devices in his car. To finally be rid of those statistics and computer screens that had bored him in Hyperion and plagued him in his new job! The cameras, monitor, and TV were turned off, one by one. Finally, at a traffic stop before the exit to a country backroad, he prepared to finally turn the navigation system off. Of course, this was the last straw in illegality. Deactivating the monitor systems was subject to massive fines, but it was usually treated as a misdemeanor as long as there were no other charges. Nonetheless, ever since the Security Crisis of 2024, all vehicles were required to have a navigation system with transponder that allowed security forces to locate them immediately. In fact, they could be remotely stopped, as well, all over the Earth. Those wild police chases on the highways that could still be seen on archaic law enforcement videos were nearly unknown now, except in the case of extremely sophisticated thieves. As he used his customized switch to create a ghost car that would fool the authorities, he pictured himself as one of those daring and usually doomed adventurers. That treacly synthesized voice, the AI that always seemed to be *too* sympathetic and nice to the owner, asked him an unfamiliar question:

Are you sure you wish to turn the navigation system completely off? I will not be able to assist you if you choose this option? Please be aware of the following legal consequences...

Sick of a lifetime of computer-assisted decisions and deadlines, Hollingsworth happily pressed the "Yes" button that appeared on the touchscreen. His omniscient electronic helper fell silent, and the car shifted entirely to manual control. He looked out over the horizon, basking in the orange hue of the setting sun, and accustomed himself to the unfamiliar sensation of putting his foot on the brake as he waited for the traffic light to change .

Finally, the light turned green. Hollingsworth felt the roar of his car's engine as he put his foot on the accelerator and moved forward through the light. A sensation that was mundane, even boring, for most twentieth century drivers felt like the equivalent of being in a Formula One race to Hollingsworth! He felt a sense of purpose, of *life* pulsing through him as he steered boldly through traffic and put his foot harder onto the accelerator. He watched as the trees and bushes on the sides of the road began to blur and the drone cars around him began to recede into the distance. Their computers, programmed for safety over speed, could never match the speed of a human driver. He heard a loud warning honk come out of one of the drones as he swerved around it. Instead of deterring him, the near accident increased his sense of confidence; he felt like he could handle anything, and stamped his foot harder on the pedal. He heard the navigation computer boot itself up again to warn him, "You are travelling fifteen miles over speed limit. Slow down now!" But he paid the computer no heed; its power over the car had been disabled, leaving him able to go as fast as he wanted.

Suddenly, a man riding a motorcycle in front of Hollingsworth began to slow down. *Dammit, this idiot having engine problems?* Hollingsworth thought. The man's bike came to an abrupt stop in front of him in the middle of the road. Hollingsworth tried to swerve his car out of the way, but there wasn't enough time.

Hollingsworth heard a sickening thud as the front of his Mercedes impacted the bike. The man was sent flying from his machine into the middle of the road, where he lay still. Hollingsworth could hear the sirens of a police car behind him, summoned by the motorcycle's automated cry for help. He rushed over to the man and felt for a pulse, but it was quickly fading; he had landed at an angle that had done tremendous damage to his spine. As the police arrived, he put his hands up in the air to surrender, awaiting his fate. Goodbye, Mercedes; hello AVM – Aggravated Vehicular Murder.

The next few weeks sped by like a bad dream. He was processed, interrogated, arraigned, interrogated some more, and eventually made bail with the help of a shyster Erica suggested to him (who else could he call for advice?) and at an expense that forced him to liquidate almost everything he owned. Once on bail, all he could think to do was to mope around his nearly empty place until the trial. Since the security forces were cracking down particularly on all mobility violations in the wake of renewed mad-dog car bombings in Texas, the prosecutors were eager to make an example of his case and absolutely gutted him in court.

His counsel, Abraham Barsamanian, had claimed to be "an experienced lawyer in murder cases," but Hollingsworth had taken a dislike to the man almost as soon as he laid eyes on him. A squirrely little fellow with bushy eyebrows and a stubble beard, Barsamanian seemed to be perpetually nervous, often fidgeting with his pencil or playing some inane game on his phone's touchscreen when he wasn't obsessing over legal documents. He rarely looked Hollingsworth in the face, often not even bothering to raise his eyes while consumed with the details of the various legal cases he was involved in. Barsamanian's neurotic mannerisms made Hollingsworth even more unnerved than he would have otherwise been during the trial, and Hollingsworth found his patience and composure nearly exhausted.

"Abe, you said something about a 'special plan' you had yesterday. What exactly is it you're planning to do? Can't you at least tell me? My testimony in court was awful, the prosecution'll eat me alive in their closing arguments! Can't you get me a plea on a manslaughter charge so I'll get a lesser sentence?"

"Ah, about that," Barsamanian sputtered. "The sentence the prosecution is proposing for your AVM charge is minimum 30 years. You'd likely be doing that in a facility like Clevenger Penitentiary, which I wouldn't recommend for a man of your age..."

"I'd be lucky if I lasted two weeks in Clevenger!" Hollingsworth shouted. "That place is full of gangbangers and murderers! Do you have any idea how to keep me from getting sent there?"

"As you know, Mr. Hollingsworth, the penalties for driving without navigational assistance, except in case of emergency or power failure, are quite severe. The prosecution has made it very clear to the judge and jury that you were joyriding, and that no power failure had occurred in the car's electronics. Moreover, you have the lesser charge of Willful Police Deception to make things worse. I'd love to be able to get you a simple manslaughter charge, but the prosecution wants to make an example of you: they want it to be very clear that hacking and hot-rodding cars will be met with zero tolerance in regards to punishment."

"Is there any way you can possibly have me *avoid* going to Clevenger? It is what I'm paying you for, after all."

"Ah, the... special plan. I do have some... experience arranging for more lenient sentencing of individuals given extraordinary circumstances, provided there is corporate backing. I've talked it over with the judge and prosecution, and we've agreed that if you plead guilty to manslaughter, you will not sentenced to 30 years in Clevenger, but life on Domremy instead."

"A *lifetime* on Domremy!" Hollingsworth yelled. "If I get sentenced there, I'll never get back to Earth! Even in Clevenger, I still stand a small chance of getting paroled, especially if I could find some con to rat out. Your 'brilliant strategy' was to sentence me to an even worse punishment!"

"You know very well that the chances of anyone incarcerated in Clevenger getting sentence reduction are minute," Barsamanian said harshly. "Getting sent to Domremy *is* a commuted sentence. The planet isn't anywhere near as brutal as it used to be, provided you get assigned to the right town."

"You make it sound routine. I didn't think any one is even being sent there anymore. I got the impression they were moving people out instead of moving them in, when they didn't just let them croak up there and save the transport fees."

"This is special. And you have some people in your former employer that may be able to arrange an advantageous position on Domremy for you."

"Was it Hyperion? Did *they* pay you off too to take this case and get me hustled off to Domremy?" Hollingsworth asked. "After all, they probably want to keep the bad PR as far out of sight as they possibly can. Great headline for them: Former VEOPO jailed in

Clevenger. They're probably afraid some of their current top staff would wind up there, too."

"I am not at liberty to divulge the actions of other clients or groups that I may or may not be involved with."

"Yeah, you keep saying that, you little shitweasel. And here I was, thinking that Barsamanian Defense LLC was just looking to get its name in the papers again years after the Klein trial. You've gotten an awful lot of business since then. How many other people have you shuttled off to Domremy with Hyperion's encouragement?"

"I am not at liberty to divulge case details of…"

"Just forget it," Hollingsworth said with a sigh. Pondering his downfall after being fired from Hyperion, Hollingsworth realized the error of his earlier reasoning. He had thought that his life was completely disconnected from his Hyperion career after he had been fired, but in truth, his corporate background would follow him to the end of his days. What had once been an opportunity for advancement, money, and power would now be an albatross around his neck that would torment him across the galaxy. Very hesitantly, he finally said, "I'll take the plea and go to Domremy." *Hyperion better have something damn good lined up for me on Domremy, or I'll die just as quick there as I would in Clevenger*, he thought.

The Dissenters used many meeting places, but the one they used most frequently in Stafford Station was an old barn grouping far outside of town. Rendered redundant and obsolete by newer buildings as agriculture around Stafford Station expanded, its silo was rarely full and often not in use, and the Dissenters had come to prefer it as a location for their clandestine meetings. Guzman remembered the dingy barn from his earlier visit, when he and Klein had tried to win the Dissenters' support for Klein's campaign. Since then, he had been to several more appointments, as he inquired about the religion and was eventually allowed to observe some larger meetings, like the one where Peebo chose his penance. But he was still relatively unfamiliar with the rules of order, if any, for Dissenters' meetings. Their practices continued to surprise him. Rodriguez, who had accompanied him lately, was even less comfortable with the ways of the Circle.

"I don't like the looks of this place," said Rodriguez. "Getting us to come out here, in the dead of night, and not showing up at the meeting spot? And we're supposed to believe there's only one guy? They could be hiding somewhere, waiting to snipe us. Muy, muy malo."

"The Dissenters aren't like that!" said Guzman. "They don't call people to meetings just to stab 'em in the back and murder them. Or would you rather take your chances with Alek?"

Rodriguez shook his head. "Still don't trust these people, or this place."

The door to the barn swung open. Guzman watched as Trevor walked in and waved. "Welcome Guzman and Rodriguez, friends of Klein. Sorry I was a little bit late tonight, but sometimes farmers like us aren't the best judges of time. After all, to a farmer, a day ends at sunset."

"To us, a day ends at sunset too," said Guzman. He whispered to Rodriguez, "That means not a word of this to anybody outside this barn!" Rodriguez nodded in response, the movement of his head almost imperceptible.

"What brings you back to us, Guzman?" Trevor asked. He was smiling and asked the question in a friendly tone of voice. "Please be honest with me. Trust is the foundation of a New Earth."

"I'm gonna be straight up honest with you," Guzman said. "We've got nowhere else to go. You know that I can't go anywhere near Site 89 now that Alek won, and Rodriguez here...he's out of a job, too. He can't work as a mankiller anymore because he can't get psych clearance. So we want to join you, leave behind our old lives and become Dissenters."

"You wish to join our faith?" Trevor asked.

"Yes, everything I have seen has convinced me more, and my friend wants to join, too," Guzman said emphatically.

Trevor studied the faces of the two men, reading their emotions through the movements of their facial muscles. He had been chosen for his duties not just for his piety, but for his ability to judge the character of other men. Guzman had a look of anxiety in his eyes, but his face seemed like that of an honest and sincere man. Trevor found Rodriguez more troubling; his brow was furrowed, as if he was uncertain whether he truly wanted to become a Dissenter. He considered how to question the two men further.

"To join our faith requires a great commitment," said Trevor. "You must be willing to relinquish all your ties to your old life before you walked on Domremy. You must be able to let go of the Sinful Earth in all ways."

"Si, si, whatever," said Rodriguez. "Got nothin' going for me now. What should I do?"

"I feel you don't quite grasp what our faith is about, Rodriguez," Trevor said sternly. "When we say that you must end your old life and begin anew, we mean that in a very literal way. You must be willing to end the path of violence your life is based on and never return. You must never speak of your old life with pride, and draw strength from your new faith. The last step in your journey to becoming one of us is to symbolically relinquish your old name, and take a new name as a Dissenter. I was not born Trevor."

"*Mierda!*" exclaimed Rodriguez. "You think I should just turn my back on all I did in my life, never take any pride in what I've done? You think I should just forget all the people I saved from those *cucarachas* on this planet? Let me tell you something, I'm *damn* proud of the man I am and I ain't giving up my name for anyone!"

"Perhaps," Trevor said, "you are not as proud of yourself as you claim. The life of a mankiller is a tremendous strain on any man who takes up those duties. Can you truly say there was *nothing* you regret from your time as a mankiller?"

"I don't need this *shit*!" said Rodriguez. "You people don't want me around, I'm leaving now! This was a stupid idea!"

"Wait!" Guzman called as Rodriguez headed for the door. "They just want you to be honest with them! How can you expect them to accept you if you don't tell them about yourself?"

But Rodriguez said nothing. He didn't even bother looking back over his shoulder at Guzman or Trevor as he charged out of the barn. He swung the weathered old door open and stormed out into the midnight darkness without a second thought. Guzman turned to follow him, but Trevor told him, "He must find his own way. Let him go."

"I can get him to come back," Guzman said. "I don't think he's safe out there."

"Our faith is based on trust," Trevor replied. "I cannot trust a man who walks amongst us against his own will. Rodriguez is still too troubled—by his own uncertainty or by the sins of his past, I don't know—to truly want to join us. As for you, are you willing to commit to our creed of sacrifice and trust, even without your friend, or do you also have misgivings?"

"Yes, I'm willing" said Guzman. "I'm dead the moment I go back to Site 89, and I want a new and better life, one without the violence that got me here. I don't know how I feel about losing my name, and acting like my past doesn't matter, but maybe I'll be able to understand what it all means better if you explain it to me. Patiently."

"We Dissenters have a saying," said Trevor. "Even the most fulfilling journeys begin with a single painful step."

"Well, this had better be a fulfilling journey," said Guzman. "Because I've had nothing but pain since Hyperion dumped me here on Domremy."

"Then let's think of a good name. What did you do back on Earth?"

"A lot of things. I drove a taxi for a while in Monterey. I worked with iron in a *colonia*. I even learned to shoe horses for a while I stayed in my uncle's village. Then I started to do bad things for money."

"Well, that reminds me of a fellow a long time ago named Lo. Let's see, Lo, Loo, Lew, how about Luis?"

"Fine. From now on, call me Luis."

There wasn't much work on Domremy for a mankiller who couldn't pass a psych evaluation. Rodriguez had roamed from town to town, trying to find a marshall desperate enough to hire him as mankiller, but the positions were often filled already, and no marshall was desperate enough to hire him once they saw the giant red "U" stamped on his psych papers. Damn the Corporation and that stamp! It had condemned him to a life of drifting between Domremy's towns taking what miserable menial jobs he could find, until either his employer or the townspeople themselves tired of his attitude and forced him out.

Rodriguez' current duties as a janitor in Site 89's bar had been a miserable, low-paying endeavor, but had at least brought a certain amount of stability back to his life. The bartender, Erskine, seemed to care little about what his janitor thought or said as long as the day's work got done, allowing Rodriguez to keep his bad attitude and vent with impunity as long as he stayed out of the way of the customers and never mentioned a word of his problems to any of Alek's cronies. The relative solitude and lack of human interaction in his employment gave Rodriguez plenty of time to ponder the misery of his situation, his mind waffling between crawling back to the Dissenters to beg for a new life among them and trying to tough it out and see if he could find a good life on his own in Domremy.

Erskine also kept Rodriguez around because he had developed quite the drinking habit, choosing to spend large portions of his meager wages on whatever beer Erskine had on daily special. After a hard day of cleaning up, he had been guzzling down "Erskine's Special Sauce," a truly putrid excuse for brown ale that a local brewer had come up with as a promotional tool for Erskine's bar. While Rodriguez pondered how such a vile draught had been created and whether the Dissenters had better brewers among them than the citizens of Site 89, he heard loud yelling and cheering coming from a corner of the bar. A raucous cry of "Renaming Day's comin' up!" resounded clearly amidst the din that the group in the corner was raising. Rodriguez gave a questioning look at Erskine, and Erskine shrugged, having no idea what the men were talking about. Still curious about what "Renaming Day" meant and why the men were so excited, Rodriguez decided to walk over and investigate. Erskine gave no objection, spinning a coin around apathetically while the yelling continued.

As Rodriguez slowly lurched over to the corner in his inebriated state, he could discern other sentences amidst the clamor. "The Corporation has given us the go ahead to make Site 89 a real town!" said a small, shifty-eyed man with a loud, booming voice. "And, here's the man who made it all possible, Aleksandrov!"

Aleksandrov stood up. Rodriguez had never seen the man in person before, but Rodriguez could tell from the way men in the bar talked about him that he had become very powerful in Site 89, had an extremely short temper, and was not a man to be crossed. Alek began to speak.

"I am proud to be here with you, my partners in my campaign for Marshall. You have all given me financial aid in my campaign, and with the new businesses I will open soon, you will all be rewarded as my partners. As for Renaming Day, the Corporation has sent me a letter saying that citizens will be allowed to vote on a new name for Site 89. What name will you recommend?"

"Xanderburg!" the men seated around Alek yelled.

"Excellent. Renaming Day will be three weeks from now. There will be a great celebration then, like the day I became Marshall..."

"What's that fuckin' beaner doin' over there, slouching around? Is he a goddamn spy for someone?" the shifty-eyed man asked. "Get outta here, goddamn it!"

"Shut up, Darryl," Alek said harshly. "You're drunk, do not fight this man...."

But Darryl paid no attention to Alek. He advanced towards Rodriguez in an ungainly, stumbling gait, yelling insults as he walked. "Fuckin' beaner, fuckin' spy...fight, you son of a bitch!"

Rodriguez's punch came more out of reflex than rage, as if he was trying to crush an annoying insect flying in front of him. It was an awkward, wild swing, a punch that had no chance of hitting a man who was remotely close to being sober. But as ugly as it was, the punch was undeniably *powerful*, and it sent Darryl crashing into a table. The momentum of the swing caused Rodriguez to stumble and fall after the punch. He could hear Darryl spewing profanities as he flailed on the ground.

"That...that...son of a bitch...he hit me! You see that?! He hit me! He had no right...I'll shoot that son of a bitch! Where's my damn gun, get me my damn gun!"

"No," Alek said. "You will do nothing. I will resolve this. Ben, Terrence, seize that man."

Two of the men seated near Alek got up and grabbed Rodriguez, roughly dragging him to his feet. Rodriguez could feel something hard and metallic being pressed into the back of his skull, and even in his inebriated state of mind, he could tell it was a pistol. He thrashed around, yelling out to Erskine, "Save me!" But Erskine made no move to intervene, and was still playing with his antique coin. "Salvame!" he yelled out to Erskine again, but there was no change on his employer's face, no movement to come to his aid. Rodriguez' mind entered a state of panic, frantically trying to burn out the alcohol as the men dragged him outside. *Ohshitohshitohshitohshitohshit*, his primordial flight reflex screamed.

The men dumped Rodriguez outside the barn, and he sprawled in the dirt, stumbling about as he tried to get back to his feet. He could see men watching him from the balcony of the bar, and Alek was standing in the doorway. "You have attacked my friend, criminal. We will duel now. As they count down from ten, we will draw and shoot. If you draw early or run, these friends of mine will shoot you." One of the men standing next to Alek nodded.

As Rodriguez finally managed to stand up, Alek walked over to him and threw a rusty old pistol down into the dirt in front of him. Once Rodriguez had seized the pistol, one of Alek's followers yelled, "Turn around and start walking! Ten!"

Rodriguez began to walk. Terrified thoughts began to flood through his brain. *Damn, damn, damn...can I run for it?* He briefly glanced at Alek's followers, and could see one with an M221 trained at his head. *He's got the local mankiller ready to snipe me!* As the man continued to count down from to nine, then eight, Rodriguez finally began to think his actions through. *Can't run, can't shoot him early...only chance I've got is to outdraw him,* he thought as his finger pulsed on the trigger. Sweat trickled down his face as the man yelled out "Two!" He could feel his heart beating like an engine's piston as his muscles tensed...

The man's shout of "DRAW!" came out far too quickly for Rodriguez. It seemed to him like he turned in slow motion, and he could see Alek pulling the trigger already as he came around. Rodriguez could feel himself dying rapidly, his limbs going dead, a terrible pain in his chest. He could hear Darryl yelling out joyfully, "You killed that son of a bitch!" as time seemed to slow down. The dizzy, indistinct pleasure of his earlier drunkenness was replaced by a state of horrifying clarity in his agonizing final moments. One final thought flicked through his mind as the blood flowed from his veins.

Dios mio! A final thought of shock, a clarity he had never known of the pervasiveness of the dangers of Domremy.

In space, the tiniest second in the lifespan of a star can be a huge chunk of the life of a man, a family, a lineage, a civilization, a race. The routine swing of a planet around a burning main sequence sun ticks off a precious finite increment from the expectations of an individual. Yet during that time, the progress of a person's existence may seem as predictable and inalterable as the invisible arc that celestial mathematics has charted for a whole world moving through the near-void. From the surface of a planet, the stars at night appear to assume their customary places after sundown, but educated beings know that this is all an illusion: their twinkling, their brightness, their relative position in the cosmos, their stability, their reliability, are all subject to an immense game of chance that only God understands and where, as in any casino, the house always wins in the end.

Entara knew this as each month she went back to the Gardens of Fulfillment to gaze at the stars with her firstborn daughter and wonder what had happened to Klein. Later, in the solitude of her room, she would often begin to sing snatches of melody that would weave themselves together into a song, but she tried to keep these to herself. In the garden, Ayan'we, now past the equivalent of her teenage years, often left Entara to her thoughts, but never for too long, trying to form from time to time questions that were not just obvious distractions or maudlin prompts for trying to push back doubt and melancholy. The garden evenings were times when they could share as equals. And why not? Ayan'we had by now completed most of her training, along with her next two sisters, and the three of them had assisted at several births of their siblings, who now numbered precisely forty-one, since Entara usually birthed triplets. Not that much was required of them, for Entara's birthings were as easy as rain falling on the ground, even with the three male children who had, after weaning, been duly turned over to the hooded emissaries of the Brotherhood to begin their male conditioning.

"How was Tays'she this evening, mom?"

"Not good, dear. The nurses had to clear his lungs twice today and the upper heart is showing signs of weakening. Ragatti brought a cardio-pulmonary doctor who said another stent was impossible at this point."

"Have you thought about afterward? They'll probably propose you as a candidate for the Eyes of Alertness Council again." Entara had already refused this honor twice, giving rather skimpy excuses. Everyone knew she was competent. Her real reason was that if she rose to the Council, she refused to appear on the podium without her husband in attendance, as was customary, though to bring the wretch to such an event would have been like dropping a turd on the dinner table. Entara had not been able to prevent her elevation from para to para-para, meaning that she was considered an exemplary leader not just for her home mahäme, but for all those of the matriline, on-planet or off. There had also been rumors lately that she would be named Entara-ji, meaning that her status would be similar in all Forlan's matrilines. Ayan'we knew that her mother had had well-concealed visits from members of the present Eyes Council, sounding her out about nomination to the Council of Nine itself, the very one where she had once confessed her actions and invited a punishment that never came.

"I've been too busy for any extra cares right now," Entara answered, stroking one of the three infants at her breasts. "What about you? You're far past the need for protecting me from anything. I could drop the Clause of the Firstborn in a heartbeat and you would be free to marry if you want to."

"You overestimate my interest in males."

"If memory serves me right, you were spending some time with one young male a few months ago. Aren't you interested in him?"

Ayan'we sighed and admitted, "He was not like any of the others I've met here. In fact, that's why we got along together as well as we did. We were both freaks. In fact, we became a little bit affectionate, in the new way, but not too far. I really didn't want him to get any expectations, but he put out some feelers in the Brotherhood, anyway."

"I didn't know that. No one contacted me. What happened?"

"Well, you know, he's the son of a Third Wife and pretty low in the hierarchy. They told him somebody like me was out of the question and that they had other plans for him. He came to me and began to talk about eloping off-planet, so I put a quick end to it. You know, as much as I love the sisters, I'm definitely not eager for mating, myself, even to someone more or less compatible."

Ayan'we was silent for a time, as she gazed at a constellation in the sky named for a lovely avian creature that had become extinct during Forlan's great ecological disasters of the previous ages. It existed now only as a legendary memory. She broke the silence to ask, "Mom, please be frank with me. I've heard about it from everybody but you yourself. It's in the songs and the stories that circulate through the matrilines. What was it like to be with Klein? How did you feel then?"

"I'm surprised you never asked me earlier. I'm not ashamed to talk about it, especially with you, my daughter, my own flesh. It's true I don't like to brag about it in public, because they always want to idolize me and make me into something I'm not. But with you I can be honest, since you know my soul and will not twist things. I was no great expert on emotions. Just the opposite. When I took a notion to become Klein's consort, it was mostly out of curiosity about his loneliness, his deeply concealed sense of need, his volatility that was so different from the crude aggressiveness of many of the humans who came to the house. I was trained to give him pleasure, of course, as we all are. Yet right away, I discovered that he responded with a gentle compassion that he tried to hide from me. He genuinely expected so little of me that I was free to be myself. So when I kissed him and caressed him and took him inside of me, it was a sort of rebirth. I understood how innocent I was myself and to be truthful, I loved that as much as any power I had over him. I didn't need to worry about controlling him at all and that's where the fun began. Human organs are much more sensitive than ours and their pleasure lasts so little that what mattered most was creating a joy that was not strictly physical. He stimulated me to laughter and to delight in my own insignificance."

"Then why didn't you hold onto him, mother? We could have found a way. Why tie yourself to that cadaver that we still call Tays'she? To a decaying body without a consciousness. All for a person we can only loathe."

"I can't loathe your father, no matter what he did to my body in mating, nor what he planned to do to us later. If I could hate him, it could only be for wanting to deprive you of your future, but to be honest, I can't even bring myself to despise him for that, since it was driven by stupidity and greed and impulses unworthy of us. As for Klein, you know I was tempted. And you were correct to think that the need to separate from him might easily have made me kill myself. I was terribly tempted. I suppose it was partly because of the ecstasy of birth. It sweeps through you in a way that is both wonderful and terrible because you can never think the same afterwards. However, I can't blame it all on my body, even taking into account the changes that mating brings about."

"What was it then?"

"The night before you came to slide a blade between his ribs, when we were trying to make love again, it was already obvious. Klein realized that the young body that had brought him physical pleasure so easily was gone. I sensed it in every move he made, in every crease on his face, in his breath, in his heartbeat -- so easy to follow when they have only one. Naturally, he did his best to appear spontaneous and passionate. He was trying so hard to compensate. The humans call that "faking it." Perhaps it's unfair to use that term, because Klein was not fully aware he was faking. He wouldn't have let himself do it. And he would have insisted on holding me and adoring me as best he could every night until the end of time if I permitted it. I might have even come to enjoy that kind of devotion, or torture, or whatever you chose to call it. But it would never have been right. It would have been the worst kind of unfaithfulness I could ever imagine, both to him, and to me, and to the joy we had shared. The only way to honor that uncorrupted feeling was to give up trying to recreate it when neither of us was capable of being the same as we were."

"Yet here we are again. And you and I are watching the stars revolve through the void and wondering what his life is like and what we can do to make it better. Mom, he'll never be away from us."

Neither had anything more to add. Eventually, Entara changed the topic. "Well, speaking of that, any news from the digisphere on our friend?" Though they were both virtually certain that Klein had made it to Song Pa, they had not been able to trace him over the years, despite convincing every sister of the Eyes of Alertness who got an off-planet pass to scour the spaceports and transfer stations, handing out gifts to any beings headed for the Song Pa system so they might contact Klein and report back.

"More of the usual, I'm afraid. Mom, I think I may want to take the search into my own hands."

"You don't have enough seniority to get anywhere near Song Pa. Besides, that place is so cut off from everywhere else. We would be helpless without a solid confirmation of just where he is. If only we knew what alias he used."

"We may have something in that direction soon. One of my old hacker friends has been working on retrieving indenture records through a hole she found in the Song Pa firewall. She says it's frustrating as hell, but she's going to keep throwing out the net until she catches something. It's become a challenge for her."

"Let's keep hoping," added Entara, drawing the infants closer. "We better get these imps back to the house. It's starting to get cool."

At that very moment, a good many parsecs away, Klein was leaning against the trunk of a tree fern and gazing up at a binary daytime sky filled with the milky stratus clouds that often hung over Song Pa, wondering about how many children Entara might have by now. It was a comforting thought to his increasingly dreary existence. Over the length of more than a decade of Earth years, he had wrestled, or rather fumbled, with many frustrating, seemingly insoluble mysteries. Even the puzzles he had encountered on Carrier 12 still remained, for the most part, inscrutable.

One thing that still tantalized him was the nature of the strange creature that the Song Pai called a "Lowly One." Judging from the likelihood that the only Lowly One he had glimpsed was hunted down and killed while he was still on the ship, he wasn't surprised that he hadn't seen any Lowly Ones in public on Song Pa, but what surprised him more was that the Song Pai never even discussed them. During his entire time working on the shoreline restoration project, not a single Song Pai had even mentioned the Lowly Ones, which made it impossible for Klein to deduce anything about their nature from the everyday conversations he observed on the work site. He was loath to ask the Song Pai themselves about it—they had very short tempers, and judging from what he had seen of their reactions when the subject was brought up, he didn't want to risk the honor they placed on his contract to a fit of irrational rage. As the project drew to its close, his obsessive desire to discover the truth finally overwhelmed his sense of self preservation, and he mustered up the courage to ask one of the overseers on the work site, "What are the Lowly Ones?"

The Song Pai was shocked by the words on Klein's screen. How could a mere *indentured servant* from another planet know of the vile Lowly Ones, a truth all true Song Pai strove to keep hidden? He flushed fuchsia in rage at the thought of the loathsome ape in front of him *demanding* the truth! Why, if the creature wasn't an indentured servant, he'd cleave it to pieces! He tensed his bladed tentacles... *The contract.* The contract was always sacred, always inviolable. Such had been said by the Elders of Song Pa, so it shall be. The muscles in his tentacles relaxed and his skin turned a sickly green color. He felt a strong sense of disgust with himself—not so much for nearly killing Klein in his rage as at the thought that the loathsome offworlder would somehow learn the truth, no matter what he said. He already knew too much; surely Klein had seen something, maybe in the ship that brought him here, maybe in the work camps somehow. But the thought of being one among the Song Pai to reveal the nature of the Lowly Ones to Klein inspired only shame and disgust, and he decided *he* would not be the one to do it.

The supervisor pointed one of his tentacles in the direction of a large, ugly building painted a faded yellow pastel color. "In there," he texted to Klein. "Go to the center of that building and talk to the Speaker-to-Idiots." The Song Pai then turned away from Klein, still flushed green with disgust.

Despite being pock-marked with discolorations and pits, the building still seemed to be used regularly; its exterior and interior lights were still functioning, and Klein could feel a chilly breeze from some sort of air conditioner as he walked down the long hall to the center. There were various alcoves and lockers in the hallways, most of them filled with the guns and ammo the Song Pai favored, and arrows on the ceilings and the walls pointing the way to various areas. Klein walked straight to the end of the hallway and came to two broad metal doors that were closed. He saw a large blue button on the wall and pressed it, opening the doors with a loud groaning sound.

The empty room had rows of tables and chairs arranged in front of an amphitheater. In the center of the amphitheater sat a gigantic texting screen that was thin enough to fit on the wall, but tall enough to span the entire height of the room. It looked more like the fabled analog cinema screens from before Klein's time than any electronic device he had seen on Earth or Forlan. A red light shone out of the side of the machine's monitor and scanned Klein's face briefly, and then he heard a loud whirring sound as the machine turned online.

"Advance, Indenture Joe. What information do you need today?" appeared on the massive screen.

He decided to experiment with a seemingly less touchy question than the Lowly Ones first. "Why are you called 'Speaker-to-Idiots'?" he typed into his text screen. The machine sent out its red light again and scanned an image of the text from Klein's screen. It then responded, "This position is not considered desirable employment for Song Pai organisms. It used to be filled by cowards and those unable to breed. Technological advancement has eliminated the need of Song Pai to fill this position."

It may be more or less accurate, but this thing has a programmed slant towards propaganda, Klein thought. However, he realized that the Speaker was probably the only thing he had found so far that would give anything remotely close to the truth, so he typed in "What are the Lowly Ones?" to his texter and held it up for the Speaker's scanner eye to see.

The machine whirred again briefly, and then more huge text appeared on the screen. "The Song Pai were one of two species derived from cephalopods on Song Pa. The second species was smaller and had a faster reproductive rate. The second race was a species that was conquered and exterminated during the Song Pai expansion."

"What do the Lowly Ones have to do with any with this?" Klein asked.

The Speaker explained further. "Some of the females of the second race were used by Song Pai males for breeding purposes, as the two species were genetically close. Future generations of Song Pai bred from these females acquired a faster reproductive rate as a result. However, among Song Pai descending from this breeding, a certain amount of children will be born with the undesirable characteristics of the second race. Undesirables are considered 'Lowly Ones' and should be exterminated."

The Song Pai's reaction to the Lowly Ones finally made sense to Klein. The Lowly One Klein had seen had been nervous and fearful...qualities the warlike Song Pai would see as cowardly. The Lowly Ones, throwbacks to a race the ancient Song Pai valued only for their breeding potential, were the embodiment of all qualities that were un-Song Pai, far more so than any Talinian or human could be. The more rapid breeding, an asset that likely aided the Song Pai in their evolution and technological progress, was directly linked to the possibility of giving birth to genetic throwbacks to the older, second race.

The Speaker asked, "Do you have any further questions?" Klein texted "No," and the Speaker turned off with a loud whir. As Klein walked down the hallway, he pondered the complex nature of the Song Pai race. How would he be able to get out of this bizarre place, a world with incredible technology run like some nightmarish antebellum plantation?

Above all, Klein had two great preoccupations -- obtaining an off-planet com link to contact Entara, or even Peebo, and locating the Song Pai guard who had molested him at the space port. He had failed miserably at both tasks. He had tried to bribe, coerce, beg, trick, and even hypnotize other indentured servants to help him obtain the com link and the closest he ever came was a short-range device that would not reach the edge of the continent and was now irreparably broken, to boot. He had never been able to get a single part to replace one of those that were nonfunctional. As for his rapist, Klein had consulted everyone he had come to trust to help him to trace the guard, but his only breakthrough had come four years back, when a reptilian servant had managed to determine that the glyphs on the badge indicated a date associated with seniority of service, and nothing more. The thing was etched with numerous little notches and holes whose purpose he had never been capable of learning.

Now he was going to try once again, hoping against all hope, to get help from another team of Talinians who owed him a favor. He had covered up their absence when they swam off to cadge some extra food one day. He beguiled the Song Pai supervisor with a cock-and-bull text story that they had gotten the wrong directions to the reef. It was time for his meeting, so he drove up to the shoreline with a load of rip-rap and made a show of delivering it to them, texting from low in the machine's cabin to hide it from view. It was easier for them to answer, since they could text from under water.

"Locate squid guard?"

"Supervisor? Over there."

"No, other. Must talk."

"No name? No job?"

"Just this. Look."

He sauntered over to the water's edge and the newts all pushed on the same stone, while he slipped the ID to the one that was texting. He snatched it and it disappeared under the wavelets. There was a big eddy, as he could tell they were crowding around to see it as they uttered a lot of "slubbrr, blubbrr." After a while, a post from the one who had texted him, "Stand by."

The whole group of Talinians began texting away with the supervisor and he could follow the exchange partially on the translator of his own texter. The newts convinced their boss they could not work at the depth last week's supervisor fixed for them and they needed to contact him. The super protested until his skin turned a bright shade of fuchsia out of anger. Sometimes you didn't need to know what a squid was saying, because his coloration changed with his emotions. He fired off a barrage of "Filthy slime worm!" messages, until he finally handed over a handheld machine Klein had never seen before. Pretending to readjust the treads on his hauler, he surreptitiously watched as his Talinian contact slid the ID bar into it.

After a minute or two, they handed the machine back to the super as Klein cursed beneath his breath at another apparent failure. But in seconds it was his turn to receive a message.

"Coordinates follow."

He could barely believe his eyes. According to this, the Talinians had succeeded in tracing his tormentor to a spot less than twenty kilometers away. It was a construction supply center where his unit was often sent to pick up materials. He would have to set to work right away, planning how to punish his enemy before they could move him again to a distant assignment.

Another text arrived from the Talinians: "Even?"

"More than even!"

By the time Klein had found his target, he had decided several things about his revenge. He would have to ambush the squid when he was alone, because dealing with more than one of the creatures would be totally impossible. He would have to do it quickly, because the Song Pai had every advantage if the struggle were to become prolonged -- their maneuverability and savagery were just too great. Finally, he would probably have to devise some weapon of his own rather than hoping to disarm the thing. To further complicate matters, he would not have much time to fiddle around with planning, for work in this area was wrapping up and crews were already beginning to depart for a mine in the mountains. He stayed watchful for days as he joined the work of closing down the supply depot. Getting revenge on the guard had become a sick obsession inside him, a crazed effort to exorcise the built-up hate of his servitude and the years of separation from Entara that had eaten away at him. He felt the desire to renew contact with Entara fading into his mental background as the imperative of revenge grew. He cursed himself for it, but couldn't seem to control his desires any more. His own body's deterioration had always fed these festering thoughts, as over the years his work injuries mounted up. He had never recovered full use of the arm Tays'she had poisoned, while other breaks, strains, and wounds just continued to wear him down. Soon he would be reduced to nothing unless he managed to redeem himself through vengeance. He fantasized on how it would look to watch the guard's blood flow out of him, as though it could wash him clean of all the dirt he had accumulated, mental and physical. The enemy's sweet blood: would it be blue, like the Song Pai's relatives on Earth? The supply base gradually emptied, but the guards stayed on. When Klein's crew was ordered to hit the road for the mountains, he managed to slip away unnoticed.

    The next day a big dust storm blew up, confining the few remaining Song Pai to the wet rooms. Like earthly octopi, their species had siphons that were used for propulsion and breathing circulation in the water. On land, they could store oxygenated water through them to last for a day or so before needing to return to a pool, a canal, or a wet room. The siphons were extremely sensitive, though, to snow, sleet, or dust. Their five eyes were sensitive, too. Storms pretty much disabled them. Klein was counting on it. As his few scavenged rations disappeared, he wracked his mind for a plan, until he spotted some gas cylinders that gave him an idea. They contained extremely compressed nitrogen used in industrial processes and he wondered whether he could ram one of these into the guard's siphon and literally blow him up. It would require him to keep the siphon tightly grasped around the hose from the cylinder while being exposed to deadly blows from the tentacles and hooks -- a plan that Klein admitted to himself was foolhardy. But his mind latched onto it like a limpet because there was just no alternative and by now he was nothing but a fool.

 He waited until the guard was alone in a wet room in the midst of the storm. The others had gone to the far end of the complex to check on something. Then he ran to the entrance and hit an alarm, texting that intruders were in the compound and burglarizing tractor parts. As expected, his Song Pai target came tearing out of the building and headed for the lot where the graders, lifters, and earth movers were parked, his rod-like particle beamer at the ready. As it turned its eyes looking for the burglars, Klein stole up with the cylinder he had prepared and launched himself onto its bulky body. He was lucky enough to grab the siphon and shove the gas tube in before the guard understood what was happening. He put what seemed to be all his last strength into a vise-like grip around the siphon and tube, having correctly guessed that the creature's body did not possess muscles in this area that allowed it to push it off. It was stunned by the nitrogen-argon blend that rushed into its body and started to be absorbed into its blood. It turned the silvery color of shock and defense, but this inaction lasted only seconds, and it soon began flailing its reddening tentacles to seize Klein and to lash him with the dreadful claws. Klein could feel cruel wounds opening on his legs, but he didn't dare to look, concentrating all his forces on the tube that was inflating the cephalopod like a balloon. Within one minute, he could feel its internal organs beginning to rupture from the pressure, but this race was accustomed from soon after birth to desperate combat and this one would hold out until the instant of death. Its head swelled and swelled, turning a dark sepia tone of despair. Klein knew that it was only instinct now that fueled the cephalopod's struggle, but he didn't dare to let go. Finally there was a horrendous ripping sound and its body exploded, spreading sticky gore everywhere and throwing Klein several meters through the air.

After a moment's mindless gloating, he felt the onrush of his own pain and found that he could not move his legs. Action was probably useless, but if he didn't die right away and didn't cover up the murder, he knew he would face unspeakable torture, should he be caught. He dragged himself on his belly to the nearest loader and pried off an engine panel. If he could short-circuit the batteries and ignite the hydraulic system, it would create a blast that would flatten the whole area. Blinking through blood, he could hardly tell if he was crossing the right wires, but he felt a manifold with his hand and pulled it back at once, for the heat told him the reaction was taking place. Useless to even try to run. The dead were mauling the dead. He rolled himself sideways, over and over, down a slight incline into a ditch that might protect him and heard the detonation as soon as he slid into it. A huge fireball spread debris in all directions, blackening the ground, as incandescent shrapnel landed on his back. He could never look up to see the aftermath, because he was already unconscious and never expected to awaken.

Ayan'we strode into her mother's rooms and pointedly asked, "Mom, do you know somebody named Elytra in the Backscratchers? We got a strange message this morning."

Entara put down her papers and shook her head. "I don't think so. It's a small matriline and I only know a few from school and training. Why? What's the message?"

"Don't get too excited, but it may be what we waited for so long. This Elytra describes herself as a pleasure worker on her way from Taluka to a new house on

Dahlgren. She says that while she was in a transfer out in that sector, she happened to see a group of Talinians transshipping and one of them ran up to her blathering something as soon as he noticed her. He grabbed her com and texted this: "Entara-para, Forlan. Clan. Song Pai. 206.5, 44.38, six years more past, gift Fatty Tahinni" and a com link number somewhere. Can we trust it to be true?"

"We can't trust it not to be true."

"It squares with something my computer friend said. That Klein might still be on Song Pa under the alias Joe Miller."

"Look, Ragatti told me she has wangled a travel permit to visit some spaceport on Song Pai, in case we ever were contacted. I'm calling her now to see if she can depart right away. It's a shot in the dark, but we must do what we can. While I do that, see if you can locate this Fatty from Tahinni so we can send him a gift."

Slowly, Klein became aware of Hell. He could hear the souls of the damned around him before he could see anything. They were moaning and screeching in torment. He realized that he was part of this moaning and screeching, that his own pain was indistinguishable from theirs. He finally managed to focus with one eye. The walls and the floor of Hell seemed to be smeared with pus and blood. It should smell awful, too. Wasn't there supposed to be brimstone? Why couldn't he smell? He couldn't move. Maybe you weren't supposed to move in Hell. This played over time and again between screams before he could make any progress. Then the horrifying thought came to him that perhaps he was not dead.

The holding area where the Song Pai had hauled his carcass was not a hospital. They didn't have hospitals or doctors, except for the unborn and the very young. Their science brooded over the preservation of ova and sperm from warriors sent out into space. The honored dead had their frozen gametes activated in the warm sheltered waters of the hatcheries, where they were carefully trained by adults in all they needed to know. Then when maturity reached its first threshold, they were released to fend for themselves. A Song Pai maxim: Beyond the sheltering reef, fight hard or die. Any desire for self-preservation from sickness or injury was a serious character defect and signaled unworthiness for survival. The Song Pai literally didn't care whether an indentured servant lived or died. Better if he died, in fact, because no final bonus would have to be paid. While servants could still breathe they were under contract. Contract said three meals a day and a place to sleep, but nothing about doctors or hospitals. Those unfit for work were put in a holding area and it was their business to walk back out. There was no effort to disinfect wounds, apply bandages, keep out vermin, or any of the most basic procedures of medicine.

Klein woke up when he felt something banging at his lower body. He was eventually able to perceive it was a fellow indenture, a humanoid of some kind, bashing away with a crutch. Then he saw what he was bashing at. A crab-like thing was tearing away at one of Klein's legs, gobbling strips of flesh. Finally the indenture made a side swing that dislodged the crab and sent it flying across the room into the darkness. The fellow inmate hobbled off on his crutch to chase the thing. Klein never saw him again. Then he once more passed out.

The buzzing woke him up. "Let me just die!" he tried to say, but all that came out was an inarticulate scream that sent up a cloud of flies from where he lay. He almost wished he could feel the maggots because he knew they were there. Seeing them, however horrible, would be better than his having to imagine them. He tried to shake his body, but nothing seemed to respond. He had no idea how much time was passing or when he had been brought to this place and he had lost all interest in any future. He kept repeating silently that he wanted to go *now*, until the mantra somehow erased his consciousness once again.

The liquid brought him back again. Burial at sea. Slide into the liquid arms of the sea and surrender. The liquid was lapping at his body and calling to him. He pried his lips apart and waited for the water to come in so he could gulp it greedily into his lungs. But that didn't happen. It was only coming in a drop at a time. It was salty but also sweet. Was this some new torture Satan had devised? Or maybe God? He tried with all his might to thrash his body around and actually was able to budge a centimeter or two before he cried out in pain again. "Shhh. Shhh," said God, as he removed something that had been covering his eyes. One eye, anyway. It could hardly be called a good eye because it refused to focus. "I need you to stop moving while I finish this," said God, pressing down lightly on his chest to keep him in place. He aimed his eye at the voice, hoping that the radiance of God would just disintegrate him.

But God had no radiance, for he was black. A sad black face that Klein tried to recall from a ravaged memory. God's name was Trevor. The liquid was disinfectant solution on a sponge that Trevor was applying in a very careful but persistent way to what remained of a human body. "Shh. That's good. Calm down. This won't hurt. As soon as I get finished cleaning you up, I'm taking you out of this dump. You are not in a good way, friend Klein. Can you understand me? Yes, I can see you do. Remember, it's Trevor and you're still in the Circle as long as I'm around. You do look positively awful. It took forever to get the bugs off you. Out of you, too. I can't do much more than clean you and move you. Before I do the moving, I got something to knock you out for a good long time – no pain. Someone else is coming who can help you more. Now you won't see this and it might give you a twinge for a second, but after that it's sleepy time, so you relax. There, there, there…"

When he was able to look up again, he was in a place with clean grey walls. Above him, something purple was moving around. "Entara!" he tried to say, but all that came out was "Eh, Eh."

"Stop trying to talk, now, I'm not done yet. There." The thing reached down and patted the area around his eye with gauze. "Can you see me now? Sorry to disappoint you. I know you were trying to call Entara."

He could see it was a Forlani with a sky-blue tunic. Not Entara. The face finally assembled in his mind. This was Ragatti. "Klein, darling, you are, as Trevor says, an unholy mess! You're just lucky you had a mating and birthing specialist to help you, because you were more exsanguinated than any pierced young wife that I ever worked on." She gave him a little caress. "But does your girl Ragatti know blood or not? I was even able to get some of your own human blood type for you. Through a little trade I worked out with some of your co-earthlings." She smirked, thinking of the series of rapid seductions and sex services she had exchanged for some type A positive. "I think I can say I've done pretty well. You should see the cute nose I worked out. But it's not all good news. You, my pet, have some things wrong that go far beyond my training. We're going to have to move you again. Right now you're in the decontamination unit at Song Pai Spaceport Three. The only remotely germ-free area I could find in this pesthole. While Trevor was watching you last night I managed to contact a medivac team that will arrive in about an hour to take you to Corlatis. I'm already cleared to visit the Epidemiology Center there and they agreed to take you as an emergency case. That place has every type of specialty covered, and I suppose they'll all want to have a little hand in your treatment. You may wind up in the surgical manuals."

The joking mood disappeared as she looked at Klein with serious compassion. "There's one more bit of bad news. You'll find out soon anyway. We had to take your right leg below the knee. There wasn't much left anyway after what you went through before Trevor found you." Her smile returned and she added, "Now if we were back at the mahäme, I'd fit you myself with a perfectly beautiful Forlani prosthesis. You'd be surprised how many girls fall out of trees or get crushed when something collapses. But the aces on Corlatis will probably insist on giving you the latest ultra-modern, top-tech thing, so we'd better let them. I can hear Trevor coming down the corridor now, and that means it's time to prep you for the ride." She reached to swab his brow again and he tried to kiss her fingers.

"Watch it, lover, none of that now till your jaw's unwired." But she lowered her face to his and kissed him tenderly on his lacerated lips, slipping a needle into his arm so that the sensation of her warm, moist mouth was the last thing he felt before he dozed off.

Recovering from his sleep, Klein could sense he was somewhere new. He slowly decided it was the low gravity, so unlike the pull of massive Song Pa. A clean, well-lighted place -- he tried to place the phrase that sprang into his head from somewhere. This was it. He had taken a couple of hours getting used to sensations from parts of his body he never expected to feel again, except in a stab of agony. He wiggled, flexed, blinked, and burped. Now he was trying to decide why a big raccoon was sitting on his bed staring at him. Maybe his brain had gone bad and they'd taken out the sensible part. Eventually the animal removed its mask, which Klein realized was a medical viewing scope. On second thought, it looked more like a giant coati, or maybe some kind of Australian critter he's seen on a nature video long ago. It began to speak through a fuzzy vocal interpreter.

"Now, Mr. Klein, I am your doctor. Please answer "yes" with your vocal chords if you can."

"Yes," Klein croaked, surprised at how unusual his own voice had become.

"Very good, now tell me if you feel it when I touch these places, and tell me if it hurts at all." Coati proceeded to give him a pretty thorough poking that excited a few twinges, but no real suffering.

"Here? Oh, very good. Here? Ok. Over here now. Nothing? That's a bit strange, we'll have to consult on that. Perhaps a little electrolytic occlusion. Over here?

Fine. All right, Mr. Klein. I'm Tatatio and I did your ventral area yesterday. Was it ever interesting! Yes, we took things out of your belly that were fascinating -- animal, vegetable, and mineral -- made a nice little film I'll show at a convention. Your intestines were a most delightful puzzle to solve, and you should have seen the beautiful bit of liver I grew and grafted in! A perfect fit. Coco138 did your thorax a few days ago, but didn't find anything very interesting, just a little touch-up and cleaning of your lungs. In most exposed places, we didn't do anything but tweak what Ragatti did on you, other than pump in a lot more fluids and pick at a little detail here and there. Can you hear me ok? How about now? Hello? Hello?"

He adjusted the volume on his translator, trying different settings. "Well, it looks like you've still got a couple of aural frequency blanks, but not too bad. After all, you'd never on your best days hear all the things I can. It was someone from your own home planet who worked on your ear and I must say, I like the way she restored that lobe. We don't get many humans up here, you know. You do realize you're on Corlatis? Part of the Coriolis system. Nice little exoplanet with just enough gravity and no atmosphere – we make our own here. Earthlings couldn't get in until a few years ago, since we're technically in Blynthian space and we still respect what you call the Quarantine Treaty of 1947. The defense forces still strictly control the perimeter, but we do admit talented individuals once in a while. After all, you humans are filled with nasty micro-organisms of all kinds and it helps to have some of your brighter minds to cooperate with once in a while. You've heard of the latest outbreak on Earth? Gruesome stuff, but so far it's been confined. Anyway, I chatter on and on. So what's next is that a prosthetic team will attach your new leg before long. All fabricated and tested of course, but they're making a few last-minute cosmetic touches to make it match as well as possible. Then Torghh will do that wonky eye of yours and we should be ready to let your friend Trevor take you away. Any questions? Rest for now, best medicine of all."

He found himself surprisingly relaxed and passive as he adapted to the hospital routine. Regular and irregular visits from all the multi-species staff, including Ragatti, who couldn't stop bragging about how much nicer a nose she'd given him than what he had before. After the leg work, there were little strolls around the room to test the prosthesis and get him used to walking again. Regular meals of "mush-in-a-bag" brought by an attendant who was no more than a girl, like the candy-stripers of old. They even managed to scrounge up some symphonies for him to listen to. He never did get to meet Dr. Torghh, because after the surgery they bandaged both of his eyes to prevent him from trying to move them too much and damage the work.

He really couldn't understand the doctors most of the time, but he liked to exchange a few sentences with the little candy-striper. He heard her enter the room. "Hi, Mr. Klein. It's me, Amanda. You feeling all right? I'm so anxious to see your new eye. I bet it will be beautiful. Torghh is a bit stuffy, but he just performs miracles on all kinds of eyes. I've got something good for you today, real solid food for a change and I know it's good because I helped cook some of it. We've got a turkey patty with onion gravy, mashed potatoes, spinach, and some real traditional cherry Jell-O. What do you want to start with?"

"Turkey, please."

"Here it comes, but mind you don't chew too hard. We don't want to loosen any of those jaw pins."

"Mmm. Delicious. A bit of the tea, thanks. Nice. Amanda, how did you get here from Earth?"

"Never been there. I'm a true space-brat. I have been planet-side, to Dahlgren and Tau Ceti Mu and Forsythe. Mostly I've drifted around ships and transfer stations. Can't go to Earth now because of the plague, but to tell you the truth, I'm not sure I want to. Dr. Tatatio told me there's a planet in this sector with unusual magnetism where there are colors dancing in the sky all day and night. That sounds so beautiful! That's what I want to see."

"What do you think of Doctor Ragatti?"

"I know you're a friend of hers from way back because she told me, but I have to say, Mr. Klein, that she is one sexpot! The whole surgery team is off right now having a party to celebrate their work on you and I wouldn't be surprised if it turns into an orgy. Doctors are pretty touchy-feely anyway, regardless of their species, but with her... she's a vixen. And that's in public – I can't imagine what she does in private. Oh, I'm sorry Mr. Klein. I shouldn't be saying these things about a friend of yours."

"Amanda," Klein replied between spoons of potatoes and Jell-O, "I think she would be flattered. I can tell you from personal experience that Ragatti is never stingy with her warmth or affection. Not many Forlani are, but she does stand out. I can't seem to resist them."

"I've enjoyed our chats. I'll miss you when you move on. You must lead such an exciting life."

"Too exciting, most people would say," commented Klein as he finished off his meal. "And now I would agree with them. Pretty soon I think I'll have to talk about my life with some friends who see things differently and I don't know how I'm going to account for myself."

"Is that why Trevor is taking you away? He doesn't seem to be mad at you or resentful. Maybe it won't be as bad as you imagine."

"The mad, resentful part will not be with him or the Circle. It will be with me. It's always been inside me."

"Well, then, I'm optimistic, because Dr. Tatatio says your new insides are a beacon for the galaxy, so they can't do you wrong. Bye now."

All told, Klein's recuperation took a bit longer than planned, due to ship schedules that no one at the clinic could control. Before Klein and Trevor left, Ragatti came to say goodbye, since she was departing earlier in another direction. She astonished Klein by locking the door, leaping up to slap an adhesive over the monitor camera, slipping off her gossamer robe and climbing into bed with him.

"I'm here to pronounce you fully cured and I intend to give you what you humans call a happy ending."

She began by kissing him on the mouth and the eyelids and then licked the side of his nose. "Mmm. Your new nose tastes as good as it looks, I must say, even if your human nostrils are so dull. If you could smell what we can, you'd realize how much I desire to please you right now. They say human noses are linked to other parts of the anatomy. My! They seem to be right. Let me just try this. Ahh, that tickles just right. I've been looking forward to having a proper goodbye to make up for that "bum's rush" you gave me on Domremy. And that gives me an idea. Get down off this bed and let's see if your new legs are up to a little exercise. Just enjoy."

Klein was completely swept up by Ragatti's onslaught of sexuality, even though Forlani females generally described these copulations as competent pleasure service or massages rather than true intercourse. Ragatti was wholeheartedly giving herself over to lavishing attention on Klein through every position and trick he could imagine and she was playing him like a Stradivarius. Suddenly she seized him with arms and tail and flipped him up to the bed again.

"Ragatti, I can't resist you, sweetheart!"

"I bet you can't." She leaned over him and stared down as her muscles completely took control of Klein's desires. "I can give you the same little things you used to enjoy so much, just as nice and moist and warm as you like. How's that? Yes! And that? Maybe this way? Just a little warmer? I can do whatever you want, mister. You just say."

Klein was so rapt with enjoyment that he couldn't manage to say much of anything that was articulate.

"Ahhh. Ahhh. Ahh! That's all you need to say, Klein. Ragatti's got you totally under her spell now and she's going to top it off right NOW!"

As Klein was shuddering and hugging her close, she kissed his ear lobe and whispered in it. "Now you've had a Forlani body that's never been ripped apart by a male in mating and never will be. I prefer to come together with you. And if you hadn't saved me by sending me away from Cashman and his goons, I would have lived to just hold onto you night after night until they killed me. I would have been happy to die right here, lying beside you. In fact, I thought about it. It would have been so easy to bring a little syringe into the room for both of us, and I would have been the last creature that Klein thought of or felt before he went into the hereafter." She whispered this because she knew Klein has already slipped away into a post-coital half-dream. "It's all right, darling, because I don't really believe it deep down. I'm just trying to persuade myself that I'm stronger than I truly am. Ragatti is Ragatti and, big medical doctor that she is today, she will always be a little bed-hopper trying to have her way with another human instead of with those things that pass for male on Forlan. But I'll tell you this, sweet. Even if I had been mated and had let my guts been sliced up by one of them, I wouldn't have let you go. If you had come across space to save me, I would have clung to you like a second skin. Even if I had felt a hundred little bodies come sliding down my birth canal and every one of them drove me wild with happiness until I was insane, I wouldn't have let you go. Ragatti would have found a place to hide you and keep you safe if she had to dig to the center of the world to do it. She would never have sent you to that shithole of Song Pa so you could blow your parts all over the surface and had to be sown up by some little flesh seamstress, clever as she is. But even as she's saying this, she knows you'll never hear it or know it, because she's afraid you still love Entara, and all the time you'd be kissing Ragatti out of gratitude and telling her she was the one you longed for, you'd still be saying it to the damned high-holy Entara-para-para, the one I would wish I could be if I were not me. And right now, me is going to leave you warm and happy and breathing lightly but strongly. I'm going to lick these little stitches on your new nose just a little, because I put them there and I'm the only one in the universe who can see them. No one else knows that about you, even Entara."

And with that she rose off his body like the morning dew and slipped into a sheer cape the color of sunrise in the desert. As she unlocked the door and slipped outside, she did not cry, because Forlani can't.

Three days later, Trevor, with the travel documents and a small suitcase, walked in front of Klein, in a hover-chair, and an orderly, as they left the Epidemiology Center on Corlatis, on their way to the neighboring spaceport and a ship that would take them, by way of numerous stops and transfers, back to Domremy. The staff had given him little gifts and treats for the trip and had assembled on the steps to see him off. Tatatio was grinning widely, showing off his pointed teeth, and squinting despite a big sun visor, because his race was crepuscular and avoided broad daylight. Tatatio had explained that Coco138, the thoracic surgeon, would not be there because he was aquatic and had actually done Klein's chest while they were both suspended in liquid. The elusive Doctor Torghh turned out to be a machine, causing Klein to wonder why a robot should be so reticent and shy of the patients whose very eyes he repaired. As Klein waved at them on the steps, he wondered where his little candy-striper was. Finally he spotted Amanda next to another human, probably the lady specialist who had done his ears. As he looked closer, he could see that woman had her arm around Amanda's shoulder in a way beyond the usual doctor-nurse standards of affection. As he moved away, he peered closer, through Dr. Torghh's excellent new eyes, and gasped. The woman next to Amanda was Helga Pedersen. He had been that close to his own daughter and had never consciously understood it.

8

The trip back from Corlatis to Domremy took over a year longer than expected. Trevor mused that it could be blamed on bad weather in outer space. Of course, he was aware that there is no weather in space, at least in the sense humans usually attached to the word – no night and day, no seasons, no perceptible variation in temperature, no rain or ice or wind or fog. But there are things that happen that affect space travel, and it so happened that a major ion disturbance in one of the star systems he and Klein had to pass through had caused the equivalent of a traffic jam to develop. While space is mostly emptiness, the anchorages that serve as transfer points for the craft that ply the Perseid Arm of the Milky Way Galaxy are usually located on the fringes of planetary systems and the suns at the center of those systems are active and dynamic reactors that vary tremendously in their output of radiation. In turn, that radiation can have a deleterious effect on the operation of the types of motors that power interplanetary ships. So navigating into a system with an ion disturbance could be likened to driving an automobile into a swollen creek. Control is soon lost and the craft becomes subject to disaster. There is not much that even the most advanced civilizations can do to take control of the radiation pattern of a star, so ships tend to line up at neighboring systems like semis at a truck stop or airplanes on the tarmac of an airline hub.

Trevor tried not to obsess about such topics as many fellow humans do. The majority of his race clung to vague notions that their opposable thumbs, upright bipedal stature, and relatively symmetrical physique confer some kind of intellectual superiority, but Dissenters realized as a primary tenet of their beliefs that human bodies were from the very beginning of the Evil Earth both a blessing and a curse -- mostly the latter. Certainly, in space travel, the vulnerability of human flesh and its almost complete insensitivity to electromagnetism and many of the other most important forces in the cosmos place the race at a distinct disadvantage to other more perceptive types of creatures.   No wonder humans had never truly discovered interstellar travel, but had simply glommed the technology from those more intelligent when the

Quarantines instituted in the twentieth century had ended.

To pay for the trip he and Klein were taking, Trevor had had to employ all his wiliness and determination. Even with the help of credits from Ragatti, Entara, and some of the generous staff at the Corlatis facility, they could not make it all the way. While Klein reclined in a space coma, Trevor had to seek out every odd job he could find along the way, even working as a guinea pig in medical experiments and selling a kidney at one transfer. One would never think that an organ that seems to be nothing more than a crude filter could be so valuable, but they couldn't be grown as livers could or replaced by machines like hearts or neuropatched like parts of the human brain. It was that kidney that paid the final stages of their path back to Domremy. Trevor was actually somewhat sad to part with it, since he had a secret nostalgia for his flesh that was not supposed to be part of the ideal Dissenter attitude. But then, his pilgrimage originally had nothing to do with Klein and was supposed to be a quest for illumination through visits to ancient religious sites. He had been more than a little surprised when messages advised him that Klein might be on Song Pa and should be aided if located. Rarely did the Circle, so often willing to accept the loss of life, reach out to one who was not within it. Trevor knew, however, that this had to do at least as much with Entara as with Klein, since she was becoming a genuine phenomenon in the entire sector and was rumored to be ascending to the Council of

Nine. The Dissenters held their alliance with the Forlani to be sacred, since the Purple Ones had been the major means of their exodus from the Evil Earth and also since the Forlani determination to restore the original health of their planet's ecology was a topic so dear to the Dissenters' way of life. Yet even without Entara, Klein held a certain special interest for the Circle because of his connections to Peebo's family and to the newly recruited Luis. Trevor himself, like several other of the most mystically inclined Dissenters, had had premonitions that Klein's destiny would have an effect on events still to come on Domremy.

Klein finally began to emerge from his space coma and found himself not at Stafford Station, but at another landing site at the far northern extremity of the established colony. He asked Trevor about it as soon as he had gathered his wits and begun to walk around.

"Why are we here instead of at Stafford? Does it have something to do with smuggling me back in under a false ID?"

"No, no," Trevor answered. "You see, most of the transfers we passed through couldn't have cared less who you were, or even if you were to be revived. To them you were a frozen human chunk with a Farm Bureau pass. Even when we made it back into the area where Hyperion had agents and check points, they couldn't identify you as Klein because of all that medical work done at Corlatis. Ragatti did more than just reconstruct your nose with love," he chuckled.

"You mean she deliberately altered me to create a cover?"

"Right, and not just her. Oh, she added a cosmetic touch or two around the eyes and jaw, just enough to deceive the identometrics. But rumor has it she also used her considerable charms to get some of the other doctors to make little changes inside and out, as well. I can't even imagine how she got an aquatic like Coco138 or a robot like Torghh to go along. I'm not even going to try to imagine. But you have enough carefully installed features to put any scanners off the scent. She put lots of pepper on the bloodhound's snout."

Klein looked around the farmstead where he was recovering from the long flight. "I expected when I started to wake up to see Peebo and some of the family."

"This was a better choice. Actually, Peebo is not at the farm right now. When he came to share his experiences in the Circle, he decided to take some time away at the research center on the southern continent to clear his conscience on your matter and… some earlier things. Beyond his original plans, he has continued to go back periodically to pursue an important research project and he's there right now."

"I could have gone to his place to wait for him."

"I know that, and your friend Luis has asked several times when you are coming."

"Who the hell is Luis?"

"You knew him as Guzman. He has joined the Circle and taken a spiritual name. You will be surprised that many things have happened in his life."

"What about his buddy Rodriguez, did he join, too?"

"Eventually, you will also learn what happened to him."

"I wouldn't mind staying with Peebo's folks and helping out on the farm while I wait."

"Felicia has quite a bit of help already. While she was willing to help care for you, she felt your presence might be a bit of a shock to the kids. Disconcerting to the younger ones, especially. So you see, this is a better solution for now."

"Sure, I see."

Despite his agreeing with Trevor in the open, Klein could not help but feel rejected on the inside. Just another brush-off in a string of them, tracing back to Entara. He had dreamt of her often in his coma, touching her motherly body, caressing her fur, kissing her everywhere, cuddling some of her newborn pups on his lap. He could have settled for never waking up at all if he could have continued forever in those illusions that were so much more satisfying that the rotten facts of everyday life. Even Ragatti had unexpectedly screwed him till he was cross-eyed and then walked off into her own future. Not to mention Helga, who had repaired his ears and not said a word to him when he could hear again. And Amanda, who had chatted with him and fed him, but then, when he realized she was partly his own flesh and blood, had waved to him from the hospital steps without ever calling him "Dad." Now Felicia was treating him like a contaminated sheep that she feared to put near her little lambs. He fully expected Trevor to put on his pilgrim's robes and traipse off to some forgotten temple any day now, leaving him to fend for himself. Klein felt a tear in the corner of his "old" eye, but not in his new one and speculated that the mechanical Dr. Torghh would not have bothered with tears. He strode off in search of beer and soon located whiskey, as well.

The booze took its toll and prolonged convalescence also had an effect on Klein's appearance as well as his morale. One day as he returned from a long walk through the settlement, he noticed one of the kids in the town staring up at him strangely.

"What's wrong? You don't like what you see?"

"You're shaggy," stated the youngster. Klein couldn't tell for sure if it was a boy or a girl. Dissenters didn't differentiate much in childhood fashions and their young ran around in coveralls most of the time until they were about ten.

"I've been travelling a lot. What do you want me to do?"

"You should see John," the kid answered without hesitation.

"And who might John be?"

"John over at the reactor.'

"What's he going to do? Atomize me?"

"He cuts people's hair. He's cheap, too," the little critic added after a second.

So this little creep thinks I'm indigent besides being unkempt, thought Klein as he strode away. Still, he had never had a haircut at a power station and there was not much else to do in town, so he decided to look up this John. After searching around, he was directed to a shack where he found a dark-haired, clean-shaven fellow at a com screen.

"Are you John?"

"Yes. That's me. And I can see why you have come. Step into my parlor," he said as he pointed to a little wooden platform with a chair on it. "Nothing fancy here. But I'm the best barber in town. In fact, the only one."

Klein sat. John covered him with a clean piece of cloth and started snipping away methodically. After a while, he had reduced the rat's nest on Klein's head to an orderly coiffure and held up a mirror so the customer could see. "How's the length? Suit you?"

"Shorter around the back, please."

"I don't think you really want that. People who know how to look will see these," he warned, touching the two little prison marks still beneath the hair line near Klein's right ear. A souvenir from the Old Country. Klein automatically tensed to spring at the barber and scanned the room for possible weapons, knowing John still had the scissors in his hand.

"Let's see," said John, peering closer, "Sicherheitbereits Münster! A political man, after my own heart. And... Athens! So you were a TV star, too. Don't worry, a bull is always a bull in any language and a con is always a con. Ispahan Number Three," he explained, showing Klein a different mark near his elbow.

"Irani? What were you in for? No Sweeney Todd stuff, I hope."

"Not exactly. After the Third Islamic Revolution, my unit was out near Karachi and we had a disagreement with some of the Revolutionary Guards. Sent a lot of them to Hell, too, before they rounded us up."

Klein could see in the mirror that John was finishing up the job. "So you're not what you appear. How in the world did you get up here, John? I thought the Ispahan prisons were pretty much a dead end."

"You're right, it's really Jahangar, by the way, but John goes over a lot easier on this rock. Yet I think the Dissenters already know some of the truth about my past and don't care. The Guards had us cleaning up a failed reactor, so I learned a few things about energy. Then Hyperion needed somebody low-cost to look after this little Swedish job in the town and they picked me from the pool." His tone changed and his eyes refocused far away as he went on. "That was just as the plague was starting to get out of hand. I didn't have any chance to get the family out. Not that they would have agreed, anyway."

"I'm sorry."

"And I'm sorry for you. I hear things in Germany got even worse. In Iran, there are out-of-the-way places where people can hole up. Not so for your people. 'Tut mir leid, mein Freund."

Klein responded grimly, "I didn't really have anyone left."

"Still," remarked John-Jahangar, "There are people who might be on the lookout for you. Yes, I have an idea who you are. No one has stopped talking about the disappearance of the number one mankiller, no matter how many years have passed. All over the settlements, people expect you to come walking out of the prairie grass at any moment. It's true, Hyperion has other fish to fry now. Since transport through Tau Ceti to Earth was suspended, they're busily pulling out everything worthwhile to relocate to Dahlgren or Double E or one of the other colonies. If they'd had more time and cargo space, they would have grabbed my little Lundquist 335, but it's small potatoes as reactors go. In a couple of years, we won't even need it here. The Dissenters got their hands on a lot of piping and pumps somehow and have started installing geothermal wherever they have a cluster of farms. A lot of individuals don't even bother to hook up to that and stick to their windmills and solar panels. It's a good thing I can cut hair, because the power business on Domremy is going to be pretty slow. Voilà, all done."

Klein fished in his pockets. "I'm afraid all I've got to pay is some transfer scrip..."

"No need," laughed John. "You've given me plenty already!" He pointed at the tufts of hair lying around the base of his platform. "Relics, Mr. Klein. Someday you'll be a historical figure, maybe even a saint. And it's authentic, DNA traceable. Don't worry, I'll keep it safe under lock and key until the last Hyperion spy has left and I can arrange a few little sales in peace. Come back any time you like."

It took Klein a couple of weeks to get over John's reaction. He was used to being a pariah on Domremy. It's true he was the exalted Teacher Klein in the mahäme on Forlan, but that was all due to Entara's damned songs. So far, the way he was being treated by Trevor and the townsfolk in this settlement had led him to think his status hadn't changed. Nevertheless, he realized that barbers are generally the bearers of all sorts of hidden truths and he was disinclined to dismiss John's enthusiasm over getting a batch of his hair. Maybe he was more than a disgusting murderer who had lost an election after all.

Although Trevor mentioned in the following days that things were going very badly on Earth, Klein remained ignorant of the extent of damage the plague was doing. After all, his thoughts were still focused on Forlan, though filtered through his harrowing experiences on Song Pa and Corlatis. Had he known more about the changes that Hyperion was undergoing, he might have been able to make clearer plans for how to act on Domremy.

Hyperion's new Headquarters of Intergalactic Operations was a dull affair. Boxy, undecorated, and located in Boise, Idaho, the building where Erica and the others involved in the Domremy program had been redesignated didn't seem exactly Spartan to her—it still had the requisite TV monitor in the lounge room, the motivational posters on the walls, and the sound system softly playing bland elevator music that some psychologist had claimed would relax employees and relieve their stress. In fact, it was probably one of the best available buildings in the Intermountain Exclusion Zone. But the building lacked the distinctive character of the old New York office Hyperion had previously assigned to the Domremy branch, and Erica missed the old building's exterior columns, reproductions of 20th Century space travel photographs, and metallic blue elevators. This was a building without character, without a sense of purpose. It could just as easily be an insurance office or call center as the locus of the once-prestigious Domremy operation. At least it was plague-secure for the moment. How the decades fly!

Although the office was having a party in her honor, Erica wasn't feeling very festive. She wandered over to a table filled with appetizers and munched on a tiny triangular sandwich. She saw Robert Salerno, one of the remaining workers assigned to her project who had not yet been reassigned, taking a generous helping of punch. "Why so glum?" he asked her, noticing the melancholy expression on her face. "It's your party."

"It's just...Bobby, don't you feel like this company's lost something? I can remember going to the party celebrating Bill's twenty years with Hyperion. Back then, they treated us like we were really valuable to the company—they even let Bill be the first one to operate the controls of the new aquadrone in that party! He was so happy to be the first one to steer an aquadrone through the ruins of New Orleans beneath the Gulf of Mexico. This party feels like it's fit for a bunch of stooges in data entry, not high-level executives."

"What can you do?" Bobby said. "You know they're not giving the Domremy project the funding they used to. At least they medevacked us out of that pesthole in the East before we were contaminated. Were you really expecting to get what Bill got?"

"No. Not given the budget cuts we've been getting lately. I was hoping for some reassurance that we still mattered to the company in the grand scheme of things, though."

"Of course we do. We're here at this party, aren't we?" Bobby shrugged and got himself another glass of punch. Tired of discussing company matters with him, Erica wandered around the office, engaging in small talk with her coworkers about the weather and what their children were doing in school, but remained pensive and preoccupied with the Domremy program throughout the party. Stories about birthdays and report cards couldn't get the sense of anxiety out of her mind, and she found it difficult to follow the conversations she was engaged in. As she was looking at a clock on the wall, hoping the party would come to a merciful end, she saw an older man motioning for her to come over and talk with him.

"Erica, could you come into my office for a bit? We need to chat," he asked.

Erica nodded and followed him away from the party into his spacious work area. As she looked around the office, a real office with walls and a door, unlike her cubicle, she noticed his computer was still running. She wondered why, if he had been planning the conversation for some time, he had left his work computer on. Had he been checking over the details of the Domremy program before inviting her in?

"Hello, I'm Ernest Samuels," the man said, extending his hand to Erica. She shook it and sat down in a chair by his desk. "You may call me Mr. Samuels. Hyperion's board of directors and I have been looking over the reports and statistics from the Domremy colony's last few years of operation. We realize that Mr. Hollingsworth, your predecessor, made it difficult for you to achieve profitability on Domremy given the state our operations were in before he left. However, it appears that conditions on the planet have not progressed, and have in some aspects deteriorated, since Hollingsworth was removed from his position."

"I'm aware of the problems on Domremy," Erica said. "It's very difficult to motivate many of those people—they're convicted criminals for the most part, not voluntary colonists, and they don't have much of a work ethic. Also, there's been a problem with drug consumption and distribution that developed in the last two years, at about the point Site 89 developed into Xanderburg. Some close-knit groups of colonists are more resistant to these negative developments than others, but we know relatively little about them."

"The Dissenters? They're one of the few truly productive elements of the colony. But they're not productive enough to make it profitable and worth the expense of maintaining our current scale of operations on Domremy. We're going to accelerate scaling back operations over the next few months, leaving just the Archive in operation so we can maintain on-planet records in case we decide to reverse course and increase our Domremy presence again. This present health emergency can't last forever, can it?"

"I would hope our Headquarters staffing of the Domremy operation would at least remain stable for the short term," Erica tentatively said, her anxiety finally getting the better of her. *Damn! I should've never said that. If they weren't making plans to fire me before, they certainly will be now. It's only a matter of time before my career is as ruined as Bill's was*, she thought.

"Oh, we'll be making some staff reductions soon enough. But if you're feeling apprehensive, you shouldn't be. We have something special planned for you." Mr. Samuels reached into his desk and brought out a large brown folder with a memory stick attached. "This is a synopsis of our post-Domremy plans for interstellar operations. There's an offer for a division transfer to our new off-world combined center on Tomakio, if you're interested. I suggest you look it over. If you want in, bring it back to me with the forms filled out two weeks from now. And one more thing… all the information in here is strictly confidential, not to be disclosed to anyone other than you."

"I doubt Bill would have been able to keep that request," Erica said with a gentle chuckle. "He was always the type to crow in triumph over the smallest hint of a prestigious achievement or promotion."

"That's why we're not offering it to anyone like him. In your current position, you have proven to us that you have all of the personality characteristics that are valuable to us in this new venture – characteristics that Mr. Hollingsworth lacked. Don't disappoint us for placing our trust in you. We'll be waiting for your response in two weeks."

Erica glanced at the nondescript brown folder. It was so prosaic in appearance that it would barely attract attention, yet packed with infinite possibilities for advancement. She guessed that all the papers were copy-secure and that the memory drive had a self-destruct, as well. Erica could feel a slight tremble of anticipation in her hands as she reached out to grasp the folder. She felt the beginning of a smile forming at the corners of her mouth as she felt the thick paper in her hands.

A week after that far-off interview, Trevor appeared before Klein in his traveling clothes, with a small duffle containing all his personal articles slung over his shoulder.

"You should pack your things to go to Stafford Station," he announced. "Someone will be coming this evening to pick you up. As for me, I can finally continue my pilgrimage now."

"What do you mean you're leaving? This is abrupt!"

"You knew the goats would have to be milked," Trevor answered in Croptalk.

"Well, I suppose I've been waiting to see Peebo and his folks again. But why should you leave? Wouldn't you be more valuable as leader of the Circle?"

"A circle has no leader, as it has no corners. And if I wanted to become one, it would be an even more powerful motive for me to leave."

Klein scowled. He had grown accustomed to Trevor's low-key advice and had been counting on it to try to readjust more fully to life on Domremy. "What good is it for you to be nosing around old temples, anyway? You should share your knowledge with the other Dissenters instead of traipsing around and devoting yourself to tourism." Klein regretted this outburst almost as soon as it left his lips. He had no right to preach to the man who had saved his life and tended him so faithfully.

Yet Trevor was not angry. He merely gave Klein a look that he might have given to a foolish child. "It's not just sightseeing. The object of my pilgrimage is to share new knowledge with the Circle about something that's a bit hard to explain. Actually, we only dimly understand it now, and that's why I was dispatched to find out more. It has to do with something we call the Spirit Substrate."

"That sounds very esoteric all right."

"Some of us have come to believe that there may be a common factor in many, if not most, religions. More than just earth-sprung religions, the concept of religion across the barriers of species, senses, and even ideas. The old Roman Catholics had an inkling of this – something they called the Mystical Body of Christ. Certain doctrines among the Latter Day Saints also pointed in this direction. So do some branches of Buddhism, particularly early Mahayana. It's even tied in with the twenty-first century economic theory of the value substrate. We're hoping that knowing more about religions across the two explored spiral arms of the galaxy can add something significant."

"Well, better you than me," Klein pouted. "I think I would have to give up quickly in such a vague quest." He didn't dare add "hopeless" to the description.

"I've found a few clues that may give me a thread to follow. For now, it's back to the ruins on Song Pa, which I was just beginning to investigate when word came about you." Trevor paused a while before adding, "Klein, my thoughts and prayers will be with you. Your path may be more vague than mine. There are things close by that may prove extremely difficult to deal with. You will have to trust your strengths and distrust them at the same time. It may call for some delicacy, which, frankly, is not always your strong suit. Please be careful. Don't make me regret turning the bull loose in the pasture. Farewell now, and hopefully *aufwiedersehen!*"

Klein watched Trevor head down the road and around the next bend, then set about packing. His articles were scarcely more numerous than Trevor's. He wondered if Peebo had taken care of the old volume of Faulkner he had left with him. Since several hours still remained before evening, he decided something substantial, like Mahler, was needed to calm his anxieties. He put on his headphones and drifted into a more orderly, more musical universe.

The second sun was headed toward the horizon when he spied a vehicle coming from the direction of Stafford Station. It was definitely home-made Domremy material: two thallops pulling a contraption of various pieces of steel welded together over a pair of wheels salvaged from an old military transport. It probably served mainly to haul grain and hay in from the fields. When it drew closer, he recognized the wizened face of an older Guzman at the reins. He went down into the road to meet him.

"Good to see you again, amigo," Klein said in greeting.

"Well, look at you. Stay right there and let me appreciate the changes. Yes, the nose, the ears, not quite the same, but not bad at all. They warned me you had a lot of surgery, but I didn't know what to expect. If I didn't know you so well before, I might not have recognized you. Hop on."

"Wait till you get a load of my prosthetic lower leg, Guzman" Klein joked, as he hoisted himself onto the seat.

"Maybe you can kick some ass with it!" chuckled the driver. He turned the wagon around and headed home. "By the way, it's Luis now. Believe it or not, pardner, I'm in the Circle now."

"A reprobate like you," mocked Klein. "They must have lowered their standards."

"When the cyclone blows, you head to the shelter," replied Luis, showing off his Croptalk. "There's more than that, I'm married and I got a family now. Many new responsibilities."

"How'd that happen?"

Luis flapped the reins a bit to straighten out the thallops, which were not the ideal creature to work in tandem. "Oigame, after I became a speaker in the Circle, there was this widow with two kids. Everybody kept mentioning her to me and suggesting all the time I help out at her place after her husband died of icing cancer. So, I started to go around there just to shut them up. And then... Things just kind of took their course. She's a little older than me, but still too young to be happy sleeping by herself. She made that very clear. And she's a very good cook. Knows how to run things in the farm, too."

"So what's the catch?" asked Klein, sensing a bit of reluctance in Luis's tone.

"She's not the best looking woman I ever screwed," he sighed.

"I'm impressed you're so up front about it."

"I gotta be. I'm in the Circle now and we're pretty honest, as you know. But since I'm in the mood to share, I'll tell you one thing more, 'cause you'll find out anyway. Sometimes I cheat a little bit. Every now and then I really get horny for one of them Forlani girls down at the house. I make up a good excuse and I'm real discreet, understand? But I'm sure Betsy knows anyway, so I told her and expected to get hell in return. Was I surprised! She says it's OK and sometimes she likes to spend some time with Cousin Al and she hopes I don't mind."

"What did you answer to that?"

"I say, make sure you let me know so I can take care of the kids and their supper."

"Ha! Pal, you've received a gift from God and if I had that kind of ability, my life would be a lot easier."

They chatted all the way back to Stafford Station and it wasn't until Peebo's place was in sight that Klein off-handedly asked, "By the way, how's old Rodriguez."

Luis's brow darkened and he bowed his head, muttering, "I'm sorry, now's not the time for me to talk about that. Maybe later."

Klein's uneasiness at this cryptic response was swept away when he was greeted by Peebo and his brood on the steps of the farmstead. They clustered joyously around him, took his bag, and ushered him into the dining room for a feast. Only Felicia remained a little aloof – polite, hospitable, and correct, but holding back something that Klein knew he would eventually have to deal with.

In the fortnight that followed, Klein got reacquainted with Peebo's children, who had grown so much since he left for Forlan. The "Number One Son" was Mel, short for Melanchthon, that cerebral reformer who had almost managed to avert the Wars of Religion back in the sixteenth century. It was an appropriate name because Mel, now over twenty years old, was a thinker who set his own pace and reached beyond the bounds of habit. He had already learned everything there was to learn on Domremy about farming and talked about going off-world to acquire new skills, prompting verbal skirmishes with his mother. "Number Two Son," Mohandes, aka Moe, by contrast had no interest in leaving Domremy and was so keen on its ecology that he had taken over Peebo's work with the Varoneys, with the old man's blessing. "Number One Daughter" Odile had staked her claim on a young fellow in an adjoining village and was already negotiating various details of her nuptials with her parents. The others who were practically babies when Klein had left were now rushing toward or through their teens and eager to show off their strong points to the distinguished guest. They knew they would in turn become minor celebrities when Klein's long-rumored return was openly acknowledged. Klein opened up to them as he had rarely done for a long time with fellow humans. Knowingly or not, he was compensating for the lost presence of his surrogate family on Forlan and for his too hasty separation from Amanda. Only Felicia, despite her veneer of welcome, seemed to refuse to accept him as a member of the household.

 The time finally came when Luis arrived to bring Klein to the inevitable meeting with the Circle. After they arrived at the chosen farmstead and the ashes had been laid out, a Dissenter named Stewart, who had played a minor role in his last encounter, took the lead in speaking with Klein. Stewart was as close to a dandy as one would find among the Dissenters, wearing a fancy embroidered vest and an immaculate Stetson.

 "Again the sun dips down, friend Klein," he began, "But the evening brings us peace. The foxes no longer roam around the henhouse and the chicken hawks don't hover in the sky." *True, Hyperion spies seemed to have all but vanished and the observer drones had disappeared with them.* "We wonder if the Mankiller can walk in such peaceful lanes. We wonder if he can see into his own mind and keep his word better than he did after last we met."

"I have been mindful of my promises about the trip to Forlan every day since I confronted the purple one named Tays'she. The fact that he threatened my life more than I did his doesn't matter much. I was totally prepared to die that day. I had lost something I doubt you could fully appreciate," he added hesitantly, thinking back to that night when both he and Entara might have died for their love for one another.

Looking more determined, Klein went on. "What I could not abide was that this hateful creature threatened lives that I cherish."

"You offer that more as an excuse than as a revelation," Felicia shot back unexpectedly. "Isn't it true that you could have immobilized your opponent, unmasked his plots, and secured your... friends, without administering a second, excessive dose of the venom? Was it any better than murder to turn that wretch into a living corpse?"

Klein was about to respond when Peebo decisively spoke out, with his eyes on his wife. "Compassion knows many forms but no boundaries. Tays'she had become so warped and sick with greed that he threatened untold numbers of his own species. I have already told you what kind of fears held me back. Thanks to Klein's mastery of fear, the purple females face a future of freedom from oppression. They irrigate their groves with Klein's blood."

"They weren't too noble to irrigate themselves with other fluids from this man," Felicia spat back vehemently. "I assert his compassion was no more than an afterthought of lust."

Cousin Al put a hand on her shoulder. "Felicia, you have proven your own worth time and again, but is it right to let your own turmoil roil the ponds of others? Please remember why we are here."

"Peebo, Al, I can speak for myself," Klein interjected. "I have sensed since I came back that I had wronged Felicia somehow. Maybe that proves I can't control where my actions lead, but I swear I had no intention to hurt her. And I know you all suffered more than I did in some ways," he added, looking around the periphery of the circle. "Because it is your nature and your will to feel the pain of sins, to want to rectify what all of us, but I especially, brought out of the Evil Earth. I don't deny it. And you, Felicia," he said, turning to face her, "what mistake have I made to anger you?"

"I hate you, Klein... Yes, I use that word because we here in the Circle must speak the truth. I hate you because of what you did to my husband. You made him a killer, too, more than once. You took him away from me when I most wanted him, all because he felt the need to atone at the Research Center." She turned toward Peebo. "I've never before revealed all this to you, but I say now you had no right to let this man's contamination creep into your soul. And now, by assuming that burden all this time, I've poisoned myself, too. But that's not the worst. Now I look at our own children and wonder if they have been ruined. Melanchthon yearns for something far away that he can't even express and I worry that he will become a mankiller. I wonder if Odile's children will carry the infection. I live in terror." She hung her head with that admission.

"And you speak from pain," pronounced Stewart. "Felicia, I know you have forgotten only for an instant that your family has strong soul. Don't we hold as the roof beam of our faith that the dharma power overcomes the pull of even the most deeply rooted sin? I've heard you yourself testify brilliantly to this fact." With that, Felicia was able to raise her face again to the assembly.

"Yet, as for you, Klein," Stewart went on, "We have no proof that you can let in the light. Only hope. How do you feel about your past actions and those to come?"

"Klein, are you ready to join us?" chimed in Luis. "Together we can help you get over all those demons. I know, man. I have felt it myself. Give yourself a chance."

"If I were a better man, maybe I could take that step," answered Klein. "But not now. I don't know exactly why, but I sense there are too many loose ends in me. Even if I give up the desire for revenge I nourished when I was on Song Pa, even if I can somehow reconnect with the ones I want to be close to, I can't be sure that I have the strength to control myself the way you want me to. There are times when it's as if I hear a horn blowing and I have to rise up and walk toward death, against all logic and reason. I have no excuse."

"We have no intention of forcing you to lie," Stewart assured him. "In my own mind, I can see you in danger once again. Not all the dragons in Eden have perished. Understand, though, friend Klein, that we are here to help you." In conclusion, he began to scatter the ashes with his boot, and Peebo walked Klein back to his home.

Farm work on Peebo's spread was helping Klein to recover his physical form, even though he seemed to make little progress in improving his image in Felicia's eyes.

A few weeks later, he was plowing a field destined for sunflowers with a mechanical tractor that some Dissenters had rigged up for the use of those who hadn't managed the art of field preparation with livestock. He suddenly saw a blur of purple far down the road. As it approached, he realized his first impressions were correct, that it was a Forlani girl out running. By her distinctive short cape, it must be someone of authority in the Local house. He stopped to watch because he had never seen a Forlani on Domremy move with the speed he had seen them use so effortlessly on their own world. He was surprised that she came straight for him and stopped at the edge of the field. When he joined her, she nodded and said, "Greetings, Teacher Klein, I have a message for you."

Her hand was trembling a bit and Klein knew it was not from the exertion of running. The little auburn hairs on her forearm told him it was from nervousness. After all, she knew who he was and this was obviously a big moment for her. She handed him a letter in an envelope and Klein looked up to thank her, but she went on quickly, "I've done my best to translate and transcribe it. I hope it's all right. It was passed from planets and transfers by word of mouth, of course, memorized. No one will forget, I can promise you that. Oh, it is a most beautiful song in our language and I would be glad to sing it for you some time if you wish."

"I hardly know how to thank you."

"Teacher Klein, it is my privilege. I realize you probably don't recognize me because I was only in one of your study groups at the mahäme for a couple of days. My name is Iquitzli. It's been a long time and I've already been on this planet for two years. I am now senior at the local house. Forgive me for coming unannounced, but your friend Luis confirmed it was you who arrived recently. I make sure he is very well cared for when he drops in and your own instructions on the psychology of clients have proven extremely helpful, of course."

"Iquitzli, I know he is quite happy with you and your friends. Can you tell me when this was sent?"

"It has taken several months because it was passed on through six couriers. I know you will want to examine it in private, so I will be going. Please come visit if you can."

"Thank you again, Iquitzli. Your matriline will be proud of you."

She sped away and Klein looked at the envelope for a few seconds before opening it, trying to imagine what the message might be and how he should react to it. He finally gave up and opened it to begin to read.

>My dear friend,
>Word has come that you are now on your way safely back to Domremy. How overjoyed I was to learn of it! I have thought about you every day – I promise it is true. Already I break my promise, it was mostly in the night. How often I have watched the dark skies, often with my daughters at my side in the garden, and wondered what had become of you. I pictured us together, happy in the past. Often I dreamt of you and would wake up and be shocked that we were not really together, that it was time to let my mind's images dissipate like a morning fog and start tending to the children or seeing to some other task that couldn't wait. In a better universe, I pictured us falling off to sleep together with no regrets for the day.

Do you know that in those first days on Domremy, I would often wake up and look at you at night and think to myself, "I've made this strange human happy and driven away all his torments. My little body magic has done more than just earn a few credits for the matriline, it has transformed him and restored him so that he can face the sunlight where he will have to kill his own and never show a reaction because he must be ready instantly to kill again. If he has to face death itself, maybe my embraces will let him do it without suffering." I was so smug in a way and so delighted not to feel the least bit guilty about it. I could skip through the day while you were away and try to imagine I was in your skin, that I was brave enough to face terrifying creatures, and helpless to change it, and witness lives vanishing before me. Now that I've had to show a little courage myself, I truly know what I was missing.

But what about you? I hope you are not still suffering from the awful ordeal you experienced on Song Pa. Trevor and Ragatti, mainly Ragatti, have told me about the condition they found you in. I can't imagine the pain you must have endured — even mating must not be so bad. To lose part of your leg. Is your new one serving you well? Ragatti seemed to think you were doing fine, and I have to admit your new nose is very beautiful indeed – she has a right to brag about it so much. Of course, she told me, and most of the mahäme as well, about the goodbye gift she gave you and I have to say I heartily approve. I know humans tend to get jealous in those situations, but we usually do not, and I am happy that you took pleasure from one who so enjoys giving it and who knows completely how to appeal to males. I spoke to her about returning to you, but she claims she is too fickle and adventure-loving to stay long with one companion. That was the same response she gave when I offered to try to arrange an advantageous marriage for her, though I must admit, she would have more willingly gone back to you than to take a place in a Forlani marriage bed. I don't know if she's more fearful of the pain of mating or vain about her youthful body. Anyway, she is remarkable and I am content that she shared herself with you.

For my part, I now have felt the joy of birth more than fifty times and even my second and third daughters are now married and pregnant. I assisted at their post-matings. My eldest daughter, Ayan'we, whom you met and who is quite fascinated by you, has no intention of marrying in the near future. In fact, she has been off-planet since shortly after your friend Fatty send word of your location. You won't find her in any of the houses, though she was judged quite qualified, for she is extremely intellectual and has grown even more so since finishing all the recommended studies. She has gone far beyond that and pursued knowledge on several worlds, moving around so quickly that I confess it is difficult to keep up with her. She told me not long ago that she wants to contact you herself through a safe channel for a face to face talk, so don't be too surprised if you hear from her.

I am usually overwhelmed with work, besides caring for the children, even though Tays'she passed away. You may not believe it, but it was not so difficult supervising his care because somehow I forgave him completely. Ayan'we always said I must be insane, because she could barely stand his presence, even though his mind was gone and there was no more evil will there. But I suppose for me the fact that his personality was totally gone relieved me of any impulse to hate him. Despite the fact that he sought the death of me and my daughters. This time it was your courage in confronting him that washed me clean of any desire to feel hateful. That's the same reason I never tried to hide him or to dissociate him from me. After all, he had a fine creative mind that ruined itself through needless greed and perversity. I was proud to be his First Wife again, as if he had been a better husband. Of course, it was not all pristine kindness. Perhaps I was just determined to be the First Wife I deserved to be. You see, this is what you gained for me. Not to speak of my daughters, who have all been privileged as a result of your sacrifice, or my three male children, who would probably all have been gelded and reduced to dumb servitude if things had gone differently. By the way, I stay in touch with them as closely as I can, given the barriers of the Brotherhood, and am on good terms with all three. The eldest seems to have inherited much of Tays'she's artistic talent without the nasty qualities.

All these family considerations don't leave a great deal of time for other activities, but I am constantly being asked by the matriline and the state to take on more responsibilities, even though I went into semi-retirement from the Passport Office, only doing consulting work with them from time to time. The Eyes of Alertness has turned me into a sort of diplomat because I work well with various other matrilines, especially Long Tails, Hands for Fruit, and Barkscratchers. There is a big ecological project called Common Groves that requires so many meetings! I've managed to dodge service on several councils by coming up with lame excuses, but every time I turn around the mahäme is absolutely requiring my participation in some ceremony or conference. Whenever I can, I try to disappear with some of the children to a place where I'm hard to reach. Do you know one of my hideaways? It's the camp that you had the assassins bomb by mistake when they were after us.

If you have gotten this far, you are probably experiencing deadly boredom. I will finish by asking you to please, please send a letter through the Dissenters letting me know how you are. Whatever you may believe, I would like to come to you if I were free, but my youngest need me and they're far from being flight-worthy. It's all I can do to stop myself from establishing a visual comlink, but Hyperion and the Brotherhood both still have death rewards out for you. I'll let my talented daughter try to find a way to get this to you without putting them on your scent. Let them go on thinking you're probably dead, if that helps you go on living. That's all I want for you. I hope you can find more happiness. Even if it may mean forgetting me, I'll understand. But do speak to me somehow, so that one of those stars will light a special light for me when I look at the night sky.

Yours with deepest feeling, E.

Klein stood at the edge of the field for more than an hour looking down at the papers. His wound had reopened and he was stunned. There was no way to react and he could not imagine what to do. Part of him wanted to rush into Stafford Station, to the com office or to the Forlani house and say something, anything, in response, but he knew his voice would fail him. Part of him wanted to be able to hate Entara, but that voice abolished itself in a nanosecond, like some subatomic particle that must spring into existence but must also vanish just as soon. Part of him wanted to find a weapon and kill himself then and there, but what was still left of himself to kill? *This must be a little bit what it felt to be the Frankenstein monster. Patched together by the will of others. Torn away from whatever attachments there originally were. Longing for a counterpart that will only be present in my imagination. Wandering around exciting terror when I want acceptance, and awe when I want nothing but to be alone. Kept alive by revenge and deprived of any kind of meaningful death. Now I'm going back to start that tractor and I'm going to till this rectangle of soil. Then I'll start looking for another one. If there is a God, he will find me something to do.*

Maybe Klein could ask Luis about God. The next day he went to his new farm to have a talk. Luis introduced him proudly to Betsy and her children, bragging that another was on the way. When they stepped away to the barns to talk privately, Klein congratulated him. Luis's answer surprised him.

"I know, you're thinking, but do you know it's your own? Well, I'll tell you I don't give a damn. They're all mine now and it doesn't matter whose little wiggler first got them going. I think all that stuff about heredity is crap, anyway. You got to choose who you'll be. I choose this. It's better than anything I ever had or would have had. We all do what we do to get this thing called pleasure and then most of us can't live with the consequences. I tell you, I love this family, no matter where it came from. It's a gift to me. Am I going to throw away the first gift I ever got from my rotten life over some stupid matter of pride?"

"You're right, amigo. You were a damn fine man when I met you, but you're twice the man now. I envy you. It's too bad Rodriguez couldn't have followed your lead. Will you tell me now what happened to him?"

"Now I've done my preaching, I will tell you the truth, just to show you honestly, I am still a sinner and a coward. Rodriguez was killed by Alek. Hunted down in the street of what he calls Xanderburg like a mangy dog. I did nothing about it. I ran away as fast as I could. Sure I want to kill him now. I want to go after him and know I could do it. I could watch for him from cover after I'd sighted in my gun and wait for a head shot. Pumpkin on the fence post, just like they say in weapons training. That's not a skull with a brain in it, it's just a pumpkin full of seeds and you're going to pop it and scatter those seeds for the little birds. This isn't a rifle sight, it's just a fence post out in the country on a fine day. If you hear things that sound like shots and people dying, that's just acorns falling off the tree and blackbirds squawking in the air. You just concentrate on the pumpkin and when it's nice and round and sitting on the fence post, you breathe out and breathe in nice and slow and squeeze the trigger nice and steady like it's half a lime you're squeezing over your moclajete. Poof, your problems are solved." Luis smiled at Klein, who was shaking his head, remembering his own training. "Only I'm not going to trade this for that. I don't need to play no pumpkin on the post. I got responsibilities that I like and I aim to keep them. So I'm not going after Alek."

"But I am."

"I know that, Klein. That's why I didn't tell you earlier. You weren't ready. Now you're as ready as you can be. Physically. Maybe mentally too?"

"More than you can know!" sighed Klein, thinking about the pages of the letter.

On another evening, Klein watched the grass softly sway in the light wind as he waited for a storm cloud to open. All day it had seemed that the entire plain had been silently waiting in anticipation of the coming downpour. Klein had been staying with Peebo for the past months, keeping far away from the dangers of Xanderburg while his broken body continued to heal. He had come to regard his prosthetic leg as feeling almost as good as his lost natural limb, and the pain and suffering from his time on Song Pa was almost gone from his body, if not his mind. Peebo was sitting on his chair on the porch, rocking back and forth gently.

"I can't stay here forever," Klein said. "Alek murdered Rodriguez in cold blood while I was off-world. I can't let him get away with that—not for my reputation, mind you, God knows that's been driven into the ground—but because I can't stand to think of myself as the kind of man who'd let someone get away with murdering a friend. Remember last night when I woke up screaming? That was a nightmare—the last thing I saw in it was the corpse of Rodriguez, drenched in blood. If I let Alek live, I swear I'll lose my mind."

"You know we Dissenters won't get involved in your blood feud. Please don't go down the same road Rodriguez did. Even if you live through your confrontation with Alek, you won't be the same at the end of it," Peebo said. "We've all seen so much tragedy come out of Xanderburg already."

"I'm not worried about ending up a different man. Hell, I can barely recognize the photos of myself before I went to Song Pa! I'm a mankiller, and when you've been a mankiller long enough, I think it becomes as much a part of you as your blood and bones. We can't just 'switch it off' and be normal—I don't think Rodriguez could ever quite manage it, and I know I can't. If anyone was born to take on the burden of killing Alek, it's me."

"And after you kill Alek, what then? Do you think Xanderburg will just collapse into the dust the moment he dies? He's got a whole regime working for him in Site 89, and they'll still be there after he's gone to carry on his work. The people of Xanderburg don't follow him because they're brainwashed—they follow him because they *want* to! Even if you get rid of him, that rat's nest he's created will still be here to plague Domremy."

"I know it'll take some effort, but maybe things will get better there after that bastard dies. Alek values loyalty in his stooges, not independent thought. If I take him out, I don't think they'll be around forever. I've been dead set on doing this ever since I learned how Rodriguez died, and I'm not about to turn back now."

"Even if the Dissenters wanted to help you avenge Rodriguez, we have almost no information on Xanderburg these days. We never had many informants inside that town, even when it was Site 89, and just about all of our settlers have been forced to leave Xanderburg for various reasons. We can't provide much info on Xanderburg and how it operates. Of course, the Dissenters strongly disapprove of violence and revenge and would never seek to enable someone with those goals in mind."

"Peebo," Klein said, "even you've killed before, though you may hate to admit it. This planet may not be as sinful or malevolent as Earth, but even here, no one is truly without sin. I'm not asking for help from the Dissenters. I'm asking where I might be able to find some information I can actually use."

Peebo had a troubled, anguished look on his face. He knew he had already killed for his friend Klein—something the Dissenters could never completely condone once they knew. Was he so different from his old friend? And if Klein was so dangerous and vindictive, why would a man of the Circle like Trevor go through such trouble to save him, especially after he had violated the Dissenters' orders? Perhaps Klein served the same God as the Dissenters, even if it was in a savage, frightening way.

"You may be many things, you may take many jobs, you may see things on Domremy that we could never imagine," Peebo told Klein. "But you will never be a Dissenter, and you will never know peace until you see your Father after the last sunset."

"I've known that for a long time. But a person like me has just as much right to exist on Domremy, and try to make it a better place, as the Dissenters do. Even if I don't walk the same path as the Dissenters, maybe it will lead to the same place in the end."

Peebo considered the place of Klein on Domremy. For all the Dissenters had done to free themselves from the Sinful Earth and its old institutions, they could be just as dogmatic and as blind to the need to change as the things they had traveled across the universe to escape. The Circle might consider Klein's words dangerous, even heretical. But perhaps this world needed savage, mercurial men like Klein to help keep it safe from those who would corrupt it. For all his faults, Klein had always strived to be honest with him, unlike the rotting Hyperion Corporation and the manipulative Alek. He made the decision to help Klein in his own way.

"Go to the Archive in Hyperion City," Peebo said. "I think the man who is in charge there might be able to get you some info. His name is Bill Hollingsworth. He used to have a better job in Hyperion than he has now, so he might know some things about Xanderburg that will be of help."

"Thank you," Klein said. "Just the lead I was looking for."

"The longest road is the one you must walk alone," Peebo said.

The clouds had broken, unleashing their torrential rains, by the time Klein got to Hyperion City. Although Hyperion City was allegedly Hyperion Corporation's "capital" on Domremy, Klein found the settlement to be sparsely populated and in shabby condition. The paint was already beginning to look faded on some the buildings, and Klein passed by many empty houses and businesses as he walked the muddy, half-paved streets during the downpour. He found the city's appearance jarring; Hyperion had been one of the few constants in his time on Domremy, a monolithic company that had governed the colony through a veil of secrecy, an organization as inscrutable as it was omnipresent. To Klein, Hyperion City looked less like a symbol of prestige and more like a ramshackle town that had already seen its best days. The townspeople of Hyperion City paid little heed to Klein as he headed in the direction of the Archive; other than an occasional curious glance, most of them seemed to be distracted, wandering through their lives in a state of weary apathy. Klein couldn't help but feel happy about the fact that, for once in many years, law enforcement wouldn't be on a state of high alert at his presence.

His good luck ran out the moment he got to the Archive. The doors of the building were locked, and a blue cyclopean guard robot was standing in the window. "Please submit access papers," the robot said in a soft, reassuring voice that didn't sound like it should be coming out of such a garish, intimidating physical form. Klein held up a bogus appointment card to the robot's glowing red eye. After briefly glancing at the card, the robot said, "These forms are not valid, Thor Harbard. Please retry or submit other forms."

"I don't have any other forms! These are the only ones the Archive sent out for me!" Klein said, exasperated. *I know this hunk of junk is too stupid to know about Norse myth, so he's just doing this out of general orneriness or incompetence.*

"Please retry or submit other forms," the robotic security guard repeated.

Klein groaned and held up his appointment card once more. The robot glanced again at the card. After a brief pause, it said yet again, "Please retry or submit other forms."

Before Klein could roar a series of profanities at the machine to vent his frustration, he saw an old man walk in behind the robot and turn it off. "Sorry about this thing. Maintenance men never came to fix the blasted visual scanner when they were supposed to. Sometimes it gets caught in an error loop like that. You're Thor Harbard, right?" The old guy winked and said in a low voice the robot couldn't register, "At least for today."

Klein nodded and held up his appointment card for the man to see. He heard a click as the old man pushed a button and the doors swung open. "Come on in, my office is this way," the old man said, motioning for Klein to follow.

Klein followed the old man through a maze of shelves and cabinets that made up the Archive. Most of them were filled not with the old classics of a 20th century library, but with printouts and diagrams of various statistics of life on Domremy. Klein could hear the steady whir of the servos of a couple of loader robots, which were used to move files and furniture about as necessary. Access to the Archive was by appointment only, and the interior of the building had acquired a distinctive musty odor due to the amount of time it spent sealed off from the public. The old man guided Klein to a small office with barely enough room for both of them to sit down in it.

"I'm Bill Hollingsworth," the man said. "I used to be the executive who was in charge of this colony. Now, I'm a pencil pusher filling out reports in an archive that Hyperion barely remembers it built."

"You said you had some info on Xanderburg for me?" Klein asked.

"Back when I was an exec, I didn't pay much attention to the details of agricultural production on Domremy. Too little for the board's taste, anyway.

Now that I've been stuck checking over these forms and filling out reports on Domremy's stats, I've been able to better understand what went wrong. It appears that agricultural productivity was flat for the majority of Domremy's population up until the point Site 89 was renamed Xanderburg. After that point, productivity declined across the majority of Domremy's population. There were some exceptions, of course."

Klein was very careful not to mention his friends by name. "Maybe not everyone on Domremy likes what Xanderburg's selling?"

"This minority group, these...Dissenters, they've made extraordinary gains in productivity. So much that it may have actually served to mask the agricultural failures of the convicts until Xanderburg really got started. I know I was arrogant, but I think all of us at Hyperion were, to an extent. We thought we could just manage Domremy with minimal intervention and not take notice when organized crime started to get set up down here."

"Has Alek been running some kind of crime syndicate out of Xanderburg?"

"By all accounts, not a terribly sophisticated one. We have been getting reports that he's been trying to come up with some kind of drug distilled from the Varoneys, but he hasn't been successful at anything that wouldn't put you in the infirmary after you took it. What he mainly seems to specialize in is smuggling in luxury items from Earth -- digitals, off-world booze, gaming devices—and making money off gambling.

That doesn't mean Xanderburg isn't as dangerous as hell compared to other places on Domremy. The murder rate there is much higher than in the other towns, and lots of people there are loyal to Alek and will kill anyone they think is a threat to him."

"Alek murdered my friend. I need to know the best way to take him out."

"There's an anniversary festival commemorating the Naming of Xanderburg in about a month. The best way to kill Alek -- the one that would be least likely to make everyone in that town try to take revenge and kill anyone remotely associated with you -- would be to go that festival, when Alek's probably let his guard down and gotten drunk out of his mind -- and challenge him to a fight to the death. As violent as Alek is, all the info I've found on him seems to indicate he values what passes for personal bravery highly, and most folks on Domremy won't try to avenge a death in "fair" combat. Of course, you have a slight limp, which makes me think you may have a prosthetic limb, so you probably don't have much of a chance anyway."

"I'll find some way," Klein said dryly. "If there's one thing Domremy's made me good at, it's been finding a way to survive."

"Good," Hollingsworth said. "If you possibly can, get that bastard for me. His criminal enterprise cost me my job."

"That's all that matters to you?"

"It didn't seem that way at the time, but after being stuck here in the Archive with only those loader bots for company, it sure seems that way now. Those memories of being in a beautiful office with a window view, having respect from my coworkers, driving around in a big Mercedes...sometimes they come back to me in dreams, and I still think I'm living that life. Then I wake up, and I end up in this dusty place. Sometimes I wonder if I died in that car crash, and this new life is actually Hell. Just hearing that Alek died would make me feel alive again."

"One last question," Klein added. He looked around the "office" one more time to see if there were any Hyperion people lurking in the shadows, knowing there weren't. "Why confide this to me? How do you know I'm reliable? I could just as easily rat you out and they'd drop you out a hatch into deep space on the next shuttle."

"Cause I know who you are. I'm not so cut off or so completely stupid not to know how to find these things out. I've been watching my own ass for a long time now, Klein. You see, I had something to do with putting you up here a long time ago. I know you're a stone cold killing son of a bitch and when you say you're going to get somebody, you'll do it. I saw the preliminary Cashman report. I don't give a crap what happens to you and I won't lift a finger to save you if you fail. And I know that doesn't matter any more to you than a yellow fart. Maybe I don't have the guts to do it myself, but I want a share of blood, too."

Hollingsworth was so self-absorbed, so lost in the prison of his own delusions and thwarted expectations that Klein found talking to him disturbing. Although the man's information would be a great asset to Klein in planning his revenge, he realized that Hollingsworth would never consider him – or anyone else on Domremy – a friend, and he would have no loyalty to Klein whatsoever. Klein reckoned that the longer he talked with Hollingsworth, the more he risked saying something that would anger the man and cause him to stop being so cooperative or even to turn on him. So he silently nodded to Hollingsworth and walked out of the Archive, back to the rain-drenched streets of Hyperion City. *I may never be a Dissenter,* Klein thought, *but I'll never fall as far as some men on Domremy.*

The train wasn't running again until the next day, so Klein hopped a motor transport filled with empty grain containers for the trip back to Stafford Station. He was headed out of town in the direction of Peebo's when a squirrely guy ran hopping over some puddles to catch up with him. He was so scrawny he looked like the weight of a weapon would tip him over into the mud. Klein was tempted to ignore him completely, but turned around with a sardonic look to face him.

"Hello! Buddy! Talk to you a minute, please? Hello?"

"What's up?"

"Are you Noseman?"

"What the hell are you talking about?"

"I work the com office and we got a live feed for a Noseman that's supposed to be passing through. So are you Mr. Noseman? Sir?" he gulped.

Klein was willing to go along with this joke at least for a while. "Well, do you see anybody else around here with a nose as pretty as mine?"

He came along into the com office, where nothing seemed amiss as the little wimp fiddled with the controls. "Coming through from way out on the Blynthian border it looks like. I don't even know how to arrange a link like that. Here it comes. You can take booth four."

When Klein stepped in and activated the screen he saw it was a Forlani female on the viewer. Even though this girl was fully mature and wearing a non-Forlani outfit, he almost immediately recognized that this was what Ayan'we looked like now that she had grown up.

"Greetings Noseman. My, the reports of Ragatti's work are right, your face is something to behold."

"Ayan'we, this is a surprise. I hope nothing bad has happened to cause you to contact me this way."

"Oh, bad things are always happening somewhere, but not to me, or the family, right now. Wondering how I got you on live link? This is Blynthian tech. I found a way to link it in with your human stuff, which is pretty primitive in comparison."

"What are you doing way out there?"

"Didn't mother tell you I was traveling? I can even fly myself now since I qualified on one of our new hex interceptors. I hold the rank of Lieutenant Ayan'we, if you please," she chuckled. "But right now I'm civilian. How do you like my Blynthian intern clothes? I had to adapt them of course, since like you I have only four limbs, not counting the tail."

"It's wonderful to see you. Congratulations on all the accomplishments. I can see why your mother is so proud. And I like the distinguished way you address me, by the way. Caught my attention and my curiosity right away."

"No reason to paint the letters C-O-W on a cow, as your religious friends would say. I know mother wrote to you." Ayan'we's face became more serious – miraculously, with only about two seconds of com delay. "Do you understand her point of view? You do, don't you? She really still cares for you like no other. Tell me you comprehend that."

"Yes, it's terribly difficult, but I'm trying to understand. I'm doing my best."

"After my father died, she was really planning to bring the two youngest with her, until one of them got sick and she discovered she was about to give birth again. It's not just the biology, Kl.... Noseman, there are feelings involved that any human is really going to have to stretch a long way to relate to."

"I wanted to get to know all of you. To find peace there. I've got a back story, too, you know."

"I may know more about it than you realize. I'm a very good researcher. I feel for you and she does as well, as much as somebody with purple skin and a tail can empathize with a neo-ape. As far as the peace goes, you may be fooling yourself a bit, but everybody's got a right to that."

"Copy you."

"Are you OK? Are you in any danger? I could come and take you away. Given a couple of months. I hope you haven't gotten yourself into any scrapes."

"I may have a bit of a scrape coming up, but it's nothing you can help with, little one. I've got to stand on my own two – well, one real and one artificial – legs now. You've obviously found plenty of useful things to do and I want you to go on. As for your mother, I'll try to think of a way of answering her, but tell her I am all right and I have no regrets."

"When shall I call you again?"

"I'll try to call you through the Forlani exchange. Don't know when. It might be a while. But if I don't call, it's because I have nothing intelligent to say. Take good care of you know who."

"Copy that, Noseman. Blynth transfer com 531-w out."

The first thing Klein heard as he stepped off the train and onto the streets of Xanderburg was the deafening yelling and cheering of a celebrating crowd. The people of Xanderburg were enjoying their Naming Anniversary with a raucous joy that reminded Klein of the day he chose to run against Alek as a candidate for Marshall. Bitter memories of the election's outcome—and the suffering he had endured on Forlan and Song Pai as a result—prevented Klein from sharing in their joy, and he walked through the streets with a harsh scowl on his face. The revelers didn't pay enough attention to Klein to recognize him, and he tried to move as quickly as he could to the Town Center without attracting attention. The town was still recognizable from its days as Site 89 when Klein had been its mankiller, but Klein could sense the place had become tainted and corrupt in the time he had been offworld. There was a seedy atmosphere to the place, a sense of concealed violence and veiled threats that felt far stronger than it had in the days when Cashman had still been Marshall. Klein briefly wondered if some supernatural curse hovered over Xanderburg, if the town was destined to have a series of ever more vile rulers until the hateful place finally burned to the ground. The thought barely registered for a second before the rational part of Klein's mind dismissed it, his muscles tensing for the coming confrontation with Alek.

Klein reached the Town Center and saw Alek on the podium, speaking to a large crowd gathered there. He could hear Alek's voice booming out above the babbling of the milling crowd.

"...and on this day, our town was named! We chose the great name of Xanderburg, to represent our new age of strength and wealth! Xanderburg, for a great future for us all! Cheers to the future of our great city!" Alek yelled. The crowd roared its approval. All except one.

Alek could somehow recognize his old adversary immediately. Klein was standing silent as a stone in one of the back rows of the crowd. Alek looked him square in the eyes and saw the smoldering flames of Klein's hatred, a look of rage and murderous vengeance. Alek met his gaze and called out into the crowd, "Who is this man, who comes with a history of bloodshed and murder, to this day of joy?"

"Wilhelm Klein. You killed my friend in cold blood. I'm here to return the favor!"

"Who was your friend? Some criminal I killed back in my early days as Marshall? I don't remember the name of every man I've killed."

"Raul Rodriguez. You killed him when he was drunk."

"He was fighting my deputy. I protect my men."

"He was drunk, and your deputy provoked him!"

"What lies do you choose to believe! Who told you what happened?"

"Someone I trust more than you. Even though you've won the election, I still have one right to contest your rule of Xanderburg—a challenge to a personal duel. I challenge you to a knife fight, Aleksandrov!"

Alek looked at the surrounding crowd. He could still hear their cheers of approval, their droning chants of "Alek, Alek," but he knew that Klein had caught him at the worst possible time. If Klein had simply snuck into town to try to assassinate him, he could have his men dispose of the intruder like the worthless wretch that he was, and his supporters would still follow him without question. But a challenge in an assembly devoted to Xanderburg's principal holiday could not be so easily brushed aside and dealt with by subordinates in back alleys. There would be no bullet in the back and unmarked grave for Klein, as there had been for some of Alek's other challengers. Only Alek himself could answer brazen defiance in public, for this was a battle to prove his own worthiness to lead as much as it was to dispose of Klein. The people of Xanderburg loved physical strength and violence, and respected above all a man who could kill his personal enemies. This had always been true, way back in the settlement days, but had ripened and burst like an infected boil thanks to Alek's uncontrolled despotism.

"Very well," Alek answered Klein. "We fight to the death. Deputies! Form a ring for us to fight in!"

Several of Alek's deputies began pushing the crowd back, clearing a small circle in the area next to the podium. Alek stepped down from the stage into the empty space, and Klein walked forward to meet him. As Klein walked into the ring, the crowd closed behind him, creating a tight human wall.

"Let me see your knife," Alek said.

Klein held up a large, gleaming Bowie knife with a razor-sharp blade. Alek's face betrayed no sign of emotion.

"Not as good as mine," Alek said. He drew an even more massive Spatznaz knife with a metallic handle and a straight blade, and held it over his head for the crowd to see.

They roared their approval with loud chants of "ALEK! ALEK!" and "KILL THE BAS-TARD!" over and over.

Alek yelled to his deputies, "We fight only with knives. He draws anything else, shoot him!" and motioned for the battle to begin.

Klein and Alek began to tentatively sidestep around the interior of the circle, their movements short and jerky, their muscles tensing. Klein watched Alek seemingly prepare for a lunge but correctly anticipated that the move was a feint. Alek's stab stopped in mid motion. The two fighters moved closer to each other, their eyes locked on each other's knife-wielding hands. The first stab came from Klein, a jab aimed at Alek's chest. Alek's thick knife parried the blow, knocking it aside. Alek countered with a diagonal cut to slash at the arteries of Klein's arm. Klein' backstepped to avoid the slash, recoiling towards the throng of spectators.

As the chants of "ALEK! ALEK!" rang in his ears, Klein knew he would have to bring the confrontation to a quick end. Alek would have been stronger than him even if he hadn't lost a leg to the horrors of Song Pa, and would ruthlessly exploit any sign of weakness in Klein—which he would easily discover if the fight lasted long enough. Klein needed an attack that would surprise Alek and mortally wound him before he had time to adapt to Klein's tactics. As Alek closed in, Klein quickly prepared to execute his plan.

Klein could see Alek's arm pulling back for another stab. He moved his knife in his right hand to prepare to counter Alek's jab. At the last second, he quickly tossed the knife to his left hand and lunged for Alek's chest, while twisting his shoulder around to absorb the impact of Alek's knife. He felt the Spetznaz knife bite deep into the meat of his shoulder and grunted from the pure molten agony that assaulted his nerves, but didn't flinch from his attack and drove his Bowie knife deep into Alek's chest. Before Alek had a chance to draw his own knife out and stab it into his vitals, Klein dodged to the side of Alek, out of range of his grasp.

Klein could see the effects of his attack on Alek. The man was howling in agony, blood pouring out of his chest as the knife remained embedded in it. Klein was certain he had hit a lung, for Alek was gasping for air, and spitting up blood. It was only a matter of time before his hated adversary died from loss of blood and oxygen. But there was still vitality in Alek; with the speed of a striking mamba, he pulled a smaller knife from his pocket and pushed a latch that turned the blade into a flying projectile, aimed at Klein's Achilles heel.

Klein knew he couldn't move fast enough to dodge the knife entirely, but he could make a choice of which leg was hit. He swiveled and let Alek's ballistic knife bury itself in the part of his prosthetic leg that would have housed the Achilles tendons, had it been a natural limb. Alek was shocked at the fact that Klein was still standing. "Fake...leg?" he asked, wheezing as his blood and oxygen deserted him.

"You're not the only one who has some tricks," Klein said, "nor are you the only one who knows about a shooting knife."

"Fucking...bastard," Alek forced from his mouth before he finally slumped down, spending his last moments in agonized silence. As Klein tore the Spetznaz knife from his shoulder, he watched as Alek's eyes turned glassy and ceased motion. Aleksandrov, the man who had driven him into space and ruined Site 89, was finally dead.

The crowd, eager to salute the superior fighter responsible for the carnage, quickly turned on its fallen hero. The chants for Alek ceased, replaced with a "Klein" chant. It began tentatively, with only a few particularly bloodthirsty individuals eager to chant the conqueror's name while the rest of the audience was lost in short-lived mourning. But it caught fire, quickly building like flames on parched-dry wood, the chant steadily mounting to a rhythmic "KLEIN, KLEIN!" Finally, other spectators began chanting "ON THE STAGE, ON THE STAGE!" and "SPEECH, SPEECH!" Klein knew what they wanted of him now—after calling for his head a matter of minutes ago, they now wanted him for their new marshall, their king pin, their dictator. Although the agony of his shoulder wound was overwhelming and Klein could think of nothing he could possibly want any more than some anesthetic and an immediate trip to the infirmary, he walked up to the podium to answer. Klein tore some cloth from his shirt to fashion a crude patch for his shoulder wound as he stood at the podium, relaxing before he spoke.

The chants of "SPEECH, SPEECH" quickly diminished as Klein held up a hand for silence. Klein looked out to the crowd again and saw the smiles of approval the savage horde were offering him. Their fury was only temporarily contained with Alek's death. They would demand more duels, more killings for their amusement, from either Klein's subordinates or Klein himself. The tradition of bloodletting had been crafted by Alek to cement his rule, but it would not simply vanish at his death. Klein knew then that Alek had corrupted this town so thoroughly that it could never be cleansed, and he felt a sense of failure that a place as evil as the Sinful Earth could exist on Domremy. He cleared his throat and prepared to give the mob the speech it deserved.

"Citizens of Xanderburg, Alek brought you the joy of killing and murder for your amusement. He was a great Marshall for you, a man who would answer to no law and no man other than himself. After my time on Domremy—and the way you choose to support me now—I must tell you that I cannot live up to his example."

"All that you care about is sadism and bloodshed. You turned on me once before, when I still thought I could bring progress and civilization to you. You turned on Alek, when he died, because he could no longer live up to the image of strength and power he projected. And I damn well know every last one of you would turn on me the moment a quicker gunman or a stronger fighter showed up to challenge me. This place is a rat's nest that deserves to get burned off the map."

The crowd's chants had turned to boos and shouts of rage. He could hear cries of "Fuck you!" and "Hang the son of a bitch!" coming from the crowd. It wouldn't be long before the crowd overcame its shock and tore him to pieces in its wrath. But Klein had just one more thing to say before he left.

"This town doesn't deserve a marshall. Even a rotten chickenshit who spends all his time cowering behind his desk in the Archive doesn't deserve to be the marshall of this place. Do whatever you want, choose whoever you want. I'm done trying to save you. Better yet, clear out of here. You can go sell your dope in the new places Hyperion is opening offworld for you. Leave now, before they forget you and cut you off forever. Get your rotten hides off this world that doesn't want you. I'm clearing out now myself. And if I find a herd of Locals out there in the prairie someplace, I swear I'll stampede them through this shithole and they can eat every last one of you down to the bone."

The crowd was dumbfounded. Here was a man who had fulfilled Alek's laws, who had killed and brought them joy, yet would not lead them. Some of them simply wanted to charge the podium and tear this weird new Alek to pieces, but others felt that killing a man who had obeyed the harsh laws of dueling and had won his fight would bring bad luck to them. A few of the more intelligent ones questioned whether killing a man who had technically won the right to be marshall would make it impossible to recruit *anyone* to the position. As Klein rushed off the podium, clutching the bandage to his shoulder, the mob had already begun to turn on each other in frustration. Klein took a last look at them over his shoulder as a massive riot began and saw their faces so incandescent with furor that they looked more like the demons of Perdition than men. Longing to get away from the disgusting nightmare Xanderburg had become, Klein headed for the old thallop stable, found it still held a few of the beasts, slung some packs of supplies on their backs and led them on foot out into the grasslands, never looking back at Xanderburg again. But the townspeople's bloodlust that day would haunt his nightmares for the rest of his life, ensuring he would never be truly rid of the horrors of that hellhole.

9

When Ayan'we walked into her mother's office suite at the mahäme, she found her feeding her newest sister and dictating messages to a secretary. Her trip back from the Blynthian frontier had been smooth and relatively swift, since the Eyes of Alertness had arranged diplomatic passage for her. As a practical Forlani, she had planned to simply take the tram from the spaceport, but had been surprised to find a gaggle of friends assembled to wish her welcome. They hired a transport and arranged a little party at a new juice bar on the way. Though this delayed her a bit, Ayan'we concluded that was just as well when she recovered her many pieces of luggage and realized how impractical her tram plans had been. She had almost no personal effects, but instead had brought back every piece of memory and every typical

Blynthian object she could get her hands on. The matriline was expecting her to begin teaching a course on Blynthian communication and culture as soon as possible, so Ayan'we felt a bit abashed at having a great responsibility on her shoulders. Much in the planet's future depended on maintaining good relations with the awesomely powerful but reclusive aliens she had visited.

"Greetings, dear mother," Ayan'we chirped, with a special ultrasonic trill at the end that was appropriate for reunion after a long trip. She gave Entara a hug and tickled the baby at one of her breasts. "Iqtho'pa, isn't it? Only one this time?" At the same time, she gave a smile to the secretary who was discreetly making for the door to afford mother and daughter a little privacy.

Entara answered, "Well and safe return," with a trill of acknowledgement. "You're a bit later than you had said in your last onboard message."

"So much to carry! Fortunately Ploondiqtha and some of the sisters from school waylaid me with a transport and dragged me off to that new Three Plums place for a little libation."

"I've been there just last week. Did you try the Pear & Spice special? Made with fruit from some of the trees the Dissenter Peebo brought to us."

"Next time, mother. So you also have been in contact with friends on Domremy?"

"A couple of times since your ingenious linkup with Klein. Did you hear what happened? As Peebo warned, there was a showdown with that Aleksandrov character and Klein wound up wandering off into the wilderness. Sometimes I just don't understand his reactions, even when I know what to expect. Surely he knew that the Dissenters would want him to stay among them. For that matter, he could have remained in that town and those barbarians would have hung on his every word. There must have been a kind of disgust or futility that I can't quite grasp."

"You'll always see him through a cloud of adoration that no other male can cause. Or deserves, either."

"Sometimes I think he left in my womb a seed of skepticism that passed on to you, firstborn. Fortunately, you are wise enough to control and manage such thoughts. I just wish you didn't take quite so many risks with yourself. I'm so happy that for once you'll be here on the home world for a good long stay teaching the novices about Blynthian ways. And maybe, with time…"

"Isshh. Please, mother dear, at least hold off a little on the marriage lecture and the matchmaking. I know I'll be in for a barrage of that from I'shan and Tolowe."

"Did you ever manage to make contact with Klein's human daughter?"

"Her name is Amanda Pedersen, and no. She and her mother left the Epidemiology Center in the Coriolis system. I couldn't track them exactly, but I am worried that they were headed for the anchorage at Tau Ceti. You know about the plague among the humans?"

"I have heard awful news passed through the houses. Oh, I hope they are not taking such a risk. One more tragedy and who knows what will happen to Klein? Maybe it's a blessing that he is out in the wilderness, away from communication. Is there any way to learn if he is still alive? At least the Dissenters seem to believe he is, but they don't seem to have any proof."

"I wouldn't underestimate their opinion, mother. They've got a lot of experience dealing with secrets – more than we do, for sure. The other humans even mumble about them having some kind of mystical powers."

"Ayan'we, please don't try to dampen my fears with a lot of mumbo-jumbo! What I want is a nice, simple GPS plot showing that he is still moving around in the grasslands somewhere."

"Sometimes one creature's mumbo-jumbo is another creature's established fact. That's what the Blynthians state again and again, based on their eons of observations. I can't help but feel that Klein will never really be alone. As fast as he tries to run away, he draws people to him. As for me, I'll keep trying. The GPS on Domremy is off since Hyperion abandoned the colony. I suppose the Dissenters on Domremy feel they know where they are and where they're going and don't see the need to tell anybody else. They only maintain a few low-tech contacts with passing freighters and their settlements on two or three other planets. You can't appreciate how much trouble I had linking to Klein. I had to hunt out a freighter in the vicinity that was headed for Domremy and when they made contact to order some goods, I piggy-backed on their signal. While I was waiting to speak with him, some other fellow kept trying to sell me something called molasses."

"Well, I have sisters in the last few houses that remain open on Domremy, but I want you to use your technical skills to keep track as well. Right now, let's take little Iqtho'pa here back to the family house, where I have some clothes for you to try on. If you parade around in that diplomatic cape, you'll never have a moment's rest. We'll have a little meal together and then, if you want, you can come back to the mahäme and spend the night with some of your chums."

After Klein stomped away from Site 89, he traveled for days before stopping to make a proper camp. Only then did he really inspect the thallop packs and discover that they contained months and months of rations. The animals could satisfy their appetites munching grass, which was all around them for hundreds, then thousands of kilometers. They also proved reliable in finding the one necessary commodity, water. If he let them follow their own long noses, they were bound to arrive within a couple of days at a little pool or pond on the prairie invisible to human eyes. Klein discovered that there was a certain type of reed on the grasslands that was almost woody in texture and burned slowly enough for a good fire. He just kept going in a more or less straight line to the southwest, knowing that sooner or later he would run into Domremy's ocean. He let his hair and beard grow and washed when it rained, naked amongst the grasses, while the thallops looked on with what seemed to be a quizzical expression at this bizarre creature's behavior. Perhaps they were really wondering why he bothered to put on those tattered old clothes at all.

In this total solitude, Klein's feelings subsided into insignificance. He began to feel he was as much a part of the landscape as the sun and the plants. He thought fondly sometimes about Peebo and his family, even Felicia, toward whom he realized he no longer had mistrust or fear or ill will. In some moments, particularly on a hot day when the air shimmered, he would imagine a mirage of a settlement ahead, as he thought to himself, "I'll just saunter up there and see if they have a nice cold beer for me." But when he reached the spot and found nothing but more of the same, he wouldn't be the least disappointed, and would take a swig of water from his canteen with as much relish as he had a frosty Kölsch on the banks of the Rhein. His only remaining quirk was that he would take care to dig a little latrine wherever he stopped and to cover it over with earth as he left the place. He told himself that this was really to cover his trail in case anyone was following him, but after a time he admitted this was a ludicrous excuse and owned up to having a drop of inexpugnable civilization left in him. Months passed, then seasons.

There was something else left in the thallop packs – a sniper's rifle and a lot of ammunition. Not as good as his old M221, but still serviceable. At first, he thought it might be useful for keeping varoneys out of his path, but in truth, amid the silence of the prairie, he found that they heard his approach from far off. He barely could catch a glimpse of them as they scuttled off into the tussocks. His first real use of the rifle was when the rations finally ran out. After living on some roots and seeds for a few weeks, he decided to kill what looked like the oldest of the three thallops and managed to butcher and smoke it inside a little tent he took from the packs. He used up all the salt and pepper he had in order to jerk it and congratulated himself that it wasn't too bad.

Even though he felt a contentment as never before, Klein's senses sharpened to the point that he could feel a presence in the grasslands beyond his little sphere of activity. Even without sophisticated goggles and sensors, his own organs had become attuned to changes in the sounds of bugs in the wild, to nuances of odor. Soon he could sniff out waterholes almost as well as the thallops. He swore he had become sensitive enough to air pressure to detect the approach of a storm without even looking for one. So he knew he was being watched and he had a pretty good idea what it was.

He had to devise a lure to catch sight of the first Local. He staked his animals near a water hole and crept around in a big arc downwind until an oily odor told him the Local was near. For hours he crouched in the reeds watching it, until his thallops began to snort to call him back. The Local must have understood this, too, because he vanished out of sight with a couple of low bounds. Klein pondered what had happened for a long time. This Local, complete with its up-close scent, confirmed what he had suspected for months about being monitored. Yet there was no hint of aggression in the creature. The Local had, in fact, placed itself out at what must have been the maximum extent of its line of observation. So it was watching, not hunting. Why had it not snuck up and attacked? Back in his days at Stafford Station and afterwards when he had worked with Cashman, Locals were quick to jump on any exposed human or thallop and carry them away to serve as hosts for their larvae. A few of these larval arrays had been exposed and destroyed after a massacre, providing humans their scant knowledge of Local reproduction. Why spare him? Wasn't he good enough to feed to their newly hatched spawn? And if they had no appetite for him, why not go for the two thallops, especially when they had been left unattended?

Later that night, as he listened carefully, he heard a far-off drone a little different from the wind and knew that the Local was communicating with its kind. Perhaps it was alerting a troop that would descend on him at sunrise. At first light he made a little scarecrow out of reeds and used it to sight in his rifle. He would hold up the human end to the last and take out at least one Local before he succumbed. He even made an improvised grenade from some explosive and bits of scrap metal in order to take himself out so they couldn't carry him away as a living host. Then he got an idea and took off his clothes to put on the scarecrow, lying it down like a sleeping dummy. He washed his own scent off as best he could before slipping half-naked into the tall grass, hoping he had not yet been seen. In this way, he hoped he could fool the beasts with an upwind approach they would not expect. Neither the thallops nor the dummy brought forth the expected pouncing attack.

After several hours, as the sun neared its zenith, Klein decided he was tired of swatting flies and moved to take the initiative. After all, this was a kamikaze mission. As he slowly crept far outside the perimeter of his camp, he finally spotted a single Local. It was moving around a little, about fifty yards away, as though puzzled about what could be happening in the inactive camp. His target was almost head-on, hiding the vulnerable spot on the back, so Klein decided to try to cripple it with a leg shot and then approach to finish it off at close quarters. His first bullet hit it square in a joint of the foreleg and it reared back in pain or surprise but did not flee. The second shot brought out a gush of fluid from the widening wound, leaving the foreleg dangling by a thin bit of tissue. It still made no move to flee, nor did it start keening to call its pack to help it and kill the human. It only stood as erect as it could and faced him as he approached for the *coup de grâce*.

What was this crazy creature up to? Did it want to die? From a short distance he shot off the rest of the foreleg. Bluish ooze dripped from the joint. The Local made no move to lunge at him, but braced itself on its remaining legs. Klein could not chase from his mind the odd impression that it seemed proud.

"You think I'm afraid to kill you?" he yelled. "I might just pick you apart limb by limb." He aimed at a rear leg, thinking he could topple it over on its side. The thing made a noise. It was not plaintive nor challenging. It wasn't really a rattle or a rasp, but something in between.

Klein lowered his weapon a bit. "Is that how you say yes?" It made the sound again.

"My name is Johnson." It stood stock still and silent.

"No, it's Willie Klein," he ventured, and the thing made the same sound a third time.

He could be imagining this whole thing. Even now another Local might be inching up behind him to grab his in its jaws, but he knew there wasn't one. "I'm not going to harm you anymore," he shouted.

The Local again made its sound of assent. Klein waved his rifle at it in a gesture to chase it away. "Now get out of here or I may change my mind. Get out, and don't come back. I mean it!" The Local began to go backwards, turned around, and crunched off through the grass, leaving its inert foreleg as a trophy to Klein's anger. He thought about bringing it back to camp, but then, for some reason that escaped him, he quickly gouged out a hole in the ground and buried it before returning to his animals.

Although Klein stayed longer than usual in that camp, three whole days, nothing further happened and he resumed his trek to the southwest. Having gotten the Local scent into his nostrils, he knew that he continued to be shadowed, but not by many, since the scent was faint and sometimes disappeared for a time. Months later, he was running out of jerky when the Middendorf Hills loomed up from the low horizon ahead of him. A few days out, he saw something in the sky that he had only seen before in old videos – a blimp. It was almost silent, making a soft, whirring sound, as it flew over him straight toward the hills. *They wouldn't take all that trouble to look for me, and didn't even circle, so there must be something up ahead.* The next night he could see little lights up in the hills and the day after that he saw some smoke. He came across the track of a wheeled vehicle, the first he had seen in maybe three years. After several hours walk along the trail, he came into what looked for all the world like an Alpine village. He had to stop and blink a couple of times to convince himself that he wasn't going crazy. He looked right and left and saw terraces with grapevines contoured into the slopes. *Shit! I must have died and heaven is in Switzerland. Or maybe it's hell with cuckoo clocks. It'll definitely be hell if they only speak Schweizer Deutsch!*

But it turned out they didn't speak any kind of German. French, Italian, Spanish, and Arabic, but no German. They were all Dissenters who had set out to grow grapes and make wine in the Middendorf Hills. They looked at him as though he were from another planet, which, technically, was true. He heard a few of them murmuring his name behind his back, but they all had the good manners not to ask for it and he didn't want to give it. They simply addressed him as Traveler, offered him new clothes (they took the old ones and promptly incinerated them), and gave him plenty to eat and drink. It wasn't Kölsch but neither the red nor the white wines were at all bad. He asked them if they weren't afraid of Locals and they said there were quite a few that migrated through the hills, but they always stayed away from humans. They explained the blimp, too. A metal shop had been set up at one of the old Sites by some Dissenters and a few clever ex-cons. They knew Hyperion had a helium well nearby that was still used to fill up balloons for passive lifts, so they cobbled together an airship and made infrequent but fairly reliable visits to the most remote settlements of the Circle. They would come for a couple of tons of wine to bring back for barter with the crews of freighters that stopped at Domremy. The vintners offered Klein his own cave-house in their settlement (the facades were Alpine, but the homes were conveniently troglodyte). He declined, swapping his older thallop for a younger one, loaded up on compact supplies, and departed in the direction of the ocean. As nice as these folks were, Klein had grown to value his solitude and freedom more than creature comforts.

The latest -- and likely last -- shipment of supplies from Earth courtesy of Hyperion had brought with it the usual contraband items for Bill Hollingsworth. Various types of "enhanced" cigarettes, cleverly disguised digital viewing devices, and junk food from Earth that Hyperion's biochemists had banned for having "no nutritional value" were all smuggled aboard. But one particular bit of contraband was something very unique, something Bill held dear. It was one of the last bottles of merlot from Argentina bottled before Earth's climate changes had altered the quality of the grapes from the region. Hollingsworth had spent almost all of his remaining credits on the illicit transactions required to smuggle the item in from Earth, but he felt very little stress from his newfound poverty. His body had been telling him that he would soon enough have no financial worries at all.

He couldn't be certain whether the stress of his trip to Domremy had prematurely aged him—he was one of the few men who had been shipped to the colony in his senior years—or whether the harsh life of a Domremy colonist had put too much wear and tear on his old bones. Over the course of the last few years, his legs had grown weak to the point that he had developed a dislike of walking, and he found that the cool of the capital city winters fatigued him more and more each season. His memory had grown increasingly erratic, and he found himself making mistakes with his calculations and forgetting the correct format and vocabulary Hyperion recommended for statements. Even with his deteriorating health, he had maintained his regular working hours up to the day his first heart attack had occurred. In the months since, he had felt wearier, more reluctant to finish his assigned hours each day. He had finally resolved to resign his position and take whatever retirement Hyperion would allow him on Domremy, only to find that Hyperion had effectively severed its contacts with the planet. He had been working for months for a boss that no longer required his services or seemed interested in his carefully filed archives.

Nevertheless, he was still a company creature. As he filled in the resignation forms on his computer's screen, his hazy memory drifted backwards, recalling the events of his time on Domremy. *That bastard Alek, he got me sent here, now he's dead. Who was that guy who visited me that said he'd kill him? Kling? Clive? Someone from a past he vaguely remembered. Too bad he rated no robot organizer. Who gives a damn, he probably wasn't the one who killed Alek anyway.*

Considering his choices of a reason for resigning his post. Hollingsworth briefly considered his short list of credible options before settling on "declining health." *Might as well tell them the truth, since it's not like they give much of a damn what happens to me anyway. Sometimes I wonder if I should have taken a chance and explored more of this world while I had the chance. It seems like I spent all day cooped up in this tiny room. Planet's probably all a bunch of deserts with nothing interesting anyway, I doubt I missed much.*

Hollingsworth had reached the point on the form that instructed him to sign his name. Such a simple command, compared to all the job interviews, meetings, office politicking, and performance studies he had gone through to keep a job with the Corporation. One small form to sign on the dotted line with that crude scrawl that he called "Business Cursive," and he'd finally be free of Hyperion for the first time in decades. He gripped the stylus as tightly as he could and slowly went through the motion, writing his name as elegantly as he ever had in his life, savoring every moment of his final victory signature.

Once he reached the "g" in "Hollingsworth," he felt an agonizing pain like a dagger in his chest. *Damn, not now!* he thought as he fell from his chair onto the floor. Blue and red streaks crossed his vision as his breathing became labored. Eventually, his vision ceased, leaving him with only the distorted memories of his past...

He saw a young child looking up in admiration at the old Hyperion building in New York City, his eyes filled with hope and idealism. A college student preparing to go into Erickson, worrying about his chances at applying to the Hyperion Development Program in his second year. An older man, neurotic with worry, struggling against younger coworkers hungry for his position...

Dammit! Always that all-consuming corporation, siphoning off all his time! Had there ever been anything in his life but his career with Hyperion? He remembered there was a woman he had briefly been with before he had been assigned to the Domremy project, but he remembered only lust from that time, not love, and it had ended quickly. No children crossed his mind, nor a pet he had loved. There were only endless piles of work and woe over the course of his life.

As the light of his world dimmed, a comforting image finally emerged in the dusk of his mind. It was a beautiful Mercedes, silvery in color, with an engine that roared like the petrol engines of the auto industry's 20th

Century glory days. It slid through the night, seemingly of its own free will, and came close to Hollingsworth. As everything else in the universe grew dim, and the mental traumas and strife he had faced during his life vanished from his mind, the silver Mercedes seemed to glow ever brighter.

What does this car mean? What happened in my life that makes me come back to this one object? Hollingsworth's mind was already too far gone to remember why he was on Domremy, or even what Domremy was. But somehow, he could remember every single contour of this car, even as the last cells of his brain suffocated from lack of oxygen. His mind came to one final realization in the auto's silvery glow before the last light left his mind.

Freedom. The only freedom I ever felt in my life was when I was with you. Hollingsworth felt himself driving down a peaceful country road inside the Mercedes, the windows open in the cool air of early spring. For the last few microseconds of his existence, there was no Hyperion, no Domremy, no anguish. There was only the open road, stretching as far as the rising sun.

As the plague ravaged Earth, Erica had watched the culture around her transform, its hedonistic openness replaced first by a withdrawn resignation to the inevitability of death, then by violent loathing and resentment of the business and cultural institutions humans had once placed their trust in. First had come the protest marches, people walking through the cities yelling and holding up signs that said **REPENT** and **SAVE US**. The ruling class had steadily lost patience with the protests until they finally began to send the police out to "ensure the preservation of an orderly society," as one of the politicians had put it. Erica had given it little thought at the time. Most of the protesters were far away from Hyperion's new headquarters in the Intermountain Exclusionary Zone. The majority of them were dying or about to die. At first actual violence was limited to looting and the occasional beating. The government thought that once the protests were suppressed by law enforcement, the movement would end, its ability to make its voice heard the only thing keeping it alive.

Once the protests stopped, Erica began to pay attention. News became rarer, as the people left outside the E-Zones dropped like flies. The few broadcasts were pre-recorded, according to rumor because media personnel were dying in front of the camera. Their chance at political reform via standard methods gone, the surviving protesters turned to newer, more vicious methods as their circles of friends and family dwindled, taken from them by the relentless plague. There was the Oakland sniper, a man who targeted only the few remaining politicians and civil servants, drowning his grief in the blood of the government he had come to loathe. There was the Kamaitachi Brotherhood, a cult of murderers from the subways of Nagoya, Japan, who had abducted and killed a series of young girls in hopes they would bring about the end of the world and relieve their suffering. And then there was the Great Fire of Washington, where plague-carrier arsonists lit a massive fire in what was left of America's capitol in an attempt to burn away the hated federal government, even though the White House and the Pentagon had long been abandoned, their staff transferred to bunkers in the E-Z's. In the aftermath of the fire, any pretense of an open, tolerant government had been forgotten. National defense forces followed instructions to shoot first, beginning with a "surgical" napalm and cluster-bomb strike against the agitators that wound up incinerating everything between Northeast DC and Laurel, Maryland. From then on, all communications were closely monitored for the smallest potential indication of a threat.

Mr. Samuels had called Erica into his Boise office to discuss what he claimed was a "very important" career opportunity for her. As she greeted him by shaking his hand, he asked her, "How's your day going?"

"Well, it's…okay, I guess. I just noticed in the *H-Weekly* that Bill resigned due to ill health. Must've taken a while for that news to get back from Domremy."

"Who's Bill again?" Samuels asked.

"Hollingsworth," Erica said.

"Oh, I guess it had been so long that I was having trouble remembering you two used to work together!" Samuels said with a chuckle.

"Part of the reason I was thinking about it," Erica continued, "was because, for a long time, I felt sorry for him because he would never be able to come back home to Earth. But after the last couple of years here, I guess I've begun to feel envious of him. Domremy seems like such a safe place compared to what Earth is turning into…"

"Are you saying you don't feel safe on this planet anymore? I'm sorry, but we can't arrange a transfer to Domremy for you. Hollingsworth was one of the last people we sent there. We've arranged for shuttles to come by to take some of the inmates to new colonies where we think they'll be more productive. They must have missed your friend. We've even shut down the comlinks to the archive on Domremy, since we won't have a presence there for the foreseeable future.

"What about the moon base office?" Erica asked. "I hear that's a pretty nice place."

"We have no openings at the moon base office at this time, particularly in relation to the Research and Development division that you work in," Samuels continued. "However, there is a very specific task related to research and development that I'd like to assign you to."

"Is it not on Earth?"

"Certainly not. However, it does involve a certain…volatile political situation, and if you somehow failed to achieve our desired goals in this position, we would have to ask to resign your position, and all the pay and benefits associated with it, immediately."

Erica considered Samuels' request carefully. After turning down the assignment on Tomakio (to her disgust, she learned the rock was overrun by Dissenters), most of her duties since the end of the Domremy program had been related to Hyperion's attempts to solve the problem of the plague ravaging Earth, from attempts to change the human genome to make it more plague-resistant to efforts to gather materials from other planets to synthesize into a cure. Her duties had been to supervise a series of fruitless attempts to end the plague's death toll. *Maybe I could have succeeded if I had been allowed to accept those sera offered by the Blynthians. But those weirdos had specified "no profits" and the company wanted all the profits from the greatest product ever produced on Earth. A product that was never produced. Now they can blame me.* Erica knew that with another failure she would very likely be considered for termination just as Bill was. Could the new position present a solution to both her problems?

"I'm willing to take the risk," she said after considering the consequences.

"You will be going to a very important diplomatic post. We want to arrange the situation in such a way that we can obtain some tech that we think could be used to boost our profits in the reclaiming of Earth. Of course, since this position involves *governments* rather than *corporations*, you would have to be sponsored by a politician on Dahlgren and ostensibly resign your position with us. On the books, at least. Off the books, you will be remunerated at the level of Assistant Vice-Director III. You'll see that this will go far on your new planet. We need new angles to exploit off-world and you can help us obtain them. There are military operations, territorial disputes, new colonization by various races, things we need to know about from the inside."

Erica took a deep breath and made what felt to her the most momentous decision of her life. "I'll do it," she said.

It was well beyond the vineyards when Klein began to feel he was being followed again. The Middendorf Hills had already faded to barely discernible humps on the far horizon. It started as a mere intuition, something he couldn't pin his finger down on. His "plains senses" were so developed by years of travel that he didn't try any longer to follow logical inquiries about changes in the environment. However, he was aware of something moving along in his wake through the sea of grasses. He began unloading the thallops earlier in the evening, while the suns were still both up, in order to mount up and take a short ride to view the northeast from a slight elevation. The first proof was dimly visible smoke from a campfire. Eventually, riding at different times, he could see lights from the fires and finally a furrow in the prairie about twenty miles back where something was moving. Obviously this was not Locals, since there was no record of them ever using fire. Plus, their movements were either widely spaced bounds or undetectable creeping in the reeds.

Klein began to wonder whether Hyperion had left behind some bounty hunters to track him down. The thought of Kinderaugen operatives even crossed his mind, though the rumors he had heard in the Middendorfs about the plague back on Earth made that possibility almost ludicrous. Could some of Alek's friends, or even Cashman's, still be hunting him, assuming that they ever had any? He decided he had to lay a trap, lying in wait as the disturbance in the prairie surface neared his camp. Hearing a muffled humming, he saw at last what had been parting the grasses – a bulky electric vehicle covered with solar panels and a single passenger. The fellow was swathed in a head scarf to disguise his identity or to protect him from the sun, but there was something vaguely familiar about the way he moved as he descended from his perch on the solar truck and nosed around Klein's campsite tentatively, calling "Hello" in an uncertain way. The fact that he stopped in front of Klein's tent and hesitated to go inside gave Klein an inkling of who the newcomer might be. Still, he held his rifle on the man and added a note of menace to his voice as he silently broke cover and said, "Turn around slowly and keep your hands high."

"Don't shoot! Look, it's me."

"Me, who?'

"Oh, yes, the scarf. Let me take it off nice and slow. See? It's me John."

"Barber John?"

"Yes, Barber John, Jahangar. Remember? From Site 36? I gave you a haircut."

Klein pointed his rifle down. "I haven't thought much about that lately."

"No, clearly not. My goodness, you have become a hairy beast. I'll have to do something about that. Right now, I'm just glad you didn't shoot me. How did you know?"

"The head scarf. A Middle Easterner's sun cream. And when you hesitated to barge into another person's house, even a cloth one, then I figured it might be you."

"I should have expected nothing less. Your preparedness and cunning are legendary, even for a German."

"So what brings you to this part of the wilderness? Who's taking care of your little nuclear reactor?"

"Oh, my little Selma has been down for over a year now. I named her after Selma Lagerlof. With all the geothermal, there was really no need for the power, especially since the trains are only powered up once in a blue moon to move large shipments of goods. A Dissenter would rather hike for two days than ride in a train alone. They wanted to keep Selma serviceable, though, in case there might be a future need. So I deactivated her quite completely and put all the rods into long-term storage in a nice, safe vault."

"Then?"

"Then I was bored as hell. I thought about finding you, just to have something to talk about with my customers in the barber chair, and then when the letter came for you, I had a good excuse to borrow this thing from a neighboring site," he said, waving his hand at the vehicle.

"What letter, John?"

"From Earth. From a lady who I believe is a relative of yours," he added, producing an envelope from a pocket in his tunic.

He handed it to Klein, who took it hesitantly, rather astonished that Jahangar could handle so casually an item from a disease-infested world.

"Oh, you needn't be afraid of germs, my friend. As you can see from all the cachets, it has passed through many security points and been certified sterile before it reached the surface of Domremy."

Nonetheless, Klein turned the envelope over and over, held it near and far, and scrutinized it as if it were an alien life form he had never before seen. It was more than a cursory investigation. It was as though he had come to doubt that such an object could even exist, as though he wondered if it would dematerialize in his fingers. Only once he had accepted its claim to reality did he begin to examine each and every stamp on the outside of the envelope. My God, he thought, it has my actual name! How could the powers that be pass on such a document? Then, as he looked more closely at the stamps, he saw that many of them were clearly not of human origin. *The links with Earth must really be so disrupted that everything depends on alien cooperation now.* Lastly, he turned his attention to a postmark that appeared to be the original, and it read Groneland Nordest. The Danish settlements in Northeast Greenland. Could it be? He tore open the envelope in a sudden frantic movement. Written manually in a hand he didn't recognize. But the first words slapped him right in the face.

"Dear Father," it read.

Klein's jaw must have dropped like a lead weight. Jahangar coughed discreetly and murmured, "I've got some things to unpack just now. I'll leave you to read your letter in peace." He sidled off towards the solar car, leaving Klein to his tears.

> It still seems so weird for me to call you that. But I definitely cannot call you Mr. Klein as I did back on Corlatis. Believe me, I would have called you father sooner if I had known. I almost ran out and hugged you when you left the medical center. I would have if Mother had not held me back and repeated to me that you needed to leave and it would be unfair to

stop you. I guess she was right. She generally is. Still, my feelings about all this are a real jumble.

Before I get into all that, let me assure you first that we are both OK. I have been up here in the Arctic Clear Zone ever since I got to Earth. We left Corlatis not too long after you did. By we, I mean most of the epidemiology staff, except for the aquatics. At first, we passed through the anchorage at Tau Ceti and worked there in triage for several months. At that point, nobody was setting foot on Earth. Blynthians, Coriolans, and a lot of other species were delivering supplies to the Exclusionary Zones by air. Then they started to drop in the decon teams of robots and immune species, beginning with your Talinian salamander friends who were given a grant in the tropical Pacific in exchange for their work, and they certainly earned it. We were with the first resettlement contingents sent into the Clear Zones – the Anzac, the Arctic, the Mid-Atlantic and the others. Mother left me here and moved right on to a transition center in Newfoundland and then down to the main triage at Tadoussac. I told her I was ready but she wouldn't hear of me getting closer to her. It's stupid, since I earned my MedTechIII at

Tau Ceti and I could do most of what she does.

Anyway, it's not so bad here. I can speak all the languages, except Inuit. They tell me the weather is better than Novaya Zemlya, so I guess I'm lucky. It's just so boring sometimes. Aside from delivering babies or the odd fractured bone, there's just not much for me to do. The MedTechI's get all the immunizations and other little stuff just to keep them busy. To preserve my sanity, I spend spare hours (lots of them) doing boat decon and refurbishing. Some of the boats do nothing but go down and bring back other boats, but they're going to ramp up fishing pretty soon to help feed the resettlers, so they always need more.

Sorry I couldn't try to get a comlink to talk with you in person, but there's still not much of that kind of machinery up here. I usually have to wait for a week even to call Mother down in Tadoussac. She sends you her best wishes. I should say her love, but you know how she is about the l-word. I have to be content with being "cherished." She never admitted how deeply she felt about being able to work on you on Corlatis and I know she would rather die than breathe a word about it to you. Of course, I can tell because I can read her like no other. She went absolutely hysterical after she told me about you. It took all three counselors to persuade her she hadn't ruined my life in some way or committed some kind of "sin of weakness." I know you two weren't together long. Frankly, she has had men in her life since then for much longer periods. You're special, though. I don't think I'd ever be here if it weren't for you. Well, duh, of course not! What I mean is that I don't think she'd ever have made the leap to having another child with any other man. That's not just flattery, it's true. Anyway, you can understand why it's me writing, rather than her. The sun would turn pink before she would set pen to paper. I'm just hoping I can corner her into a comlink somehow once technology gets back to normal.

Before I forget, I have some other good wishes to pass along. Torghh is head of treatment in Mexico now. Being 100% inorganic, he can go right into the hot spots looking for human immune survivors and come back through decon in a snap. He's going to stay on for the duration, he says. Until two months ago, Tatatio was down at

Terceira in the Azores setting up a medical college for humans, but he had to go back to Coriolis for the birth of some great-grandchildren. Haven't seen Ragatti since Tau Ceti, where she did a little stint before disappearing again, but she said to tell you she's saving something special for you if you get together again and I bet you won't have to think too long before you guess what it might be.

So back to me. Why don't I come see you? I don't even know if you still exist, but that wouldn't stop me if I could get up the nerve to leave. It's not that I'm afraid of interstellar. I do like Earth, despite all my complaining, and I think I want to make it my home, but that doesn't prevent me from taking ship for Domremy, or anywhere else for that matter. I suppose the main thing is fear. About Mother. As good as she is and the people around her, too, there is always a chance, however slim, that she will be infected. As long as there is the tiniest chance of that happening, I'm not going to go farther away from her than we are now. You've got to understand that it's not that I think less of you, but because she is almost all I've ever known and certainly all I could ever count on. In a strange way, that goes for her, too. I'm the one thing she has allowed herself, for herself, in her whole life. I want her to know I will be there for her. You will have to wait, if you can bear it.

Please, the one thing I'm asking you is to get in touch with me and let me know if you get this letter and where you are and how you are doing. Everybody in the center on Corlatis used to talk about how impetuous or reckless you could be. Ragatti told me she knew there were people on Earth, that is, on pre-plague Earth, who wanted you killed and that you had trained yourself to always be on guard. Naturally, SHE didn't think recklessness was a negative quality at all, but I think I share Mother's opinion on that score. I just hope that before it's too late, you find out I love you. Yes, I do. I can't SHOW you that, other than by writing this letter, but you'll have to believe it on your own. Knowing you're out there, knowing there's something in me connected to you forever, little twisty things in all my cells, but also the way I see and think that I share with you, that you gave me – that's something I never had before I knew the truth. It feels so damn good I just can't find any other words for it. I love you, Klein, Father. Not like your Entara, not like Ragatti (thank God!), not like anybody on Domremy probably, but like only I can love you. Remember that when things go bad, but above all, remember it when things are going well, too, because I hope they always do. There's somebody down here on Earth in these slightly frosty old fjords that loves you and just you in that way. Please answer me.

                        Love, Amanda

Klein just stared at the pages for a long time. There were no more tears in his eyes. Then he stretched back to lie down flat on the ground and stare up at the stars. They were clear in the vault of the sky, hundreds of glowing points undiminished by the light pollution cast by sprawling cities or by the stifling haze of the Europe where he had grown up, endured training, gone to war, and then dissipated his existence in drab offices and bars. He did something he'd never done before in all his years on Domremy, trying to determine if one of them was the same sun that shone on Earth, on Amanda. *Is it daytime in Northeast Greenland now? Or is it night and she is like a mirror image of myself, gazing up to look for someone she can't see?* He could distinguish clusters of stars that made patterns of constellations to which the Dissenters had begun to give names. The Hyperion claimants had done nothing but lay this sky out in a grid of dry mathematical coordinates. The Dissenters, however, were more human and they had already filled the heavens with The Thanksgiving Turkey, Buddha's Tree, and the Good Samaritan. Klein chuckled when he confessed to himself that he was too poor at physics to guess at Earth's celestial coordinates or the brightness or distance of its sun, so he picked a bright star in the head of the Good Samaritan and he said, "That is Amanda's star and from now on when I see it, I will think of her."

After several minutes, he turned toward the northern horizon a bit to a small star he had had someone locate for him a long time ago, soon after he arrived on Domremy, a star he knew because he had visited its system, the sun of Forlan. "I won't stop watching for you," he whispered. "But now, you have company."

Then he rose with a sigh and went over to the little electrical heater Jahangar had lighted as the suns were setting, to see what he had prepared for supper.

The next day, Jahangar set out all his barber implements and proceeded to attack the rat nests that were Klein's hair and beard. After spending the last few years looking like a cave man, Klein decided on a buzz cut with a mustache and goatee, giving him a look he had never had before. Examining his new face in the mirror, he complimented Barber John on another success and they shared a hearty dinner, planning to break camp promptly at sunrise and set off down the coast towards the Southern Continent. There, Klein planned to take the ferry from Fielder's Crossing over to the opposite coast and go on to the Dissenters' experiment station, while Jahangar traded his slow solar truck for a faster trip back to his home site. During the night, however, Barber John awoke Klein twice in a nervous sweat, claiming he had heard noises in the grass and that he was afraid Locals might be stalking them. Klein assured him that Locals had been shadowing *him* for months and had done him no harm, but finally he agreed to keep watch so Jahangar could get a little rest. The Iranian, who had brought a Kikkonnen with him and had never primed it so far, set it on ready and kept it by his bedroll all night. Even then, Klein never heard him snoring and assumed that he was too scared to close his eyes.

It was not till dawn when, as Klein suspected, a Local emerged from the reeds near camp and stood stock still at a distance of dozens of meters. Jahangar immediately raised his Kikkonnen, but Klein caught him in time, set the safety, and warned the barber that if he fired, the next shot would be coming his way, and Klein never missed a man target. *Unless I choose to*, he added to himself, thinking back to Cashman. He went over to within a few meters of the Local, sat cross-legged on the ground, laid his rifle on his lap, and put his hands on his knees, smiling contentedly. After a few seconds another Local came out of the prairie cover and held up a foreleg for Klein to see. It was a stump that was apparently growing back from where the end of the leg once extended.

"Stumpy, welcome," said Klein, pointing at the newcomer. The Local answered with the yes sound.

He pointed to his own chest, adding somewhat comically, "Me Klein." Again the yes.

The Local stretched his other foreleg and drew a straight line in the soil.

"One," ventured Klein, and the Local acknowledged.

Klein reached out and made a pair of lines with his finger. "Two," he said, and the Local said yes.

Klein reached again and drew three lines and said, "Two," but instead of making the yes sound, the Local waived his feelers.

"Right. So I guess we understand each other about as far as yes and no are concerned. What next?"

Stumpy gestured to the other Local, who slowly edged up until he was next to Klein, as Stumpy said yes several times in a relaxed way. Local Number Two stretched out one of his feelers in front of Klein, as if to offer it for inspection.

"Am I supposed to touch it?" he asked, and Stumpy answered in the affirmative. It was not hard and shell-like as Klein had expected, but pliable and rather soft, like a fiber-optic cable.

"You want him to do something to me with this, don't you?" asked Klein. Same answer.

"And I suspect he's not going to do anything that will hurt me and make my friend nervous?" The gesture for no.

"John," Klein said over his shoulder, "We're going to try a little experiment and whatever happens, I do not want you to be concerned for me or to make the slightest move. In fact, I want you right now to go put the Kikkonnen over by the thallops and come back where you were. Nice and calm."

"OK, I'm tip-toeing over now, and I'm placing it on the ground and now I'm tip-toeing back, but if you don't mind, I'm going to be saying some prayers right now."

"That's fine. Just remember: absolute submission, infinite mercy." He looked straight at Stumpy and said, "I'm ready."

Slowly, Number Two inserted the feeler into Klein's ear. He could feel it working around and very gently resting next to the eardrum. He was waiting for something to happen when suddenly he felt a series of mild shocks. Then another, and he saw stars in front of his eyes. *It's a good thing the brain doesn't feel anything like pain.* To his surprise, Stumpy said yes. Then he began to see images in front of his eyes, but they were weird and unarticulated, sort of like a bad drug trip.

"No, Stumpy, no. I'm sorry, I can't make out what you're trying to tell me."

"Are you all right, Klein?" Jahangar jabbered nervously.

"Yes, fine, don't worry. Momentary problem. No harm done. Stand down."

Meanwhile, Stumpy made a few new noises and two more Locals came out from the reeds. They moved over next to Number Two and the three of them went into a new pose with their middle pairs of legs slightly lifted, exposing a small aperture in what might be called their armpits. Number two put a feeler into slot Number Three and Number Three to Number Four, making the arrangement look like an animal display of a direct current electrical hookup. Stumpy said yes and right away Klein began to see outlines of images that were much more distinct than before, a savannah landscape with bunches of trees and unknown kinds of beasts.

He was moving, bouncing along high into the air. Next, he began to feel pure joy. He realized he was a Local and was bounding along with a whole host of Locals, experiencing unadulterated happiness. Creatures the size of Volkswagens, resembling a cross between a pig and a hippopotamus, ambled along fearlessly amid them, along with hordes of smaller life forms that might have been rabbits or kangaroos. There were pools of water, too, with groups of reptiles sunning themselves like giant iguanas. This was some distant past.

All at once the joy disappeared. In the sky, a slightly different tint from present-day Domremy, fireworks began to go off. However, suddenly there was searing heat and an odd feeling inside him. These were not firecrackers, but neutronic explosions.

He was seeing the day the Locals' universe died, the day Hyperion came. It was the terraforming.

Then there was a new feeling impossible to identify. It was like earthly sorrow, but something else. Local bodies and those of other Domremy creatures lay everywhere, rotting without even carrion eaters to dispose of them. Survivors were dragging half-charred victims back into holes that others were frantically excavating in the ground. Not just fellow Locals, but the other life forms, too. They were trying to save everything, but failing because now creatures were choking all over the landscape. The afflicted pulled themselves from the grasp of the charitable survivors, preferring to die immediately and end their torture. The holes went deeper and deeper but even as they were being lengthened, the excavators were dying along the way. Then there was long, cold darkness and a feeling that must have been Local Hell. Finally, there was sunlight again and the endless, monotonous plain, where Locals were leaping again, but this time they were under attack by a patrol and Kikkonnens were blasting them to pieces as they rushed to abduct human bodies. Suddenly, Klein gave a start because he was looking at himself, mounted on a thallop with his sniper rifle, aiming at the kidnapped humans as the Locals somehow said, "No, please, no, not this."

The next thing he knew, the feeler was being withdrawn from his ear and his short course in Local History was at an end. He looked up at Stumpy and said, "Do you know how sorry I feel for you? All of you? Sorry? It means compassion."

Stumpy said, "Yes. Yes."

Klein got up and went over to Barber John. "Don't worry, Jahangar, they haven't erased my mind. Instead they've made it much, much bigger. Now it's really imperative that we get to Fielder's Crossing with all speed. I've got to share what they told me with the Dissenters and see what I can do to help, maybe to atone. Let's break camp."

At the end of three months' time, Klein and Barber John reached Fielder's Crossing and parted ways. The shadow group of Locals had followed them most of the way, occasionally reappearing out of the prairie grasses, but had vanished about three days distant from the straits. Klein sold his thallops and his gear, including the sniper's rifle, before crossing over with his back pack. The ferry operators had informed him once they reached the terminal that it was only about thirty miles on land to the experimental station and he could most likely hitch a ride with any Dissenter wagon. Klein walked. He found the station to be a sprawling compound with groups of Locals all around and even inside. Walking up to what he judged to be the director's building, he was delighted to find Dr. Patak's name on the little sign. The bronze-faced man rushed up to him and embraced him as soon as he popped his head in the door.

"Mr. Klein, so happy to see you, sir, after such a long time. I must say, you're looking unexpectedly well-groomed after your epic meanderings."

"I had a great barber for the last seven hundred kilometers or so. You look well, too, Patak."

"I have to admit I'm not entirely surprised, because rumors about your survival have been buzzing around since the blimp pilots brought back word that an odd hermit had been sighted in the Middendorfs. Luis will be especially overjoyed, since he has made bets on your reappearance all over the sites. Not that the money matters more than simply knowing you still exist. I have so many people to tell that I hardly know where to begin. Will you be staying a while now?"

"Hopefully a long while. Listen Patak, I had an incredible breakthrough with the Locals. I need to tell you about it."

"And we will be most eager to hear it, since we've been conducting research along those lines of communication ourselves for some time." Patak called in some other personnel with recorders and they began the debriefing right away. It went on long through the afternoon, with tea and sandwiches brought in to keep everyone fresh and attentive. Patak's face lit up when Klein told him about the encounters with Stumpy. He began nodding vigorously at Klein's account of the ear tap, whispering hurried remarks to those around him. His eyes widened at Klein's descriptions of the telepathic visions.

When his testimony finished, Patak rolled his eyes and exclaimed, "Absolutely remarkable! You can't realize how far you have just pushed us ahead. Oh, we had been able to obtain some telepathic visions, but the quality was nothing like yours. You see, we were trying to tap through the nose and sinuses, assuming it would shorten the gap to the cerebral cortex, but there was always too much mucus and sneezing, so the most we could receive were still photos that were hard to interpret because there was no dynamic element or scale. We had never tried the triple hook-up, but I can see now in retrospect that the Locals were trying to suggest something like that. Our insistence on scientific controls had limited us to individual encounters, which did not even work well for you."

"So you think the visions were true and accurate?"

"Most assuredly. I will show you something soon that will confirm it."

"On the way to the crossing, Barber John and I had to slow down to cross several little rivers that flowed into the sea. In two of them we found bones. I brought some with me and left a few larger ones in a locker at the Crossing. I suppose they must have washed down and been buried in silt and dust, then uncovered when the banks eroded or the river changed course slightly."

"Yes," agreed Patak, "It's just like what happened with the dinosaurs, except it's only an interval of a bit over a century. We've found bone specimens here in the South Continent Hills, as well. In fact, we found some bits of hide and tissue that have allowed us to look into cloning and genetic reconstruction."

"I thought you folks didn't believe in that."

"In principle, the Circle does not. But we also believe in trying to restore the pre-terraform ecology of Domremy, so exceptions have been made in extraordinary cases like this."

"And you have personnel that can do that?"

"Not enough, alas. Mainly a few people like myself who received genetics training before joining the Circle. After so many of the GMO projects on Earth went awry, that sort of education was mostly taboo for us. However, with old timers like myself and a handful of crossovers from Hyperion operations, we have been able to get a good head start. Come see."

He led Klein across the compound to a distant building and around back to a huge corral where Klein was astonished to see two of the creatures from his vision, alive and wandering contentedly through the foliage.

"Those are the pig-hippos I saw in my link-up!"

"An apt description, and from this moment forward and in honor of your discoveries, we shall call them pippos."

"But why don't you have more if you can clone them so well?"

"It's true we did wonders with DNA from some desiccated hides found in a cave. But we didn't want to create a lot of them until we knew if we could feed them. You see, most of the flora as well as the fauna was also wiped out in the terraforming. We have parallel experiments with plants in the fields over there and we have been able to discover enough to keep these alive. When we started, we didn't even know if they could breathe the air and the first attempts failed until we could find a way of adapting them embryologically. We have enough on the way to form a small herd soon."

"This is marvelous. Look, doc, I'm no biologist, but I want to help with things here and I'd consider it an honor if you let me do something for these creatures."

"I think that can be arranged. Let me introduce you to the head keeper. I believe you've met him somewhere."

He led Klein around a corner and right up to a familiar smiling face.

"Peebo!"

"Pardner, I'm so happy to see you again. I just knew you'd come back sooner or later. I'm lucky to catch you here while I'm on assignment for a few months. Next week, I'm heading back home for a year. But we'll have plenty of time to get caught up before I do, and maybe by then you'll get to know these critters…"

"Pippos!"

"I like the name. And I'll hand over all my secrets for caring for them. But first, a tall glass of cider."

In the days before Peebo left to return home to Stafford Station, Klein tried to learn all he could about pippos and their care. He was astonished at the scientific sophistication of his farmer friend, who obviously had a deep understanding of the genetic research furthered by Patak and his team. Klein had always known that Peebo had an instinctive grasp of ecology that revealed the relationships of all living organisms. The extent of his friend's biochemical knowledge went far beyond that, putting him in a league with professors Klein had encountered in his university training, foreshortened as it had been. In any case, Peebo dubbed Klein fully qualified to care for the pippos and left several files of instructions of things to watch for and experiments to perform until he could return to the southern continent.

Months passed quickly. No sooner had Klein gotten used to his pre-terraform pig-hippos than Patak presented him with a couple more clones to raise, with a view to extending the herd. All the while, Klein was also busy with Local encounters. Each afternoon he passed his pippo duties to an assistant and went to join the team in charge of Local communication, working in an expanded new area that allowed for triple and eventually quadruple feeler hookups with a human subject. Klein trained others to do as he had done with Stumpy and company. During and after the active sessions, a group of up to ten evaluators scrambled around trying to relate the new visions, which were becoming more and more narrative, with the background material they had already assembled. They became convinced that what was being communicated was far more than individual life experiences and that Locals had the ability to share in a collective consciousness that spanned untold generations. Locals regularly did feeler hookups as part of their social life, passing on vast quantities of lived history between groups to create a racial record. It was as if humans could each possess the entire knowledge of all their species' libraries and data banks in eyewitness form. As the record grew, Klein became more and more impressed by the struggles the Locals had undergone in order to survive the coming of Hyperion and its settlers. The insectoids acquired a status of honor and even moral superiority that he had always been loath to grant to his fellow earthlings.

Throughout this busy and quickly changing time, Klein could not forget the letter from Amanda. He began and tore up a succession of responses where he tried in vain to express his appreciation for her and even the word he was so reluctant to pronounce – his love. Everything sounded trite, stupid, and contrived as he read it over. Finally, over a year into his stay on the continent, he approached Patak with the request to set up a comlink. It would have to be one-way, of course, but at least he might be able to speak to her as though they were in person. Perhaps the tone of his voice and the sight of his face could provide what abstract words seemed incapable of conveying. Patak shook his head at the impossibility of such a thing, given the Dissidents' renunciation of electronic communication with their own brethren on the other planets where they had settled. The equipment and power sources simply didn't exist on Domremy. He merely replied with his typically Asian patience and steadfastness that he would look into it and see if an opportunity could present itself.

Months later, it did. Patak came puffing down to the pippo compound to announce that a one-way comlink was being arranged for two hours later. A Blynthian diplomatic corvette had entered Domremy orbital space to make arrangements for some food shipments to the resettlement camps on Earth. They were equipped with extremely powerful transmitters and agreed to alter course for a bit over the southern continent so that the experiment station could emit a message that they would boost via contacts through Tau Ceti and down to one of the Earth receivers to relay to Greenland. It would arrive much later, naturally. Klein regretted he could not see Amanda's surprise when she played back the message. He wondered if it would have the effect he desired.

He hardly had any time to prepare. When the technician gave him the signal to begin, he suddenly forgot some of what he had intended to say and stammered through the first five minutes ad lib. When he finally caught his breath, he looked back at the notes he had scribbled and tried to fill in as best he could in order to make a coherent message. Too soon, the technician was holding up three fingers for the minutes left, then two, then one, and as Klein frantically babbled his goodbyes, the techie gave the cut sign ending transmission. Ten minutes to express a lifetime of emotions. Klein was sure he had failed.

As soon as he was summoned to view a reply, months later as another Blynthian ship passed, he was sure he had not. There was his little candy-striper, grown to blossoming young womanhood, wearing her anorak and bubbling with joy at being able to speak face to face to her father, despite so many parsecs distance and a time delay that only Einstein could appreciate. She ran on about her life and her hopes, repeatedly excusing herself for forgetting things and sounding absurd, and interjecting bits about Helga's successes with post-plague triage. By the end, she was babbling worse than Klein, blubbering too, as tears rolled down her cheeks. She threw an awkward kiss his way through the camera lens as her transmission ended.

From that point on, Klein was constantly reminding Patak and the techies at the experiment station about checking passing ships for another transmission opportunity. He made a rare personal trip to the few sites that served as improvised spaceports for supply shipments to make contacts and to enlist them in his network, as well. An added rationale for the trip was to stop at Peebo's place with his son Mel, who had been doing a four-week stint at the experiment station and was returning to help with the harvests. Peebo's second son, Moe, cornered Klein at every opportunity to pepper him with scientific questions. Having taken over the varoney project from his father and gone on to become recognized as one of the top ecologists among the Dissenters, Moe hinted so obviously at his interest in the pippos that Klein took it upon himself to invite him down to take a role in their care and eventually become the top pippo keeper. After the fact, Klein worried that he might have offended Mel, the elder child, by offering such an opportunity to the sibling, while Mel had already done valuable work on the southern continent. He needn't have worried, because Mel was delighted at the idea, revealing to Klein that he had an off-planet project he was working on that required all his attention for the next couple of years at least.

So it was that Klein returned to the experiment station with Moe, got a half-angry lecture from Patak about assuming recruitment duties himself, and began to initiate the young man to all the work the scientific teams were doing. By the third six-month training stint, Moe was not only completely up to date on the pippo situation, including the two new members of the herd and two more that were about to join, but he was also deeply involved in the flora side of genetic re-engineering with the plant folks. Klein celebrated by taking a two-week vacation to the coast, sunning himself, diving to examine sea life, and running along the beach. He was just beginning to congratulate himself on his new-found leisure time when he ran into an old friend. As he crossed the center of the station one day, a Local walked up to him and extended his foreleg, saying "Yes, yes, yes."

It was Stumpy, the foreleg now proudly and completely regrown. Klein immediately arranged a neural hookup and the two began trading information about their pasts. Each still had difficulty calibrating the other's concept of time. They mastered this obstacle by devising a code system with a couple of tablets that allowed them to sequence and re-sequence events. Causality was still an issue, particularly for Stumpy's grasp of third-party motivations. Stumpy comprehended things like the Cashman and Alek episodes without much trouble, but balked at the Kinderaugen affair. Klein guessed that this had something to do with the Locals' attitude to young people, since their own customs were much more humane than the humans. During the bad times of the hunting parties, older Locals did not hesitate to offer their own bodies as breeding hosts in order to bring more larvae to maturity, though it cost them their lives. Compared to this altruism, a Local could not readily conceive of how earthlings could bring themselves to mutilate their own young.

Even after Stumpy had left to rejoin a group of Locals migrating through the Middendorf Hills, Klein was so buoyed by the experience of their communication that he began to make elaborate plans for future conversations. It took a whole month for the debriefing team to assimilate all their experiences. Moe was about to leave, too, at that point, so Klein turned his attention to training another pippo assistant. Before the year was over, he once again found himself in a leisurely situation, when a Forlani girl presented herself at the research station with messages from Entara and Ayan'we. He persuaded the messenger to stay for a few days while he read the letters over and over again, thinking about how to respond. Entara's letter was much like her last one, full of information about her family and her increasing official duties, along with personal wishes that assured him she still held him firmly in her heart. In addition to this, there was a new twist that caused Klein to try to read between the lines. It was not that there was any danger – Entara had shown Klein that she was quite capable of talking about danger in a most unambiguous way when she summoned him to Forlan in the past. There were distinct hints that her own role had somehow changed, or at least her notion of what it should be. Klein inferred that she was working on a new project that she was not yet ready to reveal. It seemed to have to do with the structure of Forlani society on a very fundamental level. There was actually a passage in Crop Talk that intrigued him, following a customary disclaimer about how much she would like to visit him if she could. She spoke of "a hen wanting to come back to an old roost, but no one wanting it to leave the coop when it had begun to quack like a duck." Clearly, Entara did not want to alarm him, but rather to share the secret that she was up to something big.

Ayan'we's letter confirmed this impression. She complained openly that despite her pleas to be allowed to take a pause in her Blynthian classes for the mahämes, the Council of Nine had heaped extra demands on her that would keep her on Forlan for some time. She had gone so far as to appeal to the Council of Nine, minus her recused mother. A couple of members had approved out of sympathy for Entara, but the rest had stuck with the exigency of possible alliance with the Blynthians and its advantages for the planet. Having grown up in Europe during the Corporate Age, Klein was well schooled in the fact that organizations often found subtle ways to try to keep their most valued assets under benevolent close control. He had a couple of long conversations with the messenger girl, but the most he could worm out of her was that young Forlani of both sexes were excited about some "new songs" that were considered to be daringly progressive about the relations between the matrilines and the Brotherhood. Taking into account the enormous cultural influence of any songs attributed, truly or falsely, to Entara, Klein could begin to perceive the importance of what was going on. He hastened to reply to both Entara and Ayan'we, assuring them in Crop Talk that if someone even knocked on the barn door, the bull would rush out and chase off any intruder.

After another fortuitous exchange of links with Amanda, Klein decided he needed another vacation and joined the paleological unit scouring the southern continent on what he called the "bones and hides patrol." It was an expedition that might take many months, but with Peebo back at the station for another research stint, Klein knew he could leave the pippo attendants under his supervision with full confidence. The truth was that, while he found all the recent communications with his past life extremely exhilarating, it was also mentally exhausting for him. He longed for the solitude of the wilderness where he could mull things over and decide in an atmosphere of serenity whether it was time for him to leave Domremy again, either in the direction of Forlan to check on Entara and Ayan'we or in the direction of Earth to be close to Amanda. In the meantime, he became passionate about searching for animal remains as the team assembled a trove of biological specimens to bring back for analysis and perhaps future cloning experiments. By the time he got back to the station, Klein had made up his mind to look into the process for joining an Earth resettlement team.

It was then that he began to feel sick. The occasional dizziness and nausea he had experienced on the last two weeks of the expedition must have been from too much sun or too many stale rations, he had told himself. The first time he stumbled and fell coming back from the pippo enclosure, he laughed at himself for tripping over a stone in his own backyard. The second time, he cursed himself for getting old, but still didn't report it, merely dusting himself off as he glanced furtively around to be sure no one had seen. The third incident was impossible to hide. He had passed out in the middle of a staff meeting, right in front of Peebo and Patak. When he woke up on a bed in the clinic with an IV in his arm he had been irate and tried to get up. It was all his friends could do to keep him from tearing out the IV tube and walking out. Peebo had only calmed him down by promising that if Klein rested, he was going to obtain a new fake ID in case he wanted to take another interplanetary trip.

Inside, though, Klein knew something was seriously wrong. He lost appetite for most food and even had to refuse a glass of beer after the first sip disagreed with him. Patak popped in often with his usual happy face, though Klein suspected he was feverishly performing tests on all the fluids they collected from him. What he didn't know was that Patak was so worried that he had jury-rigged a comlink to several off-planet medical facilities.

After what seemed an eternity, they changed the meds and Klein began to feel a little better. When they wheeled him into Patak's office, he thought they were going to simply discharge him. He immediately knew better when he saw the thick files on Patak's desk and the serious look on his face that seemed to turn his glowing bronze a darker shade.

"So when can I get back to my pippos and check on the expedition's results?" he asked with false cheer.

"The bone and hide boys are waiting to give you an update, but it's about your own results, my friend, that we need to talk right now."

"Bad news, I take it?"

"Some good, too."

"Give me the good first."

"As you can tell, the recent cocktail we have brewed up for you has brought a very good control of most symptoms. We can expect this to continue for about ninety days."

"I think I can guess the bad."

"It's a rare prion disorder. Kept us stumped for a long time until I had confirmation from some off-planet sources. Officially, it's HPD17 and we think you picked it up on Song Pa. At least, nearly all the known cases have had some association with the planet, usually from indentures such as you were. One researcher has even speculated that it might be related to whatever wiped out the previous civilization there. Song Pai themselves are immune and so far do not seem to be carriers. You were slogging along in the mud for years, so it's impossible to know how you might have contracted it."

"So, from what I've heard, there's usually no known cure for prion disorders."

"Not this one."

Klein blinked his eyes a couple of times. "If I started right away, I might be able to make it to Greenland in ninety days."

"I'm afraid not," Patak sighed. "You would never survive icing or juicing. You would need a sophisticated hospital ship just to keep you alive."

"And after the ninety days? There will be lots of pain, I suppose?"

"It won't be pretty, and if we let things take their course, it won't be fast. The only consolation is that your consciousness wouldn't be around to feel what's going on."

"A nasty straw death, as the old Germans used to say."

"We can, of course, set up protocols so you can call the final shots."

"Very appropriate for a mankiller. He becomes his own last target, by proxy."

"I won't enjoy it," Patak stated glumly, "But that's about it."

"Then it's time for me to learn what goes on in the Incubator."

Patak gave a little start and didn't know, for once, what to say. The Incubator was the biggest secret in the station and only a few technicians and specialists entered the large building. Of course, it was known that one of the station's goals was to aid the Locals in restoring their population. There were some mysterious comings and goings, human and otherwise, that had been whispered about by long-time staff. Klein, however, already had a very good idea of what went on there, due to his linkup with Stumpy and others he had communicated with. It was a facility for experimenting with larval hosts.

Finally Patak cleared his throat and replied, "If you wish, we can start processing you for the program. I can tell you from what I know of you condition that you could make an excellent host. Do you understand what it would involve?"

"My main concern would be that I could stay alive long enough to be of some use."

"No problem there. We have done lots of experimentation. Mostly with animals at first. You see, the original species that Locals preferred as hosts was a sheep-sized grazer that went extinct in the terraforming. After that, they usually used their own bodies to incubate larvae until the settlements started. It didn't work all that well, for some biological reasons I won't go into. When humans showed up, they desperately turned to us. The first incubations were, of course, extremely gruesome, despite the fact that they inject an anesthetic substance when they implant the ova. Then we achieved rudimentary communication and began to work with them. Our friend Peebo, by the way, was one of the first to make some breakthroughs."

"I suspected he was doing more than whistling at the clouds when he walked out past the fields into the savanna."

"His patience was enough to get the exchange working and to convince them that we were more than a barbaric, destructive species. When we first set up the Incubator, we tried different hosts, mainly thallops. It was clear from the beginning that their physiology made them less than ideal. We've had some successes with other types of livestock. Then some humans volunteered – a few Hyperion dropouts but mostly Dissenters who had picked up some disease during transport. I believe your friend Luis is married to the widow of one who chose to be a pioneer. Thanks to them, we were able to totally eliminate the pain factor by using a combination of varoney venom and the Locals' own injections. Also, we were able to monitor growth and to determine that human incubation need only be ten days long. After that, the larvae can be moved to a more efficient feeding apparatus that gives us better temperature control at the same time. We were also able to develop an implantation technique that avoids a lot of collateral tissue destruction for the ten day period."

"Sounds like something I can handle."

"Frankly, the main concern is psychological. The host has to be able to deal simultaneously with its own mortality and with the awareness of a foreign organism feeding off its cells and growing inexorably inside it. Some people just can't deal with that in a rational manner."

"Rational, schmational. If I'm going to croak, and especially if I can't get to see Amanda or Entara in one piece, I want my death to be worth something. As for 'foreign species,' I don't think of the Locals that way anymore. After all, it's their planet. We're the foreign species. Time we did something other than exterminate them." Klein turned his head away and was silent for a moment. "Hell, in some ways, I'm more like one of them. A con, an outcast, an underdog. Maybe the reason I belong here is because I'm more Local than earthling. So bring it on."

"Klein, I can assure you," said Patak, nodding his head, "I've never known anyone more human than you."

"The first thing I need to do is to have a long talk with Peebo."

Ninety days seems like a long time if you count it in minutes or seconds, but it's only three months, and they can tick by like little clicks on the face of a clock. Peebo had lived for a long time with the immanence of Klein's demise in one form or another. Beyond that, Dissenters are seldom shocked by the news of death because mourning is so internalized in the observance of their religion. He immediately got the news out on the Crop Talk grapevine and every Circle meeting on

Domremy knew of Klein's condition before the suns set twice. Even their distant colony on Tomakio knew within days. Peebo felt sure that the message, spreading like wildfire, would reach Earth and Forlan soon, but probably not soon enough to let anyone travel to them in time. He didn't even need to inform the Locals. The minute they spotted Klein being wheeled into the Incubator for a first visit, feelers began twitching all over the southern continent. Couriers hurried to the ferry up the coast that Dissenters reserved for Locals -- they abhorred the memory of massacres at Fielder's and always crossed continents apart from humans. Once on the mainland, they spread like a flash among the pods in the grasslands. A healthy Local can bound along to cover six hundred kilometers in a day, so it wasn't long until all knew the truth. At night they gathered to drone their incubation chant, but this time with extra emphasis at such a significant event.

When Klein wasn't resting, undergoing prep for the implantation, or wrapping up things with the pippo crew or the team from the paleontology expedition, he wrote letters and prepared link transmissions for Amanda, Entara, Ayan'we, and even Helga. Forlani delegations from the Domremy houses came to visit him. Moe and Felicia joined Peebo at his side, explaining that Mel was off-planet already. Klein had several communication sessions with Locals from the area. One day Stumpy reappeared and they had sessions almost daily, often linking up with three or four other

Locals. Klein barely had time to himself. He spent most of it listening to his music or reading a digital copy of *Intruder in the Dust*, which he had always meant to start but had continually put off. The day his vision blurred so badly that he couldn't decipher the words of Faulkner on the screen under any magnification, he asked Moe to read the remaining section to him aloud and then called Patak to tell him he was ready.

They shot him full of happy juice for the implantation and screened off his lower body. All that he could remember afterwards was seeing the head and forelegs of an unknown Local next to him. Patak explained that they had successfully implanted four ova near his pelvis and that the countdown to Day Ten was under way in good order. Klein asked to listen to some particular Schumann pieces that he had enjoyed with Entara, but dozed off before they were done. Consciousness drifted in and out. Occasionally they fed him something or woke him up to take samples. He couldn't tell how long it had been when he awoke to find a purplish form standing next to him.

"Entara!" he whispered.

An arm with dense brown fur reached down to touch his face.

"I was on the grassland for a long time. It's time to sleep now, I think. But I want to feel you again."

The lithe Forlani body climbed up gracefully into the bed and gently pressed itself next to him.

"I feel a little bushed tonight. *Winter Dreams* is playing. Let's just listen."

There was no music in the room. The two bodies rested together for a long while until the purple form ever so silently arose and went to the chamber door, where Peebo was waiting. They went into the hallway. The Forlani slumped against the wall.

"I don't know how I feel," she said. "He thought I was Entara. I hope I did the right thing. I didn't want to disappoint him. Did I do enough to please?"

"Young lady," said Peebo, "I don't know how many clients you've had in your house, but you never pleased any one of them as you pleased Klein just now by just keeping him company for a few minutes."

"It's the most important thing that ever happened to me. I'll never forget it." She shook her head. "I'm going to have to think of something to tell the overseer at the house because I don't want to have any clients after this, ever. Do you think I will be expelled?"

"Don't worry. I think they will be very happy with whatever you decide to do. I'll make sure of it."

The next time Klein was aware of being awake, he saw two human and one Local form standing next to his bed.

"How do you feel?" asked one of the humans.

"I'm not alone here. You're the doctor. What's up, doc?" he laughed. "Alles in Ordnung."

"Any pain?"

"No pain. No pain, no gain," Klein chuckled. "Just a little crowded. Like a crowded elevator sometimes. What floor are we on?"

"It's the morning of Day Ten. We'll do the removal in a little while. Do you know what that means? You'll be sleeping after that."

"The first notes of the coda."

"The coda? What the hell is he talking about?" wondered Patak.

"It's the end of the symphony," answered Peebo. "He's a little out of it but he still understands."

"Hey, I know you. What's his name gardener. You gave me a room. A nice room for me and Entara and we didn't have to pay. Thanks, farmer. Farmer in the dell."

"Someone else is here who wants to see you."

"Green grasshopper. I know who you are, too. You show me pictures. Hold up your leg."

Stumpy did as requested.

"Stumpy wants to have a little earlink with you one more time if you wouldn't mind."

"I'm ready for Freddie."

The Local inserted its feeler up to the eardrum and concentrated just on "listening" to Klein's mind, trying to reach as far into the past as possible. Klein was already there. Images were remarkably clear and distinct. It was a shore. A beach, someplace called Rügen. Klein was a small child. He stamped around in the water. The waves lapped at his knees, then his waist, then his chest, as he squealed, "Mutti, look, this water is moving!" A human woman with yellowish brown hair and blue and white clothing tight to her body came up and took his hand as he plunged further into the sea. "Let's go! Farther! Farther!"

"Helmut, come and help!" the woman called. "He's slippery as an eel and he's trying to get away from me."

Another human with a black garment around his middle came up and took the other hand. "What are you trying to do, little fish, go all the way to Sweden?"

"Let's go all the way! Lift me up!" shouted little Willie.

They each raised an arm and held him up so he was running across the top of the water.

"Now you can be a superman," said Helmut.

"You're not my little boy anymore," said Maria. "You're Good Heimdall, the son of the Nine Waves and you will watch over a Rainbow Bridge into the heavens."

"More! I love this! Let's go all the way!"

They walked down the beach wave by wave, the three of them laughing.

Patak and Peebo watched Klein in his bed. "His lips are moving," observed Patak. "Can you make out what he is saying?"

Peebo leaned in close. Klein whispered, "Bevor…bevor…Freude." And those were the last words he said.

The young woman clasped the poncho they had given her on the ferry tight around her body because, although the rain had stopped some time ago, the wind still had that chill only moistness can give it. She moved quickly up the road, sometimes hopping puddles in the compacted earth. There was a slow, irregular stream of wagons and walkers heading in the opposite direction. These were mainly Dissenters of all ages, dressed in their best clothing, barely more formal than what they would wear in the fields or in the market. She was worried about being too late, but when she asked them, they merely reassured her to go on up to the end of the road. She felt miserable inside. *I've failed, I've failed. I've come all this way but it didn't do any good. I'm so alone.* She could scarcely understand that the Dissenters looked on her with compassion, even as they realized they should not stop her. When she got to the clearing at the end of road, the first sun had already set. In the twilight she saw a dozen Forlani girls singing around the monument. The monument was a simple stone obelisk about six feet high. She would learn later that it had been hastily made by a man named Luis. The Forlani sang on and on, voices arranged in several harmonic groups that seemed to answer each other in a complex pattern. She turned to the only human left in the open space, a Dissenter boy from the looks of him.

"Am I too late?" she asked.

"Never too late to pay your respects. The Circle met and some people spoke a while back. They've all gone back to the ferry by now, except for the ones that stay near here. I brought these girls from Site 55 with my wagon and I'm going to wait and take them back whenever they want. My name's Bart. You must not be of the Circle. Which site are you from?"

"Off-planet," she sighed. "My name is Amanda."

He looked at her with surprise. "*The* Amanda?"

"Amanda Pedersen-Klein"

"Wait till I tell the girls. Welcome to Domremy, by the way. I never did meet your dad, but I'm proud to know you. He was a great man. I don't know what we're going to do without him."

"Neither do I," said Amanda, holding back a sob.

"Here, you better take this before I forget. It's your share of the ashes," Bart explained.

Amanda reached out and took hold of a simple metal container that fit easily in the palm of her hand.

"I hope that's OK. They left it with me in case you should show up. Of course, most of his remains were buried there under the monument. The Circle wanted some for a future ceremony and the Locals asked for a little bit to mark the place where they had their first conversation with him. It's become an important stop on their migrations, probably holy."

"Thank you, Bart," Amanda said. "I'll bring it back to Earth and maybe my mother can help me think of a good place. Bremen is mostly under water and

Düsseldorf hasn't been cleared yet, but maybe we can go there eventually."

The Forlani continued to sing, moving every so often into a different symmetrical pattern to add a dance-like quality to their song. Finally they stopped and stood in silence a few minutes before moving to unpack some things from Bart's wagon. He had a few words with them and one of them came over to Amanda.

"Greetings, Amanda, First Daughter of Klein. I'm so glad you were here for our tribute song. My name is Ayan'we. I knew your father when he came to our planet. It's a long story and I would really like to share it with you sometime. But right now you look so cold. Did you come all the way from the ferry on foot?"

"Yes."

"Well, you must need some refreshment. Come join us for a little fruit and juice. Please, we would be so honored."

Ayan'we brought her to the rest of her group and introduced her. Each Forlani girl seemed thrilled and took her by the hand. They urged her to try the succulent fruits they handed her, and their sweet pulp soon began to revive her tired body, if not her spirits. Bart sat on his wagon nibbling bread and cheese and taking an occasional swig from a cider jug.

"Aren't you going to ask the boy to join us?" inquired Amanda.

"Already have," responded one of the Forlani. "I think he's afraid of being tempted." They all giggled.

Ayan'we explained. "Young men in the Dissenters generally avoid us and the houses because they've heard stories that we can bewitch them with our pleasures. Of course, Forlani always try to please their clients, but we're quite happy if human males keep to their own mates. That's why the houses here are dwindling. My fellow singers come from several different houses because we couldn't form a proper chorus just from one house or one matriline. Nowadays there are many more options for our girls. If they choose to visit Domremy, it's often because they are passionate about the lives of my mother, Entara, and your father."

"You, the daughter of Entara?"

"Firstborn," admitted Ayan'we with a bit of guilty pride.

"I'd like to know more, especially to tell my mother. She'd heard about your mother and was always curious. Not jealous, I mean. Mother's never been really attached to a single man, and often to none at all."

"I think I understand. I sort of feel the same way about males."

"Don't you ... work in the houses?"

"Well," answered Ayan'we, exchanging a knowing glance with her singers, "I've received pleasure training like all the girls in my cohort. However, I've never served in a house, mostly because there always seemed to be other things to do. As for marriage..." She made a Forlani version of a moue. "My two nearest sisters pester me all the time, as well as others. For the time being, I feel it would be more suitable to look into other things."

They had finished the meal and were putting away the leftovers. It was already getting quite dark. Amanda noticed that Bart had unhitched his team of mules and staked them to graze.

"We're going to camp out tonight," announced one of the Forlani. "Won't you join us?"

"Please do," said another. "It's much too late to get back to the ferry this evening and we can bring you in the wagon tomorrow."

"Camping out is so much fun!" added a third. "The sky is completely clearing now and we can see the stars. We all sleep together in a cluster to keep warm. It's so great, because normally we don't get to sleep with non-matrilines."

"You mean one big bed?"

"Of course. It would be silly to be all separate instead of warm and cozy together. It's not as if some male would crawl up to you and try to get intimate," she chuckled. All the group laughed together, adding little gestures toward Bart, who huddled into his sleeping bag and pretended not to hear.

The twelve Forlani started to form tiers, a couple jumping on the mattress first crying "Bottom for me!" Ayan'we stopped them and said that as guest,

Amanda should get first choice. Not knowing how it would feel trying to sleep under all those mink-like bodies, Amanda chose the top level. Actually, they did not sleep on top of one another, but slightly overlapping in three partial layers, like Greenland sardines in a can. They pulled a cover over the top. Despite its sheer appearance, it was amazingly wind-resistant. The warmth of the Forlani bodies beneath and around her soon made Amanda feel awkwardly comfortable, as the girls continued to chat with each other in their own language.

Amanda rolled over a bit to look at the monument and a tear slid down her cheek. Astonished, she felt a tongue flick out and taste it. The Forlani on her left said something and Ayan'we corrected her. "Speak English," she insisted. "It's impolite to talk so Amanda can't understand."

Ayan'we murmured to Amanda. "Don't be insulted. She couldn't help it. She was just curious." Then Ayan'we spoke a little louder to the others. "Yes, it's salty. It's the way they feel sorrow. Don't act like you didn't hear about that in training. I know it's a bad sign in clients, but for Amanda, it's a sign of grief."

All the Forlani reached out to touch her face and her hair, saying they were sorry and they didn't want to stop her tears. Amanda felt so touched that she cried a bit more, but then reassured them that she really felt well with them, better than she had felt for a very long time. They all settled down again and gazed at the stars.

"From now on, you'll be one of our sisters," said Ayan'we, giving Amanda a little hug.

The Forlani continued speaking English for her benefit, picking out stars in the sky they might want to visit and imagining what life would be like there. The girl on Amanda's left suddenly asked, "Which one is your star of Earth, Amanda?"

She looked up at the alien constellations and admitted, "I couldn't begin to tell you."

"I know which is your star," said a girl in the tier next to her. "It's that one right up there."

"Where?"

"Show her Siita, I can't reach."

The girl to her left took her hand and pointed it up to a group of stars. "That constellation is what the Dissenters call the Good Samaritan. That star in the head is the one your dad selected to be Amanda's Star. He told Moe, son of Peebo, who told Luis, who told an Eyes of Alertness in the Stafford Station house and now everybody on Domremy knows and some have made diagrams to bring back to Forlan to share because the skies are different at home."

Ayan'we whispered in Amanda's ear. "Klein couldn't give you the days he wanted to. Now he has given you a star. When you look at it, from wherever you look at it, you can remember you had a wonderful father who chose to live on in you."

Amanda fell asleep without realizing the passage of time. She would never feel truly alone again.

ABOUT THE AUTHOR

Life Sentence is the product of a collaboration between literature professor James F. Gaines and librarian John Manley Roberts Gaines, both lifelong science fiction enthusiasts from Fredericksburg, Virginia, who are at work on several more volumes in the Forlani Saga that follows characters from this novel.